CHUCK DRISKELL

This is a work of fiction. Names, characters, places, and incidents either are the product of the author's imagination or are used fictitiously, and any resemblance to any persons, living or dead, business establishments, events, or locales is entirely coincidental.

DEMON'S BLUFF
CreateSpace Edition
ISBN 978-1-4922-6561-0

All rights reserved.

Copyright © 2013 by Chuck Driskell
Published by Autobahn Books
Cover art by Sean Madden

This book is protected under the copyright laws of the United States of America. Any reproduction or other unauthorized use of the material or artwork herein is prohibited without the express written permission of the author.

First Edition: February 2013

In loving memory of Dena Driskell. What a wonderful sister.

Chapter One

April 14, 1943

Havana, Cuba

AFTER YEARS and years of toiling in obscurity, Carsten Steuben had finally landed the whale. In intelligence parlance, his collaborator was termed "loaded," meaning he possessed good information. And wasn't "good information" such a lovely understatement?

"Good information" meant the most sensitive data on earth—data on the Americans' secret atomic project.

Data that Mother Germany needed—desperately.

Time was of the essence and, at the very worst, Carsten estimated it would be thirty days before he could package his collaborator's intelligence. Following that time, it would take two more weeks of ocean travel before he could present the intelligence to the Führer himself. Carsten indulgently envisioned Hitler, sitting rapt while Carsten fed him each piece of his earth-shattering find. When finished, Carsten would bow before the Führer, asking how else he might be of service. Carsten was betting on tears of joy from the Austrian-born leader. And a promotion—a big one. Several things, however, had to happen between now and his meeting with Hitler. Carsten didn't yet have a scrap of this unequalled intelligence. Acquiring it was going to require approval from his chain of command—and money (of course.) That process started tonight with his chief, when Carsten would begin by requesting a small initial amount to pay the American pigeon.

El Restaurante de Soria was located on the south side of Havana, in the affluent neighborhood of Cerro. Requiring reservations a week in advance, the popular restaurant turned its fourteen tables three times a night. The eponymous establishment was staffed exclusively by three generations of Sorias, a family of proud Cuban natives, right down to the busboys. The Soria specialty was local Havana cuisine, primarily of the seafood and pork variety. Manuel Soria, the father and proprietor, went to great lengths to make each customer feel at home, catering to their every whim. Carsten, who split time between Havana and Ciudad de Panamá (henceforth called Panama City), certainly knew this, and had the elder Soria's über-obliging nature in mind when he'd made the reservation that afternoon (greasing the palm of one of the Soria sons in order to get it.) Fortunately, it didn't seem to offend Papa Soria in the least when Carsten beckoned him over and asked for a table with a bit more privacy.

Manuel Soria straightened, turning his brown eyes to the rear of the restaurant as his face transformed from thoughtful consideration to an accommodating smile. "Please, Señor Lancaster," he said to Carsten, utilizing the false name that comprised Carsten's cover. "We have a private family room in the back. I will be offended if you don't allow us to move your meal there at once."

Carsten dipped his head. "You're far too kind, Señor Soria. We graciously accept your benevolent offer." His accent was precisely British, spoken with a generic London accent. A slight man, Carsten appeared to have a perpetual cold. He had pale, yellowish skin, with a turkey gobbler that hung too heavily below his weak, retrognathic chin. It was not the face of a healthy forty-four-year-old man. His brown hair was thinning, flecked with gray and combed over his lumpy pate. His baldness was most noticeable as he half-bowed at Señor Soria, an Asian habit he'd adopted from his international customs training at the intelligence school back in Berlin.

The owner snapped his thick fingers, causing Sorias to appear like ants at a picnic. In rapid-fire Spanish, he instructed his children to prepare the back room immediately. The soldier-like Soria offspring hung on his every word, springing into action. Plates were whisked away. Silverware and condiments deftly moved. The eldest son appeared, carrying dual complimentary aperitifs—yellow liquid imbued with a shot of carmine red, along with a juicy slice from a locally-grown orange— while he apologized for the brief delay as if the Soria family had done something wrong. After no more than two minutes of waiting at the bustling bar, Carsten and his companion were ushered to the rear room by Manuel Soria's only daughter, a tall, brown-eyed beauty. She wore a long layered skirt, the red and orange ruffles doing nothing to conceal the shake of her perfect hips as she walked. Both men, career intelligence professionals, deftly glanced at her form, experienced at not being obvious when scrutinizing something.

Manuel Soria ushered them into the long room, bounded on both sides by antique vitrine cabinets displaying family mementos, photographs, and even a double-barreled pistol below a sepia photo of a distinguished Cuban with a handlebar moustache.

Carsten's dinner mate and section chief, Bernd von Danzig, a statuesque Prussian with bronze skin and a full head of blond hair, studied the photo and pistol, one hand behind his back as he inclined forward for a better view.

Manuel leaned over the dinner table, lighting the two candles by match, shaking it out as the sulfuric smell briefly defeated the aroma of Cuban cooking. "My father," he said to Bernd. "He fought the yumas with that pistol." A prideful smile grew on his face as he said, "There's no telling how many he took with him."

"Yumas?" Bernd asked, his head turning slightly as he continued to stare into the cabinet.

"Americanos."

Turning fully, Bernd's stony face switched to warmth. "Ah, yes, our peoples have both had our issues with those callous, poorly-bred people." He glanced at the picture again. "A handsome man, your father. I'm sure he was quite a gentleman." Bernd's warmth disappeared as quickly as it had come.

Once both diners were seated, Manuel snapped his fingers again, shooing his adult children from the room. He gestured grandly at the setup. "You have drinks, a complimentary bottle of our family wine that is imported from Argentina, fresh ice water, and your food. Will you require anything else?"

"You've been terribly accommodating, Señor Soria. We're in fine shape, thank you," Carsten replied with a grateful smile.

From a table by the only door, Manuel produced a large hand bell. "I will leave you now, for your requested privacy. If you require anything at all, ring this bell. Otherwise, we will respect your seclusion."

Carsten thanked him again. Bernd, his irritation showing, was already eating. The door clicked shut.

"Why all the damned fuss?" Bernd asked, doing nothing to hide his mouthful of red snapper. "I was about to gnaw on my arm."

An immediate flush came over Carsten's sallow skin, making him appear momentarily healthy. "This, Bernd, is a celebration."

"Indeed?" Bernd queried, sipping the wine before briefly glancing at it with amused satisfaction. "And what, pray tell, could be important enough to summon me so far from my current home?"

"Before I reveal my grand surprise, how was your trip?"

Bernd soured his face and made a shooing motion. "The Mexicans..." He shook his head, saying nothing more.

Carsten dipped his head. He didn't really care for Bernd, but Bernd *was* his superior. If only he would take the time to understand the people he lived among, Carsten thought, then perhaps he would appreciate them a bit more. Thinking better of it, but blurting it out anyway, Carsten said, "I actually like the Cubans. Family-oriented people. And if one makes an *effort* to befriend them, he will find himself paid back by an excess of their teeming goodwill."

Bernd smiled thinly. "As our Anglican friends say, 'Bob's your uncle.' Now, as I eat, you tell me about this little surprise of yours."

Carsten managed a bite of his fish, humming as he chewed. "The food here is superior." Took a sip of water. "Do you remember, back in January, when I told you of an American contact I made in Panama?"

Making short work of his fish and vegetables, Bernd shrugged. "I believe you said he was a *Trottel*."

"Indeed, at first I thought he might be a pigeon," Carsten acknowledged, adding length to the end of his sentence. "Since then, however, he has promised an intelligence windfall that could very well win us this war."

Bernd, exactly forty years old and possessing both German (Humboldt) and British (Oxford) degrees, was known in German intelligence as *Der Geist*, The Phantom. Younger than Carsten, he was his direct superior.

"Win the war with intelligence you've unearthed?" Bernd asked.

"Yes."

Bernd stared back at Carsten through leaden eyes before braying laughter. He turned his head away, his laughter dying off as he shook his head, whispering "Carsten" again and again in an admonishing tone. "Win us the war…really? Does this pigeon of yours have an army of undefeatable robots like one might see in a Saturday matinee?"

Carsten twisted the linen napkin in his lap. "You laugh now, yet you haven't even heard what he can deliver."

"And what might that be?" Bernd asked, tugging on his eyebrow, his good cheer transforming into what looked like skepticism and boredom.

Carsten tried to hide his irritation. It was widely circulated throughout the halls of the Konradhäus, back in Berlin, that if an idea didn't belong expressly to Bernd, it wasn't an idea at all. It was *Sheisse*. Perhaps that was why, Carsten mused, their small intelligence section had been tucked away in Latin America. Jünger chasing his tail, and the local women, in Brazil. Laurenz spending his days tanning himself while counting oilers on Aruba. And, other than Carsten himself, splitting time between Cuba and Panama, there was Bernd, living it up with the local *putas* while shaking down American expats for scraps of information in Mexico City. Their entire team, because of Bernd's perpetual clashing with his superiors, had been patted on the head and sent away to serve a peripatetic Caribbean existence. And, even after the humiliating deportation of their collective station, Bernd still maintained his haughty air.

While some men might enjoy living a paid existence in the tropics, it insulted Carsten. A world war was raging. He'd just read about the uprising in the Warsaw ghetto. The German U-boats, dominant in the Atlantic for so long, were beginning to lose their grip. Blood was spilling in Tunisia and Crimea and, tropical lifestyle be damned, Carsten was determined to make a difference.

And, rather than help, Bernd smirked at him. It boiled Carsten's blood.

"Now don't pout and go silent on me," Bernd chided in quiet German. "Out with it."

Carsten dropped his fork loudly onto his plate. "As I said, my American is no *Trottel*. He's an aviation executive at a private firm, very well placed."

"Our aircraft are better than theirs, Carsten," Bernd warned, sticking with his Prussian-accented German and mopping his plate with a piece of cornbread. "And besides that, we've hundreds of their aircraft we've shot down. Fighters, bombers, recon planes. We've got our own unit that does nothing but fly these aircraft. Hell, our engineers have deconstructed *every* one of them. I'm not going back to Berlin to tell them we've got some useless wing-designer on the payroll."

Carsten closed his eyes, motionless. He stayed that way for a moment.

"Look at you," Bernd chuckled. "You're a petulant child who holds his breath. Go on, take a lungful before you faint."

Carsten opened his eyes. "As I said, aviation executive, very large private firm." Lifting his eyes to Bernd, he said, "And he's not a designer, he's a key member of an *enormous* task force put together by the American government."

Bernd stopped his eating, arching his eyebrows. He looked like a bad actor attempting to play the part of an interested person.

Carsten made him wait. Five seconds. Ten. Finally he said two words: *Atom bomb.*

The baby blue eyes across from him flicked to the right before coming back to Carsten. Bernd acknowledged the words with a quick nod before buttering another piece of cornbread. Holding the bread in range of his mouth, he asked, "Is he a scientist?"

"No."

"Does this *alleged* person have anything of value in relation to this atom bomb?"

"You certainly don't think he does," Carsten said sharply, uncharacteristically challenging Bernd. He could feel a cold film of sweat growing on his head.

"Calm down, old friend," Bernd replied, popping the bread in and showing the palms of both his hands. Chewing, he mumbled, "It's my job to be skeptical. Please go on."

Carsten leaned forward as he spoke in a whisper. "He has designs of *all* their prototypes. He has their method for fission. He has the full list of elements and ingredients, and he has the narrow-range date of when they will be ready to drop the first bomb. Good enough?"

Bernd put elbows on the table, clasping his hands and steepling his index fingers. "So, *presumably*, he has most everything?"

"Yes."

"And what does this white knight want in return for this information?"

"I paid him five thousand U.S., up front, to get what I've gotten thus far. He's very bright, Bernd, demanding a hundred-thousand dollars to be deposited within one hour of his courier message at a Panamanian bank of his choosing. No doubt to ensure that it's not—"

"Not counterfeit," Bernd finished, nodding his head in an unimpressed fashion. "They all get the money part right, Carsten. Never be captivated by that."

Carsten stared at him, whitening his thin lips as he pressed them together.

"Oops. I did it again, didn't I?"

Carsten nodded.

"*Es tut mir leid*," Bernd said, apologizing in what sounded like a genuine tone.

"After the deposit, he will surface, but will be due a hundred and fifty more. A quarter-of-a-million in all. And for that, we get everything."

"Did you ask for some kind of verification?"

From the inner pocket of his rumpled gray suit, Carsten produced a three-page document written in English. He watched as Bernd bent it the other way, then flattened it on the table. He read the explosive preview slowly, taking the better part of ten minutes, absently picking at his teeth over the duration. Carsten smoked a cigarette as he waited. Finally, Bernd handed the report back, running his tongue over his straight teeth.

"Trinity," he said, eyebrows arched.

"A test," Carsten replied, nodding.

"They've come that far, have they?" Bernd asked, rubbing the back of his neck in a nervous manner.

"My contact says they're two to three years ahead of us."

"This preview could be bullshit. All of his intelligence could be fabricated, and neither you or I know enough to tell for sure."

"He checks out, Bernd. He's with Omicron Aviation, and Oscar Hausen in Ausland-SD has confirmed for me that Omicron is involved with their atomic project."

"Indeed?" Bernd asked.

"Yes."

"Those bastards set us a decade behind in Godforsaken Norway. Everyone involved in that heavy water catastrophe should be rounded up and shot," Bernd whispered. "Especially that imbecile Hahn." He was silent for a long period before narrowing his eyes at Carsten.

"How did you find this gentleman, this American?"

"I didn't."

"Explain that."

"He found me." Realizing how impotent that sounded, Carsten quickly added, "But only because I'd salted the earth to the American expats in Panama. I'd put out word that if any of them were in play, they needed to speak to my man at Rojota."

"Rojota?"

"A bar I set up as a front."

Bernd nodded. "So is the exchange to take place in Panama?"

"Yes."

"Then why did you come back here?"

"I had to wrap up two operations, and knew I had several weeks before the exchange. Plus, Bernd, I know how you like Havana."

Bernd appeared thoughtful, looking away.

"Does this meet with your approval?" Carsten asked.

Turning back, Bernd's rigid face split into a broad smile. "Indeed it does. I'm so very proud of you and I hope you will accept my apologies for doubting you." He paused, taking his white wine in hand. "A toast, old friend. This is an historic occasion…the beginning of your ascension to a level you deserve."

Carsten's heart hammered in his chest upon hearing such rare words from the younger Bernd von Danzig. He smiled in return, his words hung up in his throat. "It will be good for both of us," Carsten finally managed. "That's why I've brought you in at this early stage."

After finishing their glasses of the tart Soria wine, Bernd wolfed two more pieces of bread before gulping water, staring at Carsten over the rim of the sweaty glass. Finished, he sighed contentedly, slapping both hands on his stomach. "Quite a feast."

"Manuel is the best," Carsten agreed.

Bernd tossed his napkin on his plate, rapping the table with his knuckles in the German style. "Pay these fine people so we can go."

Carsten rang the bell two times, removing his wallet, feeling warm from the wine, warmer from Bernd's tributes. Upon paying Manuel Soria, and adding several extra pesos to the bill due to the imposition they put on him and his family, the two men stepped outside into the sticky night air, stretching and walking slowly the way two men often do after a fine meal.

They both nodded to an attractive young lady who hurried by. She gave the two non-Cubans a wide berth.

"Do you take the time to occasionally enjoy a lady?" Bernd asked, glancing back at the woman as she strode away.

Carsten motioned Bernd to the rear of the restaurant, through a darkened alley. "Car is back here," he said offhandedly. "And, regarding women, no…the temptation is difficult, but, as you might remember, I have a fiancée back in Köln."

Bernd chuckled, saying something under his breath. Carsten noticed he was walking slowly, ambling a step behind. "What a night," Bernd murmured, head tilted up to the sky.

Carsten glanced over his shoulder at him. "How's Mexico City this time of year?"

"Mixed," Bernd replied with a rueful shake of his head. "Just so filthy, and with the altitude, April is hit or miss. I'd much rather be here. Clean air. Warm temperatures. The ocean."

Carsten led Bernd through the alley and to the left, into a darkened lot. He jingled his keys as he pulled them from his pocket. Bernd had gone silent. Carsten turned to see him walking around the car, his hands in his pockets as he still looked skyward.

"Look," Bernd said, gesturing upward. "You can see *der Grosse Wagen* perfectly here."

Carsten paused, prepared to get in but glancing up in deference to his superior. "Sometimes here in Cuba you can even see *das Chamäleon* in the southern sky." He slid into his seat, unlocking Bernd's door and cranking his engine. As the car idled, Bernd lingered outside, his torso visible. He appeared to be lighting a cigarette. After a few moments, he entered, a broad smile on his face.

"I'm slowed this evening because I'm stunned, Carsten," Bernd said, speaking German in the privacy of the Chevrolet. "Giving me wonderful news, a superior meal, and inviting me to this beautiful land. What else could you do to make me any happier?"

"Perhaps a nightcap of genuine Ansbach and a comfortable bed?" Carsten suggested. "My guest room is turned out nicely. Then, tomorrow, as I brief you on the particulars, maybe we'll take a drive to Morro Castle. While it's certainly not as historic as Schloss Braunfels or even Gleiburg, the setting by the sea is stunning. The spray over the rock walls, when the light is right…"

Carsten noticed, as he spoke about the castle, Bernd was looking over Carsten's shoulder, his face darkening. "*Sheisse*," Bernd said in an annoyed tone, motioning past Carsten. "What the hell does Señor Soria want now?"

Following his eyes, Carsten turned around, looking out the driver's window and seeing nothing but the moonlit weeds in the dark lot. Just as he was about to turn back, he tensed at the python-like sensation of a powerful arm clamping around his throat. As both of Carsten's hands shot to the muscular arm, a wet cloth moved over his mouth and nose before utter…

…blackness.

Chicago, Illinois

IT WAS a chilly April night with stripping wind blowing in from the lake, pushing through the channel of the river and watering Roald "Rollie" Donahue's eyes. The April cold made Rollie wonder why he didn't try to transfer somewhere warmer. A whole country existed out there, at least half of it warmer than Chicago. Being a weeknight, with a war on, there wasn't much happening in the city. Liquor was scarce. So was gasoline. A few horns could be heard and, several blocks away, an L-train clicked and clacked on its recently refurbished tracks. In the distance Rollie watched as two sailors—they looked like kids, probably fresh from recruit training at Great Lakes—staggered by the river, doing a fine job of holding one another up, arguing about something or someone named Chartreuse. A hooker approached them from the shadows, beckoning them to one of the many hotels dotting the area. They must've forgotten all about Chartreuse because they followed her like two puppies. Rollie shook his head resignedly—just another mind-numbing night of surveillance.

He'd positioned himself in a familiar spot, awaiting Richard Hampton's exit on the south sidewalk of Wacker Drive, three blocks west of North Michigan Avenue. Rollie was more than ready to hang it up for the evening. Seven months of watching this asshole had confirmed two things: One, he was unpredictable. And two, he wasn't to be trusted.

The five bus came and went, Rollie waving the driver on and catching a dirty look in return for standing under the bus shelter. He pretended to smoke a cigarette, not inhaling, keeping his head down just enough to keep a vigil on Richard Hampton's building. The streets were shiny slick from an earlier rain shower. There were ripples on the puddles from the brisk wind. People hurried down the sidewalks, their hands holding their coats together at the neck, the look on their face not unlike Rollie's, certainly wondering why they lived here. Much of the U.S. actually enjoyed April, especially the second half of the month. But here, tonight, it felt like December. Funny, Rollie thought, twirling the prop cigarette as the bus turned north on Michigan, if this was a January night, we'd call it warm.

"Perspective," he muttered. And right now, his perspective on this evening was that of a waste of time. "Five more minutes," Rollie whispered to himself as another forty-degree gust buffeted his body, "and then I'm going home." No sooner had he gotten the words out than Richard Hampton appeared through the revolving door, his bronzed skin out of place in sun-deprived Illinois. Hampton buttoned his tan overcoat as he stepped onto the street, toting the light brown briefcase he'd only started carrying a week earlier. Rollie glanced away as Hampton walked in his direction, going past the bus stop and the alley where he should have turned to retrieve his car. He was headed somewhere else.

This wasn't entirely unusual. There were problems in the Hampton household. Richard Hampton often stopped off for a few drinks and, occasionally, took a room at the Blackwatch just across the river. When those nights out first began occurring, using only the limited skill of a week-one detective, Rollie filled his miniature camera with images of the prostitutes as they negotiated the carpeted hallway in their stiletto heels, heading to their illicit interlude with Hampton. In fact, Hampton had hired so many hookers in Rollie's more than 200 days of surveillance, Rollie had quit taking pictures and simply noted the visitors for his end-of-week report that flew to Washington in the federal courier bag.

Remaining motionless at the bus stop, Rollie watched as Hampton crossed the McCormick Bridge, headed north on Michigan. He continued to glance back, checking for a tail. This was new behavior and it was painfully obvious. Waiting until Hampton was across the river, Rollie crossed Wacker Drive and watched his target from the river railing, his fingernails nervously scratching at the peeling paint of the rail. Still heading north, and with the flagrance of a rank amateur, Hampton stopped once every block, pretending to look at something in his briefcase as his eyes searched for a tail. Making an educated guess, Rollie reluctantly purchased a cup of steaming Postum from the newsstand a block away, but only for the warmth. As he sipped the molasses-tinged beverage, he passed through the alley that led to Hampton's car. Parked on the far side of the lot, which was just off LaSalle, Rollie slid into the front seat of his own black Ford two-door, drinking the substitute coffee as he waited. A quick glance at his Mido wristwatch showed Rollie that Hampton had been walking now for twenty minutes.

"And it's windy and about forty degrees," he said to himself. "And Hampton's grown used to the good life."

The scars on Rollie's torso were on fire. The dryness of the artificial heat in wintertime always did an absolute number on him. In a well-practiced move, he reached into his coat, removing the small brown bottle, adding just a few drops of the liquid to his drink. He downed the now cool Postum before he crumpled the thick paper cup, tossing it into the floorboard of the passenger side (along with the rest of the refuse typical of a surveillance car.) It only took a minute before the silky sensation of the morphine hit Rollie's bloodstream. A disciplined man, Rollie had used a very small dose. But, like a file over freshly cut fingernails, the dosage was just enough to smooth the rough edges created by Rollie's ever-present pain.

No sooner had the pain dissipated than Hampton emerged from the alley, headed straight to his burgundy Lincoln, cranking it. Rollie peered through his door window, seeing Hampton leaning over slightly, no doubt placing the heat on its highest setting. Rollie then allowed his subject to drive away without following him.

Five minutes later Rollie exited his car, walking back to Wacker and to the payphone near the bus stop. He spoke with the operator, placing a collect call to an Alexandria, Virginia phone number, telling the lady his name was

Simon Berry. While the phone rang and the operator hummed an off-key tune, Rollie dipped his head at the sight of an attractive young woman approaching him. She tapped on the glass, gesturing in all directions and saying, "Hey mister, do you know where Henry's is?" She was, of course, asking about the well-known eatery. Afraid to join eyes with her, Rollie gestured north.

"Up Michigan three or four blocks and left on Ontario. You'll see it."

She lingered, hands in her dark wool coat. He glanced up to see her smiling. "Thanks so much," she said in the tone of voice of someone who wants to keep the conversation going.

He nodded once before turning his back on her, exhaling in relief as he heard her heels clicking away.

The operator was speaking to Nicholas Penland who, in a curt voice, agreed to accept the charges. A click and the tone-deaf operator was gone.

"Sir," Rollie said. "This is Kestrel."

"Wait one." There was a long pause and the sound of rustling as Nicholas had to be checking today's sign and countersign. Finally he said, "Pilot."

"Sandwich," Rollie instantly replied, feeling silly at the precaution. Had he said, "Trimmer," it would have indicated duress, and gotten a completely different response. But "sandwich" did nothing but authenticate his identity, so that now he and his boss could communicate about routine matters over an unsecure, but likely uncompromised, common phone line.

"What is it?" Nicholas asked, clear annoyance in his voice.

"Our boy has suddenly gone on high alert."

A long pause. "And what makes you say that?"

"He was plenty cavalier before his trip to God knows where. Now he comes back with a ridiculous tan and takes a frigid walk to do nothing more than look behind his back every twenty feet."

"Don't *tell me* you got burned…with your scars and all I've told you a hundred times—"

"Give me a break," Rollie said, cutting him off. He felt the flush in his cheeks as he was reminded—again—about the abnormality visible under his chin.

"You're sure he didn't make you?"

Rollie took a calming breath, enunciating his response slowly and clearly. "No, he did *not* make me."

"Did his passport show up anywhere while he was gone?"

"Negative. I ran a search and they're pretty good nowadays with the war and all."

"Maybe he just went to Miami?"

"I don't think so."

"What are you saying?"

"I think he's close to making a move."

"So, what are you recommending?"

"At least a three-man team, twenty-four-seven. Taps, too. Cooperation from mail service, home and work. Radio wave sweep. Snatch team in place. And I need your team to find out where he went that brought him back tan and paranoid. That should tell us a great deal."

"Not happening, old boy," Nicholas answered, laying on his northeastern accent. "We can barely spare you with this damned war on, and if you think I'm hitting Dillard up to ask for all that—based on a trip, a tan, and a touch of patented Kestrel suspicion—then you're crazier than I thought. Now listen, I've personally scoured this fellow's background. He has information on his outfit's particular aircraft and nothing else. In fact, I'd hazard the Germans or Japs wouldn't pay a reichsmark or a yen for anything he has in his entire brain."

Rollie squeezed his eyes shut. "Well, if he's that benign, why follow him at all?"

"Because, dear Kestrel, he's definitely in play and everyone loves to burn a traitor. You know that. It shows we're on the job." A lighter could be heard clicking, followed by the scant crackling sound of a deep cigarette inhalation. "Just stay on him. He tries to leave town again, this time you follow."

"How do I know if he's leaving when I'm only on him for twelve a day? I'm only one man."

"You'll figure it out." There was a click as the line went dead.

Rollie jammed the phone into its cradle, desperately wanting to pick it back up, call Penland again, and scream "Prick!" back into the receiver. He stepped from the phone booth, tilting his head back to the night sky, eyes closed as he attempted to calm himself. After a moment, Rollie walked to the bridge, peering up North Michigan, able to see the girl he'd given directions to, her bright red polo coat and band beret setting her apart from the light crowd. She turned left onto Ontario, headed to Henry's, having already easily forgotten the man in the phone booth. Leaning against the gilded column by the river, Rollie imagined himself with her at a dark Henry's table, his hand on hers as he said something clever that made her laugh. He imagined telling her about his life, about his adventures in the Pacific. After dinner and a few drinks, they would leave. He would suggest a nightclub. The girl…her name would be Valerie…no, Veronica…would grip his hand tightly in hers, moving in front of him as she breathily asked to see his house. And there, after a few discreet candles were lit, Rollie would slowly, lovingly bring her to a state of undress. He would kiss her sweetly, gradually moving down her trembling body, both of his hands locked with hers, satisfied as she arched her back in pleasure just as he buried his head in—

"Stop torturing yourself," he growled, feeling his chapped lips tighten over his teeth. In the pockets of his overcoat, Rollie felt his hands sweating. He could also feel the sheen of perspiration on his forehead, despite the cold.

Rollie told himself the sweat was from his condition and the constant pain of his injuries—not morphine cravings. But deep down, he knew the truth. The dosage he'd just given himself was far less than his body desired.

Disgusted with himself, the low-level intelligence agent hurried back to his car, driving twelve miles to the northwest, as he'd done so many times before. Peering in from the picture window behind Richard Hampton's sprawling Lincolnwood home, Rollie found his subject sitting shoeless on the cabled sofa, the radio on and a glass of neat brown liquor in his hand.

Hampton's wife, Vivien, a real looker, blew into the room. She was wearing a modest blue gown and saying something to her husband that didn't appear to be pleasant. Hampton made a dismissive gesture back to her, yelling something about unwinding and leaving him the hell alone. The wife had already disappeared, her blue gown trailing behind her in the distance as she ascended the stairs, shouting something in return that Rollie couldn't make out through the window. He did, however, watch as Hampton gestured to the ceiling with dual raised middle fingers.

Situation normal in the Hampton household.

Shaking his head in the cold shadows of the patio, Rollie was thankful there were no children in the mix. He backed away from the window and headed back to his car, again halting his mind as it pictured himself with the girl in red.

Finally home, he caught himself daydreaming again as he stored his things. But he wasn't thinking about the girl in red. The star of his fancy wore blue this time—Vivien Hampton, Richard Hampton's wife. Frustrated and unloved, perhaps she might overlook Rollie's flaws to allow herself to be cared for.

Maybe if I could get him prosecuted, legitimately, thought Rollie...*then she'd be there, all alone, just waiting for—*

"Stop it!" Rollie snapped, his voice echoing through the empty turn-of-the-century home. With dogged determination, despite his cravings, he set about his evening rituals. But before he left his bedroom, he removed the false rear of the drawer in the bedside table, spiriting away his nighttime bottle.

Just the view of it halted his sweating.

Rollie placed the bottle beside his bed.

Havana, Cuba

"COME ON now, wake up," were the first words Carsten heard. A slap in the face was the first thing he felt. The words were being spoken in German, but with a heavy Prussian accent. The horrific headache throbbing in Carsten's head confused him, causing him confusion over where he was or who was speaking. He blinked rapidly, trying to clear the blur from his eyes. Then things began to come clear, both literally and figuratively.

Standing above him was Bernd von Danzig, saying something about the hangover-like aftereffects of chloroform. The area was shadowy, the sliver moon providing indigo light, displaying thick tropical forest all around them. Between the gaps of the trees Carsten could see the stars Bernd had waxed over earlier. Crickets and cicadas chirped loudly. Bernd had shed his coat and button-down, now wearing only a tight undershirt over the powerful musculature of his torso. He held a cigarette in one hand as he continued to slap Carsten's face with the other.

"Okay, okay," Carsten said, pulling his head back and feeling it thud against something solid. He turned side to side, realizing he was sitting in a clearing, the glint of his Chevrolet parked well behind Bernd. Below him was moist Cuban earth and, behind him, as he fluttered his cuffed hands, was no doubt a small palm tree. But Bernd hadn't secured him to it for some reason. The palm was *behind* his hands and his wrists which, while cuffed together, were free of the tree. An amateur mistake from someone as thorough as Bernd von Danzig? If only he could stand and perfectly time a kick to Bernd's groin…

"Carsten," Bernd said calmly, squatting and flicking the cigarette into the surrounding flora. "I'll give you one chance to tell me everything. I want your American's name. I want the rendezvous. I want the dates. I want every scrap of information, and I want it now."

Carsten sucked air through his snotty nose. "Why are you doing this?"

As was his habit, Bernd showed his palms in a gesture of innocence. "I'm going to let you go, Carsten. But I need to sweat you first…it's my job—this is how I'm trained. You've never found anything of substance before, so it's understandable that you haven't been through a debrief such as this. And the choice is yours: you can do it with or without pain." His chin lifted in an arrogant manner as he said, "The Reich cannot afford to let any one man possess such critical information."

"So why not just ask me over a cup of coffee?"

Bernd patted Carsten's knee. "I would have, old friend, but I'm a believer in greed as a powerful motivator. I think you would have withheld information from me to ensure all the glory for yourself—and there's always the concern you might flip. You're a gentle man and have grown to love these local savages. Who's to say you wouldn't use this intelligence as a bargaining chip to set yourself up in a new life?" Bernd smiled warmly, like a friendly uncle giving his favored nephew career advice. "These intoxications, Carsten, are too much for only *one* man to be entrusted with. So I needed your complete cooperation, and this…being out here…ensures it."

Carsten's head was pounding but his thoughts were clarifying rapidly. "What if someone finds us out here, speaking German? Do you have any idea what they do to gringos who break the law? And can you imagine what they'd do to two Germans? This isn't Mexico, Bernd. Here they tie you up in the town square, and after they've lashed you to a bloody mess they—"

"I'm Prussian."

"They won't care. But if we're caught they will—"

"Ayúdelo!" Bernd stood and yelled, cutting Carsten off. He yelled it three times, very loud, a broad grin plastered to his face. "Helfen Sie ihm!" he shouted, again three times, cackling with laughter as he waved his arms, gesturing to Carsten. Then, "Hey…anyone…we're two *spies* out here, having a major problem…help this one that's tied up!" The only response was a rustling in the trees beside them, probably birds or lizards startled by the sudden noise.

Bernd squatted down again, laughing to himself, spiriting a gnat from one of his eyes. "You see, Carsten, there are no locals here. No one at all, other than you and me."

"You're crazy," Carsten whispered, feeling his headache being replaced by cold fear.

"I would have to be crazy to believe you landed a loaded whale. And what was that you said…'salted the earth'?" An indulgent chuckle. "That's good, Carsten. 'Rich,' as the Brits would say. This fellow walked up and smacked you in the face with his bounty of information, didn't he? The old saying is, 'better to be lucky than good,' and I guess that's true." Bernd reached to his right, producing a rope as thick as a man's finger. He began to pull it taut as his tone flattened.

"But the luck ends here. You found him, but you damn sure don't have what it takes to run him." He measured Carsten with narrowed eyes. "What do you weigh?"

Carsten's lips parted as he eyed the rope. It was still mostly slack, the sound of it moving over something audible from above.

"Don't feel like telling me? Well, let me take your load and I'll guess it like the man at the circus." With that, Bernd took several steps to the side before he removed the slack.

Suddenly, Carsten felt his arms elevate behind him. "Wait!" He scurried to his feet to prevent the pain but, on the second pull, he felt himself being lifted by his arms. Not only did the steel handcuffs cut into the tender skin of Carsten's thin wrists but, because his arms were cuffed behind him, it caused the entire weight of his body to flow through his shoulders. On the next tug, he was off the ground, his body bouncing from the excruciating tension on his shoulder joints. The pain was so intense that Carsten wet himself while screaming loud enough to rupture his vocal cords.

"My guess is seventy kilos," Bernd said academically. He held tension on the rope by securing it around his waist before tying it around a small curved palm.

"You already pissed yourself?" Bernd laughed, staring at Carsten's pants. "I've worried myself over what might happen if you ever got burned by the opposition but, well…I didn't realize you'd cave this easily."

Carsten clenched his eyes shut, trying to shut out Bernd's rebuke as well as the pain.

"Tell me about him," Bernd warned. "Tell me or I'll make the current pain feel good compared to the hell you'll endure tonight."

He's not going to let me go, Carsten realized with a surprisingly lucidity. *This sick bastard is going to squeeze the information out of me before he kills me. Then he's going to play dumb to Berlin about my whereabouts while he reaps the rewards of Samuel Fields, the American with the atomic secret.*

As Bernd's voice grew, warning Carsten about the agony he would soon endure, Carsten said a silent prayer of thanks for the odd and excruciating dental procedure he'd endured a year earlier in Fortaleeza, Brazil. He pushed at his second lower molar with his tongue, pressing out and up as hard as he could manage. Tears welled in his eyes from the pain of his shoulders as well as his anguish over the finality of his plan. Carsten pressed hard enough to cut his tongue, his mind awash in memories of his parents back in Mainz, of his little sister who'd died of pneumonia as a child, and of sweet Katarina back in Köln, the only woman he'd ever loved.

Panic seized Carsten as he couldn't get the tooth to release.

"So, you're going to try to hold out, are you?" Bernd asked from the ground. "I thought you'd give in immediately when I saw you piss, but I'll give you some credit, Carsten…you've since belted up and are doing better than I thought." He grasped Carsten's knees, bear-hugging them. "But let's see how you do once those shoulders give way." Bernd clutched Carsten's legs with all his might before pulling downward, hanging from his bony legs, applying all hundred kilos of his own weight to the thin man's frame.

The shoulders popping sounded like brittle limbs cracking in an ice storm.

Carsten Steuben's mouth opened wide, his shriek so shrill and high it was actually quieter than those before it. Lightning pulsed through his body as he hung straight, the tendons and ligaments of his shoulders shredded like overcooked spaghetti. Bernd then let go, adding even more pain from the simple vibration of Carsten snapping upward on the tensed rope. Admiring his handiwork for a moment, the Prussian finally stepped to the tree, tossing the rope in a spiral, making Carsten plummet to the ground with a thud.

Lying there on the damp dirt floor of the jungle-like forest, Carsten shook with sobs as he tried to adjust himself, his arms as limp as empty sweater sleeves. He lifted his eyes to Bernd, seeing him standing there, casually lighting another cigarette, wearing the same expression he would in a staff meeting or at a coffee shop. Killing his colleague with the same countenance he might have when ordering a pastry.

Doing it all in the name of glory. His glory.

With one more great effort, Carsten dug at his tooth with his tongue, letting out an appreciative grunt as it mercifully snapped open, ejecting the miniature glass ampoule filled with white potassium cyanide. During a few panicky seconds, he nearly allowed it to fall back into his throat. Carsten caught it with his tongue, manipulating it forward as he rolled to his back. Jolts of pain fired through his body from his disjointed shoulders, but the agony was partly quelled by the shock that had already begun to set in.

"Bernd," he said hoarsely, lifting his head and trying to find his voice.

Bernd was pulling on the cigarette, staring down at him. Carsten used his tongue again, moving the ampoule from the safety of his cheek to the front of his mouth, clenching it between his teeth and tightening his lips backward to give his captor a full view.

"No!" Bernd screamed, tossing the cigarette and flinging himself onto his subordinate.

It was too late. Recalling how the dentist said the ampoule was sturdy, to prevent an accident, Carsten crunched into the thick glass with all the force his jaw could muster. He immediately swallowed the poison and the tiny shards of glass, doing so just before Bernd's grubby hand roughly probed the inside of his mouth to no avail. For good measure, Carsten bit downward again, feeling tissue rip and bone crunch as Bernd snatched his bitten right hand backward. Resting his head back on the ground, Carsten began to laugh a loud, relieved laugh, tasting Bernd's blood as it mingled with the bitter almond taste of the poison.

The Prussian leaned back on his haunches, rubbing his hand on his trousers, cursing.

"Now you'll never know," Carsten chided.

Bernd breathed deeply, both men sitting there for a half a minute, allowing the finality of Carsten's action to set in.

But then Bernd stood, working his bloody right hand. Staring down at Carsten, he reached into his pocket, producing a folding straight-razor of the shaving variety. Using his left hand, he held it in the scant light, twisting it back and forth. "Poison takes a few minutes, Carsten, old friend. So let's see what we can learn before you expire."

"Good God, man, can't you just let me die?"

"You're going to die anyway."

Bernd went to work, carving.

Carsten held out admirably, providing only snippets of information between the cuts. First was the name, of course. He also gave a rough description, the best he could manage under the duress of the slashes and building effects of poison. But when it came to a rendezvous, Carsten—the razor under his scalp, scraping across his skull—managed to moan the word "letter". Bernd didn't stop, still carving his underling, producing slaughterhouse quantities of blood. Finally, just after Bernd severed Carsten's left ear and promised to go for the right one, Carsten whispered about the existence of a safety deposit box in Havana.

"The keys are under the spare tire," he rasped, his mouth working open and shut as he gasped.

"What else, Carsten?"

Carsten's eyes were shut. His breaths short. A gurgling sound could be heard in his lungs.

"Can I find him with what you've told me?" Bernd growled, an inch from Carsten's clammy face. "Tell me, damn it!"

Carsten's eyes fluttered as the poison enveloped him.

Gripping Carsten's bloody lapels, Bernd shook the slight man. "Tell me something, Carsten…anything. Give me one final clue."

Carsten wet his lips, his voice a croak. "He loves…"

"Loves what? What does he love?"

With the trace of a sardonic smile, Carsten breathed the word "women", managing a raspy laugh as his life escaped him.

The poison should have taken five or six minutes to kill Carsten. With Bernd's blade slicing him like a cured Virginia ham, and Carsten's poor health, he was dead in three.

Bernd straightened, repeating everything he had learned to himself, burning it into his brain. The three most important items were the man's name, the existence of a safety deposit box and, Bernd said aloud as he dragged Carsten's corpse back to the Chevrolet, the fact that this man named Samuel Fields "loves women."

He would dispose of the body quickly and rifle Carsten's apartment for any relevant items; then he would sleep.

Tomorrow was to be a busy day.

ROLLIE DONAHUE lived in Skokie, a suburb just outside the shadows of Chicago's skyscrapers, and just far enough away to have a hint of small-town Americana. About half of Skokie's denizens were Jewish, many of them recent immigrants, fleeing the rampant hatred in much of Europe, coming to America to find things marginally better. Their presence also lent a unique European feel to Skokie, offering all manner of delicacies and crafts not typically found in the United States.

While few of the townspeople knew Rollie personally, many, if questioned, would certainly recall the tired-looking man who occasionally was seen coming and going, lugging his battered wooden toolbox up and down the village streets. With a neck-enveloping scar under his chin, who could mistake him? As he'd awaited his current assignment, he'd done handyman repairs on the cheap, but lately had been gone on most days. When asked, he'd tug on his cap and mutter, "More work downtown. Pay's better."

Things must have been better because now Rollie, who went by the name of Linton Rucker, even owned a car. A beat up old Ford, but a car nonetheless. If anyone were to question him about it, he planned to tell them his sister died and left it to him.

No one asked.

For a year and a half, Rollie had spent his days blending into the village of Skokie. With dark circles under his vivid blue eyes, the local women would often shake their heads and admonish him after he requested odd jobs for pay. "The lush" they called him. Three times a week, and somewhat obviously, Rollie would emerge from Benton's Main Street liquor store, right at five on the dot, carrying a large brown sack of joy back to his dilapidated rental house over on Concord Lane. But it was what went on inside that house, if those women knew, that would truly amaze them.

After keying the door, Rollie would straighten from his forced poor posture, stretching for a full ten minutes. He would then head straight to the sink, pouring the bottle of liquor down the drain, flushing water behind it to carry away the cloying smell. It wasn't that he didn't like to drink; he did enjoy the occasional beer or glass of wine, though certainly not two-bit rye whiskey. While at the sink (unless he planned to go back out), he would use the hand towel to wipe away the dark greasepaint from under his eyes.

Once the blinds and curtains were shut, Rollie always removed his "uniform" of filthy overalls. Then, perhaps the most important of his daily rituals, he would rub the scars of his neck and torso with prescription lotion. Because he couldn't reach much of his back, Rollie had created a device—essentially a washcloth on the end of a stick—to apply the lotion to the scars while he watched in the mirror. Once the lotion was applied, Rollie would stare at his deformed body for a moment, imagining the horror a woman might experience if she ever saw his skin in the light. The scars ran in all directions, courtesy of hundreds of skin grafts performed by the military and civilian doctors.

Usually Rollie twisted his head around, eyeing his back, ruefully comparing himself to a kindergartener's clay rendering of the boogeyman. His muscles had eventually recovered, though, due to atrophy and trauma, they were somewhat misshapen.

Finished with his ritual, he would don a pair of shorts and always a clean undershirt, crew style so he didn't have to see the majority of his wounds. For sixty to ninety minutes straight, six evenings a week, he set about a rigorous calisthenics program, alternating days to allow his muscle groups to recover. He'd learned the technique from a strongman on the isle of Kauai, a solid block of a man who'd first worked with Rollie to regain his strength.

On this night, after Hampton's odd behavior and Rollie's frustrating call to Nicholas Penland, Rollie exercised as usual. The night before he'd focused on his legs, back and biceps. Therefore, tonight would consist of exercises for his chest and triceps muscles, and, as always, his abdomen and lower back. First came thirty push-ups, slow and deep. Rollie then rolled over without rest, doing sit-ups with his feet wedged under the dormant radiator. Then came diamond push-ups, with his hands so close together the area between his thumbs and index fingers made a small diamond shape. He'd seen all these exercises before, but it was the procedure of how they were done that was so effective.

What he hadn't seen before, also taught to him by the Hawaiian, was an exercise called a canoe. To do a canoe, Rollie laid prone on the floor in a Superman position, then simply raised all limbs (and head) six inches from the floor, holding them that way, making the body arch in the shape of a canoe, all his weight resting on his stomach near his belly button. He did ten, each lasting ten seconds. Following these four exercises, he started again, declining in repetitions until he was physically spent. There were other exercises he used, constantly changing up his rotation: chin-ups, outward tension, barbells, dumbbells, and an agonizing set of exercises involving an old pipe, a length of rope, and a five-pound weight. While it might have looked ghastly, what remained of his body was rock hard and nearly devoid of any excess. Best of all, due to the exercises breaking up the scar tissue, he was without joint or muscular pain.

Other than the psychological pain, Rollie's aches occurred at the skin. The lotion took most of the pain away. But when Rollie failed to coat his scars, small splits would occur. It was like having hundreds of paper cuts.

When finished with his routine, Rollie cooked a small dinner for himself, eating it by the radio. Last year, when he was home early in the summer months (after donning his coveralls again), he would occasionally sit out on the back porch while listening to the city's beloved Cubs finishing their afternoon ballgame. Since it was early spring, the Cubs had played much earlier today, and had lost. So, instead, in the darkness, Rollie tried to listen to *The Hermit's Cave*, unable to get into the rambling story as he thought about the brown bottle by his bed.

Sometime around ten he switched off the radio, listening to the silence. There were a few crickets chirping out back. More would be coming as the days warmed and grew longer. He stretched out on the threadbare sofa, staring up at the ceiling as he rested his head on his interlaced hands. In his eighteen years of government work, Rollie had always done as he was told. First as a Marine, then as he worked his way through the ranks of federal law enforcement. Eighteen years is a long time. Rollie wondered what he would do outside of government service. A void pressed into his mind, a great black hole. Not one idea came to him, as if life outside of his career didn't exist.

But it was during those eighteen years, two of them spent recovering, that Rollie had crafted a keen instinct. And right now, that instinct was telling him—screaming—that Richard Hampton was up to no good, and it was somehow bigger than selling some low-level foreign agent a handful of designs of his company's newest fighter plane.

Though he wasn't tired, Rollie retired to bed without ingesting any of the liquid from the brown bottle. He laid there for a half-hour, hearing his pulse as his heart-rate steadily increased.

Memories of Gran Chaco, bombs, burns.

The smell of burning flesh, the smell of death.

There was no use.

Flinging his feet from under the sheet, he sat on the side of the bed and uncapped the dropper from the brown bottle. Filling the dropper full of the morphine sulfate solution, Rollie leaned his head back, squirting it into the back of his mouth, swishing the awful tasting compound around before swallowing it. This was three times the dose Rollie had taken earlier.

What followed, unfortunately, was quite blissful.

Hallucinogenic time passed as he stared at the whirling ceiling, free from himself.

But, oddly, sleep wasn't to be found. At 11:30 he stood, unsteadily walking to the kitchen, hand resting on the earpiece of the wall phone. His head lowered to his upper arm, resting there.

"No," Rollie whispered.

But there was no use. Tonight he was giving in to all his vices. He lifted the earpiece and dialed the five digits he'd long ago memorized.

"Hi," he said nervously, though he'd made this call a hundred times. "Is someone available to come soon?" He listened. "Good. My address is one-thirty-eight...oh, you knew it by my voice? Well...how long?" He mumbled his thanks before hanging up. As the most intense portion of his morphine high abated, he took a very quick shower, reapplying the lotion afterward. After donning fresh boxers and a black undershirt, Rollie turned out every light in the house. Only a strip of light shown through above the heavy drapes, bleeding in from the outside. He waited by the door. She arrived twenty minutes later, heavy with perfume, her young voice scratchy from too many cigarettes.

He led her inside.

"Kinda dark in here, isn't it?" the young woman said. She was from the South. Kentucky, or maybe east Tennessee.

"I like it that way."

"Yeah, that's what Silvie said. She said you're real sweet, too."

She couldn't see him in the darkness, but had she been able to, after she got over the scars on his neck, she'd have surely been puzzled by his expression. His eyes were squeezed shut, a grimace on his face. It was an expression of self-loathing, one Rollie knew well. When he gathered himself, he took her hand, leading her to the couch.

"This won't take long," he said in a reassuring voice. "I have to get up early tomorrow."

"It's your dime, mister. Take as long as you want."

But it didn't take long. Rollie's actions, as they always seemed to be after he dialed those five familiar digits, were purely mechanical. He was gentle enough, wearing a prophylactic although it wasn't required. He pinned her wrists above her head, but not to be rough. He knew if he didn't she might feel his scars through his undershirt. The woman, as all the skilled ones did, added in the requisite moans, gyrating her body over the five minute duration of their interaction.

Finished, as he sat breathing heavily, the woman fumbled with something from her purse.

Bright light exploded as she surprised him by lighting a cigarette. He twisted so violently his swinging arm accidentally spun her from the couch. The lighter went out, clattering across the floor.

"Was it that bright?" the woman asked, laughing nervously.

"I'm sorry," he said, relieved that she hadn't seen his body. He stood, crossing the dark room, finding the lighter and the two bills from the table, pressing all of it into her hand. Even in the dark, obviously well-practiced, the young woman was dressed in a flash. With an uneasy thank you, she allowed him to lead her to the door, exiting into the purple of the night as he stood behind the door, out of view. When she was gone, Rollie leaned his head against the door. He stayed that way for some time, eventually filling a glass with water and heading back to his bed.

Typically after a large dose of morphine and a session with one of the call girls he fell right to sleep. But not tonight. He tossed and turned, eventually feeling hot, the sweats returning. He kicked the covers back, his mind flashing pictures like a slide show, the images starting quickly, replaying, winnowing down until only a final few features played on the screen of his mind: the coquettish woman in red from earlier, the firm young woman who had just been under him (even though he hadn't seen her, he'd felt enough to draw a solid mental picture); and the final image, the one that stuck there until sometime well after 1:30 A.M., Vivien Hampton, tall and blonde and regal. There was something about her, something alluring, something he couldn't quite discern.

Without taking another dose, Rollie replaced the bottle in the back of the concealing drawer, thankful that his mind wasn't racing about Gran Chaco.

It was ten of three when he last looked at the clock. Tomorrow was to be an early day. Rollie knew he was going to be awfully tired.

And while he knew tomorrow would be a long day, what he didn't know was what the day might hold.

If he had, he might have taken that second dose.

Chapter Two

April 15, 1943
Havana, Cuba

THE FOLLOWING morning began with a gorgeous sunrise. Bernd von Danzig greeted the sun's arrival from his painted balcony, smoking an American cigarette and enjoying a fine cup of room-service coffee in the cool whispers of the Cuban morning. He sat on the spindly wicker chair, wearing only the hotel robe, rubbing the small key to the bank box nervously in his left hand.

The sun's welcome appearance set the whitewashed buildings to his east aflame. While happy to finally see the sunrise, there were still yet another three hours before the bank would open—an eternity to an impatient man dying to finalize the plan for his life's masterwork. His bare foot was propped on the lower rail of the balcony railing, tapping nervously.

Three long hours. Verdammt!

Rather than sit still for what would be a terminal amount of time, Bernd crushed out the cigarette, donned the previous day's clothes (minus the sport coat, which was unfortunately ruined by Carsten Steuben's sickly blood), and walked down to the ornate lobby of La Habana Magnífica. He found the extremely pleasant concierge busy behind his Victorian desk. Speaking his British English, Bernd requested a shave and a shoe shine, sliding three Cuban pesos to the avuncular little man in order to hurry his actions. The concierge nodded politely before he made a phone call, speaking native Spanish so rapidly that Bernd—who was fully fluent—hadn't a prayer to follow along. The call appeared to be quite terse. But when he hung up, the concierge's features seemed to relax as he smoothly informed Bernd that the hotel barber would arrive shortly. In the meantime, the concierge donned a canvas apron and personally applied a glossy black shine to Bernd's Oxford caps, taking care to remove dirt from the soles along with what looked like a few scarlet tomato sauce spots that seemed to have spattered from somewhere on the tops of the shoes.

The barber, a young man, arrived soon after. He was heavily obese with sleep lines on his face and forehead, and was waiting by the time Bernd's shine was complete. Bernd again tipped the solicitous concierge generously, whispering something to him that resulted in an approving nod and a wink.

"Sí señor, that can easily be arranged."

"Even at this hour?"

"In Havana, señor, anything is possible."

"Very well," Bernd replied. "Please have her wait in the sitting area by the lift, on my floor."

"She will be there," the concierge replied, hurrying back to his desk to make another urgent phone call.

The barber took Bernd to the rear porch of the hotel, overlooking a lovely garden, the morning birds providing a cacophony of tropical song. Bernd lay back, his eyes closed as the Cuban provided a close shave, downward, then, after another lathering, upward. The young man produced clippers, carefully snipping and sanding each of Bernd's fingernails. He was especially careful with Bernd's bandaged right hand, Bernd telling him dismissively that he'd been bitten by a stray dog. Finally, the barber finished by shampooing Bernd's hair before giving it a light trim. After the trim, he rinsed the blond hair, toweling it and combing it severely with the help of old-fashioned Makassar oil. Finished, Bernd tipped the man before ambling back to his suite, getting a miniature salute from the grinning concierge. A check of his watch showed only ninety more minutes remained. Just enough time for a morning romp and a relaxing bath.

On the fourth floor landing, just to the left of the elevator, sat a fresh-faced young woman, wearing a cheap sundress and a wide-brim hat. Her shapely legs were crossed as she sat: very ladylike. Had Bernd squinted his eyes, blurring his vision, he might have thought she was a young lady of society. But he didn't squint—instead, he leered at her, drinking her in. She couldn't have been more than nineteen, with an unlined face and the taut olive skin of Cuban youth. As Bernd stared, he could feel his excitement forming tangibly. He smiled, more to himself than her, proffering his hand. "M'lady."

She accepted his hand, flashing a dazzling smile marred only by slightly crooked teeth. "Señor."

He led her to his suite, quickly learning that she spoke very little English. Having no desire to converse with her, his actions were deliberate, if not a bit rough. Whenever Bernd enjoyed a prostitute, especially a young one like as this, he always sought to provide her a genuine climax, if only to prove to himself that it was possible. To give a woman, who had sex for a living, pleasure—*while* having sex—showed genuine prowess and virility. After going through a multitude of positions, he situated her on her back. Using his powerful hands, even with the bandaging on the right, he gripped her hands above her as he went to work. When he saw what looked like a pained expression on her face, he increased his speed and pressure, satisfied to hear her breaths cease for long periods as she held her mouth open, concentrating. Next came the moans, deep guttural sounds as the young woman lost all sense of self-consciousness and succumbed to sheer pleasure, her trim abdomen undulating with each wave of the coming climax. And, on this occasion, the señorita's pleasure was certainly genuine, resulting in a fit of shuddering that left the young woman momentarily paralyzed before she reached up and cupped Bernd's face in her hands, murmuring some sort of colloquial praise that involved his being compared to a governor.

He finished in short time, completing his act without any sort of prevention, hoping (as he did with every woman he slept with) that she might wind up pregnant. The earth would be a much better place with more Bernd von Danzigs—or, so he thought.

She bathed him immediately afterward, soaping every inch of his body as she followed the washcloth with small kisses, making him feel every bit the governor she thought he was. During the bath, Bernd spoke Spanish to the girl, learning that when she turned *eighteen*—which had been only a few weeks before—her father had sent her into the city to make money for the family. She worked for a madam, a truly wicked woman to hear the young woman's tale. Bernd was only her third "date".

Believing her account, he commanded her not to go back to the brothel. After toweling off, Bernd made a dinner date with her for eight in the evening, giving her five pesos and telling her to buy a new dress. He called downstairs, arranging a room for her, telling her to spend her day relaxing.

The man known as *Der Geist* then sent her on her way. It was time to get dressed. After more than three long hours of wakefulness, there was finally business at hand.

Chicago, Illinois

DARKNESS GREETED Rollie, along with a piercing headache. The headaches were common, and he knew how to deal with them. He stood, sliding his hand on the wall in the creaky hallway, guiding his way to the small kitchen. Once he'd managed to open his eyes in the harsh overhead light, he loaded the top of the percolator from his rapidly dwindling stash of Chase & Sanborn coffee. Two cups were all he needed and he reminded himself to start checking his sources to acquire more.

While the coffee brewed, Rollie guzzled three glasses of water, feeling his headache briefly intensify. That was okay—it would be gone in a few more minutes. When the coffee was ready, he carried a cup out the back door to the small fenced-in yard. The cold seemed to have blown out during the night, leaving the morning cool yet pleasant, with the promise of a true spring day. The sweet smell of early-blooming phlox wafted on the gentle breeze from his neighbor's backyard. Something about the scent, and the strong, earthy coffee, whisked his mind back to where it had been headed last night when sleep had first evaded him. His mind went far southward, to the Chaco Boreal of South America.

The memories that dominated his nightmares revolved around the largely unknown Chaco War. Rollie, a Marine, had taken part in the war, before his disfigurement.

The Chaco War was, and remains, one of the great charades of the 20th Century. A war between Bolivia and Paraguay, two of the world's poorest countries, supposedly fighting over ownership of the region known as Gran Chaco. Rollie was there, his Marine service undercover while he acted as a mercenary, unknowingly leading innocent men to their deaths while he and the rest of the cadre were misled by Washington assholes and robber barons in well-appointed boardrooms.

Rollie sipped the coffee, remembering the final day when he and his remaining platoon had been pinned down, jammed into that wedge of a ravine with nowhere to go but up. He and Stinson were the last two Americans of the bunch and, just before they heard the airplane, the rocky ravine echoed with the voices of their assailants.

The voices were English, speaking in American accents.

What they'd suspected for so long had been true.

Fearing confusion, Stinson had yelled to the opposing force, telling them they were shooting at Americans. He was greeted with curses and a burst of full-automatic fire.

That had confirmed all of Rollie's suspicions.

And, soon after, the dark blue night sky of the Chaco Boreal displayed one of the most fearsome sights to any ground fighter. It was the blackness of a swiftly moving airplane, swooping in from high like a hawk closing on a defenseless rodent. The aircraft, as Rollie later learned, was a state-of-the-art Curtiss A-12 Shrike, piloted by an American. It roared down, diving into the canyon, propelled to top speed by its death-defying descent. And just before it would have smashed into the wedge of the canyon's end, it pulled rapidly skyward, simultaneously releasing two 122-pound incendiary bombs from the racks underneath its wings.

Rollie clearly remembered the two bombs' arching descent, tumbling awkwardly to his men. He recalled his yells urging cover, and his final glance at the assailants. They were standing on the ridge, no longer concerned over being shot. Just before the bombs struck, he saw one of them raise his hands like a football referee signaling a touchdown.

Americans.

The memory of the screams and the smell of sizzling flesh were thankfully interrupted by the neighbor's barking dog. Rollie had dropped his cup and was holding onto the railing of his back porch, preventing himself from falling. Mere feet away, separated only by the knee-high fence, the neighbor's brown and white mutt yapped at the street, probably set off by the paperboy.

"Good boy," Rollie breathed, thankful for the intrusion.

He turned, staggering back to the door, knowing it was probably half-past six. Time to go to work.

Putting the thoughts of Gran Chaco aside for now, Rollie went inside, trembling hands and all, pouring his second cup of coffee and preparing a simple breakfast.

He checked the clock, vowing to be out the front door in a half-hour.

BERND VON Danzig, having sent the newly-rich young prostitute on her way, dressed in his finest glen plaid suit, tailored of extremely light tropical wool, feeling nothing less than dashing on the twenty-minute walk to Carsten's bank. Though the day promised to be quite warm, the air was not yet thick with the sweat-producing humidity that would later cover Havana like a unwelcome blanket. When he neared the bank Bernd's muscular chest began to tighten as it did with every operation that had a remote chance of failure. There had been no bank book at Carsten's apartment. The bastard had hidden it somewhere. Therefore, what Bernd planned to do was incredibly delicate and would require balls of brass. Fortunately, he had two of them. He slowed, closing his eyes for long periods, rehearsing his lines, bolstering his certainty that he could pull this off. Especially since he'd found Carsten's small stash of bribery cash.

Making the task more difficult was choosing the proper banker to deal with. It was critical that the banker wasn't familiar with Carsten or, as his papers read, Harold Lancaster. And one needed always worry over people remembering Carsten—his volubility and puppy-dog nature typically cut a wide swath of toadying goodwill wherever he'd been.

I'll know soon enough.

The bank was large and quiet, lacking in appearance compared to what a person might find at a similar-size bank in Germany or the U.S. It felt more like a gutted Edwardian home than a financial institution, and Bernd purposefully didn't allow himself to be sidetracked upon entering. He walked to the center counter, the one with pens and slips of deposit, furtively studying the different personnel and tellers. He wanted to avoid the senior bankers and the sharp-eyed whippersnappers of the group—he was looking for the harried middle-aged banker of the institution. The employee every office has, fearing for his job but still not working hard enough to impress, utilizing a strategy of hope and nothing more. Bernd rotated his head. *No. No. Definitely not. Maybe. No…*

There!

Overweight, chin bulging from his sweat-stained collar, the banker sat in a small office, a cigarette burning in an ashtray and a half-eaten piece of sugared bread next to his hand. He stealthily held a newspaper just behind the lip of his desk, too stupid to realize that the edge of the page protruded beyond the side of his desk. The excess weight. The slovenly appearance. The effort at not working. Bernd would no more let the man manage his money than he'd hire him to wash his car. With his crooked tie, stained shirt, and cluttered office, the banker was the picture of incompetence.

He was perfect!

Wiping a film of sweat from his upper lip, Bernd stepped smartly to the man's office, noticing the nameplate and committing the name to memory. "Señor Landa? Buenos dias. Habla English?"

The fat man nearly jumped from his skin, rising quickly after his start, probably unaccustomed to being sought out by bank customers. Beside him, the fútbol section of the newspaper fluttered to the floor. Using his hoof-like foot, Landa slid it under the desk as he stuttered his affirmation that he knew limited English.

Bernd removed his gray fedora, smoothing his freshly-oiled hair with his hand. "Señor Landa, I was referred to you by an accommodating gentleman at my hotel."

"Who might that be?" Landa asked, trying to conceal his surprise and failing miserably.

"I didn't get his name, but I will send him your compliments, good enough?"

"Sí señor. How may I help you?" Landa leaned forward, offering up a toothy smile as he deftly deposited the sugared bread in his top drawer.

"I have two items of business to attend to. They're quite private," Bernd said in a low voice. Nodding, Señor Landa stepped around him, closing the door.

"Better?"

"Thank you," Bernd said. "I certainly don't want to appear rude."

"Rude in what way?"

"Well, when I opened my account here, I didn't really care for the banker who helped me."

"Oh?" Landa asked, a note of satisfaction in his voice. "And who was that?"

Bernd showed his palm, shaking his head. "Please, I don't want to make an issue of it. In fact, I've already forgotten the man's name." Seeing Landa's face cloud just a bit, Bernd went in for the kill. "Anyway, I have an additional ten thousand dollars to deposit which, if I'm not mistaken, enjoys a one-to-one exchange with your Cuban peso. I was hoping you, Señor Landa, could help me and become my personal banker."

Landa couldn't manage to keep his mouth closed. His jaw fell open, further pressing his mass of chins onto his straining collar. After several audible breaths, he nodded and managed a smile. "Yes, yes, of course."

Making a shooing motion, as if it were of little importance, Bernd also said, "And I need to add just one little thing to my safety deposit box." He produced his key, pressing it onto the desk with a click.

"Of course, of course," Landa said, rubbing his hands together, undoubtedly unconcerned with the deposit box as his mind was awash in the stunning sum this man planned to deposit—just as Bernd had planned. "May I please see your bank book?"

The undercover Nazi agent automatically tapped the breasts of his glen plaid suit, a rueful expression on his face. "I searched my chamber this morning and seem to have misplaced it. This was another reason I felt it urgent to come and see you. I don't want anyone accessing my account but me."

Landa's pudgy face was stern, his eyes narrowed. He punctuated the air with a fat finger and said, "Normally, this would be a problem, Señor…"

"Lancaster."

"Señor Lancaster. And this is why your hotel caballero did well to send you to me. For you I will, as you say in English, *twist* the rules, yes?"

"Your English is magnificent."

Landa stood. "May I have your identification?"

Bernd handed Carsten's British passport and Visa over, having substituted the photo page with his own.

"And may I also have your deposit check?"

"Is cash acceptable?"

"Oh, yes, of course," Landa breathed.

Bernd removed two hotel envelopes, each containing fifty American hundred-dollar bills, adorned with gold certificates, denoting their age as being issued shortly after the financial crash. This was Carsten's bribe money, and he still gripped it as Landa held the other end of the envelopes. "Please, Señor Landa, keep my presence quiet this morning. I don't want that rude man to come and claim me as his client." Bernd released the money.

Señor Landa paused at the door, his bratwurst of a finger over his lips in a gesture of solemn silence. He disappeared, pulling the door shut behind him. Bernd sat ramrod straight, trying with all his might to remain focused on the mission as his mind kept wandering to the olive-skinned prostitute. She was quite different than the dumpy Mexican hookers he enjoyed several times a week. While, probably due to her age, she was overly deferential, there was something slightly haughty about her persona, and that drove Bernd mad. He put her out of his mind by firmly decreeing to himself that tonight he would do things to her that she never dared dream, things that would ruin all future experiences with any man. He would wreak havoc on her nubile body, leaving her begging for more of the convulsive, quivering pleasures that only he could provide.

About fifteen minutes passed before Landa returned, a cobalt blue bank book in his hand along with the Lancaster identification papers. "You dealt with Señor DeLeon before." He sat, the wooden chair groaning under his girth. "I'm not at all surprised that you didn't enjoy his presence. He's far too serious about things. Just so uptight."

Bernd accepted the book, seeing the previous deposit of 250 pesos—probably the minimum to warrant a safety deposit box. Just below that was today's deposit. He looked up, smiling at Señor Landa. "You've been incredibly helpful today."

Landa bowed his head. "The pleasure was mine, Meester Lancaster."

"Is there anything else?"

"Two signatures, please."

Bernd had practiced the signatures for an hour after finding the identification and switching the photo page. The trick to a good forgery was speed and muscle memory. Doing it slow would make it appear disjointed, the easiest tip to a trained eye. Most people complete their signature in less than two seconds. Bernd took only a second for each one, handing the pen back while motioning out into the bank.

"Now my deposit box?"

"Oh, yes," Landa replied, shuffling the papers. He led Bernd across the floor, handing the papers to an older woman sitting at a clerical desk. On the far end of the old building sat a man behind gold-painted bars. Landa asked to see Bernd's key, squinting to see the number. He asked the man behind the bars for the matching key and led Bernd into the vault containing the boxes. Both men inserted the small keys into the box cover. Landa pulled the small door open, sliding the rectangular box from its cubby and placing it on the center desk.

"Would you like to deposit your item here, or would you prefer a private nook?"

"A nook, if you will. Just for a moment."

A moment later, Bernd was alone behind a purple curtain, a high, roundel-style barred window casting morning light into the small room. The movement of the curtain had propelled dust into the air, dancing by Bernd's eyes as he stared down at the box, his hand resting on top. With a sharp breath, he lifted the lid, eyes widening at the minimal contents.

The first item he noticed was the passport. It was Canadian. He opened it, allowing fifty folded pesos to tumble to the table. After tucking the money into his pocket, he marked the passport as an additional cover for Carsten and set it aside. The second item was a letter without an envelope. He opened it, reading the syrupy feminine German writing, realizing immediately it was from Carsten's fiancé, Katarina.

"What a dumbass," Bernd breathed. Possessing any type of cover-blowing paraphernalia, even letters from fiancés in safety deposit boxes, was expressly forbidden. Had he not already murdered him, Bernd would have loved to have castigated Carsten in an official reprimand that would be carbon-copied to a number of Berlin desks. He placed the letter on top of the passport, making a mental note to sleep with the fiancé the next time he was near Köln. The third item was obviously a photo, face down, the scalloped edges of the photo paper a dead giveaway. Bernd turned it over, his face transforming from severe concentration to a grin immediately.

He was staring at the image of a handsome man in a tropical wool suit. The man's coat was over his arm, his fedora kicked back on his head. The shot was taken at a profile angle, giving an excellent view of the subject's features. He appeared to be purchasing fruit from a street vendor, and as he drank in every detail of the photo, Bernd whispered, "Hello, Mister Samuel Fields. I now know what you look like."

But it was the last item that provided the great mystery to Bernd von Danzig. A key, about half as long as Bernd's index finger, and without any markings whatsoever. It was brass and appeared well-used. He studied it in the cubby; he studied it on the walk back to his hotel; he asked the concierge if he had any idea what the key might open; he made a list of possibilities back in his room. Bernd napped that afternoon, sleeping fitfully. When he awoke, the key remained a question. He had no clue what its purpose was.

DESPITE THE cold and damp of the day before, the southerly night winds ushered in a glorious day that was essentially a sneak preview of May: warm and beautiful, with a clear blue sky and temperatures in the upper seventies. Richard Hampton sat high above downtown Chicago, his green eyes gazing in the direction of Lake Michigan and the touristy pier area. The Omicron Aviation executive, no longer concerned with doing any work, daydreamed. He recalled the ballyhooed day he was promoted to Senior Director, one of only twenty-two in a company of three thousand. Outranking him were just six vice-presidents, and beyond them only the president himself. Though he'd expected the promotion, his ascent hadn't been easy.

Richard remembered first catching the eye of his division vice president. Richard had purposefully outworked his associates in a year-long grind of early mornings and long nights—probably the first nail in the coffin of his crumbling marriage. Following his promotion, which had occurred two years earlier, he spent numerous weeks and weekends in Champagne, listening to droning conversations about the challenges of dropping an atomic device. After that were the blasted weeks down in Oak Ridge, staring over white-coated shoulders at relayed yards of ticker tape readouts. He recalled trying to concentrate as the scientists lamented over fractional differences that were meaningless next to the loss of Richard's personal wealth.

And, somehow, probably due to Omicron's arrogance, they'd not run a financial check on Richard in over five years. Even when they'd promoted him. Doing no follow-up checks on Richard didn't surprise him all that much. His company, despite the way it ginned money—because of the war and their president's government connections—was poorly run.

After growing up in abject poverty, Richard appreciated money—and he invested carefully, at first. When the big crash had come, he'd had his money tied up in company stock. And, in the late 1930s, as the market recovered, the company grew healthy again. He sold the stock when he was allowed to, at first wisely buying blue chip stocks in an effort at diversification. But that's where the common sense had ended.

Shortly after his promotion, he began searching for values, buying low-priced stocks in his search for gems that could double overnight. A few big hits were followed by numerous misses. When that dragged his fortune down by a third, Richard went looking for an aggressive investment that could create ten times his money. He soon found it. While he called it an investment, "an incredibly high concern" was the term used by that overstuffed sycophant down at the bank. He'd advised Richard not to invest a single dime, but the foundering copper company had seemed so promising. Richard made an enormous investment, pledging everything for a quarter of the business and a seat on the board: all of his stock, all of his cash; even the equity in his home. The company, able to make its payroll because of his investment, failed in only seven months. Richard had only gotten to attend one board meeting—a bunch of yelling and hand-wringing—and they didn't even provide lunch. All he'd labored for was gone.

He should have listened to the sycophant.

But Richard, not an engineer or a physicist, possessed a manager's practical mind. He had a way out of all of this, and the key to his way out sat inches from his hand, resting on the blotter of his desk. Traitorous as his plan was, his mind wasn't troubled. Like all of his peccadilloes, he'd rationalized it away as he'd created his ingenious plot.

Occasionally in a person's life, a moment comes along that's so precipitous, so life-changing, that he or she has to sit back and view the moment for what it is—good or bad. It could be a professional peak, toasted with champagne—or the first dark night of a long prison sentence. Such highs and lows are distinct—they aren't ever missed, and they're rarely forgotten. And while he had once been living the quintessential American dream—the familiar rags-to-riches tale every red-blooded American loves—Richard Hampton, with all the wealth he had once amassed, hadn't yet had his moment. But he would. He most certainly would. Because, as far as everyone in his life was concerned, Richard Hampton would cease to exist in just a matter of days.

And that would be his moment. The start of it, anyway.

The windows of his Omicron Aviation office were up, the stuffy high floor made pleasant by the temperate lake breeze blowing three hundred feet above bustling Wacker Drive. It carried with it the scent of the lake Richard so loved. Twenty-seven stories below, children danced in the frigid waters of an open hydrant in River Park—thoughts of treason far from their dripping heads.

Richard turned and allowed his hands to linger on the supple calfskin briefcase. Inside was everything he needed for future bliss. There was, of course, a well-used passport in the name of James Samuel Fields. The name sounded a bit bland, which is exactly what he wanted when he created it nearly a year before, just when his copper investment had begun to evaporate. Richard had used the new passport to make a run to Mexico and, on two occasions, to his favored haven, Panama. It was in Panama where he struck veritable oil. He'd been there once before, back in December, on his real passport, surprised at the clash of cultures that existed in the narrow isthmus country. Their former president had been a fascist, thereby paving the way for numerous Axis agents.

And that was why Richard—Sam Fields, actually—had become a favored visitor.

Just below the passport was a handsome russet folio, buttoned tightly. Inside the two covers of the outer binding, sewn between the silk lining and accessible only by cutting away the stitching, was the sum of $2,000 all in brand new $20 bills, taken from the advance he'd received from the pale little Englishman in Panama City. The bills were distributed evenly so as not to be lumpy, nested there for insurance in the unlikely event he needed the money for an in-transit bribe. Even if he didn't need to make a bribe, the money's presence would allow him to sleep better on the ship that would sail from Galveston in two days' time. And below the folio was a petite bank book, the gilded letters on the front written in Spanish. But it wasn't the letters of the book Richard was concerned with. No. It was the numbers, universal in most any language. The sum total of all of his meager deposits down in the lower right corner of the second page. The one that read *B/.3,000*, displayed in Panamanian Balboas which (like the Cuban peso) enjoyed a one-to-one exchange for U.S. dollars (readily accepted in Panama.) Richard ran his thumb over the total, feeling the slight depression where the typewriter had hammered the paper, the typist backing up and striking it two or three more times for emphasis.

Richard liked emphasis, especially when it came to money. His money.

That 3,000, added to his bribe-ready 2,000, was essentially all he had to his name. Not counting his home, which would likely be in foreclosure soon, he was more than $10,000 in debt. He'd spent his recent salary on his travels and preparations, hiding every trace of his financial peril from Vivien, his wife. She'd find out soon enough—it would serve well as his suicide motive.

He did wonder, with mixed feelings, how she would eventually deal with the loan shark representing the notorious Chicago mobster Sean O'Bannon. Richard's "bridge loan" was overdue, not that he truly cared. Perhaps they'd show her some sort of leniency. Though he doubted it, his mind was far too cluttered to concern himself with such inconsequential worries.

In the bottom drawer of his desk, under lock and key, were his personal financial files. He'd spent nearly a year cultivating this event, papering the files in such an obvious way that the investigators would certainly believe his suicide was genuine. In his untraceable queries at the library, Richard learned that nearly a third of the persons who went missing on Lake Michigan were never found, dead or alive. They would almost certainly find the note first, then the boat, drifting aimlessly in the unpredictable spring currents. Richard planned to shear a piece of nautical rope, leaving remnants of the severed cord on the deck. He would drag a concrete block over the rail, gouging it deeply. At that area of the lake, given its depth, the investigators would be forced to assume he tied a block to his ankle, taking the plunge over the side. They would search for a cursory amount of time before they would collectively shrug, offering a hollow condolence to the striking widow whose husband had apparently squandered his fortune and taken his life. Then they would move on to something far more pressing—probably something to do with the war effort.

The war effort. His saving grace.

But what he would give to see the exchange between Vivien and the investigators. He'd give a tenth—maybe even a fifth!—of his bounty to have a picture of her expression. He leaned back, envisioning the very first question that would be uttered through those painted, bitchy lips of hers:

"How much insurance did my husband have?"

The investigators would glance at one another.

"What's the problem?" she would ask, voice shrill over her growing consternation. Vivien was an expert at reading expressions. "He *had* insurance, didn't he?"

"Had a corporate policy, ma'am, but he took his own life, so…and I'm sorry to tell you this…but the insurance company won't pay a dime, not on a suicide."

"What?" she would scream, grabbing the lapels of anyone in her vicinity. "*What?*"

"Afraid so, ma'am."

"Get out, all of you!" That's when they would hear her breaking things inside, cursing Richard to the high heavens.

Richard laughed, deeply warmed by the imagined scene.

Good old Vivien and her short-fuse Irish temper. She could sell her jewels and the Lincoln, certainly enough to prop herself up for six months. With her looks, and that cozy little spot between her legs that she'd used to ensnare him a few years back, Richard couldn't see how she would have any problem whatsoever trading in his faded memories on some graying widower millionaire from Edison Park or Rockwell Crossing.

Hell, maybe she'd even have to reconcile with her dad, a prick of a Navy admiral stationed back east somewhere. Ironically, their falling out had come because of his reservations over Richard. She'd argued that Richard's early business successes, and his run up the corporate ladder, proved him as a changed man. But the admiral had run a background check on Richard's military and college years, and had insisted to his daughter that he was a skirt-chasing cad, not to be trusted. Since then, father and daughter had been estranged.

"You should have listened to the old asshole, Viv," Richard murmured with a smile.

He lifted his Panamanian itinerary, booked in the name of J. Samuel Fields. The destination read *Colon, Panama*, though to Richard the destination was actually *freedom*. He studied the times and dates before twisting the linen paper three times, creating a tube. From his pocket he produced his state-of-the-art Zippo lighter, sitting on the sill of the open window, holding the lighter just under the paper, his thumb on the flint-wheel. He stopped himself just as a smile came over his angular face.

What the hell am I doing?

This was cause for a celebration, especially after the gut-wrenching year he'd just endured.

This *was* his moment.

Standing from the sill, he crossed the room and opened the door, telling his secretary to keep everyone at bay because he needed a quiet half-hour to complete a sensitive report. The once-wealthy executive untied his shimmering silk tie and unbuttoned the top two buttons on the handmade, crisply starched white shirt. Chuckling at his own cleverness, giddy about his new life, he crossed the carpeted area of the office, stepping onto the hardwoods in front of the bar cabinet. From underneath he produced a pillow-sized humidor, once chock-full of fine cigars, now nearly empty. Knowing this day would someday come, he'd saved one, his favorite brand, a Bolivar Inmensa, left from his trip to Havana. After smelling its length and gnawing off its end, Richard clamped it in his mouth and moved back to the sill, lighting the cigar while holding the paper itinerary at the ready.

The soon-to-be-missing executive sat there, puffing away, looking over the skyline as if he were the creator of the entire kingdom. Just beyond the spire of the Wrigley Building, directly across from him, Richard noticed a B-17 lumbering into the warm April atmosphere—probably originating from Scott Field—heading east out over the lake. He tapped the cigar, wondering if that bomber might ever drop a bomb like the one he was about to sell the details of.

"What do I care?" he asked aloud, rotating his head down to the travel plan, drinking in the six letters that comprised the three-syllable word Panama. What did that tropical country hold for him? Would he be a land-owner in the Bocas del Toro area, revered by the village of peasants around him? Or would he settle near the numerous beaches of Comarca Kuna Yala, just another rich gringo hiding from his past, pretending there wasn't even a war on? And what women awaited him? Young ones? Mature ones—the type who knew what they wanted, vocal and bawdy? Would he have a favored bar, where the owner made his drink as soon as Richard darkened the door? All of this swirled together in Richard's mind, creating an intoxicating sense of mystery. But what wasn't a mystery was where Richard's money would come from. A single exchange was all it would take. No more work. No more investments. Just sit back, relax, and live on the interest.

Not typically a sentimental man, he thought back to his boyhood as a sharecropper on the southern Illinois corn farm. When tuberculosis claimed his father, his sickly mother had to give him and his sister up. The state split them up, sending him to a boys' home down in Quincy. Their mother died soon thereafter. He remembered the visit to the mortuary, the one that took indigent embalmings for whatever amount they were reimbursed by the state. Even though the cotton-packers had caked cheap makeup on his mother, it was obvious her body had decayed for some reason. Richard recalled the hollow-eyed old mortician. He'd pulled the sheet back on Richard's mother, lacking sympathy when, after reading his face, he told Richard his mother had been found dead in her bed. Wooden in appearance, like so many morticians seem to be, the man made sure to tell young Richard that she'd lain dead for "several hot days" before she was discovered.

"But how did she die?" Richard had stammered.

"From all I hear she was just poor and crazy," the ghostly old man had recalled, scratching his chin. "Now get outta here, kid. I got a job to do."

Richard joined the Army as soon as they would take him, spending a year of sheer misery in the trenches of France. And when he'd left the service, his left leg loaded with shards of German artillery shrapnel, they'd denied him even a single percent of disability.

The left leg seems fully functional despite the heavy scarring, was the final analysis in the brief health summary.

Bureaucratic pricks.

But he'd showed all of them, knifing through Lombard College over in Galesburg in just three-and-a-half years. Lombard had been on the ropes at the time, taking Richard as a provisional veteran on the promise that he'd pay back his student loans in ten years. Too bad they'd gone under soon after he received his diploma. And while he'd gotten out of paying full tuition, had Uncle Sam actually supported him with disability, maybe he'd have gone to Chicago or Northwestern. Who knows where he'd be now?

No, the U.S. had never looked out for Richard, so why should he be any different? He pulled a footstool from underneath the desk and propped himself up on the window frame, left leg dangling outside, right leg steadying himself on the stool. He stayed in the same position for a full half-hour as he enjoyed the Cuban cigar and the late afternoon breeze, watching as another B-17 faded to a speck in the eastern sky.

Richard dug out his Zippo again. He held the tube of damning itinerary outside the window, lighting it with the flickering flame from the Zippo. He waited until the paper singed his hands before dropping it, watching as it shed ash, burning in the breeze as it whipped east.

Standing inside, puffing away, Richard surveyed the skyline, certain that he'd never miss it. With a broad, self-satisfied grin, he closed the window and prepared to leave for the day.

Leave forever.

This, indeed, was the beginning of Richard Hampton's moment.

Chapter Three

FAR BELOW Richard Hampton, across the river and perilously close to where the children, eager for summer, played in the cold hydrant, sat Rollie Donahue. He was on a south-facing park bench, a newspaper folded over his lap, his head craned upward to where Hampton sat perched, dangling a leg from his penthouse office. This was where Rollie usually waited on Hampton, especially during pleasant weather. He'd acquire him as he left the front of the building, normally between five and seven P.M. It had been sheer luck that Rollie had arrived early, mainly to savor today's weather, and it surprised him to no end to glance up and actually see his mark sitting on his window sill like a man preparing to jump. Rollie eventually saw the puffs of smoke. He removed his mini-binoculars from his pocket, seeing the long cigar and pondering what brought on this odd period of reflection for Richard Hampton.

Next to Rollie, the school-age children splashed and played, enjoying their first day of Easter holidays. Easter, occurring in a little more than a week, fell extremely late this year, on April 25th. And, here in Chicago, it wasn't at all uncommon for spring break to be cursed with a wet snow, so the kids were indeed getting a rare treat today with the balmy temperatures.

Several gulls swooped over Rollie, circling for a moment to see if he was throwing bread. He turned his Barr & Stroud binoculars to them, just any fellow killing time on a beautiful day, watching the birds. After a moment, Rollie twisted them back to the top floor of Hampton's building, again scrutinizing what he saw. Still puffing away, Hampton seemed to be staring off to the northeast, leg casually dangling as if he had nary a fear.

Something was up. Rollie had felt it the night before and here he felt it again. For more than six months Hampton had acted one way—stressed mainly. Sure, he was an odd duck with the hookers and all, but his behavior had at least been consistent. But then he disappears for over a week, coming back bronzed, acting surreptitious, looking for tails, and now smoking cigars reflectively while dangling from high-rise buildings?

Holding the glasses to his face for one last look, he watched as Hampton held something out of the window. Something white. Then…flames.

Rollie cinched the binoculars to his eye sockets. Hampton was burning a sheet of paper. The flames licked upward, causing Hampton to release it. Rollie tracked the paper, whipping to the east and around the alleyway, propelled by the whirling wind. He remained focused on the paper, dancing, swirling, descending. The alleyway was a windbreak and, even though he lost sight of the paper, it had been descending rapidly after making the turn.

Running from where he sat, Rollie took a dousing as he sprinted through one of the hydrant's streams, earning surprised yells from the gathered children. He hurried across the bridge, nearly got run over by a bus on Wacker, and arrived in the shadowy alleyway, dejected upon seeing the amount of refuse cluttering the damp ground of the sun-shaded backstreet.

Taking a calming series of breaths, the federal man hung his fedora on a broken-off steel stud and, doing what any good investigator would do, he began searching the trash and scraps of paper one by one.

Thirty-five minutes later, Rollie found the scorched remnant of a sheet of linen paper. The left side of the paper was gone, the right side mostly intact, marked by black char marks on the left edge. After slowly studying the remaining words and word fragments, he carefully carried the paper to his old Ford, awaiting Richard Hampton's departure from work. While he waited, he reread the partial paper three times.

It was clearly a travel itinerary, destination Panama. The dates were gone, burned with the left side of the page.

Panama…

Rollie closed his eyes, recalling the mandatory continuing-education class he'd taken back around Christmastime, sitting in a smoky federal building auditorium with twenty other agents. The lecturer from D.C. had listed the current havens of foreign agents, speaking at length about Cuba, Brazil, Argentina, and—of course—Panama. Travelers to and from these destinations were being quietly flagged by the State Department. If suspicious activity was suspected, their name would be passed on and they would be placed under surveillance in the interest of national security. It had been trips to Havana and Panama, and his job as a military contractor, that had initially earned Richard Hampton a federal tail by the name of Roald Donahue.

And now, for whatever reason, it seemed Hampton was planning—or perhaps had already taken—another trip to Panama. Rollie thought about his sudden absence and the onset of his unseasonal tan.

His interest steadily rising, he settled into the worn seat of the old Ford as he awaited Hampton's departure.

Havana, Cuba

PERHAPS IT was because his mind was in high gear, but the evening with the young prostitute didn't turn out like Bernd had hoped. His thoughts were still occupied with Carsten's mystery key and what it led to. Little phrases or snippets of conversation from other tables would set off brief explosions of ideas in Bernd's mind. He would jerk his head to the side, thinking for a moment about a potential use for the key, then dismiss the thought while his frustration mounted. Usually disciplined, he was drinking heavily, also. The drinking was partly a toast to his own cleverness in accessing Carsten's safety deposit box. It was also part medicinal—a suppressant to the anxiety he felt. But, despite the challenges that lay ahead, despite the mystery of the key, Bernd had to locate Samuel Fields and attain the information. No matter the cost.

He refocused on his date while her droning continued. Bernd massaged the bridge of his nose.

The final, and perhaps chief, reason his evening hadn't turned out to be very special was his date's incessant talking. She'd been so quiet in the morning, so demure, but now simply wouldn't shut up. Perhaps he shouldn't have given her that orgasm. Through all her blabbering, Bernd learned her given name was Mayra, also discovering she wasn't exactly the sharpest knife in the block. When, at one point, he asked to see the wine list, Mayra embarrassed him by asking the waiter what made wine so different from regular old grape juice. Bernd had cleared his throat, smiling as he sent the waiter on his way before providing her with a terse answer that left no room for follow-up.

Later, after digging in her clutch, she produced a yellowed picture of her teeming family. They were nothing more than rural Cuban pig farmers and somehow, as occasionally occurs, Mayra had defied genetics and been born beautiful. The rest of her family could be described as nothing other than ugly. Perhaps, Bernd imagined, Mayra's mother had bedded a handsome (and almost certainly blind-drunk) passerby while her husband was out in the slop.

When his brief fantasy ended, he found her still prattling, now about the non-sexual goings on at her Cerro brothel. This particular doldrum of a story was about her roommate, Alicia, and her incessant snoring. Apparently the snoring was loud enough to earn yells of protest from the residents—in the house next door. Bernd smoked a cigarette, his blue eyes darting around the restaurant, looking for something (anything) more interesting, as he wished she would shut up and finish her fish. He eventually stopped her with a sharp motion of his hand, pulling the key from his pocket.

"Do you know what this is?"

"A key."

He pinched his lips together momentarily. "*Gracias*. But do you have any idea what it might open?"

"A lock?"

Bernd cleared his throat. He tugged on his cheek, gathering himself, finally speaking very calmly. "Due to your omnipresent density, I'll assume your responses aren't intentionally obtuse." He spoke these advanced words in Spanish, albeit slowly.

"I don't understand what you just said."

A tight smile. "And that, my dear, proves my point."

She wrinkled her nose, flummoxed.

"Mayra," he said, placing the key flat on the table with a click. "Do you have any thoughts or ideas as to what, exactly, this key might open? A door? A safe? A hotel room?"

She reached across the table, lifting the key, cocking her head as she studied it. Her eyes briefly flickered. She reached into her small clutch, producing a ring of several keys and holding Bernd's to one on her ring. Smiling, Mayra lifted the two keys, displaying their similar profile for her date. Other than the pattern the keys were a perfect match.

Bernd could barely breathe as he stared, transfixed. "Better to be lucky than good," he whispered.

"What was that?" she asked.

He made a dismissive motion, feeling his pulse increasing. "Listen carefully, Mayra. What exactly does your key open?"

She took a quick sip of her wine before hiccup-burping loudly, giggling and covering her mouth with her hand. "Wellllll…" she said, deliberately drawing out the moment with a sophomoric grin.

Bernd's good hand shot across the table, gripping her wrist like a vise. "Say it!"

Like she'd been slapped, she peeled his hand away and pulled her arm back, lip trembling as she eventually spoke. "To be registered as a legal prostitute we have to have an address." Tears welled in her eyes. "Papa didn't want me to disgrace the family, so I had to get a post office box and make up a last name."

Bernd sat back in his chair, surprised at his sudden fury as a wave of relief flooded him. He slid his chair over as he softened his face, gently rubbing her back and murmuring apologies for his actions. He turned away, biting his lower lip in a wide grin.

A post office box, of course!

Leaning his head back, he closed his eyes, laughing silently as his hand still rubbed his date's back. The relief had immediately washed away his mounted tension and, as he brought his eyes back level with Mayra's, he felt himself hardening. Yes, she was stupid, but she was still quite beautiful, young, and could more than serve her purpose. Mayra looked away as he gulped his water, staring at her, his mind warring between what could be awaiting him in a Havanan post office box and what did await him between her shiny caramel legs.

Acting as though he cared, he asked her to eat a bite of her dessert, trying to salvage the evening. She continued to whimper. He slid her wine in front of her. She rubbed her wrist. Bernd finally decided it was of no use. She'd probably been abused at some point in her life, and his violent action had shut her down. It was a shame, too. Earlier, before he'd learned how simple she was, he had flirted with the notion of taking her to Panama. She was certainly alluring enough to keep him occupied until he would eventually pimp her in an effort to ensnare Samuel Fields.

That idea, due to her lack of intellect, was long gone. But there was something about this young woman, perhaps the innocence of her youth and rural upbringing, that had an effect on Bernd. He wasn't an animal, after all. He didn't want such a beautiful creature to have to spend the formative years of her adult life being subjected to sex with savage men. Plus, she couldn't help being born into a family of simpletons. If for no reason other than her looks, Bernd felt she deserved better. And perhaps he could help.

After he paid the considerable bill, the Prussian led her from the restaurant, peppering her with compliments. When her barrier finally began to crumble, wasting no time at all, he took her in a nearby alley, her face and chest pressed up against a damp stone wall as he noisily worked from behind. His suit pants were around his knees, her new dress hiked up as they moved together just inside the blackness of a backstreet shadow. It took only a few minutes, but she began to warm to his actions, probably remembering the pleasure he'd given her on the morning. She'd acted only as a receptacle at first, but once he began licking the back of her neck, he felt her arch her back as her hips began to move with his.

Biting his lip to blood, Bernd struggled to hold out, doing his best to see that they both enjoyed the moment. Her soft gasps transformed into loud moans as he eventually found success, having to hold her up as her knees weakened from the bliss. There were other sounds after they'd both achieved climax. From somewhere up above, while Bernd rested his sweaty face on Mayra's damp shoulder, applause and laughter could be heard over their collective deep breathing.

Afterward, they stepped back onto the deserted street, the ambient light making Mayra all the more beautiful as her glow of perspiration sparkled. She combed the wisps of her sable hair backward, raking her hand over his chest, telling him she wanted to stay the night in his room. Mopping sweat from his brow with the bandage of his injured hand, Bernd dug out Carsten's loose money and pressed it into her hand.

"This is fifty pesos."

Her climax seemed to have erased her earlier tension. But the mention of such a considerable sum visibly shook her, making her eyes widen as she stared down at the wad in her petite hand. Such an amount was no doubt at least twice what her shit-covered father earned in a single year.

Her head began to shake back and forth. "What is this for? They will only take it from me back at—"

"Now listen to me," Bernd interrupted in smooth, Mexican-accented Spanish, lifting her chin with his index finger. "You should go back to your home, but hide the money before you arrive. Hide it well. Put it under a large rock in an unused field. Then go to your father and tell him you have fifty pesos, and you will give him *half* if he lets you return home. Then you tell him—"

"But he will beat me!"

Bernd, still rubbing her chin, let out a frustrated breath. "Not if he thinks he *won't* get that money. You have to be very clear about that. Tell him you're done whoring and he will never see a single *centavo* if he touches you again." Bernd tilted his head. "Find a nice boy and use that money to make him yours. Maybe the son of a doctor or a merchant. Don't tell him what you did here in Havana. Just let him know that you have that money, then make good love to him after he proposes." He released her chin, briefly rubbing her cheek before gently nudging her away. "Go on now. Don't go back to that brothel, either."

Her head was down.

"Buy a gun if need be. Shoot the floor next to your papa, but be insistent that you have that money and he won't see any of it unless he treats you well. Do you understand?"

She nodded hesitantly.

"Go on, Mayra. Go to your home, see your family, and find that husband."

Twin glistening streams of tears on her face, Mayra turned and walked down the narrow street.

Watching her shuffle away, Bernd felt magnanimous, like a nobleman who has sacrificed a piece of himself for the good of his people when he had no obligation to help. Even though he knew Mayra would probably screw it up somehow, still, at least he'd put forth the effort.

This was how Bernd von Danzig justified himself. For all the bad he did, to him, little situations such as this one made him believe he was a decent man.

Glowing, Bernd turned and walked to the south, to his hotel that was only four blocks away. He didn't want another early morning anxiety episode like today's, so, upon his arrival, he drank cerveza in the bar until after two. The following day promised to be busy. Bernd had no idea how many post office boxes existed in Havana, but he vowed to check every single one of them if necessary.

Chicago, Illinois

DAYTIME TURNED to night as Rollie awaited Richard Hampton's departure. His curiosity aroused by the burned paper he'd salvaged, Rollie waited longer than normal, until after eight. Because Hampton's burgundy '42 Lincoln Zephyr was still parked ten spaces away, Rollie decided his mark must have taken a room at one of the nearby hotels to enjoy one of his prostitute friends. Despite Rollie's onset of sweaty palms, he wasn't quite yet ready to go home. On the off chance Hampton had taken the bus, Rollie cruised to the north, to Hampton's Lincolnwood home.

Upon taking up a post far down their otherwise vacant residential street, Rollie watched the sole house, the tranquil Hampton manor, until after ten. While waiting, he took a partial dose of morphine, just to quell the sweats.

Feeling normal again, he studied the Hampton home. Vivien Hampton's car was parked under the carport; Richard's car, of course, was not at the house. Just as Rollie had done the night before, he decided to approach the building from around back. Carrying only a hidden, leather-wrapped blackjack, he walked down the street, stopping at the edge of Hampton's yard, which was bounded by a trickling brook. He turned right just past the brook, following its bank behind the house.

River oaks leaned over the small creek, their new leaves providing dark shadows for Rollie to navigate through. After about fifty yards, he climbed the steep second bank up from the brook's flood level and crouched behind a rotting log. The quarter moon, straight above, cast dim light down on Hampton's sprawling back yard. A few crickets buzzed their nightly song. The only other sound Rollie heard was his own light breathing. No signs of life anywhere other than a solitary rectangle of honey light coming from the patio door at the back of the Hampton home.

Rollie advanced on the mansion while using the black shadows of three large oaks that led him to the patio courtyard. When he reached the walled-in court, he looked down to see his shoes, wet from dew, leaving a trail of dampness and pieces of cut grass on the stone enclosure. Licking his lips, Rollie eyed the house and the light that was coming through the patio door. The view from where he stood was limiting. The only way to get a feel for what was going on inside was to cross the patio. Doing his best to lessen the trace he might leave, he wiped the leather soles of his shoes on his pants legs before noiselessly advancing.

After flattening himself against the house, Rollie became aware of muffled music. As he neared the paned door, he heard a tinny-sounding man's voice: the evening host from WMAQ. The light was beaming strongly through the glass, meaning, as soon as he craned his head to have a look, he'd be exposed if anyone happened to be looking in that direction. Rollie waited, hearing the music begin again—*Sleepy Lagoon* by Harry James. Swallowing thickly, he removed his fedora, crouched very low, and took a peek.

Thankfully, Hampton's wife was facing away, lounged on the same sofa her husband had sat on the night before. A napkin-wrapped bottle of beer was on the end table next to her, a cigarette burning in an ashtray next to the beer. She was thumbing through a large book and, after adjusting his angle, Rollie realized it was a catalog of some sort.

The phone rang, making Rollie jerk backward when Hampton's wife stood to answer it. She crossed the room and turned down the music before lifting the ear-piece, facing the door while doing so. Rollie backed into a shadow, getting a view of her from a distance, away from the cast light of the door. In the quiet of the night, he was able to half-hear what she was saying, filling in the blanks of what he didn't hear by reading her lips.

She was angry. That much was obvious. She asked when the caller would be home. *Richard.* Then she yelled, "Working all night—*again?* Do you think I'm an idiot? Who is she, Richard?"

As Vivien Hampton listened, she knotted her painted lips and cocked a finely plucked eyebrow. "Fine, then," she said curtly. "You can stay with your little harlot all week for all I care."

Again she listened, eventually making an agonized face, as if she was more than ready to get off the phone. She ended the call by saying, "Why don't we quit pretending and just end this farce of a marriage!" Vivien

Hampton slammed the receiver down, standing there with her hand still wrapped around the handset.

Over a period of a minute, her face transformed itself while Rollie observed from a distance. It went from sheer anger to a look of dismay. Then the dismay softened to an odd kind of relief. She walked back behind the sofa and lifted the beer, taking a long sip. Her eyes seemed to focus on a spot on the wall, as if her mind were far, far away. Still standing in the same place, Rollie watched as she eventually kicked off her shoes and unclipped her earrings. One final swig of the beer and it was gone. Considerably shorter without her shoes, she carried the bottle to the kitchen. He moved back to the door.

Craning his neck to the right, Rollie didn't see her for a full minute. Just as he began to wonder if she was sitting at the kitchen table, he saw her coming back from the kitchen. His heart lurched when she veered left, in the direction of the back door. He had, perhaps, three seconds to hide himself. Feeling his adrenaline spike, and drawing on his training, he flung himself into the wet grass just outside the patio. Lying prone, one side of his body covered in dew and blades of cut grass, he heard the lock click, followed by her voice. She yelled the word "Samantha", in a singsong, pet-calling manner again and again, eventually shortening it to "Sammy."

The cat!

Damn it to hell, Rollie thought, chastising himself. He'd seen the cat before, never realizing she let it out the back door. He should have remembered that. His carelessness could have been disastrous.

"Sammy! Come to mama, sweetie!" There was a distant jingling and, in a blur of white and calico, a cat sprinted through the yard, thankfully approaching from the far side of the terrace. After twisting through Vivien's legs, the cat bolted into the house, jumping straight onto the back of the sofa, wet paws and all. This earned protests from the woman of the house as she walked in and absently slammed the door without locking it, gesturing for her beloved Samantha to remove herself from the sofa. Rollie peered from his ground position as the cat shot from the couch and disappeared somewhere further in the large house.

"She'll lock the door," he whispered into the dewy grass. "She'll come straight back and twist the deadbolt." Instead, he felt his heart rate increase again as she shed her cardigan sweater, lifting her shoes and walking to the far side of the room and into the main hallway. Rollie stood and caught a glimpse of Vivien as she turned to climb the stairs, followed by Sammy the feline. Seconds later he could hear the unmistakable sound of water running through the pipes of the house.

Making sure he wasn't mistaken, Rollie made his way back to the door and turned the knob—it was indeed unlocked. The rushing water sound was quite loud. More than a simple sink faucet. She must have been running a bath. She'd probably brush her teeth afterward, then sit in front of her vanity, applying cold cream to her face, or whatever it was women did. Rollie certainly didn't know. When she was done readying herself for bed, she would undoubtedly come back down to switch off the lights. And that's when she would check the locks.

The water upstairs stopped. The bath was full. Rollie chewed a fingernail, staring at the warm light of the den, his mind awash in curiosity over the Panama itinerary and a rushing feeling in his body as he couldn't prevent himself from thinking about Vivien Hampton.

He twisted the doorknob again.

It's now or never, buddy.

Shaking his head at this unprecedented crossing of an ethical line, he bent down and slid his dewy loafers from his feet, hiding them behind a planter and depositing his hat on top. Taking several deep breaths, he again turned the knob, this time pushing the door open. Realizing the cuffs of his pants legs were also wet, he rolled them up to prevent leaving any trace of his presence. Glancing around, he was immediately aware of her scent. It wasn't the store-bought smell of a freshly bathed person, but rather the lovely scent of a woman that simply occurs from living—a mélange of hair spray, lotion, and femininity—and something about it made Rollie's skin tingle.

Realizing he might only have a moment, he moved into the kitchen, finding the carport door. There was a deadbolt on that door, as well. As he struggled with whether or not to hide himself there—*would she lock the carport door, too?*—he heard footfalls on the floor above. *Was she already out of the bath?*

Rollie stared upward, listening to the sounds moving through the ceiling. There was a click, sounding like a closet door being shut. Things went quiet for a moment. He assumed she was in the tub. Rollie eyed the room off the kitchen, padding in that direction.

Suddenly, appallingly, he heard rapid footfalls.

She was coming down the stairs!

Glancing around and making a split-second decision, Rollie opened the pantry, using his sock feet to slide canned goods aside so he could stand inside and close the door. He twisted the knob and pulled the door shut, just as Vivien breezed into the kitchen. She was singing *Sleepy Lagoon* softly, beautifully, her mind still influenced by the radio she'd been listening to earlier. She was at the *La-Da-Da-Da-Da* part, her smooth alto voice as finely-tuned as any voice or instrument he'd ever heard.

Surprising himself, Rollie felt his eyes glistening.

Blinking the wetness away, Rollie mashed his left eye against the pantry door and peered at Vivien through the lattice-work. She retrieved a bottle of what looked like Scotch from the cabinet. *Sleep aid?* He watched as she hesitated, appearing to struggle with whether or not to drink it.

Believe me, Vivien, I understand.

She poured two fingers. Gunned it. Breathed the word "shit" to herself, her chin to her chest. This was an unhappy woman. Rollie suddenly felt miserable over his reckless intrusion, making her unknowingly share her private moment. She replaced the bottle and rinsed the glass, then set about what looked like evening chores. He couldn't get a good view of her as she washed a few dishes, but when she went back into the den, his straight-on view was transcendent.

She wore an ankle-length, filmy jade gown. Her long hair was up now, woven above her head like a princess's, presumably for sleep. After flipping the switch on the radio, she stopped at the rear door, turning the deadbolt and standing there long enough to give Rollie a jolt. Did she see something outside, like wet footprints? He pressed downward on one of the slats and realized she was actually pausing because she was crying, her hand resting on the doorknob for support.

Sammy the cat jingled in from parts unknown, snaking around under her owner's feet. Vivien bent to lift the pet, standing there and whispering affirmations in a language only the cat could understand. Rollie continued to drink in the scene.

Vivien was probably in her early thirties, at least ten years her husband's junior. According to his intelligence report she'd borne no children, leaving her with a body of a woman ten years *her* junior. As insensitive as he felt for his intrusion, Rollie was still a male, and he studied her form carefully, committing her firm stomach and medium-sized ski-slope breasts to his permanent memory. The gown, thank goodness, was quite sheer, allowing him to see a hint of the lovely delta between her legs. As she stood there, petting Sammy over her shoulder, Rollie watched as Vivien shifted her stance, crossing one leg over the other. It occurred to him that, despite her long blonde hair, the mound he was transfixed on was quite dark. This non-mission critical, yet seemingly incredibly important, observation allowed Rollie to deduce that Vivien likely colored her hair. He barely managed to swallow when she lowered the cat and moved out of sight. A reprehensible feeling came over Rollie as he realized the intensity of his own personal arousal. He was here for work, not to be a despicable peeping Tom. All the same, how could he ignore what he'd seen?

Vivien was moving around, switching off the lights. When she returned to the kitchen, she was wiping her eyes with a tissue. Rollie closed his own eyes for a moment, imagining himself emerging from the pantry without a word, walking across the floor as confidently as Bogey might. He wondered what it would be like to be that bold; to brazenly appear and pronounce that she deserved better; to ignore her protests and grab her by her upper arms and join eyes with her; to lean in and kiss her gently, pressing his tongue into her warm mouth as his strong hands moved downward, caressing her beautiful hourglass bottom and pulling it close so she could feel his pulsating response to her powerful allure; to walk her back against the wall, his stiffness holding her there while his hands roamed upward, her breaths coming in desperate gasps as he kneaded her breasts before moving one hand into position under her jaw, gently pulling away, ending the kiss as beautifully as it had started, lifting her and carrying her off to bed.

But Rollie didn't move a muscle.

He stood there. Aware of his own breath. Aware of his rushing blood. He reopened his eyes and stared through the slats, waiting, hearing a few glasses tinkling to his right. Cabinets opening and closing. She ran the faucet and could momentarily be seen breezing out with a glass of water. His eyes went straight to her shapely rear-end, making his breath catch in his throat. The ancient Greeks, with their thousands of human statues, could never have hoped to create anything that might capture the beauty of the living, breathing female form. She paused at the den, looking it over before extinguishing the last light, leaving him with complete darkness. More footfalls could be heard on the stairs as she climbed, most certainly headed off to bed. Sammy's collar bell jingled and grew distant.

Rollie stood there, breathing heavily, not one bit scared or high from the adrenaline rush he'd experienced. If anything, he was down with disappointment. Because, secretly, deep in some prehistoric chamber of his mind, he'd hoped she would have opened that pantry door.

It would have given him the excuse he'd needed, and waited for, his entire life.

After remaining in the pantry for ten more minutes, he emerged and stayed in the Hampton house for over an hour. Searched the kitchen and found nothing. Den, nothing. Same for three other downstairs rooms. A half-hour after exiting the pantry, when Vivien was hopefully soundly sleeping, he examined the cluttered office. He found plenty of old files and stateside travel documents, but none that were helpful. In one of the file cabinets, he discovered a bank account that, in 1939, was closed after a massive withdrawal. Rollie noted it on his pad.

Just when he was about to leave, he reached into his pocket and removed the burned paper he'd salvaged earlier in the alleyway. He stared at the partial itinerary on the right of the page. The name of the traveler wasn't visible; it would have been on the left side, although he assumed it was in Richard Hampton's name. The itinerary, however, was mostly intact. It included the destination of Colon, Panama and the price of $213.45. He tucked the paper away again, going back through the files one more time. Nothing on Panama. Returning everything to its normal position, Rollie switched off the lamp and headed to the rear door but stopped cold, his eyes on a bookshelf. Littered amongst the hardcover books was a large book with gold lettering, illuminated by the street lights. The book was simply titled *Panama*. Rollie slid it out and, under the pleasant light of the desk lamp, flipped through the book, noting the turned down pages and underlined sections.

At the rear of the book, in the recommendations section, the reader had underlined a section about a Panama City neighborhood called Calidonia, "teeming with American expatriates." Rollie thumbed to the front of the book, to the weather and average temperatures. In the black ink of the underlining pen, someone had accentuated the month of April.

This month, of course, was April.

Extinguishing the lamp again, he tucked the book under his arm and headed out of the house. Surely Mrs. Hampton would discover the unlocked back door tomorrow morning, remembering that she had paused and locked it. Given her distress over the situation with her husband, Rollie laid good odds that she would write it off as her own mistake. But she wouldn't miss the book. The shelves contained hundreds of them.

Book in hand, he left the way he came, tired but confident in what he'd learned. Starting tomorrow, whether or not Nicholas Penland planned to give him any support, Rollie couldn't let Richard Hampton out of his sight. He placed the book in the passenger seat, pressing in the clutch of the car and letting it roll silently backward before he cranked it. Rollie had decided to spend his own money on a cheap hotel room downtown. That way he could acquire Hampton first thing on the morrow.

As the car continued to creep, he touched the book beside him. Despite its considerable length, today had been a good day. He'd learned a great deal.

Twin headlight beams on the adjacent road caused Rollie to halt the Ford with the handbrake.

"Is this Richard, coming home late?" he asked the car.

THE AUTOMOBILE wheeled left onto the Hamptons' street. When the lights hit Rollie's rear-view mirror, he was already down in the seat, holding the car in place with the handbrake to prevent his tail lights from illuminating. The car slowed next to his Ford, probably as the driver glanced over to see if anyone was inside. Rollie rose up after the car had passed. It looked like a '40 or '41 Plymouth Coupe, black as a lump of coal, idling down the street, its straight six ticking quietly. Then, well before reaching the Hampton house— the only home on the street—the car slowed before the driver switched off the engine.

Clearly, it was not driven by Richard Hampton.

Rollie eyed the car, able to see the outlines of two heads inside. The Plymouth was fifty yards ahead of his Ford, on the opposite side of the street. As Rollie watched the occupants, he saw the dual orange glows of cigarettes.

Then, after about a minute, both cigarettes spun from each side of the car, one sparking on the street, the other in the damp weeds. Both doors opened.

The two men who emerged, judging by their silhouettes, were quite large. The driver reached back inside, grabbing his fedora and tugging it on. The passenger, the larger of the two, wore no hat. He was carrying something long and slender.

They walked toward the Hampton house, their eyes on the domicile. Judging by the way they moved, picking their feet up instead of dragging them, indicated that they were trying to be quiet.

Normally, Rollie wouldn't have intervened. But Vivien Hampton, a woman he didn't know but liked a great deal, was in that house all alone. Tilting his head back to the cloth-covered ceiling of the Ford, Rollie blew out an exasperated breath, cursing his luck, hoping that whatever this situation was wouldn't somehow blow his cover. He slid the .38 Super government model into his shoulder holster and palmed the blackjack.

The men were already at the Hampton driveway.

Rollie exited the Ford, silently moving in their direction, staying behind their field of vision.

Having obviously decided there were no nearby threats, the driver of the car lit another cigarette, standing at the rear of the Cadillac series 60 and keeping his eyes on the house. The passenger, carrying a long rod, was under the carport and had gone to work on the driver's door of the Cadillac.

They were stealing the car.

Seeing no weapons, and having no idea what was behind this action, Rollie chose to leave his .38 Super in its holster. He curled the leather blackjack back so it would be in line with his arm and purposefully scratched his feet as he walked halfway up the driveway, ten feet away from the man in the hat.

"What in the hell do you two think you're doing?" Rollie asked, speaking a few decibels below normal. Both men whirled to him. Once he'd gotten over his surprise, the one in the hat took a few steps in Rollie's direction.

"Stop," Rollie said calmly, pointing his left finger at him.

"Who the hell're you?" the man asked, speaking in a heavy south-side accent. He adjusted his elbow so it slid his jacket backward, indicating to

Rollie that he was armed. And if he was armed, Rollie had to assume the other one was.

Rather than wait, Rollie fast-drew the .38 Super and aimed it at the nearest threat. Rollie cocked the hammer, telling each man to slowly place his hands on his head.

His actions, and their calm responses, told Rollie something. It was apparent that both men were used to having guns pointed at them, especially judging by the way they hardly reacted. The only real reaction came from the man at the car door, who released his slim jim, causing it to clatter to the pavement.

"I *said* put your hands on your head," Rollie warned, keeping his voice even. "I'm not a cop and I'm not above dusting you *both* right here on the spot."

The two men complied, slowly, while the man in the fedora said, "You're making a big fuggin' mistake."

Ignoring him, Rollie wagged his pistol and said, "Walk this way." Giving them clear directions, he made them walk down the driveway and to the rear of their Plymouth. He had them both assume a perpetrator's stance, using his left hand to pat them down over their mumbled curses. Finished, it looked like a mini gun show on the quiet Hampton street. Just from the quick pat-downs, Rollie came away with a Colt Fitz Special, a Colt Police Positive, a tiny Garrucha pistol from an ankle holster, and a nasty little custom .22 pistol, suppressed. Rollie removed a bullet from the pistol and twisted it in the low light. It appeared to be a low-speed, rimfire hollow-point.

"The hell are you doing with this?" Rollie asked the man who'd carried the pistol in his blazer. He was the man who'd been picking the lock on the Cadillac. "This is an executioner's pistol, pal, designed strictly for quietly killing people at close range."

With dark bags under his eyes, and a permanent scowl on his face, the one who'd carried the .22 joined eyes with the man in the fedora. "He'll tell you."

Rollie looked to the other one. He had a heavy five-o'clock shadow and was swarthy and somewhat handsome—a bad boy with looks. "That car in that driveway is ours," he said, tilting his head toward the Hampton home.

"Yeah? Why do you say that?"

"The guy who owned it, Richard Hampton, pledged it against a loan we made him."

Rollie wheeled the .38 Super to the back of the man's neck. "You're lying."

With his eyes squeezed shut, the man said, "I'm not lying. Hampton's into us for two large."

"Who's 'us'?"

"My boss."

Rollie peered from behind his pistol. "I'd strongly suggest you start speaking in specifics."

"Sean O'Bannon."

Like most local citizens, Rollie knew of O'Bannon. A dapper mobster controlling much of the south and west sides, he was most known for his lofty position in the city's narcotics trade. "So you say Hampton is into O'Bannon for two thousand dollars?"

"Yeah."

"Well, you and Mister O'Bannon are going to give Hampton a week's grace, got it?"

"I can't do that," the man in the fedora protested.

Digging into his left pocket with his free hand, Rollie dug out a wad of bills, $28 if he remembered correctly, tossing them onto the ground at the intelligent one's feet. "There's all the juice you're getting for this week. If I see you here again inside of a week, I can promise you that the next time we will *not* talk." Rollie took a few steps backward. "Scoop up that money and keep it in your hand."

As he did, the mobster asked if they could have their guns back.

"You," Rollie said to the dopey one. "Step over onto the grass where I can watch you. And you, very slowly, get your keys and open the trunk."

"Keys are in the car."

"Okay, then, get them from the car." Rollie followed him to the driver's door, alternating his eyes to the one standing in the grass. The pistols were on the pavement behind the Plymouth, well out of reach. As the one in the fedora opened the door, Rollie noticed him furtively glance back, marking Rollie's position. He rested one hand on the bench seat as his left retrieved the key. Then, a tinkling sound announced the keys as being dropped. When the man in the fedora reached for them, Rollie saw his hand, quick as a snake, reach under the seat. And that's when Rollie struck.

With his right foot, he jammed the mobster in the ass, making him lurch forward, striking his head on the passenger door of the car. Then, after glancing at the other stunned mobster, standing aghast with his hands still on his head, Rollie unleashed a jacketed round from his .38 Super, purposefully hitting the driver in the lower left leg.

The man howled like a beagle at a full moon.

Using his foot, Rollie shoved the wounded man into the floor of the passenger seat. Keeping his eyes on both men, Rollie reached into the driver's side floorboard, finding another .38 revolver, this one with worn tape around the busted grip. He smacked the injured mobster in the head with it, telling him to sit up and take the pain like a man. Then Rollie called the other man over, telling him to get in and drive.

When the dopier of the two was seated in the driver's seat of the Plymouth, Rollie alternated his pistol between the two men as he spoke. "Richard Hampton belongs to The Enforcer, you stupid baboons. I tried to make nice, giving you a week so I could sort things out, but then you insulted me, and The Enforcer, by going for that piece."

Through his evident pain, the smart one, both hands clamped over his wounded leg, said, "You didn't say nothin' 'bout bein' with Nitti."

He was referring, of course, to Frank "The Enforcer" Nitti, the figurehead for the Chicago Mob after Capone's arrest. Though Nitti shared power with others, he was in charge of nearly all strong-arm operations. Nitti was greatly feared—and that fear showed on the faces of the two mobsters.

"Did I break it?" Rollie asked, gesturing to the leg.

The mobster had removed his tie and was knotting it over the calf wound. "Went clean through the muscle," he said through gritted teeth. Then he smiled, marked by foamy spittle in the corners of his mouth as he grunted, "Thanks for not shooting me in the thigh."

"Don't mention it," Rollie said flatly. "Now listen up, both of you. If I hear you two so much as wave to Richard Hampton in the next week, I'll personally come find you. As far as what he owes, that'll get taken care of." Rollie glanced at the Hampton house. No lights had come on after his gunshot.

"But why're you out here?" the driver asked.

"The Enforcer wants Hampton protected. Beyond that, I don't ask questions." After scooping up the pistols, Rollie came back to the driver's door. "Now back up, nice and quiet, and get the hell outta here."

"Yes, sir," the driver said. "And we didn't mean no disrespect to Mr. Nitti."

"Haul ass."

When the two hoods had puttered away, Rollie found his fedora on the street, donning it while cradling the tangle of pistols under his left arm. If Hampton's situation had gotten so bad that he was into the street for two grand, it would certainly provide motivation for a traitorous sale of information.

Rollie stared up at the Hampton house, still dark and quiet, hoping the week he'd just bought Vivien Hampton would hold out. He tugged on the brim of his fedora as he whispered to the house, saying, "Good evening, ma'am."

Chapter Four

April 16, 1943

Havana, Cuba

WHILE OCCASIONALLY sexy and mysterious, Bernd's job was often downright boring. And this morning—this terminally long morning—had been beyond that. To a man like Bernd, who craved action, the tedium he'd just endured was sheer torture.

The Guanabacoa Post Office, located in east Havana, was the final possibility. Thankfully, the post office boxes were accessible at all hours. Like yesterday, Bernd hadn't been able to sleep well. His already-injured right hand now had blisters on his thumb and index fingers, rubbed raw from checking thousands of postal boxes at Havana's three main post offices. Guanabacoa Post Office was his final stop. Unable to sleep, Bernd had started at five this morning.

Now, on his final row of boxes in a stuffy alcove of the post office, Bernd rudely made two people wait as he finished. He inserted the key into the last box, trying to turn it, growling as the key stayed straight up and down. Bernd dipped his head, steadying himself as he tried to summon patience. After a few moments he stood, massaging his lower back. Irritated, he passed back through the rows of boxes to the service area, his thick brows lowered over his eyes as he pushed to the front of the line.

"Where's the manager?" he demanded in Spanish.

The postal worker had been helping a woman with a package. Hearing Bernd's authoritative query, he dipped his head and disappeared into the back. A few minutes later, the worker returned with a dark-skinned man sporting a pencil-thin moustache of stark white whiskers, matching the cropped helmet of white on his head.

"May I help you, sir?"

Bernd glanced at the locals in line, all staring at him. The two desk workers had even stopped what they were doing. "Mind your own business!" Bernd snapped.

He turned to the manager, showing him the key. "Since before sunup, I've checked every single post office box in Havana and this key doesn't fit a damned one of them."

The manager's face was puzzled. "You didn't have to check every box. Please simply show me your identification and I can look up the box that's assigned to you."

"I've tried that. This key was given to me by a man who is mailing me a very important package. The box must be registered to him."

"He didn't tell you the number?" the manager asked.

Bernd ran both hands over his face. "Can't you tell that I've forgotten the number?"

"Well, what was the man's name who gave you the key? I can—"

"I've *tried* that, too."

Without another word the manager turned his right palm up, taking the key. He motioned for Bernd to follow, leading him to the far end of the counter. Crouching, the manager opened the cabinet before the unmistakable sound of a large key ring was heard. Standing back up, he placed the massive ring on the counter and donned wire-rimmed reading glasses from the cord around his neck, comparing Bernd's key to each of the master keys. The manager hummed as he worked, alternating his somewhat grating tones as he appeared to come to some sort of conclusion. In time he nodded decisively and pointed to Bernd's key.

"You see this hump?" he asked.

Bernd narrowed his eyes, peering at the tall hump of the key pattern closest to the round area designed to be held in a person's hand. "Yes, so?"

"Look, here," the manager said, slowly going through the large ring of keys. "None of ours have such a hump. In fact, the tumbler pattern is located at the tip of the key on all of our keys." He straightened, lowering his glasses.

Bernd noticed the master keys were each etched with a letter/number code. "Why don't you put the box number on the keys you issue to the public?"

The man smiled. "If it were up to me, I would. But the boxes are shipped to us that way. If someone loses a key, they pay for one of our extras."

"You said the boxes are shipped here? Shipped from where?"

"Come around," the man said, stepping through the side entrance to the counter area and unlocking a door. Bernd entered, following the man behind the backside of the rows and rows of post office boxes. Many contained letters, slanted in the upright cubbies. There were rolled magazines, postcards and, in one, what looked like a wrapped bottle of liquor. On the back of each box was a small ring with a number of extra keys.

The postal manager again donned his reading glasses, his thin finger pointing to a stamped silver nameplate in the center of the largest section of boxes. "Standard Postal Products, Atlanta, Georgia," he said slowly before again removing his glasses.

Bernd's cheeks expanded as he let out a long, slow breath. He thought back to the things he learned at the Soria's restaurant. Carsten had said he was due to meet his contact in Panama.

Once again, Panama…

Carsten had said his contact was very precise about how he was to receive payment for the information. And if he was so circumspect about that, he'd probably be more so about the rendezvous.

Bernd punched his left hand with his injured right, sending a welcome volt of pain through his body.

The key matches a post office box, all right. But not here, not in Havana.

The box is in Panama!

Without a word of thanks, Bernd left in a rush, rudely shoving through the line of people. His mind raced as he walked, assembling the scraps of information like puzzle pieces, trying to put together a recognizable image.

If Carsten's American pigeon was as careful as Bernd worried he might be, even if he received a letter naming the meet, he would no doubt set the meet in a conspicuous location, expecting to see Carsten before he showed himself. Even a rank amateur would be smart enough to do this and such wariness could ruin everything. Carsten and Samuel Fields might have even enabled a pre-set code, meaning Bernd would never even know where the meet was to take place.

Damn you, Carsten. Cyanide vials. Atomic recipes. I underestimated you.

As Bernd fretted over the conundrum, one thing continued to niggle at his mind, the final clue Carsten had given him. It was the clue that produced a final smile on Carsten's sallow, sufficiently butchered mug.

He said the American, this Samuel Fields, loved women.

Bernd suddenly halted. He checked his watch—it wasn't even ten in the morning. Nearly back to the center of Havana, he stood there, turning in a slow circle as the framework of a plan came together. If this Samuel Fields loved women, it meant he really craved "muschi." "Muschi" was German slang, equivalent to the English word "pussy." Bernd, being of the same ilk as this Mister Fields, was quite familiar with both versions of the word, as well as their equivalents in French, Italian and, of course, Spanish.

"Well, maybe I'll just have to provide this Samuel Fields with some *muschi*," Bernd said to himself as he began walking again, this time at a more leisurely pace. He decided to go back to the hotel where he would enjoy the buffet breakfast before sitting in his room, alone, piecing together the initial elements of his burgeoning plan. Had Mayra the whore had any brains he would have taken her along and taught her how to effectively lure a man with what she'd been blessed with. But this operation would be far too delicate and, for several reasons (for one, he would probably have to eventually eliminate his bait), Bernd felt it would be best that whomever he hired not know his face.

Not yet.

As he neared his hotel, Bernd was struck with an inspiration. There was a man here in Havana, an Englishman named Philip Carlton, a preferred provider. He'd been helpful to Bernd's section in the past, always crowing about his intelligence network and knowledge of the simple Americans—but most important to Bernd was the woman Carlton constantly bragged about. He said she was beautiful and skilled, the classic "honey-pot", a gem of the finest cut and clarity.

Bernd stepped into a store, purchasing a fine cigar and lighting it with the counter lighter. Wetting its end, he puffed it, nodding his approval to the ancient woman behind the counter. Then, deciding to move forward with his idea, Bernd removed his little black book and found a phone booth.

As he chatted with Philip Carlton's answering service, there was a smile behind Bernd's cigar. Because, provided Carlton accepted his meeting request, Bernd planned to hire the Englishman's honey-pot.

And employ her in Panama.

Chicago, Illinois

LAST NIGHT, using a bottle of the morphine sulfate he kept hidden in the foam of his rear seat, Rollie had taken a three-quarters dose and managed four hours of fitful sleep in a ramshackle yet quiet Printer's Row hotel. He was back on point by sunrise this morning, his head pounding.

After checking Richard's Lincoln, parked exactly where he'd seen it the night before in the lot behind his office, Rollie ambled over to Poor Boys, a greasy spoon diner on Wacker with a good view of the North Michigan intersection. Along with a single cup of blissfully genuine coffee, Rollie wolfed a generous portion of ham and eggs. Since it was so early in the day, he received the benefit of the heavily-rationed items. Just before eight, nearly obscured by the morning rush of people, he spied an unshaven Hampton ambling across the bridge, wearing a smug look that only an asshole who got laid all night could wear. Leaving two bucks on the table, Rollie hurried from the café, picking up Hampton's tail from a block away. Surprising him, however, Hampton concealed his face and walked past his building, taking a left down the alleyway in the direction of his car.

Is he taking a Friday sick day?

He must have been because, before Rollie knew it—and with some fancy driving—he was three cars off Hampton's tail, cruising north on Lake Shore Drive. Going opposite the morning rush, Richard Hampton drove home.

Rollie passed the turnoff to Hampton's street, allowing five minutes to pass before he doubled back. Diagonal from the Hampton house, and four lots down (right where Rollie had put a bullet through the leg of the Sean O'Bannon collection man), was an under-construction home, the only other structure on the quiet, wooded cul-de-sac. Like many homes under construction when the war had begun, the framework seemed in disrepair. Due to the war effort, a number of non-critical construction projects had to be slowed due to lack of supplies. Some, such as this one, were stopped altogether. Rollie backed the Ford well up into the tall overgrowth, obscuring it from anything but a very observant eye. He exited the old car, thankful for the cool spring morning as he settled into a well-camouflaged thicket of high weeds and scrub brush. Two cardinals, the showy red male and brown-pink female, worked on a nest in a nearby dogwood, repeatedly diving to the ground to retrieve hay and twigs for their new home.

As the temperature slowly warmed, Rollie sat stone-still, watching the birds, smelling the grass, waiting. For an hour there was no action at all, although, at one point, he thought he heard muffled yelling from the home. Just before ten, the front door opened. Vivien Hampton emerged, high heels clicking as she hurried down the drive and retrieved the newspaper, taking it with her. Doing his best to stay focused on his target and not the target's wife, Rollie managed to resist the temptation of watching her through the high-powered binoculars but, even at a distance of fifty yards, her long legs were clearly visible, forcing Rollie's mind to hearken back eleven hours. He thought about the vision that was her body; he remembered his fantasy. Swallowing thickly, Rollie was almost glad when he saw her in-jeopardy Cadillac series 60 back out from the carport, turning onto the street and, because of a curve in the road, heading straight towards him. He crouched down as the oil-slick Detroit product roared by, blasting dark smoke from the tailpipe, the carburetors dumping more fuel into the cylinders than the spark plugs could burn.

As soon as Vivien's car had blown by him, Rollie lifted his binoculars to watch as Richard Hampton almost immediately sprang into motion. He emerged from the house tugging on a captain's hat, wearing a blue polo shirt, khaki pants and deck shoes. In one hand was the light brown briefcase. In the other, a black hand grip with a maroon stripe down its center. He tossed both items in his trunk. Giving Rollie almost no time to react, Hampton cranked the Lincoln, backed out and, with a bark from the tires, sped by Rollie before squealing onto Racine and heading south.

As Hampton's car raced by, Rollie lifted his head enough to see him, watching as he held the car's lighter to a cigarette in his mouth. The way he'd exited in such a hurry at first made Rollie think he knew he was there. But his casual posture in the car defied that notion. Rollie lurched from the weeds, cranked the Ford and gave chase. After picking Hampton up farther down Racine, Rollie stayed well back, unworried about losing his mark in the light mid-morning traffic. Twice at traffic signals, from several cars back, Rollie was able to see Hampton clearly. He didn't appear to be searching for a tail at all. But given his hand's nervous tapping on the sheet metal of the car through the rolled down window, he appeared to be a man in a hurry. But a hurry to do what?

After eventually turning left off Racine, Hampton headed east, almost to the shore before he turned southeast on Indianapolis, following the curving lake well out of Chicago, driving several miles inside the Indiana border. Rollie had to keep his distance due to lack of traffic. When Hampton turned down a dead-end road at a tree-filled promontory marked by a sign as Whiting Park, Rollie was forced to keep going or be seen. He sped down Front Street, wheeling the car into a U-turn before slowing as he drove back, able to see Hampton's Lincoln stopped in the park at a distance. Rollie eased his car onto the side of the road, holding the binoculars to his face. He saw the trunk was up and watched as Hampton appeared to be stacking cut evergreen branches beside the car. Thirty seconds went by before Hampton was back in his car, roaring out of the park and speeding seventeen miles to the southern edge of the city of Chicago, to a marina in the McCormick area.

During the entire drive to the marina, Rollie pondered what in the hell Hampton had been doing in that park.

Havana, Cuba

PHILIP CARLTON, as he did most every morning, read an imported copy of *The Daily Telegraph* that was precisely two weeks older than today's actual date. He'd done this for a period of years, ignoring all other sources of news so, to him, the information in the paper was completely relevant. While he touted himself as an intelligence expert, he specialized in individual cases, mentally absolving himself from competing in the day-to-day rat race he remembered. Escape was his primary reason for leaving the intelligence service and going out on his own.

Originally from Cambridge, in England, Philip had lived in the Americas and Caribbean for nearly twenty years now, this being his sixth in Havana. The name he used wasn't his Christian name and, for obvious reasons, no one in Cuba, or the Americas for that matter, knew his true identity. A tall man with a prominent, patrician air, Philip could have easily been mistaken for a literary professor or perhaps a museum curator, given his wildly flowing silver mane of hair and slightly upturned nose. He was known throughout his Miramar neighborhood simply as El León, *The Lion*, and spent enough money with the impoverished locals that, despite his somewhat haughty nature, he enjoyed royal treatment most everywhere he went.

He sat placidly on the third floor of his Colonial-style home, out on the south-facing balcony, a demitasse of thick coffee before him—his replacement for his tea habit of a decade earlier. He took a dainty sip of the strong liquid, folding the paper, leaning his head out of the pitched roof's shadow and allowing his bronzed face to take on the radiant late-morning sun.

It had already been a good day, his morning surprise being a boorish blond Burgandian who'd brought him a fat envelope loaded with crisp American dollars. And while Philip despised the Nazis and all they stood for, he had to give them credit that at least they now knew they were over their heads when working away from their precious Germanic soil. Philip didn't have all the details, but there was an especially delicious rumor making the circuit that, sometime last year, by U-boat, Berlin had delivered four of their finest under full cover into the United States. The men had been sent to create havoc, destroy factories, upset elections and, of course, to assassinate key figures: senators, congressmen and the like. All activities that would be consonant with that madman Hitler's megalomaniacal wishes. Seemingly overwhelmed by their seductive surroundings, the four Nazis immediately lost contact with their fascist handlers back on Prinz Albrechtstrasse. As the story went, they were found weeks later, laying up naked in a gilded Miami hotel in the company of a troupe of voluptuous African prostitutes. As a final juicy detail, the men had supposedly smoked so much American reefer that, even after they were found by their German handler, they all fell asleep on their way to their executions.

Philip had been preaching to his Havana-based Nazi contact, a man posing as a Brit and supposedly named Lancaster, for three full years, "If you want to catch a particular fish, the bait used is of highest importance." It had been hard to resist mentioning the rumor to the Nazi's steely-eyed boss today, a man who came in specifically to hire him. But he'd brought Philip a sheaf of good money. And a chance. And a chance was all Philip needed, daunting as this one sounded. If he could pull in something meaningful here, he could only imagine where it might lead. All his hard work as an independent would finally pay off in a flood of Phoenix-like triumph. The foolscap paper next to his coffee had four figures in its upper left corner, neatly printed in pencil. The bottom figure, the sum, was all Philip truly cared about. It was a projection, the total of his current savings added to what he could earn in the coming year as Hitler's unwinnable war reached its tipping point. Philip closed his eyes, his mind awash in visions of a yacht-based Caribbean lifestyle, sailing island to island, eating, and living like a veritable king.

The squeaking of brakes halted his daydream. He opened his eyes and peered downward, and that's when he saw *her*, having arrived courtesy of the BSA motorcycle Philip had taken in on trade. A quick glance at his watch confirmed her punctuality, giving him no surprise whatsoever. He sipped the remainder of his cooled coffee, lighting a long cigarette and waiting. He slid the American cigarette into a silver holder—one he only used as a societal badge when he had company—listening to the steel toes of her boots strike the steps as she climbed. As he awaited her ascent of the thirty-nine steps, Philip gazed out over the buildings and homes between his house and Havana Bay, all oranges and whites as the sun set fire to the east-facing buildings during its slow climb. He breathed deeply, smelling cooking corn and roasted fish from the street-side vendors. He shifted his chair, adjusting his profile to the most flattering angle, pinching the cigarette holder in his hand as he sat regally in the breezy morning, the quintessence of Caucasian success. The boots had reached the three-story summit, now crossing through the bedroom behind him, halting at the threshold. Without turning, Philip spoke.

"Maria, my dear, so very glad you could make it on time."

Her voice was bright, as it usually was around Philip. "You said eleven, I'm here at eleven."

"Even so," he answered, as both of them spoke native-quality Spanish, "your consistent punctuality has been one of the many pleasures you've brought my rapidly-dulling life."

Maria stepped onto the balcony, coming into view, leaning against the painted wooden railing. "Where's Enrique?"

Philip smiled, knowing his expression probably appeared wan despite his best effort to mask his true feelings. "He's in the center of the city for a few days," he said through an exhalation, "visiting his sister."

"Don't tell me you two had another fight," Maria said, lifting a banana from the bowl of his terrace table. She peeled it and took a large bite.

Philip made no response.

"Don't fret," she said, mouth full. "He's crazy about you."

"There was no fight," Philip replied patiently, unable to tamp down the thread of irritation. "And that's certainly *not* why I called you here today."

"You two battle worse than an adulterous Cuban couple after the first night of Carnivale," she remarked, flashing brilliant teeth.

Making his look stony, Philip put the cigarette holder down and crossed one hand over another.

Maria moved behind him, massaging his shoulders. "Very tense."

"*No estoy tenso!*"

"See what I mean," she said, massaging him for another few seconds. She moved around to face him. "I'm glad you called me over. We haven't seen each other enough lately."

"As you progressed, I had to cut the proverbial apron strings, darling. I told you this."

She eyed him. "You're my father. I should be able to see you."

Philip lifted the cigarette, dragging on it, studying this gifted girl of twenty. Like many locals, Maria Fuentes was short, standing just over five feet tall. Her raven black hair was woven behind her head, the tightness of the braiding hiding the hair's length and luster. Her face, holding only the hint of a native tan, was rounded, dominated by full lips and large brown eyes. Maria would be described as incredibly beautiful by most men, and with her diminutive stature—even with her large breasts and shapely figure—unthreatening to most women. Unthreatening, that is, until she turned on her charisma and wore garments designed to accentuate her features, not hide them as she usually did. Camouflaged by her striking looks was her sagacious nature, a combination deemed uncommon, and unwelcome, by the world's male-dominated civilizations. And right now, Philip decided, the charisma portion of her gifted character was decidedly turned off. She was acting needy—something he understood. After all, it had been Philip who had saved her from a life on the street. While he had no interest in women, Philip prided himself on a sterling career of studying people and their motivations. And had he been a man who possessed a weakness for the softer sex—

especially after she'd blossomed around the age of sixteen—Maria would be the perfect mark to send his way.

"So you don't want to talk about you and Enrique quarrelling," she said with open, expectant hands, leaving the phrase open-ended for him to complete.

"Correct."

"What, then?"

"Well, my dear, I've been approached regarding an assignment of great importance." Leaving the cigarette, Philip stood, walking into the bedroom and holding the door until she came in. When she did, he closed both French doors simultaneously. He turned, able to read the unchecked excitement on Maria's face, though—unlike him a moment before—she was doing nothing to conceal it.

"Tell me," she breathed.

"It seems our Nazi friends have been most pleased with my work, one-dimensional as it's been."

"Oh?"

"Indeed. In fact, they've enquired about a task of discovery which, had I not known better, feels as if it was patently designed with you in mind."

"Don't tell me this is another job where I've got to be a date to some disgusting old man just to listen to him brag about his own ancient history."

"Panama," Philip said softly, bored of hearing her protestations over his occasionally using her as a non-sexual escort. Men, especially when intoxicated with wine and pretty women, have a tendency to speak loosely, no matter how high their position.

Maria cocked her head. "Where did you just say?"

"Panama," he said at length, enunciating each syllable separately. "You've heard of it, I'm certain. Central America. A well-known canal."

"What about Panama?"

"You'll be traveling there...traveling there and ensnaring a man."

She blinked rapidly, swallowing visibly. "Ensnaring a man in Panama? A local—a European—an American?"

"American."

She closed her eyes. "How old?"

"Forties and, in my expert opinion, *quite* handsome."

Maria's eyes popped open. Her exhilaration was evident as her breaths became short and audible. "You're sure? I'm not going to get there only to find out he's old and wrinkled?"

Philip made certain his affirming nod was almost too slight to register.

"And this isn't just reconnaissance again?"

Again, a slight head movement, this one back and forth, with closed eyes. "Never before by the Nazis have I been paid to do anything other than opine and appraise. This is the first field job." He allowed a smile. "And *you're* working it, my dear."

Maria's considerable chest heaved now with great breaths. "I'm running your *first ever* field job for the Germans?"

Philip lifted his long index finger, wagging it in admonishment. "Not *the Germans*. The Nazis. And, Nazis or not, from now on, they'll be known as *our friends*."

"Our friends who pay us handsomely?" she asked.

"Indeed, my dear, but only if you strike oil. Now…are you ready…and willing? You'll need to be very willing."

Maria tilted her head to the right, giving him an "are you kidding?" look that couldn't be interpreted any other way.

"This promises to be quite difficult."

"Is it feasible?"

"Certainly, dear. I wouldn't send 'my daughter' if it weren't."

"Then, I'm in."

"Very well then, darling," he said, taking her hand. "Shall I put on another pot of coffee while we sort it out? I'd advise you to enjoy it now because you'll likely not find any coffee in Panama City."

"Why?"

"Because there are so many Americans and Germans hiding there, they'll have bought up the entire supply."

They descended the steps of the mansion, sitting in the breakfast area, discussing the man she was tasked with finding. His name was allegedly Samuel Fields, although it was possible, if not likely, that he would be traveling under an alias. Philip informed Maria that the Nazi they'd been hired by was actually Prussian, ferreted out by Philip's tuned ear when he'd heard the man speak German. And the Prussian didn't know where in Panama City this Samuel Fields would be hiding but, given the potentially hazardous environment for an American, Philip assumed he would be in the neighborhood of Calidonia, in the center of the city. He'd be there—sunning, eating and drinking—along with every other field agent and spy, counting ships and watching each other.

The Prussian had provided a picture of Samuel Fields, grainy, taken on a Cuban street. In the photo he was buying an apple from a street vendor, wearing a light suit, his fedora kicked back on his head. Maria studied the photo, finding him quite attractive. She traced her finger over the man's face.

"As soon as you arrive, you'll have only one week to find him."

Continuing to study the photo, Maria nodded, replying in tone-perfect American-English. "I'll find him."

Philip's urgency shone through as he gripped her wrist. "You must find him, my dear. There will be no compensation for us if you don't, and I wouldn't rule out something far worse."

Maria snatched her wrist away, rubbing it while scowling at Philip. "I said I'll find him."

He pulled his own hand back, touching it to his tanned forehead. "I'm sorry...this is such an opportunity. Add to it my quarrel with Enrique." His hand found her wrist again, gently massaging it this time. "I'm simply on edge, dear."

"I understand." She lifted the photo. "So, am I expected to report in when I locate him, or do they want me to work my magic?"

"He's likely to be jumpy, my dear. When you do find him, they're expecting you to corral him, to act as a local and make him feel very comfortable before you ensnare him. Whatever happens, he cannot get away."

Maria eyed her superior. In a swift move she unbuttoned the top two buttons of her chambray shirt, spreading it open to reveal the upper half of her tan bosom. Reaching behind her head, she unclasped her long dark hair, raking it out and allowing it to cascade over her shoulders. "Do you honestly think I'll have a problem *corralling* this man?" she asked, twisting her lips into a smirk.

Philip indulged her with a smile. He gave her the Nazi-provided handbag containing a host of implements to disable Mr. Fields when the time came, including pharmacological measures and restraints. After that, he provided her with a packet that included her tickets for this afternoon's voyage and contact information for the man she was to summon when Fields was in her grasp.

"Is my contact the Prussian Nazi you met this morning?" she asked, tapping the coded sheet of paper that contained the proper phone number to call.

"He wouldn't say, but I would assume so."

"Do you trust him?"

"Of course not, my dear. Take all precautions."

They walked out into the Miramar neighborhood, buying her a new wardrobe, covering every contingency in their hushed conversation. Two-and-a-half hours before she was due to board, Maria prepared to bathe in Philip's guest room. Before he took his leave, Philip stood before her, eyeing her carefully, drinking in her form.

"Find Samuel Fields, Maria. Find him and sack him so you and I can enjoy the life we were always meant to live."

Maria opened her arms majestically. Then she backed into the bathroom, hand on the white slat door. Giving him a simple nod, she closed the door, leaning against it as her eyes squeezed tightly shut. While her face seemed to grimace, on her mouth was a decided smile.

Two hours later, joining a group of passengers who had boarded in New York and Miami, Maria walked the gangway onto the SS Regina at Bahía de la Habana. The Regina set sail a half-hour later, part of a large convoy of civilian and military ships.

Their destination was Panama.

Chapter Five

Chicago, Illinois

RICHARD HAMPTON couldn't have asked for a more perfect day to "die". He'd worried the day might be too calm, similar to the windless conditions that typically occurred in Chicago in July and August. After a still morning, this spring afternoon, however, while warm, provided a steady ten knot wind from due south, gusting to twice that. The swim was going to be icy cold; the wind would make it worse. But it was a small price to pay for throwing the investigators off his scent. Never once worrying to check his tail, Richard was far more concerned with making a memorable appearance at the marina. He allowed the valet to park his Lincoln, going out of his way not to act himself. After stepping from his car, he donkey-kicked backward, scuffing his door with his deck shoe. He twisted his face into a snarl, making sure to add a disgusted growl for full-effect.

"Something wrong, Mr. Hampton?" Leroy the valet asked, taking his keys and staring at Richard with concern.

"Let me think about that for a second, Leroy. Well…nothing, really, other than the fact that I married a certified cunt."

Blinking several times, old Leroy dipped his head, probably unsure how to respond.

Richard stepped to him, clasping his shoulder and giving it a friendly shake. "That was uncalled for. I'm sorry to trouble you with my problems, Leroy. You know I've always liked you."

"Thank you, sir. Thank you," Leroy murmured, his eyes still down. He did lift his head, though, when Richard emptied his billfold, pressing the unheard of tip of three twenty dollar bills into the old dark-skinned man's hands. Leroy stared at the bills, his head shaking. "Oh, sir, this is far too—"

"Take it all and enjoy yourself, Leroy. Buy your wife a nice dress. Go get drunk on me. Hell, do both."

"I can't accept this, sir. It's too…it's jus' too much."

Richard's hand moved from Leroy's shoulder to his cheek, patting it affectionately. "You take care of yourself, Leroy. You were always one of my favorites." He walked away, passing by the dock master, arranging his face in a scowl.

"Mornin' Mister Hampton," Gilbert, the dock master called out, his Irish accent dripping from the salutation.

Richard stopped, took a few steadying breaths. "Am I paid up, Gil?"

"Beg pardon, sir?"

"Am I paid up?" Richard asked, using a testy voice. "I don't owe anything, do I?"

Gil frowned, surely unused to such an odd first question from the normally good-humored Richard Hampton. "They don't keep the ledger out here, Mister Hampton, but if you still owe for April, there'll be a yellow envelope on the slot at your slip."

Richard turned his gaze to where his boat floated. He squeezed his temples, softening his voice. "Just wanted to make sure I'm debt-free, Gil."

"Yes, sir."

"So long, Gil," Richard croaked, "And sorry I was so short. You've always been good to me." He somehow managed to create pools of tears in his eyes before one rolled down his cheek. It was a masterful performance.

Down at the covered slip, Richard hurriedly unmoored his twenty-six-foot gleaming teak Chris-Craft Runabout, cranking the Chrysler inboard before heaving to and backing into the slipway. As he motored slowly away, Richard turned, staring back at the gleaming Chicago skyline while the boat pressed into the choppy spring waters of Lake Michigan.

"I'm doing it," he said. "Today's the day and I'm actually, *finally*, doing it." As he applied full power while headed straight out into open water, Richard flipped on the Philco car radio, tapping his feet in tune with Jimmy Dorsey's *Tangerine*.

It was all he could do not to laugh aloud. One of those great, maniacal laughs, like the one heard in the popular radio show, *The Shadow*. Richard could even yell out while laughing, asking, "Who knows what evil lurks in the hearts of men?"

With all the noise and his distance from shore, Richard—finding no harm in having a little fun—did his best rendition, laughing himself nearly to tears.

"Okay," he told himself. "Now, focus."

He planned to navigate ten miles to the east before turning hard back to the southwest. The ten miles would take some time, done so no one from the shore would see his true destination. Sitting now, Richard leaned back, basking in the sun as the music blared.

The way everything had come together had been incredibly fortuitous. His travels, halfheartedly considering selling his secrets. The situation at home getting worse, living paycheck to paycheck. Then, sitting in that dark bar in Panama, having what started as an innocent conversation with the frail little Englishman.

The chat had seemed benign until the man edged closer and asked Richard a question. "What exactly are you doing in Panama, friend?"

Richard had fingered his warm glass, staring into the amber liquid. After some time he looked up at the expectant fellow, deciding to let the cat out of the bag. "I'd read Panama was a haven for intelligence types."

The man's thin lips twitched. "Indeed?"

"Yeah." Richard gulped the remainder of his drink, smacking the tumbler back on the bar. "Ridiculous, huh?" He had fumbled in his pocket, tossing the last of his cash on the bar, staggering out into the balmy Panamanian night.

The Englishman caught up to him just before he'd reached Parque Urraca, politely stopping Richard by his sleeve. In the pitch black at the edge of the park, as the crickets chirped and a tropical bird screeched high in a tree, the Englishman had asked him a pivotal question: "What, if I may ask, were you planning to do if you met one of those so-called intelligence types?"

And Richard had known, right then, he'd found his man. There had been an initial spike of fear—consternation the fellow could be working for the Allies, looking to burn Richard. But if one wanted to reap the rewards, he had to be willing to take the risks. He and the fellow talked until sunrise. The following afternoon, after a nice nap and a sumptuous lunch, Richard produced his briefing—devoid of names and critical facts, of course—and it was enough to earn him the cash advance right on the spot. When he'd told the alleged Englishman what he wanted in return for the information, the man had put a finger tightly over his lips, his eyes turning away in a thinking gesture.

After considerable thought, when the waiter had cleared the dishes away, the Englishman said, "Assuming I can compensate you as you desire, when, my new friend, will you be able to deliver?"

Richard had replied confidently, "Six weeks." He already had his disappearance roughly figured out, but needed the six weeks to pull it—and the information regarding the Manhattan Project—together.

"Meet me in the Parque Urraca six weeks from today," the Englishman said confidently, getting the exact date from a card in his wallet. "Be there at six in the evening, feeding the birds on one of the benches by the central columns."

"Six weeks to the day is too exact."

"Do you think you can be there around that time?" the man asked politely.

"Most likely."

Again the Englishman pressed on his lips, his pondering gesture. He nodded after a moment. "Take a room at the Hotel Manna. Leave a message downstairs with the—"

Richard cut him off. "Sorry, pal, but I'm not going to open myself up like that. Who says you won't snatch me if you know where I am?"

"What do you suggest, then?"

Richard produced a slip of note paper and a small key. "That key is for a post office box, number seventy-one, here at the main post office." He slid it over.

"What shall I do with this box?"

"I will mail a letter when I'm ready, but not *before* six weeks. When the letter arrives, you will follow the instructions regarding the deposit, and then our meeting for the exchange."

That Panamanian lunch had been the turning point of Richard's life.

Pleasant lake wind rushed over his head. He pulled his sailing cap back on, smiling at his foresight. Setting up the post office box had virtually assured his safety in Panama. And, in the event his contact was watching passengers enter through customs, Richard had a plan. First, he hadn't shaved in two days. By the time he reached Panama, he'd have a nice beard growing. Added to the beard would be a new pair of thick-rimmed glasses and a posture adjustment. Though he didn't expect the Englishman to be watching for him, Richard felt he would easily slip into Panama undetected.

He turned, barely able to see the figure of the Roman mythological goddess Ceres on the top of the Board of Trade Building. Satisfied, and seeing no other craft nearby, he made his turn, immediately taking spray as he began to chop back into the brisk wind. From a compartment below his seat, Richard removed an Indiana state flag—something he wouldn't typically fly on his boat—and posted it on the aft pole, pleased as it popped straight back in the wind. Being a common type of boat on Lake Michigan, any boaters who were later questioned might recall witnessing a twenty-six-foot Chris-Craft heading sharply to the southwest. But the flag, mostly blue and quite different than Illinois' largely white flag, would rule out Richard's boat, which hopefully would eventually be found much farther north.

Richard tossed his sailing cap in the water. He donned a black ball cap and stripped off the polo, wearing his white undershirt. This, too, was by design.

Flying a new flag, wearing a different outfit, Richard cruised slowly to the southwest, aiming to a spot just to the left of the path of the setting sun. He had the landmarks burned into his brain. As soon as the sun passed the horizon, he would enter the water and begin his long journey to the south. To Panama.

And free will.

EARLIER AT the marina, Rollie followed the burgundy Lincoln to the entrance, pulling left onto a side street and exiting his own car. Pulling his fedora down, he moved away from his car, buying a newspaper at one of the multi-purpose newsstands that dotted the Chicago shores of Lake Michigan. He leaned against a weather-beaten clapboard building, pretending to read the front page as he peered at Hampton, having a close tête-à-tête with the valet.

Hampton patted the man a few times before walking onto the quay, ambling with his head down.

What Rollie had feared, especially given Hampton's attire, was about to come true. And unless he could gain access to a boat, Rollie was about to lose his target. Tossing his paper, he hurriedly crossed the street and ran through the front of the marina. The rapid movement sent stabs of pain down his neck and torso as some of his scars had begun to split. When he didn't apply the prescription lotion—like last night—tiny fissures would often develop.

You don't keep lotion in the car, but you sure do keep some opium in there, he chided himself, a measure of his Irish heritage somewhat thankful for the pain he was enduring.

"You guys rent boats here?" Rollie yelled at the dock master as he approached the covered stand.

"Gotta go up to the Pier area you want a rental," the man answered brusquely through a genuine Irish lilt. He gave Rollie an up and down, curling his sun-blistered lip. "And unless'n you're a member or a guest, I'm afraid I'll have to ask you to leave th' premises."

Rollie took a deep breath and made his face amiable. He reached into his pocket and pulled out his wallet, previewing several crisp bills for the Irishman. "Come on, pal, I know how to handle a boat out on the open water. What say you and I make a little deal here?"

The dock master stared at the wallet before lifting his green eyes to Rollie. With his left hand, from an unseen spot behind the weather-beaten counter, he lifted a telephone, eyes still locked on Rollie's. After one spin of the dial he said, "Chicago Police, please."

"Oh for cryin' out loud," Rollie growled. He turned and stalked out of the marina, pausing at the top of the hill to watch as Richard Hampton cruised straight out into Lake Michigan in a gleaming teak boat. With little traffic or ambient noise, Rollie swore he could hear Richard laughing. Actually, he was cackling.

"You're hearing things," Rollie mumbled to himself.

After weighing his options, he decided all he could do was wait for Hampton to return. The dock master evidently didn't follow through on his call to the police (either that or the cops simply didn't bother.) Having no desire for another long stakeout, Rollie took a short stroll and, thankfully, discovered a tidy little deli a block away. After purchasing three sandwiches and a large container of potato salad, he regretfully situated himself in the old Ford, watching and waiting for Hampton to quit dicking around out on the water on his day of hooky.

There were numerous boats out on the lake, at least half of them sailboats, truly a beautiful sight. Their owners, surely aching to sail after a long winter, seemed to be taking advantage of the pristine conditions. But Hampton had gone out on a gas-operated motorboat. Fuel was rationed. He was alone. Hampton would be back before too long, Rollie reasoned.

Knowing he had the time, Rollie self-medicated with his morphine sulfate, greatly easing his pain. He then took a two-hour nap. When he awoke in the late afternoon, Hampton's dock slip was still vacant.

By the time darkness fell, Rollie began to worry.

Gulf of Mexico, near Cabo de San Antonio, Cuba

THAT SAME evening, and just over 1,000 miles to the south, aboard the SS Regina, several hours underway from Havana and steaming southwest on the glassy waters of the Gulf of Mexico, a striking young lady sat at her assigned table in the elegant dining room, surrounded by serried tables of wealthy Americans on holiday. Her dining table was set for eight, and the only other solo traveler at the table, a silver-haired toper, was seated across from her, leering at her as he droned on with story after story about hunting adventures that had purportedly carried him all over the world. He wore a bright red carnation on the lapel of his double-breasted jacket, the red of the flower matching the burst capillaries of his florid nose.

Doing her very best to ignore the lurid old churl, Maria kept her head on a swivel, trying to enjoy her second trip away from her stifling homeland. She studied the five hundred or so travelers, wondering where each one had come from. Who were they? How did they make their money? Why did they choose to travel to Panama?

She focused on a husband and wife, seated at the starboard end of one of the center tables. They ate in silence. The man chewed his fish, occasionally looking around, sipping his wine, eyes back to his plate. His wife's food was mostly untouched. Her gaze was harsh, directed at him.

Cuba was chock-full of brothels, and the brothels were chock-full of voluptuous sixteen year-old girls. That man, Maria imagined, had visited one during the two-day docking, and had been caught. Judging by his smart suit, he had money, so his wife probably wouldn't leave him over his dalliance. In fact, this wasn't the first time he'd been caught. Or the second. Maria was certain, after studying the couple for several minutes, that she was correct in her assumptions. The man was a scoundrel.

A typical man.

Maria loved to hypothesize people's backstory, and this particular musing made her smile.

Shaking her from her reverie just after the dessert course had been served, she felt her table-mate's thinly-socked foot (rough with callouses) clumsily rubbing at her calf and knee. After closing her eyes in a moment of revulsion, she focused on him. His breaths were ragged as he cocked a bushy eyebrow. "Getting to you, am I?"

Maria turned her eyes down the table. The other couples, who all seemed to know one another, were deep in a conversation about the horrid crimp the untimely war had put on their leisure travels. One man went on and on about the Germans, professing support for the Nazis and their ideals. "Damned England," he growled. "Imperialistic bastards can't leave anyone well enough alone. We ought to let 'em twist, if'n it were up to me."

Maria brought her eyes back to the hideous man sitting across from her, wetting his cracked lips with his tongue as he ogled her. At the beginning of the evening, before the remainder of the table had tuned him out, he informed the seven others he was Welsh, now living in Maine solely for the grand hunting. He claimed, in between massive quaffs of his wine, to have killed game on every continent, as if he should have gotten a standing ovation. Now his foot was moving past her knee, probing further up her skirt as he sank lower in his chair. Had he not been so obnoxious, Maria might acquiesce to such a bold sexual advance, even despite his lack of visual appeal. It wasn't that she was averse to older men, but rather men she couldn't tolerate.

This trip, however, promised to be somewhat boring, given the fact most of the cruisers appeared to be married. Perhaps, she thought while suppressing a smile, it was time to have a bit of fun. Such playfully reckless action was deep inside her character. Philip had tried like hell to train it out of her, telling her she would eventually pick on the wrong person and get herself killed. But Maria had lived five years in an abandoned shack with a dozen other street children. The church had done its best to care for them, but it's difficult to counteract such a rough upbringing. Maria's practical jokes went well beyond good-natured and, although she knew she shouldn't monkey around while on this mission, she simply couldn't help herself.

Maria dipped her fingers in her ice water, flicking it on her upper chest, making her own breathing heavy as she leaned forward, giving the old man a front-row view of her extraordinary, and now glistening, décolletage.

"You're going to make me do something I shouldn't," she panted, pushing her accent to high Cuban. "I have a husband, you know."

"And where might that lucky lad be?" the man asked, sinking in his chair as his big toe pushed nearly to her crotch.

"Back in Havana," Maria gasped, feigning a brief spurt of ecstasy. "I had to get away from him, to clear my head for a few weeks."

Her words had the prescribed effect on him, his bleary eyes bulging. "Darling," he whispered, sounding like he had gritty gravel lodged in his throat. "If he knew how happy I could make you in the bedroom, he'd give you license to stay with me forever."

She pressed her lips together, visibly suppressing what looked like a naughty smirk. "If anything's to happen," she said quietly as she leaned further forward, momentarily dislodging his foot from her body, "I'll need plenty of drink, as my excuse." His hand went for the bottle of Burgundy before she stopped him. "A triple gin and tonic in a large glass, if you will."

"The man'll be by directly," he answered, flicking his hand in the direction of the galley as his foot resumed its motions, probing up and down on her panties.

"That could take too long," Maria panted, her hand rubbing at the rivulets she'd splashed on her chest, "I can't wait. It's been…" The big toe of the man's foot had finally found its home, rubbing furiously. She balled her hand into a fist, briefly gnawing on her index finger's knuckle, "…it's been so long since I've…since I've quaked with pleasure not provided by my own two hands." Her hand shot to her forehead as she bit her lower lip in horror. "Oh my dear, listen to me. I sound like a harlot after all this wine. We must stop. I'm not even drunk yet." She dropped her hand to her lap, shoving his foot and bony leg away. "Please put your shoe back on."

"Wait…do you still want that drink?" he asked, clearly panicked.

Her eyes turned away.

"Darling, you've a right to pleasure," he cajoled, his hand reaching over and rubbing the top of hers.

Swallowing visibly, she turned her eyes back to him and nodded.

The man pushed his chair back with such force it slid the table a few inches, causing water and wine to splash onto the tablecloth and earning a chorus of indignant protest from the older couples seated to his left. He hurried away, his arthritic joints propelling him to the long bar with surprising speed.

While the couples had been too absorbed in conversation to notice their scandalous exchange, the woman seated next to Maria, an aged southern belle who threw off a superior-to-all vibe, turned to Maria, curling her lip. "What, little lady, seems to be all the fuss between you and that hideous old drunkard?"

Maria studied the sixtyish woman for a moment, allowing her eyes to move from the showy fan-front turban, to her gaudy chunk-gold earrings and pearl necklace, to the swooping neckline desperately displaying two tired old jugs that probably hung below the bat's navel by now. Maria fluttered her eyes, smiling broadly as she said, "Why don't you mind your own business, you used-up old hag?"

The woman's head pulled back as her jaw lowered, her mouth transforming into an indignant O. She started to say something when Maria whispered through her own clenched teeth, saying, "Turn around and *do not* speak to me again."

With that, the woman jammed her linen napkin into her lap and turned, huffing her breaths loudly as she complained to her indifferent, Nazi-loving husband about the way she'd just been abused by the spic trash seated at the table's end. As the woman went on about anyone with skin a shade darker than hers, Maria reached into her clutch, flicking open one of the numerous capsules hidden in the side seam. She stood and leaned across the table, retrieving a basket of bread with her right hand. As she was rudely reaching, expertly using her considerable breasts as cover, she dumped the powder contents from the capsule into the nearly empty glass of Burgundy belonging to her grotesque "date" for the evening. Drawing disapproving glances from the women of the table, she sat back, mouth open in a smile, obnoxiously chewing a large bite of the bread as she purposefully made eye contact with their husbands, winking at each one.

By this time Henry was back, proudly carrying the tinkling oversized gin and tonic, sliding it over the white table cloth. Maria gulped half of it, nodding her approval. "Now finish that wine," she commanded.

He straightened. "In a hurry, my dear?"

"Yes, I am." She leaned forward and whispered, "I can't wait to be alone with you."

His breathing picked up again. She noticed a vein pop out on the side of his forehead—probably mirroring another rush of blood elsewhere. Yuck, Maria thought.

Henry turned the wine up, gulping the last few swallows before letting out a loud sigh, attracting more judgmental glances from the now avidly watching women.

"I'm going to take this on the fan deck," Maria said. "Won't you join me?" She flashed a dazzling smile, wanting to make him believe his crude seduction had paid off. The two joined hands, weaving through the rows of tables, exiting the dining room through the aft French doors.

SITTING TWO tables away, wearing an impeccably tailored double-breasted blue blazer with embellished gold buttons, sat an unaccompanied man of approximately forty years of age. He was dabbing a linen napkin to the corner of his mouth as he finished his superb Baked Alaska. According to the ship's manifest his name was Lawrence Wembley, of England. In reality, however, his given name was Bernd von Danzig, and he'd been the first aboard today in Havana, paying a porter to take his bags while he lingered at the rail, assessing the other new passengers, focusing on one young lady in particular. In his possession was another identification, that of one Harold Lancaster. *Der Geist* was handsomely turned out this evening, appearing quite regal on the first night of his cruise.

He nodded politely at the well-fed elderly couple seated across from him. They'd just jointly finished an hour-long tale detailing the mind-numbing accomplishments of their five Ivy League-schooled grandchildren.

"Isn't that splendid?" he said to them both, leaning forward as he spoke in a precise middle-English accent. His eyes flicked to his left, watching as the voluptuous young lady led the red-nosed man from her table, headed to the doors that led to the fan deck. Seeing no reason at all to follow her, Bernd, feeling somewhat masochistic, tilted his head to the expectant twosome and said, "Please, tell me more."

As the couple started in on another wearisome saga, this one about their colonial summer home in Vermont, Bernd lit a cigarette and massaged each of his eyelids individually.

Himmel hilf mir...he couldn't wait until they arrived in Panama.

Chapter Six

Lake Michigan, near Whiting, Indiana

WHILE MARIA seduced the eager old Welshman, and Rollie swilled bad coffee in the front seat of the government's Ford, Richard Hampton idled within sight of Whiting Park, his Chris-Craft rolling on the wind-borne chop of Lake Michigan. His nautical track had been aided simply by navigating directly toward the two looming smokestacks towering over the park, both with flashing red lights on top. He'd already shredded the nautical rope, leaving plenty of remnants on the deck as well as his jack knife, blade out. Now he hefted a cinderblock, scraping it roughly over the side rails, satisfied as it made a final plunk before sinking to the lake floor.

Richard turned off the boat's power, extinguishing all lights. Taking the Indiana flag with him, and with a final glance to make sure no one was nearby, he eased himself over the gunwale, nudging the boat to the north, satisfied as the breeze and current began to push it that way, naturally.

By the time he reached the shore, the boat was a dark speck on the deep purple northern horizon. While providing him with a chill, the breeze from his back made Richard smile with satisfaction as he viewed his beloved boat, a symbol of better times in the Hampton household. And the harder the wind blew, the further north his light boat would drift. He glanced at his waterproof Rolex Oyster, unable to read it but estimating the time to be around nine in the evening. Unless the boat was found during the night hours—which would be highly unlikely—it would probably average a few miles an hour of northward movement overnight. If pressed, Richard would bet on a morning discovery of the boat, hopefully twenty miles north. Back at the house, he'd placed his suicide note somewhere Vivien wouldn't stumble upon it unless she was looking. So, in his best estimation, a true search for him (or just his body) wouldn't occur until after noon the following day. The investigators would know his boat had drifted, but they'd have no idea he'd jumped out near the shore—near the genesis of his new life.

And, if all went to plan, by the time they discovered his death, he would be somewhere in the skies over the heartland.

Like a bolt of lightning, he remembered a crucial detail he'd forgotten to take care of.

The book!

Richard stopped walking, craning his neck back to the heavens.

He'd been so careful, so meticulous. But he'd left the damned book about Panama in his home office. He tugged on his wet face with both hands. Then, with a resigned shake of his head, he started moving again.

"Nothing I can do about it now," he mumbled. Then he cursed his carelessness. He'd studied books and articles about murders and high-crime. And criminals usually forgot one little thing that led to their ultimate arrest.

He stopped again, talking to himself. "Forget it and move on. Focus on the here and now. No one's going to find you in Panama."

Richard found the suitcase hidden under the fragrant tree boughs and toweled off. He donned the plain working man's dungarees and jammed the long ticket into his breast pocket, setting off for the main road with an old porkpie hat tilted back on his head. Given his tired mien, his burgeoning beard, and his pauper's outfit, he wouldn't draw a glance from a soul: just any old Indiana farmer looking for work along the road. The Greyhound bus to Indianapolis was due to stop at the nearby diner just before midnight. Once there, he jammed the flag under assorted refuse in a garbage barrel. After a sandwich and a piece of delicious pie, Richard Hampton—now traveling as Samuel Fields (but just call me Sam)—sat on the bench at the front of the diner, stretching his legs out, hands laced behind his head.

His eyes were closed.

He was smiling.

It had been a long, yet productive day.

Gulf of Mexico

THE SS REGINA knifed through the tepid gulf waters, the warm breeze only a half-hearted respite from the stifling heat. Because of the warmth, the fan deck was crowded with people, in their midst a swaying elder joined by a striking Cuban beauty. Despite Henry's growing impairment, his arthritic hands doggedly fumbled at Maria's bare shoulders, his eyes unfocused red slits. Knowing he didn't have long before he hit the deck, Maria Fuentes leaned back against the teak rail, jutting her chest outward and murmuring, "Why don't we skip these silly formalities and go straight to your cabin?"

Henry was only able to moan his assent. He led her by the hand, tripping to the floor when they entered the cabin section from the fan deck. After helping him up, Maria took his key, noting the room number as she hurriedly led him through the narrow passages of the medium-sized ocean liner.

His room was four levels below decks, on the same hallway as hers. The hallway contained the smallest cabins on the boat. Henry's was essentially the size of a narrow closet, with a single bed to the right held off the wall by two mooring ropes. On the outer, port wall of the ship was a round portal window. Stacked underneath the window were four hard-buckle cases in varying sizes, no doubt containing Henry's hunting weaponry. She looked to her left, to the microscopic lavatory, as Henry stumbled to the deck again. As he staggered back to his feet, Maria commanded him to get undressed.

"My dear," he slurred. "When you shay you're ready to cobbulate, you really mean you're ready, don't choo?"

"Get naked now, Henry. We need to do this quickly, so we don't let those other biddies from our table on to our little game."

Henry, drunk and about to succumb to the capsule of chloral hydrate, started with his shoes, fumbling at them as he gabbled on about the pneumatic pounding he was going to bring to her lithe body. He managed to get his old brogues off, as well as his pants and boxer shorts, before falling backward, spinning off the side of the bed and thumping loudly on the deck. That was it. He was out. From what she'd learned during Philip's many lessons, especially given all the red wine Henry had downed, he'd be unconscious for at least five hours and probably the entire night.

As the old man lay there, unclothed from the waist down (other than his over-the-calf argyle socks, with mended toes) Maria rifled through all his possessions. She counted $68 in cash in his wallet, leaving it. In the top case she found a first-rate Webley revolver with pearl grips, loaded. She located three boxes of complementary ammo in his shoulder bag. Then, in one of Henry's two floor grips, she discovered what looked like a painted piece of rock or wood with a hole in the center, the name "Luis" etched into the surface.

Maria froze, eyeing the item.

Carefully studying it in the artificial light, she realized, with a measure of shock, what sort of keepsake it was. She'd never seen one, but had heard tales of hunters taking them as souvenirs. In Cuba it was known as a *Hueco del Ojo*, translated directly as a Hollow Eye, the carved-down remains of a human skull taken from the area around the eye socket. Wealthy land barons in the Las Tunas province were rumored to hold illicit manhunts, often using purchased prisoners as the quarry. As the story went, they would set the prisoner free in the jungle, weaponless and hungry, while teams of armed codgers like Henry, loaded for bear, hunted the defenseless prisoner down.

Earlier, she'd felt old Henry was not a nice man and was simply going to leave him here, stoned on the floor. Oh, sure, she'd also planned on having a little fun with him. Things like throwing one sock from each of his pairs out the window or hiding his money in hard-to-find places around his cabin. But now, as she glared down at his snoring nude form, a wicked idea formed in her mind.

It's time to teach this murdering hijo de puta *a lesson.*

It took her only a moment to find his passport, containing stamps from all over the world. After taking his money, she tossed the wallet and passport out of the porthole. She stuffed his money and revolver into her purse, along with an extra ten rounds for the .455 caliber Webley. Then she dragged the diminutive man into the cramped hallway. Maria used all her strength to slide him aft, stopping at the carpeted companionway stairs leading above decks. She propped him up on the second step, accentuating the appalling scene by opening his knees wide and wrapping his right hand around his pathetic little tool. Stepping back, she smiled at her handiwork. The deviant little human hunter snored there, blissfully unaware of his impending humiliation.

After shoving Henry's key into his coat pocket, she retrieved his pants and shoes, scattering them in the hallway. Just as she pulled his cabin door to, she heard people coming from around the corner. Maria quickly put on a crying face, pushing past them with fake tears of distress. On the main deck she found the second officer; she yelled in unintelligible hysterics to the English-speaking Greek until he managed to calm her down. When she finally was able to speak coherently, she told him of a shameless older man from her dinner table. He'd seemed harmless at first, telling her exciting tales of his hunting. But later, when they were walking alone, he forced himself on her. He groped her. He exposed himself to her. He ran through the passageways while rubbing himself. "It was absolutely horrible!"

"I must go," she said, beginning her tears again. She took a few steps before stopping, aiming a rigid finger at the wide-eyed mariner. "And I will not be dragged into an embarrassing hearing so I won't press any charges, but please *do not bother me* with this any further. If you do, I will go straight to the newspapers and them about this floating ship of perversion and I'll tell them your name, Mister Malamatos!"

The second officer, eyes wide to show white all the way around, made a calming motion with his hands, assuring her he would take care of everything.

Before she turned in that evening, Maria broke the pistol into its smallest form, carefully hiding the parts and bullets throughout the secret cavities of her luggage. As she lay in her bed, sleep evading her, she could hear hushed, important voices as heavy feet stomped up and down her hallway. Maria knew, as she stifled laughter, that deviant old Henry, the man-hunter, was getting his.

During the remainder of the three-day voyage, Henry wasn't to be seen among the passengers again. On the last evening, just before Maria finally succumbed to the charms of a handsome Canadian gentleman, she saw Henry, after the dinner meal, wearing leg-irons and being shuffled across a passageway by two large men to the galley. She froze, telling her panting Ontarian suitor to stay still and shut up while she spied through the round window of the galley door. They were feeding Henry at one of the prep tables, both men standing guard over the tired old man while he picked at his food.

Their ship had been scheduled to pass through the canal, meaning the debarking passengers wouldn't have to endure transportation from the canal's north end, at Colon. They were able to go ashore just outside of the city. After debarkation, once she had breezed through customs with her false Panamanian passport, Maria laughed quietly as she watched the haggard old Welshman yelling at the port's customs officers. Yelling that his treatment aboard the ship had been an outrage. Yelling for his congressman, or senator, or someone to speak on his behalf. Yelling that he'd been robbed. Yelling that it had been done by some voluptuous young hussy. Yelling that he was now an American citizen and possessed a library-full of human rights.

The two customs officers holding him ignored his protests, staring at another more senior officer who was absorbed with a folder in his hand. Finally the graying Panamanian looked up from the report, curling his lip. "Sir, eet says here you were cot masserbating on a sarewell?"

"That's preposterous!" Henry roared. "It was the woman! She was a temptress, a wicked quean, using her sex as a bloody weapon. She robbed me and..."

As his protestations veered from the voluptuous young whore to allegations of drugging, then to Cuba, back to Maine, and somehow—oddly enough—to King George, from a distance Maria caught Henry's eye, giving him a wink and a small wave.

When he began to gesticulate, pointing at her while shrieking that she was the one, Maria casually handed a taxi driver her luggage claim, stepping to the outer door of the customs hall. And, as the indifferent customs officers dragged Henry off to see a tired *magistrado*, Maria informed her driver that her destination would be El Carmen.

While well-trained and bright, she was mischievous and it showed in her unnecessary little game with Henry the Welshman. And because she was too preoccupied with getting in one final jab, Señorita Fuentes never noticed the tall, blond-haired man entering a taxi two cars behind hers.

The man never told his driver to follow her cab. Instead, rather expertly, *Der Geist* directed the cab driver utilizing excellent Mexican-accented Spanish, following Maria from a discreet distance while acting as if he was recalling his own directions to a place whose name he couldn't recall.

Thirty minutes later, both he and Maria reached El Carmen at the center of Panama City, checking into the same hotel.

April 17, 1943
Chicago, Illinois

A FEW HOURS after Maria had played her wicked game with Henry the Welshman, Rollie found himself genuinely sick. It was after midnight; he was long overdue his full dose of nighttime morphine and had just vomited his stomach contents on the sidewalk across from the marina.

Staggering back to the Ford, he stared at the blackness of the lake, knowing Hampton certainly wouldn't be back that night. Taking a calculated risk, and desperately needing morphine-aided sleep, he drove to the nearest motor lodge, waking a grumpy desk clerk to pay cash for one night in a ground-floor room. He was in such bad shape that it was difficult to concentrate, but Rollie did recall seeing the windows of a small cabin on Hampton's boat. It was conceivable, especially with the nice weather, that his mark was spending his night anchored on the water. Perhaps he fished at night, although Rollie wouldn't have given good odds on Hampton being an angler.

The large, welcome dose of morphine sulfate helped Rollie to sleep until eight. After a quick and cold shower—cold to help numb the growing splits on his scars—Rollie felt decent again as he sped back to his spot across from the marina. In his hand was a paper cup of tepid, yet genuine, coffee.

Sitting in his car, in the same spot as yesterday, Rollie listened to the radio report. The United States and the British had bombed Bremen overnight, with the U.S.'s Eighth Air Force providing over a hundred B-17's for the mission. Whistling softly, Rollie closed his eyes, recalling what it was like to be on the receiving end of just two bombs. He couldn't even fathom the hell a hundred bombers could bring. Trying to put unproductive thoughts out of his mind, he craned his neck to the marina only to see Hampton's boat slip was still empty.

Though his head was pounding, Rollie felt surprisingly lucid and, after thinking over the situation, he saw two possibilities. One, Hampton anchored last night and should be back in soon—no big deal, just a well-off man enjoying his summer toy out on the water. Two, and a bit disconcerting, Hampton knew he was being tailed and knew the boat could be used to make a clean break. This, combined with Hampton's peculiar actions earlier in the month, troubled Rollie. Perhaps Rollie should have gone over Nicholas Penland's head and demanded more support.

"But what's done is done," Rollie mumbled to the cabin of the old Ford. He punched the ceiling, cursing loudly as bits of the rotten roof liner tumbled down around him.

At 11 A.M., with still no sign of Hampton, the Department of War agent crossed the street and walked back into the marina. The same dock master sat in the same hut, reading what looked like the same newspaper. He shot a bored glance as Rollie approached, eyes back on his paper as he spoke.

"You again? Want me to fetch the police this time?"

His head still hurting, Rollie was in no mood to stay undercover. He dug into the hidden inner fold of his jacket, producing a set of credentials and holding them near the man's nose so he wouldn't miss them.

"Department of bloody war?"

"Yeah, and if you so much as stutter this time, you and I are going to have a major problem."

"Why didn't you say so yesterday, me ol' mucker?" the dock master breathed, an obsequious smile coming over his broad face.

"Because I'm supposed to be undercover, *ol' mucker*, and if you utter a word of that to anyone…*anyone*…I will arrest your ass here on the spot and make it my mission to have you held in general population at the federal pen down in Gary."

The Irishman made a pained face. Rollie knew he now had his attention.

"Richard Hampton left here yesterday afternoon."

"Aye, sir, he did."

"He normally stay out all night like that?"

The dock master folded his paper. "Since the ration kicked in people do all kinds'a queer things. Don't get to use their motorboats often so, when they do, sometimes they stay out. 'Specially it's this unseasonably warm."

"Could he have docked at a friend's place?"

A nod. "Reckon he could've."

"Would that be normal for Hampton, and would you typically see him head out on his boat alone?"

The man gnawed on his blistered bottom lip, a thoughtful expression. "Well, ya know, now that I ponder it, afore'n the war Mister Hampton used to set out with his wife. But in the past years, well…"

"Yeah?"

"He's usually shoved off with other *companions*, if'n you know what I mean." The dock master cocked an eyebrow and tilted his head.

"Other women."

"That would be accurate, m'kind sir."

Rollie licked his lips, preparing another question as something from the water caught his eye. It was a fishing boat, a trawler, weathered and sturdy, of the type that dotted the lake all year round. Its motor was on slow idle, chugging slowly into the no-wake area of the marina. Behind it, towed by a rope, was what looked a helluva lot like Richard Hampton's gleaming boat, manned by a bib-wearing fisherman.

The dock master leaned over the counter so he could follow Rollie's wide eyes. He nearly fell over when he saw what was in his marina. Lurching from the screen door of his hut, he rushed down the quay yelling "Ahoy!" to the fisherman.

Rollie, however, stood stone still—catatonic—listening unflinchingly to the exchange that followed.

Found the damned boat drifting empty…'bout keeled over when we seen the knife, them rope remnants and this here out of place gouging on the rails…boat's a beauty otherwise…afraid the sumbitch musta did himself in…radioed the Coast Guard and they told us it was registered here and since they were all on patrol asked us to tow it in. They'll be here directly…

As the dock master took the line and secured the boat, and as he got the names of the fishing boat's crew and the boat's name and where they hailed from, and as the trawler left and the dock master stared at the scant evidence in Richard Hampton's Chris-Craft, Rollie Donahue leaned propped against the dock master's hut, his head down, taking deep, steadying breaths.

How in the hell was he going to explain this to Washington?

Galveston, Texas

LATER THAT afternoon, at 4 P.M. local time, a gleaming Chicago & Southern DC-3 touched down at Galveston Airfield, chock-full of passengers headed to the SS Arosa Star, ready to get underway over at the Port of Galveston. Since the plane was slightly behind schedule due to the headwind blowing from the south, the porter outside gladly agreed to ferry everyone's luggage to the docks, and was tipped handsomely for it.

Forty-one minutes after touching down, Richard Hampton—now Samuel Fields—sipped an icy Pearl Beer near the bow of the ship, watching as the last of the items were towed aboard by the enlisted military passengers. When he first boarded, Richard chatted with one of the senior Army officers. He learned the unfortunate enlisted soldiers were confined below decks, and only allowed fresh air for a few hours each day around sunrise.

"Poor bastards," Richard said while watching them. Then he shrugged.

I did my time, now it's their turn.

He took great breaths of the sticky salt air, feeling freed from his bonds but bolstering himself for what lay ahead.

Yes, he knew the damage he could cause to the U.S. by selling his secrets. It was an unmitigated act of treason. But, having been a soldier once (just like those poor sons of bitches down on the dock) he didn't think it would do much harm in the grand scheme of things. The krauts were going to lose this war regardless. How could Richard giving them the twenty-two sheets of paper change anything? Unless their scientists were miracle workers, it couldn't. But it *could* change his fortunes mightily.

And, most importantly, to be guilty of treason, one had to be caught. Richard wasn't getting caught. No way. He'd die first.

The book, a voice in the back of his mind reminded him.

Richard closed his eyes, willing the voice away.

Trying to get his mind off such weighty matters, he winked at a rosy-cheeked young lady who had taken up a position ten feet away from him, guessing her to be in her early twenties. She carried some extra weight, but at that young age, and from his considerable experience, the spare pounds were still held firm by the glorious tension of youth. She smiled at his gesture, looking away shyly before glancing back a moment later.

Here we go.

Richard sidled over, leaning over the railing next to her, facing to the southeast.

"Traveling alone?" he asked.

"With my two girlfriends," she replied in a drawling Texas accent.

"And where are they?"

"Oh, they already met some new friends," she replied with a note of well-practiced despondency. "They're having a drink with them at that table over there."

Richard followed her pointing hand, seeing the postcard scene of two attractive girls, festooned in their first-day-of-the-cruise sundresses, requisite fruity drinks in hand, eagerly chatting with two handsome fellows about their own age. He turned back to the young lady. So this was the ugly duckling of the bunch? She certainly wasn't as fetching as her friends, but to his near half-a-century-old eyes, she was a painting. Doing his best not to laugh at his typical good fortune, Richard clinked his bottle of beer with her drink and said, "You know…I hoped I would meet a gorgeous young lady on this trip. Hoped beyond hope for months." He pulled his head backward and looked her up and down, widening his eyes. "But I never thought I'd be so lucky to meet her before we even left the *dock*."

A hopeful look passed over her face just before consternation swept in. "You're just saying that."

"Honest, I'm not!" he insisted forcefully, for effect. He allowed the silence to linger before leaning close and whispering to her. "In fact, would it offend you if I told you something incredibly personal?"

She blinked rapidly, obviously wondering what he might say and eventually shrugging. "Why not? You seem like a nice man."

"It's a bit embarrassing, but I want you to know that my attraction to you is the real McCoy." He straightened, turning slightly. "So you'll pardon me for," he lowered his voice to a conspiratorial whisper, "displaying my excitement. But it is an automatic reflex. Us men, we have no control over it, you know." His eyes flicked downward to his midsection, beckoning her to do the same.

The young Texan glanced at the bulging area of his slacks. Her cheeks flushed immediately as she quickly looked away. But then, the girl who probably always played third fiddle to her friends turned back and, wide-eyed, drank in the ribald sight. After several seconds, she suppressed a giggle and again turned away. He could hear her breathing deepen as her pale skin blotched on her chest and neck.

He moved shoulder to shoulder with her. "Do you believe me now?"

"Oh, yes," she answered, bursting into good natured laughter, covering her mouth with her hand as she continued to look in the other direction.

"And you don't think of me as awful?"

The young lady turned, face-to-face this time, still laughing. "No, not awful. Honest, yes! But not awful." Her laughter ceased as her eyes flicked down again. "In fact, and I can't believe I'm saying this but, I'm terribly flattered."

Richard clinked his beer with her drink again, staying tightly against her, making sure their bodies continued to touch. And, as they steamed from the port, he learned her name was Frances, from Waco, Texas. Though he didn't know it then, Frances from Waco would certainly make Samuel Fields' trip to Panama go quickly.

So grateful. So willing.

Fort Sheridan, Illinois

ABOUT THE TIME that Richard Hampton was gingerly sweet-talking plump Frances into disrobing, Rollie Donahue sat before a military short-wave radio at Fort Sheridan, north of Chicago. Since he'd been unable to raise Nicholas Penland by phone, Rollie had bulled his way through the various levels of security and bureaucracy, finally ordering the deputy post commander to provide him with a private room and a secure radio. Since arriving, the wait had been excruciating. Rollie was uncharacteristically smoking from a pack of cigarettes purchased at the canteen on the way in. His scars were throbbing and the constrictive effects of the nicotine added a small measure of relief to the pain—something he typically used as a last resort. His hair was wet with sweat, his head cradled in both hands as he listened to the humming from the radio's cooling fans.

The room was built of cinderblock with a concrete floor and ceiling. A bunker, essentially, with no windows. The walls were painted olive-drab, the ceiling and floor bright yellow. It was a hideous combination of color that had been used back during Rollie's service, and was unfortunately still being paired together.

Behind him, a heavy steel door was tightly shut; on the outside an M.P. stood guard, holding his service Colt in his hand. Rollie had stationed him there seventy minutes before, calling the communications room at the Pentagon and informing them of his coded identity of Kestrel. Once he'd been patched through to his section, known as Division Blue, and was informed that their signal was secure, Rollie told the operator he had flash-traffic for Nicholas Penland. More than an hour, and three harsh cigarettes, had since passed while the Pentagon located their section man.

Just as Rollie was stubbing out the fourth Chesterfield, the radio popped twice before he heard Penland's voice, sharp as a razor as he said, "Authenticate Kestrel."

Rollie recited six two-digit numbers from memory. Saying them incorrectly would have resulted in the radio being shut down on the other end. Transposing any one of them, however, would have indicated duress. The conversation would have continued, and would have either focused on disinformation, or location, if the field agent felt a rescue was possible. This exchange, however, because of Rollie's correct authentication, would now simply be a routine interchange over a securely scrambled radio.

"Roger, Kestrel, copy that," Penland replied, having surely scrawled the numbers on a scrap of paper. "Stand by." There was a pause of another minute before Penland asked, "Authentication verified. What's the damned emergency? I was on a hot date with a freshly-widowed, non-grieving, twenty-two-year-old floozy."

"My mark is *reportedly* dead."

Another pause. "Say again."

"Hampton is reportedly dead."

"How?"

"Suicide." Rollie released the thumb-trigger on the handset before quickly keying it again and saying, "Allegedly."

"Give me the full story," Penland replied with a frustrated exhalation. And Rollie did, starting with his first contact of Hampton's wife. He explained that Hampton didn't come home and held nothing back regarding his infiltration of Hampton's home. Rollie explained the numerous financial files he'd rifled through, all showing a systematic depletion of what had been a sizeable nest-egg several years earlier. Countering the signs of suicide, he also told Penland about the half-burned paper displaying the Panama itinerary.

Penland interrupted only a few times as Rollie patiently explained everything. He detailed Hampton's finally coming home the morning before, and how he was on the run mere minutes after his wife left. Finally, Rollie told him about the solo boat voyage, and how the empty Chris-Craft was discovered this morning. Rollie explained how, working with the police, they'd discovered a suicide note in the top drawer of his home desk, coinciding with the evidence on his boat.

Rollie talked for the better part of twenty minutes, holding only one critical piece of information until the end. "Before he went to his marina, just before…the target went to a park on the south shore of Lake Michigan, slightly past the Indiana border."

"And?"

"He concealed something there under some pine boughs. I couldn't make it out due to limitations beyond my control. I marked the spot by memory and proceeded to follow him as he raced to the marina, where I held vigil until his boat showed up with no sign of Hampton."

"Did you go back to the park?" Penland asked.

"Yes."

"What was hidden there?"

"Nothing at all. The cut pine boughs were scattered about, but there was nothing there."

"So what was he doing there?"

Rollie lit his fifth cigarette, stared at it a moment, crushed it out. "When the target left his house, he was carrying a distinctive hand grip. I didn't see him hide it in the park, but he was partially obscured by his car and raised trunk lid. And he definitely did not carry it on to the boat when he left."

"Could it still be in the car?"

"That was the first thing I checked when they towed his boat in. Jimmied the trunk, too. No hand grip." Rollie grew silent and allowed his boss to piece everything together.

"So you think the target faked his death, swam to that park, took the suitcase and vanished?"

They don't pay you the big bucks for nothing. "Yes."

"You feel completely confident about this?"

Rollie keyed the handset, enunciating the two affirmation syllables clearly. "Roger. He had to have left the grip in the park. It is nowhere...say again...nowhere to be found."

"Copy that, Kestrel." There was pause of static. "Here's what I want you to do. Write two reports. The first needs to be everything you've relayed to me here, but use the target's name, and his wife's. Use location names, exact times, et cetera. Be as detailed as you can."

"Copy."

"Then write a second report—a detailed description of Hampton, and feature his possible destination of...where was it, Costa Rica?"

"Panama."

"Roger. Write up the description and possible destination so that we can get it out on the wire within the hour. In fact, write that one up first and get it to me by teletype."

"Roger. What else?"

"Do those two items pronto and beat it back here tonight on the late bird. We're stretched thin as it is and I'm probably putting you up in New York for a similar—"

"Whoa, whoa, whoa. You're yanking me?" Rollie yelled into the handset.

"Kestrel," Penland said soothingly. "That target you've been on is small beans. What's he going to tell the krauts, how big a frigging aileron is? The horsepower of a P-51 Mustang? Who gives a shit? If he did fake his death, then we'll deal with him when he resurfaces, but you're needed here, *now*."

Rollie stared at the handset, aware of his own pulse pounding against his temples. He blinked rapidly, his eyes darting around. This was wrong. All wrong. He keyed the handset. "Say again, Kingfisher." Halfway through Penland's recitation, Rollie keyed it again, loudly scraping his feet on the floor as he modulated his voice. "Losing you Kingf—*static as he dragged the open handset across the beat up wooden table*—will report in when I know more—*blew into the microphone loudly*—piece of shit Army equipment's smoking!"

"Kestrel, you sonofabitch! Don't even think about trying to freelance this thing when I've given you explicit ord—" Reaching behind the table-sized radio, Rollie grasped a handful of wires and jerked them, pulling his hand back as he got popped by amperage-heavy twenty-four volts. Purple smoke wisped upward as Nicholas Penland's diatribe was stopped cold. After sucking on a small third-degree finger burn for a moment, Rollie removed his keys and, using one as a punch between his balled fist, he smashed two tubes hidden on the bottom side of the short-wave device. It would likely be some time before the radio worked again.

He tapped on the heavy door, nodding when the military policeman unlocked it. "Thanks for the cover, sergeant. Oh, and your radio's on the fritz."

The deputy post commander, a brigadier general who Rollie pegged as a paper-pushing sycophant, appeared from an adjacent room with an expectant look. "Was everything satisfactory, sir?"

"Sure, until your piece of shit radio bugged out. I see the Army still only buys the best."

"I can take you to another secure communications center, sir, and I do apologize."

Rollie tossed his pack of Chesterfields to the M.P. before fake-smiling at the general. "No need, sir. I was able to say all I needed to say."

The general nodded. "And, ah, if you will please note my name for the record back at the Pentagon. I'd like to be noted as having assisted you."

"Your name was mentioned on the call before I uttered another word."

The brigadier beamed. "Thank you, sir."

"Anything for my pals in the Army," Rollie said, walking away. It was pitch black when he walked out of the building, flashes of lightning popping inaudibly in the distance. He decided to bed down for the night. Penland probably wouldn't come after him immediately, especially if he was as short-handed as he said he was. Rollie decided he had twenty-four hours, forty-eight tops, before Penland's patience would run out.

"Detective work tomorrow, old boy," Rollie said to himself as he set out for a quick run by his house. He certainly couldn't stay there, in the event Penland sent someone. But he wanted to get his medicines.

And he planned to pack a bag.

Chapter Seven

The Pentagon, Arlington, Virginia

BACK IN the Pentagon, Nicholas Penland sat stone-still in the windowless communication room. Though outwardly appearing calm, his mind was actually racing. What on earth might Rollie Donahue have unearthed in Chicago? Nicholas thought back to the précis he'd read on Richard Hampton. Like all Nicholas's domestic targets, Hampton was low-priority. The fact that everything under Nicholas's charge was low-priority was another story altogether. Over the past year, Nicholas had begun to grow wary that he'd been deliberately cut out of sensitive projects. Admittedly, it was easy to feel this way when working for the O.S.S. inside the Department of War, especially at the new Pentagon. Cases were supposed to be eyes-only. You were either in the loop, or you weren't. Still, Nicholas had begun to have the unsettling feeling that he was being played.

Having not moved from the radio for ten minutes, he eventually exited the room and lit a cigarette. The room was in sub-basement one, on a corridor filled with rooms just like it. Nicholas waited on the attendant, a buck-toothed WAC, scribbling his out-time on her clipboard as she grinned at him. He left without smiling. Hurrying, he made his way back upstairs and exited the Pentagon at the mall entrance, finding his car in the large lot, still full with overworked day workers and those assigned to evening duty. It was raining. He paused outside his car.

Go back home for more sex or attend to duty?

He tilted his head back, allowing the rain to patter on his face.

She'll still be there later.

Nicholas drove to the northwest, past Arlington National Cemetery and its uniform rows of fresh graves. He impatiently drummed his steering wheel as he endured a small traffic jam in the bedroom community of Pimmit Hills, eventually passing through and finally parking on the street in neighboring Tyson's Corner.

Nicholas stood under an awning on the sidewalk, just in front of a noisy bar, glancing up and down the street, unsure of the way to go and wishing he'd checked his notes to refresh his memory. He walked to the south for three blocks, turning abruptly before heading back to the north. The rain intensified as he passed back through the center of town, quite alive on a Saturday night, finding his way and turning left on Wolftrap Road. He counted the houses, all tidy, two-bedroom-type deals containing requisite newlyweds, professors, bachelors and twin old maids who shared rent. Halfway down the street, Nicholas suddenly turned, checking his tail. No one. He proceeded, eventually recognizing the correct house, opening the white-washed wooden gate and crossing the lawn.

Following his six well-spaced knocks on the door, a shuffling could be heard in the house. After a moment, a graying man opened the door, holding it on the chain. He held Nicholas' gaze for a moment, finally saying, "What in God's name are you doing here?"

Nicholas, tongue pressing outward on his cheek, tried to appear contrite, unable to contain a grin. "I realize it isn't exactly kosher, given all the competition between our divisions, but this is important."

The man undid the chain, leaning out and peering around Nicholas, glancing both ways. After what seemed a moment of internal conflict, he pulled the door wide.

Seated in the tidy den, Nicholas accepted a snifter of warm brandy from the man known as Liam Winterbourne. Liam walked back to the wet bar, pouring his own brandy before coming back to what must have been his favored reading chair. He sat, cupping his libation, staring harshly at Nicholas. Next to the chair a hardcover book lay face down and open near a pair of thin-rimmed reading glasses.

It was obvious Liam wasn't going to say anything that wasn't solicited. Again, making an effort to sound genuine, Nicholas said, "My apologies for interrupting your reading, but I have something that could be potentially urgent."

"And now, after all this time, you want my help?" Winterbourne asked icily.

"Our country's security is bigger than our feelings."

"Fancy hearing that from *you*," Liam Winterbourne, reportedly Scottish-born, answered straight-faced. Liam was a senior intelligence official with the Department of the Army. A year earlier, when the Office of Strategic Services (O.S.S.) began to form, only select individuals were chosen to create the new intelligence enterprise. In true military and bureaucratic fashion, the remaining intelligence arms of each governmental department duly forwarded all of their working cases to the O.S.S., but continued to gather intelligence on their own. When anything of significance arose, they were immediately supposed to forward all material to the O.S.S., who had the authority to choose whether or not to take it on. The collaboration occurred—but resentfully, and always at a glacial pace. It wasn't uncommon for the O.S.S. to get a lead that the Department of the Navy (or one of the other departments) had been working for six months. Given the ongoing war, despite threats from the O.S.S. and the Joint Chiefs of Staff, the problem still existed, which was why Nicholas was here.

Nicholas removed his cigarettes from his damp suit jacket. "Mind?"

Liam gave an uncaring wave of his hand and said, "You look like shit."

Nicholas looked down at his rumpled shirt and wrinkle tie. "I was getting laid before I took an urgent call."

Liam frowned his disapproval.

After a deep inhalation of his cigarette, Nicholas gulped his brandy, showing veins and tendons in his neck as he winced.

"That's not the way it's meant to be enjoyed," Liam admonished. According to his service jacket, he'd lived in the States since he was sixteen, well over forty years. Only a hint of his Scottish brogue remained, though it was certainly discernible when he was angry.

Settling into the sofa, Nicholas frowned importantly. "If I were to say a name, would you know if he's a live play in your department's investigations?"

Liam snorted.

"Come on, Liam."

"A name?"

"Yes."

"Even if we're on the person, I still mightn't recognize it. We're investigating many leads."

"How many frigging names are you guys working?" Nicholas asked with a note of exasperation.

Liam smiled thinly. "Hundreds. Say the name."

"Richard Hampton, Chicago, Omicron Aviation."

Eyes narrowed, Liam cupped his brandy to his belly and stared down into the liquid. His head moved slowly back and forth. "Omicron, you say?"

"Yeah."

Liam stared dead ahead, the look of a man holding a high pair from the deal. After a moment he shrugged. "Nothing. Doesn't ring a bell. Why, what's he up to?"

Nicholas wrestled with himself over whether or not to tell the truth. "I've got nothing concrete on him other than a few trips to intelligence hotbeds. Circumstantially, I've got a report about Hampton meeting with a turned Panamanian, one of President Arias's boys."

"Circumstantially?"

"Yeah."

"I thought you said the Panamanian was turned. Won't he give you a statement?"

"I'd ask the fellow but he's dead." Nicholas was referring to the initial reports on Hampton that he was seen meeting with a low-level former cabinet member of the fascist-sympathetic Arnulfo Arias regime. The Panamanian president had been ousted several years before, but his reign had caused Panama to become the preferred breeding ground for Axis agents as well as dastardly dealings.

"How did the Panamanian die?" Liam asked.

"He appeared to have killed himself—found hanged in his home months ago. According to the locals, it was a genuine suicide."

Liam nodded. "Right, Nicholas. And *la policía panameña* are such a credible institution."

"Look," Nicholas said, leaning forward. "The Panamanian is dead. That lead is gone. But my target's trips, and the fact he met with the former

Arias man, is what turned us on to Hampton in the first place. You with me?"

"So, you think Hampton had something to sell and was down there, pitching it around?"

"Potentially, yes." Nicholas lifted a single finger for emphasis. "Here's where it gets interesting. A while back, before I came to the conclusion that Hampton was a nobody, I got word to our man on the ground in Panama. He gathered what he could and learned that the dead Panamanian had indeed met with a man matching Hampton's description, and they did discuss the sale of critical information. They had one meeting, and shortly thereafter this Panamanian winds up dead."

"Was your Panamanian unstable?"

"Highly. I truly believe he offed himself. So did our guy in Panama."

"Who *is* our guy in Panama?"

"Carsten Steuben."

Liam shrugged. "Never heard of him."

"You know Bernd von Danzig, known around Department D as *Der Geist*. He's Prussian. Carsten works for him."

"I know who *Der Geist* is," Liam said.

"So, once we knew Hampton was in play, Carsten made contact with him."

"What happened then?"

"Carsten sent word to me through a short crypt that Hampton's a nobody. Said he was trying to sell worthless intel on aircraft."

"Then what?"

"Hampton came back."

"So you put your D.O.W. people on him?"

"We were already on him, at a low level. I couldn't risk escalating it for fear of drawing too much attention. But I still wanted to nab him. I could use a promotion."

Liam smirked. "But now you think Carsten lied to you?"

"Of course," Nicholas said, opening his hands plaintively. "If Hampton did have something good, Carsten could have been keeping it for himself."

"The oldest trick in the book." Liam seemed pleased. "Have you reached back out to Carsten?"

"He's not responding."

Liam swirled his brandy, taking a small sip. Nicholas could tell he was enjoying this.

"Thoughts?"

Liam eyed Nicholas. "What's this Hampton chap got to give?"

"Omicron," Nicholas answered with a shrug. "Aviation and avionics. They've got nothing incredibly sensitive that I can find…I checked it personally."

Liam didn't reply for a moment. "So, why are you here?"

"Because, what if I'm wrong?"

A thin smile appeared on Liam's face.

"Here's the worst part." Nicholas dragged hard on the short cigarette, crushing it out afterward. "Hampton *himself* went missing last night. Suicide by drowning. Chicago P.D. found the requisite note and all the trimmings. Cement block tied to his ankles. They think."

Liam made no response. His jaw visibly tightened but he remained silent.

"Due to a number of peculiar things my Chicago field guy has learned, he's insisting Hampton faked his death."

"Who's your Chicago field guy?"

"Rollie Donahue—an ever-present pain in my ass."

Liam sat unmoving for several moments. His eyes crinkled at their corners, his mouth breaking from its smirk and turning upward as his belly began to shake. Then, full-on laughter. His mouth parted as he tilted his head backward, a person clearly enjoying himself.

When the laughter subsided, Nicholas leaned forward and rested his elbows on his knees. "What is so damned funny?"

The question caused another brief outburst as Liam's arthritic finger crooked in Nicholas's direction. "You," he managed. "You're the funny one. Only you, Nicholas, could publicly stab a man in the back and then have the sheer brass to come and ask him for help, when you're mired in a quandary that seems to have been mishandled from the get-go."

Nicholas maintained his composure, allowing Liam's self-indulgence to fade away, waiting until he quieted. "Perhaps I *am* crass for being here, and perhaps I could have helped you get on with the O.S.S.. If you want me to say I'm sorry again, I will." He reached for the cigarette, grunting when he remembered extinguishing it. "But in the end, you and I owe it to our shared belief to cooperate on this type of thing. C'mon, Liam, I'm on tenterhooks here." The last question he asked monotone. "So do you, or do you not, have information on *Richard Hampton...Chicago...Omicron?*"

Liam shook his head. "No, I do not." He quickly raised his hand as if he'd realized something. "But wait, there are two things."

"Yeah?"

"Of lesser importance," Liam said, dipping his head in deference, "it's been very nice speaking to you in my native tongue. It's been over a year since I spoke German and it still amazes me that the Scottish accent I learned for English bleeds into my Deutsch."

Though he could have cared less, Nicholas nodded. "And the second item?"

"This one's more important...something I failed to say earlier," Liam said, using a warning tone.

Having felt like the butt of Liam's joke for the duration of their meeting, Nicholas held his guard up. "What is it?"

Pulling his quilt up over his legs, Liam held Nicholas's gaze. "What I didn't say is what I should have said when you first came in...and that's 'Go to hell, Nicholas.' To hell with you—to hell with Hampton—to hell with that dead Panamanian—and to hell with your field agent, Donahue, in Chicago. If you can't see this Hampton guy has taken you for a dandy ride, you should be out on Pennsylvania Avenue with a cane and a tin cup."

Nicholas took the insult with no expression. He used the side of his hand to wipe a smattering of ash from the mahogany table. He carried the snifter back to the well-stocked bar, placing it there and donning his fedora. He left the house without a word.

As Nicholas crossed the lawn in the light rain, he could again hear Liam's laughter, continuing until he was past the front gate.

April 18, 1943

UNFORTUNATELY FOR Chicago, the breezy summer had transformed back into what felt like mid-March on this Palm Sunday morning. As Rollie drove north from the motor lodge where he'd bedded down, he glanced at the thermometer mounted on his door mirror. It registered only thirty-eight degrees—so much for an early summer. The azure sky was gone, replaced by a low gray ceiling of thick cloud. The budding leaves of the trees whipped in the heavy Chicago wind, the air tinted yellow from the emerging pollen.

The brakes on the Ford chirped as he parked in front of the Hampton house. It felt strange not to be hiding his car down the street. Rollie was a tad satisfied when he saw the Cadillac parked in the driveway. Next to the loan-shark-pledged Caddie was Richard Hampton's Lincoln, probably ferried there by the Chicago PD. And behind the Lincoln was a run-down '37 Nash replete with bald tires and dented fenders, each dent laden with the paint of other automobiles. Tilting his favorite charcoal fedora back on his head, Rollie took a few deep breaths before he walked through the winter ryegrass yard and rapped on the door. It was opened after a moment by a woman, probably in her late twenties. She wore a pinafore playsuit and, upon seeing him, pulled the door wide and stuffed her hands into her pockets. She arched her eyebrows disapprovingly.

"Yes?"

Rollie thought she was probably Vivien Hampton's younger sister. Slightly shorter, her hair nutmeg rather than dyed blonde, she could almost pass as Vivien's twin. Perhaps it was only because she was protecting her sister, but right away there was something harsh about her demeanor—an edge. Rollie flashed his credentials, hoping she didn't want to scrutinize them. His first sentence was designed to conceal his familiarity with the resident of the home as he said, "Yes'm, very sorry to bother you, but I'm here to talk about your husband's passing." As he did by habit, he turned his head to the left to hide the worst of his neck scarring.

"He *wasn't* my husband," she replied, the biting distaste for Richard Hampton dripping from her voice. "My sister *was* married to him."

"I see," Rollie replied, pleased with his mild ruse. "Is she in?"

The woman flicked her eyes to her right before bringing them back. "Your fellow cops were here all day yesterday. Can't you just let her rest?"

"I understand, ma'am. I promise I won't be long. I've only got a few questions."

The sister pulled the door back and hitched her head to the right. Rollie decided her edge was probably forced, a defense mechanism. He stepped in and looked around the door, seeing Vivien Hampton on the sofa, her legs pulled up underneath her. She was holding a small ashtray, smoking a cigarette, looking a bit older as lines of stress and worry wrinkled her forehead. While she appeared exhausted, he immediately sensed she wasn't grieving her loss. In fact, if anything, she looked rather cross. Rollie removed his hat.

"Morning Mrs. Hampton, I'm Rollie Donahue. Might I have a few minutes of your time?"

She gestured to the chair adjacent to her. Rollie sat, studying her, remembering…

The way she'd swept into the kitchen in that filmy gown. The things the gown revealed…

Stop!

He clenched his eyes shut, quickly shaking his head.

Her head tilted as she looked at him quizzically. "Something wrong, detective?"

"Sorry, just the pollen. I've had itchy eyes and the sneezes since the leaves came out."

"You'll have to excuse my smoking. I know some group of do-gooders has made the decision that it's in poor taste for a lady to smoke, but I'm grieving, you know." Her slightly uptilted mouth showed him that she retained her sense of humor.

"It's not the smoking."

"Val, give him a box of tissues, will you?" she asked her sister. Rollie noticed Vivien looking at his disfigurement before politely turning her eyes away.

Her sister was standing near the front door, arms crossed. She walked to him with a gilded box of tissues, depositing them on the table beside him with an unnecessary clunk. Eyeing Rollie for a moment, she turned to her sister. "Need me in here, Vivien?" She said it fast and familiar, sounding like *Viv-yin*.

"No. Why don't you go take a nap?"

"I'm not tired."

"But you've been up all night."

"I'm fine."

"Well…if you're bored, you could run to the grocery."

"Grocery stores won't be open today."

"Bello's, up north of here in Deerfield, will be."

"Are you sure they'll be open? It's Palm Sunday."

"It's outside of Fort Sheridan," Rollie said, remembering his radio chat from Fort Sheridan just last night. "They open every day because Fort Sheridan doesn't have a post exchange."

"I'll make a list," she said, disappearing through the hallway behind Rollie.

"And I'll try to be quick," Rollie said.

"Don't mind her—it's not you she's irritated with. She's irritated with *my* situation."

"Well, I can tell she's protective of you. Are you twins?"

Vivien didn't miss the compliment but smiled only with her mouth. "She's younger. Lives in Detroit and drove all day yesterday to be here for me. Stayed up all night, too. She's got to be exhausted."

"Nice lady." Rollie softened his face. "But how are *you* holding up, Mrs. Hampton?"

"Rollie, is it?"

"Yes, ma'am."

She licked her lips. "Rollie, do me two favors, okay?"

He nodded.

"First, don't call me ma'am. It makes me feel old."

"Sure."

"I don't like to feel old," she said, again wearing the forced smile. "And second, don't call me missus. You'll pardon my being frank, but my husband was a scoundrel and a bastard and all he did by taking his life was end our marriage ahead of schedule." She clamped her lips on the cigarette, pulling on it as she shook her head. As she exhaled twin lines of smoke, she breathed the word "bastard" again.

"Why do you think he took his life?"

"Maybe he was tired of cheating on me."

Rollie offered a sympathetic smile. "I promise to get out of here soon Mrs....I mean Vivien."

"Really, you don't have to rush."

"Thank you. It seemed you were about to say something else."

She stared at the wall. "Other than his rampant philandering, I've just learned in the past day he squandered our savings. Pissed it all away. Now I'm left with no way to support myself. And his life insurance is not going to pay on a suicide."

Not knowing how to respond, Rollie opened his flip pad and pretended to study it. "Anything peculiar from Richard in, say, the past year?"

Vivien crushed out the cigarette and lowered her legs to the floor. "We couldn't stand each other, detective. Excuse me if I can't really help you with particulars. I thought he acted strange all the time."

"Did he travel?"

"Yes."

"Did he travel more frequently recently?"

There was a pause as she chewed on her lower lip. "Yeah, he did. Why?"

"Just confirming what I've learned elsewhere."

"Where did you hear that?"

"From a colleague."

She turned away disinterestedly.

"Do you know where he'd been going?"

"New Mexico."

"Really?" Rollie asked, making a note to obtain Richard Hampton's work travel schedule. "What was he doing there?"

"I've no earthly idea."

"Did he travel overseas that you know of?"

"No, never for work."

"You're sure?"

She was about to answer but paused. "If he did, he lied to me about it."

"He *never* went to Panama that you're aware of?"

"Not that I know of," she said without hesitation. "But he was interested in it."

"How do you know that?"

"He bought a book on Panama a while back. I would often see him reading it." She grasped a tin of Old Gold cigarettes, snapping the case open and removing one. Her head tilted quizzically. "Why did you ask me about Panama in particular?"

Rollie didn't blink, staring at her through even eyes. "There was something in his downtown office about Panama. I noticed it and am just closing all loops."

She lit the cigarette, studying Rollie for a moment before nodding.

Changing tack, he asked, "Did he have a passport?"

She eyed him for a moment. "We both do."

"Go anywhere?"

"We went to London back in thirty-eight." She dragged on the cigarette. "God, it was a nightmare. Lost a full day of vacation when we got stuck on the Queen Mary, in sight of London, while they searched the ship for some fugitive who never turned up."

"Neil Reuter."

"Who?"

Rollie dismissed it with a wave of his hand. "I knew the man they were looking for…knew him a long time ago. It's nothing." He glanced around the room. "Vivien, would you mind getting Richard's passport?"

She stood, padding barefoot through the house, Rollie in tow. He couldn't help but again recall how, just a couple of days before, she'd paraded around in that glorious green gown. As they passed by the passageway to the kitchen, Rollie could see the sister at the table, writing out a list. Vivien went into the top drawer of the office desk Rollie had rifled through, digging into the back, producing two slim passport booklets.

"Here're both."

He thumbed through Richard's, seeing the entry stamp from the U.K. and the return U.S. Customs stamp. On the next page were the Havana, Cuba and Colon, Panama trips from last year that got him flagged. Vivien wasn't paying attention so Rollie didn't mention the trips.

"Mind if I glance through these drawers?" She waved her hand to them in assent. Rollie glanced through the lower right drawer, knowing those were the house files and receipts. He pretended to be momentarily interested before opening the lower left drawer. Behind all of the financial files, many of them demonstrating Richard Hampton's investment failures, was a file he had not seen before. It was titled "S-F". He leaned forward, using two fingers to spread it open.

It was empty.

The file had not been there before. He would have certainly remembered it because all of the other files were clearly labeled with full names. This was the only one with initials.

"What's wrong, detective?"

Rollie glanced up, licking his lips. He shook his head, trying not to appear puzzled. "I don't understand why…" He hung on his words.

"Why what?"

"This one just seems out of place. And it's empty."

Vivien Hampton frowned, leaning forward as she removed the S-F file. She opened it, quickly handing it back.

"Have you seen that file before?" he asked.

"No, but I rarely go into Richard's desk."

Rollie thought about it silently. "The suicide note was in this desk?"

"Top drawer," she said, tapping the desk with a painted nail.

"So he obviously went in it when he came home the morning of his suicide."

She appeared surprised.

"Something wrong?" Rollie asked.

"How did you know he came home in the *morning*?"

He felt his eyes fluttering instinctively. "You didn't tell the investigating officers he spent the night out?"

"No, I most certainly did *not*." She took a half step closer. "So, how did you know?"

Not missing a beat, Rollie said, "Because I found his name on the register at the Blackwatch Hotel."

"Oh," she said flatly. "With one of his whores, no doubt."

Rollie pressed his lips together, pulling them inward, not replying.

Vivien ground out the cigarette, whispering an audible curse.

"May I ask a question of a more personal nature?"

Her green eyes met Rollie's. "Sure, detective, you can always ask. I just may not answer it."

"You said you and Richard despised one another, and the marriage was due to end anyway. If that's so, why does his spending the night with another woman bother you so much?"

She stepped to the window of the office, staring out over the box hedges to his Ford and the empty street, one arm folded over her body. "I'd like to think we all want to be wanted, detective. Do you know what I mean?"

"Yes, I do."

She turned, gesturing with one hand down her body before coming back up. "Am I so hideous, detective? Am I so grotesque that a man should find me repulsive enough to shun me for disgusting hookers?"

Rollie's eyes moved to the floor in embarrassment. "Pardon my saying so, but in cases such as this, the lack of attraction usually isn't physical. Typically it involves years of arguing, differences, growing apart…that type of thing."

She paused before again offering up that thin, acerbic smirk she wielded so well. "Well, pardon *my* saying so, but rather than hearing the psychological answer, a girl would sometimes simply prefer to hear a nice compliment."

Rollie licked his lips. "Okay," his voice croaked as he struggled with how truthful to be. As the words began to escape his mouth, he couldn't stop them, as if they were being played by a phonograph behind a protective glass, preventing him from knocking the needle off the record. "If you were mine, Vivien, I'd have a hard time *ever* leaving this house for my desire to constantly be in your intoxicating presence." When it was out, he couldn't believe what he'd just said. In the moment of silence that followed, Rollie thought his heart might explode as it hammered at his ribs.

"Well," she finally breathed. An unmistakable flicker of happiness passed over the new widow before she dipped her head and took several steps toward the kitchen. "What else do you need from me, detective? My sister's about to leave for the market and I'd really like to be alone for a spell."

Rollie pushed the drawer shut. "Will you be here for the rest of the day?"

"I should, but I may want to get out of the house for a bit."

He nodded, walking to the front door and opening it. Turned back. "Mrs. Hampton—sorry—Vivien…is there anything about your husband's death that you find remotely suspicious?"

Her jade eyes cut away before coming back. "Yes, one thing."

"And what's that?"

"The fact that you're here, going through his files, asking about *travel*, about *Panama*. Especially after last night, when the police said it appeared to be a straight suicide and explicitly told me they wouldn't bother me today." She closed the distance between them. "I know how busy the police are, Rollie. You wouldn't go to all this trouble if there wasn't more to it."

Rollie held her gaze, unsure how to respond and choosing silence instead.

"It's okay, detective. I know my husband was a dirty man. You're probably not involved with his suicide. You're probably working on something else he was involved with."

"Dirty in what way?" he asked.

"Financial," she responded without hesitation.

"We've a few suspicions," Rollie replied soberly.

She moved beside him, taking the doorknob in her hand and gently nudging him to the threshold. "For now I just need a nap, but after that you can come back anytime you like."

"Thank you, Vivien." He dipped his head before looking up at her again. "Are you sure you're going to be okay?"

She nodded but he didn't feel the conviction. Rollie tried to smile reassuringly before he passed through the front door.

"Rollie," he heard her say as he stepped onto the lawn.

"Yes?" he asked, turning.

"I can tell by the way you constantly turn your head, by the way you tuck your chin, that you're self-conscious about that burn on your neck."

Rollie couldn't breathe.

"Don't be self-conscious," she said brightly. "You're a handsome man, and that scar is a piece of your character. I *like* character." She shut the door.

Rollie's knees wobbled. He feared if he stayed still he might collapse on the lawn, so he turned and walked to the old Ford, getting inside and pulling the door shut. In the silence of the car he gripped the steering wheel and squeezed his eyes shut. After a half-minute of collecting himself, Rollie cranked the engine and drove away.

AFTER HER sister had left with her ration coupons and five dollars, Vivien Hampton filled a glass of water and climbed the stairs to her bedroom. She released the gold tassels on the heavy drapes, darkening the bedroom and lying on top of the bed with the throw blanket pulled over her legs. Sleep nearly found her before the wave of questions interrupted her solitude.

While the detective's visit had aroused a few peculiar suspicions, Vivien's worry was primarily over money. She hadn't yet heard official word from Omicron, but earlier in the morning, Norris Huff, the senior vice president, had called to express his condolences. It was almost as if he'd been too embarrassed to mention the word suicide, only calling it "Richard's misfortune", but making veiled reference to the fact that Richard's corporate life policy wouldn't pay. Giving her a small measure of hope, Norris said they would calculate Richard's final paycheck on Monday, and he would recommend them adding a "little something to it" for the unfortunate one he left behind.

Feeling the tension in her lower back, she stood, stretching by the bed before going to the top drawer of her bureau. From inside, she lifted the small bank book and carried it back downstairs, sitting at the kitchen table and lighting a cigarette. Richard gave her an allowance every month. When they'd first gotten married Vivien always spent every dime, usually going the last week of the month without money. But several years back, when the marriage had begun to go south, when she'd known he was cheating, Vivien had begun scrimping and saving what she could, squirreling it away each month. She now had $540 in the bank.

Curious, she went to Richard's desk, finding his pay stubs in a thick file, placing them on the desk. After thumbing through the most recent stubs, she found the final stub from 1942, realizing Richard had made nearly $11,000 dollars over the course of the year.

Dejectedly, Vivien realized she didn't even have a month's pay.

Taking her time, she began going through each of the files, trying to determine if there was any money anywhere else. She'd heard Richard bemoan, time and time again, that they'd lost a great deal of their fortune (he'd always included her, saying *"we* lost it") after the crash. She'd known things were difficult but had no idea it had been this calamitous, confirmed by the paltry statements she'd found from the various brokerages and the bank. But what about the house? They'd made a nice sum when they sold their last home, plowing the equity into this, their dream home, as soon as it had been built. She located the folder labeled "mortgage", trying to understand the most recent statement. The red ink at the lower right of the paper leaped out at her. It was written longhand, in a male script:

Either pay the past due amount immediately or the foreclosure process will begin!

Feeling her heart rate spike, she looked at the top of the statement, following the numbers down the page, again noting the past-due amount before finding the balance.

There had to be a mistake.

The balance was almost exactly what she remembered the sale price as being. But that was impossible! Their last home, which had been large but not near as big as this one, had sold for $5,700. Richard had been so proud that he'd been able to pay off their previous mortgage ahead of time, thereby using the entire sale proceeds as the down payment on this home, which had cost nearly $15,000. So how could the balance still be $14,780, and how could she now owe a whopping $970 in past due payments?

Scanning backward, she found the reason on the November statement: a home equity disbursement. Trading a point of interest in return, there was a transaction on November 12th, a loan of nearly all of the home's equity.

Hating herself for crying, Vivien was powerless to stop it. She put her head down on the desk, shuddering as deep sobs consumed her. Her husband had leeched every dime from their household and then gone off and ended his life without ever having to deal with the fallout. Why had she ever gotten involved with him, especially given the warnings from her now dead mother and her close friends?

Even her career sailor father, now an admiral, had warned her in the strongest terms, having done a check on Richard's military background. She remembered how ominously his note read, especially the ending:

"By all accounts, Vivien, Richard Hampton is quite bright. He's a quick study, a solid manager, and he's clever in corporate politics. He's also skilled with women and an unmitigated cad. Though you rarely listen to me and seem to harbor ill-will over my lifetime of absences, I forbid you to marry him, Vivien. I hate that I was gone so much and I'm beyond sorry over how I let your mother down. But you must set that aside and take my advice this time. Richard Hampton is trouble."

Coincidentally, her father had "let her mother down" by having an affair. When her mother found out, she divorced him and died a few years later. Feeling her mother's broken heart contributed to her eventual death, Vivien never forgave her father. She never listened to him, either.

Now, she wished she had.

After the tears subsided, when she heard her sister's car rattle to a stop in the driveway, Vivien stood, sagging as she left her former husband's home office.

A fastidiously tidy woman, she stopped at the threshold, backing up. The built-in bookcase was stacked floor to ceiling with bound volumes. Having never desired a house-cleaner (because she never found one who could do it as well as she did), not a week went by when Vivien didn't straighten and dust the bookshelves. She could see there was a book missing from the bookcase, evidenced by the tan book to the right tilting into the void. The book to the left was *Of Mice and Men*. The book to the right, the one leaning into the gap, was one of Vivien's favorites, *Rebecca*, by Daphne du Maurier.

The missing book was *Panama*. Of course.

She never liked the book on the shelf, due to its out-of-place subject and the gaudy gold lettering. Vivien hurried to the den, looking at the decoratively stacked books on the end and coffee tables.

It wasn't there.

Standing still, eyes narrowed, she recalled the detective's asking her if Richard had ever been to Panama.

"Vivien, something wrong?" her sister asked, standing in the door, her arms loaded with bags.

Vivien blinked several times, her mind in high gear. She went into the rear of the top drawer, finding Richard's passport. On the fourth page she saw the stamps from their trip to England. She flipped to the next one and there on the first page was a yellow and red stamp marked Havana, Cuba. Opposite was a stamp, in blue, denoting Colon, Panama.

Her breath caught in her throat.

She slid the passport back into the desk, searching each item from every drawer. In the back of the top drawer she found a cigarette case Richard sometimes used when traveling. Upon opening it, she was surprised to discover a pack of matches from a place called the Hotel Azul in Ciudad de Panamá. Vivien studied the matches, adorned with a toucan against a field of black. She placed the matches in her pocket and left the office, helping her sister. When they were done putting the groceries away, Vivien crossed her arms, giving her sister a look.

"You don't look happy," her sister said.

"I've discovered more lies."

"What now?"

After a moment of thought, Vivien said, "Something doesn't add up from today."

Her sister shrugged. "What do you mean?"

"Let's take a ride and I'll explain."

UPON LEAVING the Hampton home, Rollie went directly to the nearest coin-operated phone. This would tell the tale. If his little radio-malfunction stunt with Nicholas yesterday had earned him a forced recall, he'd get stonewalled as soon as he reached the appropriate person at the Federal Bureau of Investigation. Afternoon sunshine had poked through the thick clouds, beaming to the ground in buttery pillars of soft light. Rollie had to close the door of the booth to hear the operator on the other end of the line and, despite the chilly temperatures, the greenhouse effect made the booth quite stuffy. He pulled off his fedora, placing it on top of the phone as he negotiated the maze of operators.

After reaching the Bureau, he asked for Sam Linkletter in International Operations. Even though it was Sunday, Rollie felt Sam would be in the office. Everyone involved with the war effort was essentially working seven days a week. Following a few clicks he was patched through to Sam's assistant.

"Whom shall I say is calling?"

"Just tell him it's an urgent field call."

"We need a name."

"Tell him it's Donald Oswald White," the name being a poorly concealed acronym for Department of War.

"Yes, sir." Another click.

"Linkletter," came a brusque voice after nearly a minute of waiting.

"Sam…Donahue here." Rollie cringed as he awaited Sam's reply, expecting to get a harsh rebuke followed by, "Get your ass to the nearest Federal Building, pronto!"

Instead, there was a pause before Sam said, "Who's this?"

"Rollie Donahue," Rollie replied with a touch of exasperation. He and Sam had worked together a number of times.

"Hmm, I'm sorry, sir," Sam said, "I'm afraid you have the wrong number." At first Rollie feared Sam was trying to protect him, but Sam's tone was clearly jocular.

"Smart ass," Rollie finally replied, tilting his head back, eyes closed, relief flooding through him. "How're you doing, old buddy?"

"So overworked with zips and fritzes I hardly see my family anymore. Seems every nosy resident in the whole damned union has called in with a supposed foreign spy living next door."

"That's why you joined up, isn't it?"

"Oh yeah, having the time of my life. I'm not so sure it wasn't easier during the big one, living in the trenches and eating boiled rats." Sam cleared his throat, his tone switching to business. "Kinda line you on?"

"Pay phone, random."

"Last I saw of you weren't you in the doghouse, again, and being relegated to some piss-ant field post?"

"*Was*, until a few days ago."

"I presume you're back?"

Rollie paused, forming a leading hint with his tone. "Not exactly."

"What do you mean? What happened a few days ago?"

"They're probably going to recall me very soon, with prejudice. I'm freelancing at the moment. I take it you haven't seen my name anywhere?"

"No, but that doesn't mean anything. It could be lost in the shuffle. There's major goings on in Tunisia, Italy, Germany, and we shot down a Jap Admiral's aircraft over New Guinea." Sam snorted. "No offense, old boy, but I'm not sure your recall is going to get moved to the top of anyone's stack."

"Roger, understood."

"What are you working on?"

Nudging the accordion door for some air, Rollie said, "They had me soft-tailing a citizen who was possibly trying to broker something of value to the enemy. Problem is, no one thinks what he has to sell is worthwhile."

"Do we have anything hard on his efforts?"

"No, not yet."

"So why did they recall you?"

"He's dead."

"Sounds like a good start."

"Not exactly."

Sam cleared his voice. "I'm a little confused."

"I don't believe he's dead, Sam. I believe he faked it."

"You know this?"

Compressing the story to about a minute, Rollie told him about the supposed suicide, the half-burned itinerary and the book he'd taken.

Sam summed it up. "You got no body. A dropped-off suitcase, *maybe*. An itinerary he thought he destroyed, and a picture book with turned-down pages."

Rollie laughed at how thin it all sounded. "Pretty thin, huh?"

"And your gut says he's running?"

"Yeah, Sam. It does."

"Then go with it, man. Go with it. This country needs more of its people to use their balls."

"Thanks, Sam. Now to the reason I called you."

"Yeah?"

"How could my guy get to Panama?"

The phone crackled as Sam exhaled into the receiver. "I don't know for absolute sure, but I'm pretty certain it would have to be by water unless he has a charter flight from the southern U.S. My guess is all civilian flights to Panama are booked with military."

"But there are sailings?"

"Plenty. It's actually a popular destination at the moment. The cruise liners are making constant runs to carry troops and the shipping lanes, with the canal and all, are probably as secure as any place on the planet."

"Could he get there by rail?"

"He could make it part of the way by rail, but at some point, I guess down in Mexico, he'd have to make a transfer and go by air or sea."

"Thanks, Sam," Rollie said, pondering this. "Listen, I don't want to get you in trouble, so when you report I called you, just be a little slow with that contact report."

"You got it, old pal. I'm covered up with paperwork as it is." Sam cleared his throat again. "But you didn't call me *just* to ask me what you asked me because you could'a figured that out on your own."

"I trust you, Sam. I admire your efficiency…always have."

"Here it comes."

"Sam, old buddy, I need you to run something down for me, very quickly."

"Nice, starting with the flattery like that."

"You like that?" Rollie laughed.

"I love it, pal. But how quickly?"

"*Now*-quickly."

The phone crackled again as Sam breathed an unconvincing curse into the phone, followed by, "What is it?"

Rollie whipped out his flip pad, staring at the notes from his illicit night in Hampton's office. "Could you check the flights for me, then check which ships sail to Panama, and run my guy against all the flight and ship manifests?"

"Jeez, Rollie, that could require culling a few thousand names."

"I realize it's no small request but I don't want to run off to Panama if he's not there."

"What's your fellow's name?"

"Richard Hampton, although I'm quite certain he's under alias."

"You're talking a day of work, at least."

"Surely they'll have some personal info on the passengers, won't they?"

"Gimme his vitals."

"Mid-forties, could be there under a disguise. He's about six feet tall, dimpled chin, tan golfer's skin and sandy hair that he wears loose. He resembles that actor Alan Ladd and he's probably alone."

"I'll see what I can learn."

"Sam, please...keep this quiet."

"Keep what quiet? I'm not sure who I'm even speaking with," Sam replied in a mock innocent tone.

"Thanks, buddy. I owe you."

"I accept payment in single-malt, aged properly, of course."

"Of course."

"Call me back in three hours but, I'm warning you, it could take a full day."

"You got it." Rollie hung up the phone and opened the booth door all the way, walking to a street-side elm tree and leaning against it, his mind wandering in three directions. Waiting was the worst damned part of his job. He hated it, deciding to keep moving. His first order of business was finding a package store, which he lucked into a block away. Dropping four bucks on the counter, he purchased a fifth size bottle of Scapa, paying the old codger behind the counter two bits to package it softly and securely. Rollie followed the man's directions to a post office two blocks away, mailing the package to

Sam Linkletter, Federal Bureau of Investigation, Department of Justice Building, Washington D.C., idly wondering if one of the war-wounded down in the F.B.I.'s mailroom might pocket the expensive bottle.

With ninety more minutes to burn, Rollie drove the old Ford to Chicago's Municipal Airport, parking in the center of the long-term lot. Inside the airport, feeling his sweats already coming on, Rollie splashed cold water on his face in a bathroom sink. He purchased a newspaper, asking for three dollars' worth of coins. Five minutes before Sam's instructed time to call, he dropped a nickel into the payphone, spinning the rotary dial from the zero position.

He reached the operator.

She patched him through to the Department of Justice.

The F.B.I. operator put him through to Sam's secretary.

She put him through to Sam.

"Linkletter here."

"I waited three hours."

"There have only been a few flights and your boy wasn't on any of them."

"Good."

"But there was a large ship sailing to Colon, Panama, the SS Arosa Star. It's Panamanian-flagged and sailed from Galveston. That's the only ship that sailed in the last few days."

"When?"

"Yesterday. Over the next week there are other civilian sailings, too. Like I said, the cruise ships are used as troop carriers for Panama, and civilians can also buy a ticket just like a normal cruise."

Rollie pinched the receiver between his face and shoulder, wiping his sweaty hands on his suit pants. Sailed yesterday. The timeline was tight but Hampton could have made it. He'd have probably flown to Galveston.

"How many passengers on the one that sailed that could be our boy?"

"I don't have anyone stationed in Galveston, so I had to call a helpful local-yokel. He scoured the list and found twenty-nine possibilities. Although, if we stretch Hampton's age younger or older, which he could certainly be doing with a disguise, the number leaps."

Rollie growled in frustration. "If he were to make that ship he would have had to have flown. Did you happen to check to see—"

"As you know, there aren't as many civilian flights with the war on. There was one flight from Chicago, a Chicago & Southern flight yesterday morning, booked into Galveston. No one on board, however, was traveling alone. All were either military or couples except one fifteen-year-old kid. And unless your boy is the Great Blackstone, I don't think that's him."

"Shit," Rollie breathed, thinking about other airports near Chicago. "That suitcase he hid was over the Indiana border so he might have flown from somewhere else. When does that ship dock in Panama?"

"It's a slow cruise with a few stops. They're scheduled to port Wednesday morning."

Rollie's eyes had turned to the ticketing counters. He lifted his hand bag. "Thanks, Sam. Thanks a ton."

"Are you gonna chance it?"

"Why not?"

"Be careful in Panama, Rollie. With the war on, it's an intersection of all types. There are some bad people down there."

Rollie never heard Sam's prescient advice. He'd already hung up and was walking to the ticket counter.

BLUE SMOKE burped from the single exhaust of the old Nash as it squeaked to a stop in the diagonal spaces in front of the Lincolnwood station of the Chicago Police Department. It was dusk, the night promising to be quite cold as a brisk wind swept up the street, buffeting Vivien Hampton's coat as she hurried up the stairs of the old station. The lobby was mostly quiet, done in green on green. The middle-aged desk sergeant, who appeared to be on the verge of sleep, brightened when he saw her coming.

"Evening ma'am. Help you?"

Vivien rested her purse on the thick oak counter, smiling politely. "My name is Vivien Hampton. Unfortunately, my husband, Richard Hampton, took his own life a few days ago and since then things have been a blur."

"Are you *just* reporting this?" the policeman asked with sudden gravity.

"Oh, forgive me," Vivien said. "It's already been reported and investigated. In fact, there was a Lieutenant Ashland at my home who said he would be back in touch."

Appearing relieved, like a man who doesn't want to do any work that's not forced on him, the desk officer's shoulders relaxed. "He's gone for the day but I can get one of his officers up here if'n you like."

Vivien reached over the counter, gripping the policeman's forearm. "Rather than do that," she said, flashing her teeth, "perhaps *you* can help me."

"Do what I can," he replied, seemingly pleased by her touch.

"There was a man who stopped by today and…goodness me…in all this grief and confusion, I was napping. My sister greeted him, but she's uncertain if he was a policeman, or maybe he worked with Richard, or perhaps he's a family friend."

The officer stared back, face open. "You need to find him?"

"Yes, officer. He said he has important information about Richard."

"But you don't know who he is?"

"I'm ashamed to say, I don't. Like I said, he could be a policeman. I have his name, but even if he were a friend of Richard's or one of his co-workers, I probably wouldn't know it." Vivien lowered her voice, making a regretful expression as her hand continued to play on the policeman's forearm. "We were having troubles, officer. Marital troubles."

"Sorry to hear that," he replied, arching an eyebrow as he appraised her more carefully. "And you do know the name of the man you're looking for?"

"So you *will* let me know if he is a policeman?" she asked hopefully, hand still on his arm.

"Course, ma'am," he replied, lifting a massive bound volume with his free arm, not moving the arm she held.

"His name is Rollie Donahue," Vivien said, watching as he flipped to the D's. She fought to maintain her smile as the policeman moved his finger at a snail's pace, starting at the beginning of the D section. She wanted to tell him to go straight to "D-o-n" but kept her mouth shut; he got there eventually.

"We got a Domkowski and a mess of Donalds…Irish lads over in Glenview. But, nope, no Donahue," he said, thumping the page. "Wouldn't you know him, at least by name, if he was a friend?"

Vivien shook her head. "I should, but my husband and I weren't on the best of terms. You're sure there are no Donahues?"

"Positive, ma'am," he replied.

"Then I appreciate your help." With a final squeeze of his arm, she turned and walked out, watching the reflection in the glass as the desk officer stood and craned his neck, admiring her form without knowing she was watching him.

Back in the Nash, Vivien pulled the door shut with a heavy thud.

"Well?" her sister asked.

"He was no cop," Vivien seethed, already clamping a cigarette in her teeth and pressing the cigarette lighter into the receptacle. "I knew…I absolutely knew that sonofabitch was up to something."

"Richard, or this Donahue fellow?"

"Richard!" Vivien yelled. "Sorry," she immediately whispered, holding the orange lighter to the cigarette. She leaned back, holding one hand to her forehead. "Let's just go."

"And you really think he could have faked his death?"

Vivien twisted her head to stare at her sister. "I wouldn't put anything past him. He's a snake."

"So, who was this Rollie Donahue?"

But Vivien didn't answer her. In fact, she stayed quiet all the way home, her mind racing. It began to occur to her that it was possible—only possible (for now)—that Richard had siphoned their money away, hiding it in Panama. Perhaps his "losing" the money was simply a ruse. And it would make sense, too.

A year earlier, about the time when Richard began to bemoan their financial difficulties, he ruthlessly questioned her about Lyman Smith, the golf pro at their club. Lyman had come on to Vivien no less than ten times. He was a shallow, albeit beautiful, specimen of a man—one who had probably slept with every willing wife in the club registry. She'd rebuffed him like she did to all men who made a pass at her, even after she began to get proof of Richard's own indiscretions. But Richard had been too jealous, too indignant. All that bad acting made her suspicious now—had he been laying groundwork for his "suicide"? And if he hadn't lost all their money, if he'd siphoned it away instead, he could certainly retire to a third-world country such like Panama. Retire with no worries. Retire with no financial pressures.

Retire with no wife.

Chapter Eight

April 19, 1943

ON MONDAY morning, after she withdrew her pittance of savings from the main branch of the bank, Vivien, dressed to the nines, ignored the protesting secretary and strolled directly into Willard Kenworth's office. He was a senior vice president of her bank, a man she'd never met before. Willard bolted upright, smiling solicitously at Vivien before hardening his face and waving his secretary back to her desk. He ushered Vivien into one of his visitor's chairs and, quite informally, took the chair adjacent to her.

Arranging her long legs strategically, Vivien easily persuaded the vice president to make some inquiries about banking regulations in Panama. That afternoon, just after lunch, he called the house and told her, yes, Panama claims lightly-regulated, discreet banking—perfect for embezzling money with no questions asked.

"They have no overseeing body, my dear. Uncultured peoples rarely do," he'd said, finishing his report and suggesting a clandestine dinner. Vivien thanked him for his help then politely declined, telling him she would be out of town for a few days.

After hours of thought, she called Richard's cold-blooded sister in Peoria, bluntly telling her of his suicide, saying nothing about her own suspicions. "And there's no body," Vivien said monotone. "If you or your relatives want to pay for a proper funeral, have at it."

Following a few moments of stunned silence, Richard's sister said, "Vivien, as crushed as I am to hear of this unthinkable tragedy, I'm equally floored that you're asking *me* to take care of his arrangements. I believe the responsibility lies with the wife in this—"

"Oh come off it, Dottie. He jammed his dick into anything with heels and left me flat broke."

The sharp sound of sucking air could be heard, followed by Dottie saying, "After telling me my brother is dead, how dare you talk—"

"The Lincolnwood Police can give you the rest of the information," Vivien said, cutting her off.

There was a long pause on the line. Finally, Dottie said, "I'll leave in the morning to come up. And I want to speak with you about your reprehensible accusations."

"Speak all you want. I won't be here."

"Where are *you* going?" Dottie demanded.

Vivien lifted the travel section of Sunday's Tribune, staring at the 16-point line of copy on the lower left of the page. "Somewhere warm, Dottie. Somewhere nice and warm."

The Pentagon, Arlington, Virginia

NICHOLAS PENLAND just knew his boss was going to tear the report in two. Lawrence Dillard's two powerful hands, clamped at the edges of the paper, clenched and twisted the two-page document each time a phrase or supposition set him off. He appeared to be on the bottom of the second page, having taken his time despite his penchant for brevity and the report's excessive number of flowery assumptions and recommendations. Finished, he visibly swallowed, gently folding the final page over before adjusting the paperclip. He lowered the report to the table and removed his reading glasses, squeezing the bridge of his nose with his eyes closed.

The two men were in a closet-like office of the spanking new Pentagon building. The smell of strong coffee was nearly overpowering in the cramped, unventilated room Dillard kept for ultra-private meetings. Located in a cordoned-off area of the Pentagon's basement, the space was designed for secrecy, not comfort.

Dillard, a man known unofficially as "Uncle Spook", was officially an employee of the Office of Strategic Services, the head of their Interior

Intelligence Unit. He crossed the small room in three strides, poured his scarce Royal Luncheon coffee, and spoke without turning.

"So your boy, Donahue, thinks this Hampton fellow faked his death."

"While Hampton is somewhat of an irrelevant figure, the fake suicide is certainly plausible. The absence of a body bolsters the theory."

Dillard finally turned, resting his considerable girth against the stilt table with the percolator, making it wobble precariously. "Doesn't that concern you?"

"It might if Hampton were a person of interest."

Dillard stood very still, staring intently at Nicholas.

Nicholas noticed the glare, and the subtle cocking of one bushy eyebrow. "What?"

"I want you to think about something, Nick. And think long and hard before you answer." Dillard slurped the coffee audibly. "What if this Richard Hampton *has* something of value?"

Nicholas was immediately ready to speak, but paused since he'd been told to think long and hard. After sufficient time he said, "Sir, I trust our gathering unit. They've rated Hampton as low risk...a pigeon. Yes, he's with Omicron, a valued contractor, but one thing we're *not* concerned with is the kraut Luftwaffe learning our aviation secrets. They can barely get power to a factory these days, much less improve their designs." Nicholas dropped one hand, which had been pointing east, lifting the other hand with a finger to the west. "That goes for the Imperial Japanese Air Force, for the same reasons."

Dillard was silent, drinking his coffee with a roguish twinkle in his eye.

"Is there a problem, sir?"

"Well...what if Hampton knew—or *knows*—more than you thought?" Dillard shifted his weight, holding the mug against his narrow tie, the steam flitting upward, briefly clouding the silk pattern.

A cold shiver ran down Nicholas' spine. He'd seen Dillard do this to others on numerous occasions. Like so many in intelligence, Dillard liked to play with his victims: torturing them the way an alley cat teases an injured rat.

"Speak, Nicholas," Dillard said

"Sir, I can only go on what I know."

Dillard took a few steps forward, tapping his finger on the report. "True, but you sure as hell took a razor to this Roald Donahue going *only* on what you know. From all I've heard, Donahue is a hard-working field man."

"He broke with his orders and has stopped reporting in."

"Maybe he was telling the truth about the radio."

"If so, why didn't he call back on *another* radio?"

Dillard shrugged again, seeming unconcerned with Rollie's behavior.

Nicholas pulled a sharp breath into his aquiline nose. *So that's it. He's out to defend Rollie frigging Donahue. Figures. For a man who should have been put out to pasture years ago, Rollie certainly has a hell of a support system—old Marine cronies and friends of friends who still look out for him, even as pathetic as he is.*

"You don't like my castigations of Donahue?"

"I don't personally know him."

"Surely you must have met him, sir. Goes by the nick of 'Rollie,' has a nasty scar on his neck, acts a bit queer."

Dillard's eyes moved as he appeared to search his brain. He shrugged. "Tell me about him."

"I inherited him and wouldn't have requisitioned him had I been given a choice," Nicholas said pointedly. "The way I gleaned it, he got on with the D.O.W. because someone felt sorry for him or owed him a big favor. I've tried to read up on his full background but whatever happened to him, whatever he was doing when he got those scars, is sealed tight."

"There's a sealed file?"

"There has to be." Nicholas perched an unlit cigarette in the corner of his mouth. "Because visible in his files is a presidential citation from Roosevelt."

"Citation for what?"

"The citation only mentions heroic combat service while serving our great nation. It's incredibly non-specific." He removed the unlit cigarette and poked it in Dillard's direction. "In fact, the rumor is that Donahue was hospitalized and couldn't accept it personally. Two impeccable sources tell me that he sent a message from the hospital that Roosevelt should shove the citation up his wide ass."

"Have you asked Donahue about this?"

"Yes, sir. He brushes it off in that abnormal way of his. Says it's just for something routine he did when he was a Marine and then clams up."

Dillard's eyes were averted as he drank this in. "Interesting," he eventually mumbled.

Scratching a match across the sanded strip on the matchbook, Nicholas lit the cigarette. He puffed thoughtfully, feeling somewhat better. Dillard wasn't setting him up after all.

"I've nothing personally against Donahue," Nicholas said airily. "He seems to resent me a bit, the way an older worker often will when he has a younger boss thrust on him. But to be frank, he's obstinate and never communicates the way he should. To boot, he's incredibly banged up from whatever put those scars on him. So much so that I personally don't think he's fit for his job." After another drag of his cigarette, Nicholas steeled his gaze and went for the kill. "Donahue is a liability, sir. When we find him, I'm not advocating his arrest, but he should be censured and quickly put out to pasture. Perhaps he could carry the mail or be a guard at a federal pen."

"Seems obvious to me you despise him," Dillard retorted.

Shit. Overplayed it. "No, sir, not at all," Nicholas replied, softening his voice. "I just hate to saddle a section with someone not up to task. Look at him now. While he's out gallivanting around on an incorrect hunch, everyone else has to pull his slack."

"So, why would he risk his government pension by illegally chasing this Hampton character on a hunch?"

"I can't say for sure, but I would guess he wants to nab Hampton selling something, no matter how trivial it is. Donahue needs a victory. I told him, regardless of what Hampton is doing, I needed his presence for more important priorities." Nicholas patted his briefcase. "We've got threats to government officials, servicemen on the take…I'm even starting to hear theories of Nazis covertly serving in *our* own damned military and assassinating senior officers under the cloak of battle." Nicholas made sure to take on a worried look. "We've certainly got a full plate, sir."

"Hmmm," Dillard mused, definitely unimpressed.

There it is again. Shit! What does this sonofabitch have up his sleeve? Nicholas leaned forward, crushing out the cigarette, smiling affably. "Sir, I'm picking up on something here."

"Good. You should be."

Nicholas licked his lips. "What are you trying to tell me?"

"Richard...Hampton."

"What about him?"

"How deep did you go on him?"

Feeling a welter of panic, Nicholas breathed a sigh of relief when he remembered bringing Hampton's file. He reached into his briefcase, pulling it out, flipping it open. "I'd rather be accurate, sir." He licked his thumb, flipping to the third page. "Full background, his wife, military service, travel. Went to Havana and Panama, met with the former Panamanian official, and that's what got our attention, but nothing that he knew stood out. All standard stuff."

"Standard, huh?"

Sonofawhore, this is going to be bad. Very bad. Nicholas glanced back down at the folder, frantically flipping through the pages. "Gathering Unit checked everything, sir."

"Did they talk to Omicron?" Dillard asked, sitting and twisting his mug on the table.

"I'm certain they did, sir."

"Certain? Or did you and your boys assume they just make propellers and bomb bay doors?"

"Omicron is *not* listed with our sensitive contractors."

"Who made the list?" When Nicholas didn't answer, Dillard asked, "And how long ago was that list created?"

Nicholas stared at the file, as if the answers to all these questions might magically appear.

"Mister Penland," Dillard said crisply, "are you sure your little team didn't have such a feeling of familiarity with Omicron, since they're exclusively a defense contractor, that they didn't bother checking further?"

"This was done before I took over, sir."

"Ah, passing the old buck. I thought you'd know better than to try that." Dillard's face glowed as his trap was now set. "You know, as well as I do, that you cannot blame a predecessor for this. You've had more than enough time to repopulate all threats, especially when your predecessor was known to have been sloppy about things other than his keen instinct."

Knowing he was soundly defeated, Nicholas knew there were now only two choices: continue to spar with Dillard, making his defeat worse, or get in the boat with him and row in the same direction. While he wasn't at all worried about advancing from his current position—he'd climbed far enough—Nicholas didn't want to risk some sort of reprimand, or worse. It would ruin all his plans. He would have to salvage this situation, bad as it might be.

"Sir, in all deference, it appears from your pointed questions we've missed something. I accept full responsibility and beg you to include me so I can rectify the situation."

Dillard listened to the mea culpa through sleepy eyes. Finally he said, "You're aware of the Manhattan Project?"

Nicholas felt a trickling bead of sweat gathering steam on his temple. "Yes, sir. Of course."

"Omicron Aviation is handling the airworthiness portion of the project. They're essentially charged with the weapon's delivery from aircraft to ground." Dillard smiled thinly. "Did you know that?"

Nicholas wanted to scream curses and flip the table. He wanted to dump the boiling coffee on Dillard's big head and bash his face in with the percolator. He wanted to leave Dillard comatose and speed over to Georgetown to beat the ever-loving shit out of every one of those under-educated commoners at Gathering. Then he would come back, beat Dillard some more, urinating on him afterward.

Easy, boy...easy.

He reset himself, speaking evenly. "I don't know what to say, sir."

"There's no guarantee your boys would have caught it," Dillard replied, releasing measured tension on the noose around Nicholas' neck. "This project has been about as compartmentalized as any in our history, especially for its scale. But if you hope to atone for your sins here, I'd suggest you find your boy Roald Donahue, and instead of trying to finish *him*, you need to adjust your aim to this Hampton traitor. Quickly."

Nicholas nodded eagerly. "Do you have any explicit orders on Hampton?"

"If he faked his death and is still alive, we have to assume he's making a play. So neutralize him, and do it quickly."

"Would he know everything about the Manhattan Project?"

"No," Dillard said at length. "In fact, what he knows is very likely inconsequential." Jabbed a finger into the air. "But, combining what Hampton knows with what the Krauts know, and may have already gathered, could be disastrous. It could be that one tiny little shard of information that he gives them that could tip the scale."

Dillard sipped his coffee. "Think about the Nazis and what they pulled off back in thirty-nine. The ferocity of their attack, their so-called blitzkrieg—it took the world by storm. They've still got that fierceness, Penland. Imagine what they would do with an atom bomb."

Nicholas stared past Dillard. "Yes, imagine."

"I'm not so worried about the Japs, but our intel in Germany says, despite the success of Operation Gunnerside in Norway, Hitler's scientists are very close to having the bomb." Dillard poked the table with a rigid finger. "We can't give them a scrap of information."

Nicholas had been studying his hands, mind racing. He looked up at Dillard. "Sir, when did you find this out?"

"I've known about Omicron's involvement for months. When I read your report, I realized the damage that could be done." Dillard took a cigarette from the pack on the table and lit it with a match. He inhaled deeply once it was lit, holding it away and looking at it admiringly. "If Hampton faked his death, where do you think he's headed?"

Nicholas' blue eyes cut to one side. "I'm not sure just yet. He took those trips to Havana and Panama, so that's where we'll start." He raised his hand to stop Dillard from speaking. "Sir, while we're on the subject, how close are *we* to perfecting the bomb?"

Dillard dragged on the cigarette, exhaling as he answered. "When I said this project's compartmentalized, I meant it. They haven't told me a damned thing." He stood abruptly. "I want updates every morning. Put everyone from your level-four group and above on this." He took several more deep pulls on the cigarette before crushing it out. "Shit," he breathed. "I'll have to gargle some Listerine on my way back. Carol will cut my balls off if she smells fags on me." Dillard's long-time affair with his secretary was one of the Pentagon's most poorly-kept secrets.

"Get to the bottom of this, Penland," Dillard commanded, pulling open the steel door and glaring at Nicholas. "Do it fast or you're finished. That's my promise to you." He left the door open, his sawdust-coated cordovan brogues clicking down the basement hall, most likely headed to one of the executive washrooms—all of which were outfitted with jars of Listerine.

Nicholas slumped in the chair, watching the swirls of lacey smoke left in Dillard's wake. There was no time to wince over this punch in the gut. He had to take this disaster and turn it into something transcendent. Assuming Hampton had indeed faked his death, he'd have certainly made arrangements for a new identity. So, rather than focus on Hampton, it was Rollie who Nicholas should go after. Being a career undercover operative, Nicholas had to assume he, too, owned a second identity. And he knew the time and place Rollie had gone to ground, so that's where he had to start.

Sprinting through the lower hallway, he raced up the stairs, stopping at the first office he came to. After telling the secretary to take a hike, he closed her door, sitting at her desk as he instructed the operator of the extension he needed. Once connected, he spoke with the ferocity of a Gatling gun.

"Yeah, listen up and don't speak. Roald Donahue, Rollie, you know of him? Good, because he's running. He's—" A pause. "Damn it, I said don't speak!" Heavy exhalation. "He's running, probably from Chicago. Take Kilgo, Whitmire, and Womble…use a priority red and take a bird to Chicago and canvas outward in all transportation hubs. Start with air, then train, then bus. Search his name, any known alias, and especially his description. He shouldn't be hard to find with that massive scar." Nicholas lit a cigarette. "Put Whitmire on communication and commandeer whatever you have to. Relay the number back to my office and I will call you in exactly eight hours—mark it. And don't breathe a word of this to a living soul."

The action having made him feel better, he replaced the phone and twisted the dial on his Marinemaster watch. Nicholas then opened the door and gestured the still-startled secretary back in to her office. "Sorry, darling," he said with a wink. "Just had to make an urgent call."

Nicholas left her, walking back to his office. He would tidy up a few things, give his level-fours a critical, yet misleading, problem to solve, and head home. On the way to his apartment, he planned to stop at the American Express to send a seemingly routine telegram. Then he would pack a suitcase for destination unknown. Finally, after filling his wallet with cash, he would have a nice steak before the drive to his private aircraft in Philadelphia. By that time Whitmire should have some news—and Nicholas would be in a hotel room by the airport, ready to leave.

Ready to catch up to Rollie.

Texas

THE LOCKHEED Lodestar was as comfortable as any aircraft Rollie had ever flown on. According to one of the two pilots it was only a year old, smelling no different than an off-the-lot car—brand new leather and carpet, none of it yet imbued with stale cigarette smoke or the sourness of spilled drinks and human sweat. Rollie was all alone in the rear of the aircraft, the sixteen passenger seats empty save for the co-pilot who was sleeping in a forward seat, his cap tilted down over his head.

Rollie had spent nearly all of his savings to charter the aircraft from Dallas, paying cash to the senior executive of the regional airline in exchange for the highly-illegal, yet very fast, transport to Panama. He'd shown the man his Department of War credentials, telling him that his mission was to be kept silent, then offering the payment in cold hard cash.

The executive's protests were minimal.

Rollie was on the floor in the back of the aircraft, earlier having been instructed how to best take a snooze on the nearly-empty aircraft by the resting pilot. "Grab yourself four seat cushions and fashion a little mattress. Use these, too," the pilot had said, retrieving a pillow and a blanket from an overhead compartment. "Might as well get some sleep. Flight'll be about ten hours, maybe a little more, depending on wind."

They'd departed Dallas at seven in the evening. Rollie had made his pallet before sitting in the rearmost seat, watching as the sun set over the broad expanse of west Texas. When blackness finally swallowed the sky, he stood, wincing from the pain of his stretching. The bathroom was aft. He grabbed his bag and stepped into the room's cramped confines, morbidly realizing it was about the size of an upright coffin. He pressed the button for the light, grimacing as he removed his shirt and undershirt. A few bumps of turbulence made Rollie pause as he carefully probed the grafted skin of his chest and shoulder, seeing the small cracks that had formed due to his failure to look after his old injury. He pulled the bottle of prescription lotion from his shaving bag, taking time to liberally coat his skin, hoping to prevent further splitting.

After the doctors had performed the massive section of skin grafts, for whatever reason, his body failed to provide the nutrients necessary for his skin to lubricate itself. Therefore, whenever Rollie went too long without looking after it, the skin would split, creating painful, bloody fissures, just as it had when he slept in the Chicago hotel. Over time, naturally, he'd neglected himself on numerous occasions, resulting in permanent striations and scars on scars, making him (in his own mind) more unsightly than before. His own worst critic, Rollie stared at his grotesque form, remembering the first time he'd seen the results of the grafting.

"Will this improve?" he'd asked the doctor as he had stared aghast at himself in a hand mirror.

"No, it won't, not visually. You ought to be damned happy to be alive," the brusque surgeon had answered in an admonishing tone.

Rollie had stood from the crisp white sheets of his hospital bed, staring at his new body. Starting with his neck, just where the chin tucked back under, he had new skin. It reached down his neck on his left side, covering the entire front side of his body to his groin. The skin was pink and looked like finger-shaped putty. Waxier than normal skin, hairless, and without any moles or pores. He no longer had a nipple on his left pectoral muscle, and much of the muscle itself had been destroyed, repaired by stretching the muscles of the shoulder in its place.

"We managed to save the use of your left arm," the surgeon had said, hooking his thumbs in his belt as his own chest swelled. "Most surgeons wouldn't have been able to connect it the way we did. It'll be taut, but with good calisthenics you'll stretch it out over time."

Rollie recalled the painful self-rehabilitation he'd put himself through, determined not to let the tension of the muscles and tendons to cause him to carry his left arm in anything but a normal manner. Day after day, defying his doctors, he endured painful stretches and exercise in his quest to retrain his arm. When he was finally able to travel, he left Washington D.C., eventually going back to where he'd been stationed in Hawaii, working with the strongman, a man who'd suffered burns over his entire body. His alternative approach not only helped Rollie recover, it allowed him to resume a normal life.

Save for the morphine.

Leaning on the small sink, his scars cast in the harsh light of the tiny bathroom, he was awash in the painful recollections from 1935. While he'd managed to defeat his physical infirmities—he'd never overcome the visual stigma. And, in Rollie's mind, he never would. Whenever Rollie would meet someone for the first time, invariably their eyes would immediately be drawn to the scarring on his chin and neck, leading below his collar. He would watch their eyes flick over the hideous blemish, their lips parting slightly, as they no doubt wondered what sort of horrid disfigurement lay below his clothing.

Just like Vivien Hampton had done.

Before the bombing, Rollie had been well on his way to a career in the Marine Corps. The mission of the Marines, and those he served with, suited him. He'd never been gregarious in his social personality. Never a man of many words. Rollie preferred action to discussion—as did the Marines. It only took a few years before his prowess was noted and he was sent to a specialized reconnaissance company situated on Oahu. Until he was "called up" to mercenary service in the Chaco War, his life had been exactly what he had hoped.

But after Chaco, after the bombing, he'd become quiet almost to the point of being laconic, sometimes coming off as curt in his economic manner of speaking. He went out of his way to avoid meeting new people, and did so only when necessary. That's why his job, working undercover, was perfect. It allowed him to live in his own little world. To stay away from the memories. To hide.

Feeling nauseous, Rollie capped the lotion. He pulled on his undershirt, buttoning his over shirt before falling to his knees, vomiting in the toilet.

He'd not had morphine sulfate in more than a day and was determined to kick the habit. All things considered, despite the shakes and sweats and nausea and haunting visions, he was doing pretty well.

Rollie staggered from the bathroom, fell into the rearmost seat and glanced out the window. Though the sun had set, there was enough violet light remaining to see the tan and orange rocks of South Texas.

It looked very similar to Gran Chaco. Without warning, Rollie had an abrupt vision of that American Shrike ground-attack aircraft releasing its bombs on him and his men.

"No," he breathed to the night sky. "Not tonight."

Sometimes interaction could stave off a haunting recollection. Rollie dropped his tackle bag in the seat containing his overnight bag, making his way forward on the lowly-lit aisle of the aircraft. The co-pilot was still slumbering, the door to the cockpit ajar. Rollie opened the door to find the captain reading a magazine with the aid of an overhead light. Rollie tapped him on the shoulder.

The pilot started, turning with wide eyes. "Yes, sir? Everything okay?"

Rollie nodded as he glanced at the empty co-pilot's seat. "Just checking on you. I'm going to try to sack out now."

The pilot read Rollie's eyes. "Don't worry about us, pal. I'm wide awake for the next four hours." He lifted a mug of coffee as proof. "We'll get you there safe and sound."

The instruments were lit with green backlight. Rollie noticed the large cluster, showing an airspeed that was around 190, though he didn't know if it was registering in knots or miles per hour.

"You feeling okay?" the pilot asked, speaking loudly over the engines.

"Yeah," Rollie lied. "Why?"

"We're cruising at about thirteen thousand feet." He tapped the oxygen mask that hung an inch below his chin. "Usually stay below this altitude with passengers, but due to the range needed to get to Panama, we jumped up here for more favorable winds. I'm getting some oxygen from this here mask. You sure you're not lightheaded?"

"I'm fine," Rollie said in return.

"You look bad, buddy. Look in the first overhead compartment and get an oxygen bottle. All you have to do is hang the mask real loose near your face and just turn the oxygen on to a trickle."

"That's not it...I just get a little airsick sometimes. Now, if you'll excuse me, I'm going to go hit the hay."

"Hey, pal," the pilot yelled, halting Rollie. He gestured to his own chin and neck. "What's that on your neck? Is that a burn or did you have a really large goiter removed?"

Rollie glared at the man. It wasn't entirely uncommon for people to ask about it, but usually only occurred when someone felt they were close enough to him to break with social grace by broaching the subject. Rollie despised having to explain it—the precise reason he kept to himself in his daily life. Out-of-character, near-murderous thoughts flashed through his mind as he visibly swallowed. "I was in an explosion," he said with finality, turning and walking aft as he heard the pilot yelling a follow-up question.

Rollie ignored him. *Nosy prick.*

In the rear of the aircraft, he lay on his temporary bed, praying he could fall asleep without the morphine. Typically, when he took a regular dose, a minimum four-hour coma would ensue. But he couldn't chance that tonight, not with two strangers an arm's length away. Feeling his breathing pick up, Rollie shifted from one side to another, feeling the lotion on his scars slide over the fabric of his shirt.

Visions flooded his mind. The unmistakably acrid smell of cordite filled his nostrils. He heard bursts of Spanish and the distinct Southern Quechua of the Bolivian natives. Squeezing his eyes shut, Rollie willed the memories away, pulling the blanket over his head, making himself briefly smile by imagining himself chucking the nosy pilot out the rear door of the Lodestar.

With a parachute, of course.

Forcing himself to think about something else as he continued to search for sleep, Rollie's memories went back to Pasadena, the place he'd spent his teen years. Those memories, thankfully, were quite pleasant. A true western boom town when Rollie arrived at the age of twelve, Pasadena transformed into a city of culture, of grand hotels and beautiful Spanish architecture. Rollie recalled the occasional trips into Los Angeles, him and his cousins crammed into his uncle's Model T, laughing hysterically and raising Billy hell. His aunt and uncle were fine people, and never treated him any differently from their own children.

Like his parents, however, his aunt and uncle were now dead. His cousins occasionally sent Rollie letters, through his post office box, of course. But like so many other relationships Rollie had once had, he'd allowed them to disintegrate. Never rudely, of course. Rollie had just kept to himself, only replying if there'd been a major event such as a wedding or a birth. Over time, due to his lack of communication, his cousins had stopped trying.

The oldest of three children, Rollie had grown up north of Dayton, Ohio, in a small town on the Miami River. From a hard-working farming family, Rollie learned the ins and outs of manual labor at a very young age.

His parents were second-generation Irish, good people, quick to humor and always showering love and affection on their children.

When he'd just turned twelve, Rollie's family planned a weekend trip to see his aunt, on his mother's side, down in Cincinnati. His father, having had a good year on the farm—especially with soybeans, their primary crop—had sprung for a train ride on the famed Mercury Express. But Rollie, beginning to feel the independence of his teen years, had asked his father if he could stay back. In those days, a twelve year-old boy staying alone wasn't cause for much concern. In fact, due to some of the late fall chores the farm required, his father had been quite eager to accept Rollie's proposal.

Doing so had spared Rollie's life.

He'd never forget that Sunday night in the fall—it felt like January outside, what with the wind. It had blown with such force that Rollie worried the window-panes might give in. Normally he would have closed the shutters, but he was waiting to see the lanterns of the wagon turn down the drive. At bedtime, three hours after his family was due, twin headlamps appeared down the long drive. They were bouncing quickly, and shone more brightly than the wagon's lanterns. Rollie had stared out the window, watching the sheriff's dark McIntyre automobile wheel into the turnout in front of the broad shotgun porch. Rollie opened the front door to shed some light on the old sheriff and another man, the parish priest.

Even at such an early age, Rollie had read their grim faces before they'd stepped over the threshold.

After the sheriff had situated Rollie in the kitchen, the priest relayed the news of the tragedy. The Mercury had derailed, perhaps because of a problem with the track, or maybe it had been going too fast. Many of the passengers escaped without injury, but those in the forward Pullman, along with the engineer and fireman, were killed when their cars plunged off of a trestle and into the Miami River.

"Are you sure?" Rollie had asked. "Are you sure they were all in that same car?"

The priest had turned to the sheriff, whose voice cracked as he said, "I identified them myself, son."

A week later, when Rollie went back to school, he remembered how most of the other kids avoided him. Kids are like that—they have no idea what to say. From the moment he'd walked in that morning, Rollie could tell their teacher had prepared them, and she'd made a big fuss over getting him situated and caught up in his studies.

It had been about a week after he'd come back, however, when Theo Beasley, son of the Miami county coroner, just couldn't hold out any longer. They'd all been walking home, enjoying a somewhat temperate November afternoon, when Theo had begun to question Rollie. At first he'd sounded concerned, asking how Rollie was doing while living with his father's top farmhand. But then Theo had gotten on to the train accident, querying Rollie with probing questions designed to get a rise out of him.

Just as they passed by the small building housing the sheriff and his two deputies, Theo had turned to the other kids and told them he heard his father say that Rollie's family boiled to death.

Rollie would never forget Theo's words. "No shittin'. My old man said that locomotive was so damned hot it set the entire Miami to boiling, killing every fish and snake in a quarter-mile circle." He'd turned to Rollie, shaking his head even though he couldn't conceal his smirk as he said, "Sorry, Rollie, but the only thing louder than that metal twisting were the shrieks of your family as they boiled to death."

Theo was quite fortunate to have been right in front of the sheriff's building when he'd spoken those words. Otherwise Rollie, even at the age of twelve, would have killed him. By the time Deputy Whitself pulled Rollie off, Theo had already garnered a fractured skull, three broken teeth, a smashed nose and a severely lacerated eyelid.

Soon after, while Theo recovered in a Dayton hospital, Rollie's aunt arrived by train and took him back to California. Though his twelfth year was certainly marked by the horrible tragedy, the years following in Pasadena were full of good memories for Rollie. Then, after two middling years in college, Rollie had joined the Marines.

Whenever Rollie caught himself in a moment of self-pity, he would recall Theo Beasley's words, about how his family had boiled to death. Rollie had never gone back to try to find out if it was true. Regardless, what happened to his parents and his little sisters made his own situation pale in comparison.

Tossing and turning with the memories of his family's death, and without the benefit of the morphine sulphate, Rollie didn't sleep a wink.

He didn't vomit again, either. Instead, he remained on his pallet—tossing, turning, thinking, sweating—until he felt the clunk of the landing gear coming down.

Chapter Nine

Panama City, Panama
April 20, 1943

THE STREETS of Panama City weren't too unlike those of Havana. The city itself, in Maria's mind, wasn't quite as charming as her own, but she knew she was biased. She studied the Panamanians critically—packed ten deep, the flow disorderly, shoulders bumping everywhere. Moving out of the fray, she bought a banana from a corner vendor known as a *fonda* and clambered up on a whitewashed wall to eat the fruit.

The smell of barbecued meat, *carne en palito*, hung heavily in the air, making her hunger more than she knew the small banana would be able to quell. She ate it anyway, still studying the teeming crowd, surprised at the number of light-skinned men interspersed among the throngs. After tossing the peel to a roaming dog with protruding ribs, she decided upon a test, counting the faces until she reached a hundred, keeping track of the white ones with her fingers. By the time she reached eighty, she'd used all ten fingers, eventually deducing that there were twelve whites in the hundred she'd counted, all male. It wasn't easy finding pale skin. The sun blazed in Panama, and many of the Caucasians claimed a tan that was nearly-native. That considered, it was entirely possible that she'd missed a few. Maria removed a few coins from the pocket of her purposefully dingy shift, buying *anticuchos de pollo* from another street vendor, ambling through the narrow streets as she familiarized herself with the city and its people.

Passing by a church, Maria smiled at the monsignor, changing the wooden letters on the sign out front. Behind him, his young helpers mischievously thumped each other's ears, both looking sufficiently admonished when he turned and uttered a few sharp words. She continued to walk, homing in on a distant din, climbing a gradual rise to what turned out to be a lively quarter.

Prostitutes were everywhere: on the street, on balconies, on rooftops, beckoning throngs of civilian ship workers and military sailors fresh in from the docks. A fistfight erupted next to Maria, making her push away a tubby American sailor who had been shoved into her. The sailor then took a vicious right cross from what might have been one of his cohorts—they were certainly wearing the same uniform—and went down in a heap on the dusty street while the fight raged on between sailors and merchant marines. The locals watched the spectacle without even a cocked eyebrow.

An hour later, stopping in the hilly Parque Omar, Maria leaned back on a sun-drenched bench, allowing the sun to warm her face and upper chest. As she'd walked through the residential areas, she figured that her initial count of twelve white faces was accurately representative of the current makeup of most of Panama City's population. The area with the bars and prostitutes was obviously higher—probably made up of at least fifty percent white—but they would likely be gone by morning, headed to wherever their respective ships might take them. Just before reaching the park, Maria had walked through the tony Calidonian quarter, stopping and performing her count again, this time with the aid of a pocketful of pebbles. Each time she saw a white face—which was often—Maria would drop a small pebble in her pocket from a stack she'd placed on a convenient window sill. Finished, she counted nineteen pebbles. She repeated the process on another Calidonian corner, this time coming up with twenty.

Twelve percent white in the poor areas. Twenty percent in stylish Calidonia.

Appreciating how difficult finding Samuel Fields was going to be, Maria remained on the park bench for several hours, turning only with the sun, setting her skin aglow for the evening. While she remained outwardly calm, her mind was actually moving with great speed. She was creating her plan. Earlier, in the middle of the day, during siesta, Maria walked the five blocks of Calidonia, counting the hotels. There were thirteen of them, ten of which looked inviting, even though there was no guarantee that this Fields fellow would be staying at any of them. But Americans were pampered and, from what Philip had told her, Calidonia would afford them the greatest level of comfort (such as running water and indoor plumbing) for a tenth of what they might pay back in the United States.

After querying a few friendly locals—each of them said Calidonia was the only quarter for a wealthy American—Maria decided to assume Samuel Fields would be found in Calidonia. It was a calculated risk, but one Maria, overwhelmed by the population, had to take. If nothing else, that's where she would begin.

She left the park, walking to the restaurant at the Hotel Florio, studying the hostess and the few women seated at the bar. Glancing down at her current getup, Maria wondered how quickly she would be asked to leave if she stepped inside. Deciding to test it, she hadn't gotten past the open porch doors before a squat, tuxedoed local with a pencil-thin moustache appeared, rudely telling her to leave or he would have her thrown out. After cursing the man loudly, she walked away with a smug grin, finding a large street stand with beauty items, cosmetics and toiletries. She purchased nearly two dollars' worth of makeup, making sure she had the tints and shades that seemed to be in fashion here.

Small paper bag firmly in hand, Maria hurried back to her El Carmen hotel. She took a luxurious and hot bath in the hallway baño, taking time to shave her legs, ignoring the person who continued to knock on the door. It was a woman, speaking English, complaining to anyone who would listen that "this rude person thinks this is their own private bathroom." Thankfully the biddy had moved on by the time Maria exited, unashamedly walking back to her room with the towel covering only her lower half. An older couple passed her in the long hall, the man ogling her bare breasts as Maria dried her shiny black hair with her smaller towel. As she keyed her room, she could hear the old man's wife giving him the business, berating him over his rubbernecking.

After liberally coating her radiant skin in palm oil, Maria dressed in a flowery sundress, wearing platform Haiti sandals and no underwear whatsoever. She felt tingles of excitement as she left the hotel smelling of soap, shampoo, and the rich palm oil. Maria had always loved this time of day, when the lingering equatorial twilight made everyone's appearance dusky and flattering. Dusky or not, she knew she looked dazzling. It was confirmed by the unabashed stares of the men on the street. Women, too.

Unless something happened to change her mind, tonight was about acclimation only. She planned to work only a few of the Calidonian hotels and, because she was quite simply in the mood, she planned to take a lover. Tomorrow evening she would be more disciplined, estimating she could easily cover four or five hotels, finding some sort of pattern she would use in her search for the American.

Maria Fuentes was satisfied that tonight, regardless of whether or not she found her man, she would get lucky.

TEN SECONDS.

That was the limit of Rollie's concentration. Though he was lucid enough to test it, he was powerless to do anything about it. As the fan whirled above him, he lay on his bed, the mattress soaked of his sweat.

When will it end?

Rollie's hand fell from the bed, touching the pail he'd used throughout the day.

If he wasn't better by tomorrow, he would have to break down and take a dose of the morphine. He couldn't come all this way, probably ruining his career, simply to kick a habit.

The morphine, feet away in his grip.

No...

Yet again, as Rollie retched into the pail, his mind darted in a different direction.

His decision to stay sober had taken ten seconds.

Philadelphia, Pennsylvania

THE FOOTSTEPS in the hallway approached. Feminine footsteps. The type that were bound closely by a constrictive skirt or skin-tight dress. *Click-clack. Click-clack. Click-clack.* Three knocks on the door followed. Nicholas Penland had been sitting on the end of the bed, elbows on his knees, wringing his hands as he waited. He stood, walked to the door, opened it. She was more delicious than he could have imagined. Face painted in makeup. Full lips. Green eyes under raven black hair, coiffed above her to make her appear even taller. She appeared to be doing a worthy (albeit trashy) imitation of Joan Bennett. His tongue ran over his lips as he looked this pay-by-hour Amazon up and down, his licentious train of thought shattered by the ringing phone in his room. Nicholas beckoned her in as he lifted the receiver.

"Yes?"

"Your request should be arriving at any moment, sir."

"She's already here. Excellent work, Sully. Your tip will be generous."

"Please let me know if I can be of any further help, Mr. Brown."

"There is one other thing," Nicholas said. "Would you please connect me to…" He provided a local number.

"Get undressed," he whispered to the tall hooker as the phone buzzed in his ear.

"Philadelphia Federal Building," came the reply on the other end of the line.

"Yes'm, this is Lawrence Dillard of the War Department. I'm here in Philly, at a phone booth, and I have no money with me. I need you to immediately patch me to…" Again he recited a number from memory.

"Who did you say you were, sir?" the operator asked in a nervous voice.

"Put the call through lady!" he yelled, faking rage. "This is a War Department emergency!" He winked at the now undressed girl, motioning her to put her heels back on.

The operator didn't reply. He could hear her moving wire jacks to their proper holes, mumbling something about the fact that every self-important jerk manages to get her as their operator. There were finally a series of clicks followed by more buzzing. It sounded as if the phone were picked up. Then another click and more buzzing. Nicholas motioned the girl over.

He closed his eyes, muffling his grunts as he leaned his head back.

Finally a voice came on the line, answering like someone might from a residence. "Hello?"

Nicholas opened his eyes, stammering for a moment as he tried to concentrate. "Hey buddy, I'm out and about, what are you up to?" *Whitmire, I'm on an unsecure line. Give me a situation brief.*

"I've been pretty busy," replied Whitmire. It sounded like any old conversation between two friends. "I found something closely resembling that item you wanted from the catalog. I called their phone number and they said they definitely had it in stock and it would be mailed from Dallas." *We found someone who's most likely him. He's traveling from Dallas.*

"Really? Any idea how long that'll take to arrive?" *When will he get to Panama?*

"No, but they did say it had shipped. Air mail, special delivery." *I'm not exactly sure, but he's traveling by chartered air, so assume he'll be there quickly.*

"Wow," Nicholas breathed. "Okay, you did well. Keep looking for everything else we need. I'll be home before too long. My trip might have just been extended a bit." *Don't slack up a bit. I'm headed to Panama.*

"Safe travels. All's well here." *We'll stay on it.*

"See you later." *You'll be assigned to Nome, Alaska if you don't.*

Nicholas jammed the phone down so hard it fell to the floor. He lifted the woman, staring at her glistening mouth before turning her around and shoving her on the bed.

While he would have liked to have taken his time with this leggy siren, he simply couldn't afford the delay. He hurriedly disrobed, launching himself on the bed with her.

"This has to be quick," he said.

Because he was in such a hurry...

Because every second counted...

Because his aircraft was ready and he really should just go right now...

He stayed another hour.

The Pentagon, Arlington, Virginia

NINETY MINUTES later, the real Lawrence Dillard, Uncle Spook, answered his office phone, spinning his chair to stare at the dark evening Virginian woods. The caller was his chief deputy for counter-intelligence, a former field agent named Buckley, notorious for his terse manner and his irritating habit of speaking in incomplete sentences.

"Penland's moving," Buckley said without preamble.

Dillard sipped his coffee. "Routine?"

"Negative. Ordered a damned C-87. Philly."

Dillard stared at the phone for a moment. "A C-87-Philly? Never heard of it."

"No, sir," Buckley said patiently. "Penland ordered a C-87 for a high-priority D.O.W. flight—the C-87 is the VIP-version, a converted B-24. And he's flying from Hog Island...*in* Philly."

"I wish you'd have just said that the first time," Dillard said crossly.

"Apologies."

Dillard thought about this for a moment. "What's his destination?"

"Listed as classified."

"You're like a frigging telegram. You should add *stop* after each of your sentence fragments."

"Apologies."

"I want your thoughts, Buckley. Do you think he's trying to run?"

Buckley hesitated. "No. No, I don't because why would he requisition our aircraft to do it?"

"Maybe that's the genius part of it."

"I don't think so."

"What *do* you think?"

Buckley paused for a moment. "Penland turned his section inside out for travel laid on by his Chicago field agent, Donahue."

"Roald "Rollie" Donahue...we just met about him. And what did they find?"

"Among other things, he went to Panama."

"What other things?"

There was a chuckle. "Apparently, Donahue single-handedly jacked two mobsters who'd come to collect an auto from Richard Hampton."

"Say that again?"

"Good bit of chatter on the street said Donahue caught two of Sean O'Bannon's men at the Hampton house. After a bit of a tussle, he blasted one in the leg and sent them away with no joy."

Dillard snorted. "And he's gone to Panama?"

"Yes."

"Let me think for a moment." Dillard finished his coffee, rolling a stray coffee ground around his mouth on his tongue. He crunched it, allowing the bitter taste to spread through his mouth. "Buckley, you're absolutely certain Hampton's informa—"

"Is absolute garbage. The only thing he has that's tight is the bomb's delivery method. And the Germans, based on what we've gathered, have every bit of our airworthiness and triggering technology, if not more."

"You're sure Hampton couldn't have gotten anything useful on all of his trips to Oak Ridge?"

"I'd stake my life on it. Hampton's a gifted bullshit artist. He probably got some Nazi's panties all wet with his hollow promises. When he hands over his intel, the Nazi bastard will probably gut him on the spot."

Dillard ran a hand through his thinning hair. "So Hampton's in Panama; Donahue's in Panama; and you think Penland is now headed there, too?"

"Penland's an arrogant prick, for sure. He has no idea that we know he's a Nazi mole. None. And once you fed him your line that Hampton was carrying intel on the Manhattan Project, he shit his pants. Imagine it, sir…the most sensitive intel on earth and Penland, a Nazi, is in charge of the man who went off the reservation to *prevent* the Nazis from getting it."

Lawrence Dillard couldn't help but smile. Allowing Penland, a Nazi they marked a decade earlier, to ascend in the O.S.S. at the Department of War, feeding him purposefully bogus intelligence along with meaningless scraps of genuine intelligence, had been a master-stroke. Every year or so they'd tested Penland's network, giving him marked intelligence that no other person had knowledge of. It was always the type of information that would affect a visible change from the Nazis, such as the one they used earlier this year, involving the planned Allied bombing of Wilhelmshaven. Within twelve hours of the intelligence falling into Penland's hands, the naval port at Wilhelmshaven began putting its ships to sea.

Penland's network was alive and well.

It was an incredibly difficult challenge to manage a mole without tipping the mole off that they'd been made. But it helped when, like Penland, that mole was a narcissist.

"Can you get to the pilots of the C-87?" Dillard asked.

"Sure."

"Good. If he directs them any place other than Panama, that aircraft lands with mechanical difficulties."

"Understood. And if Penland orders them to fly to Panama?"

"Let him go. We can cinch up his outs, keep him from running from there."

Buckley was silent for a moment. "That's doable, but what about what he does while in Panama? You're going to let him run a manhunt for our own man?"

"Yeah."

"Why?"

"Because who knows what, or who, he'll stir up?"

"But your man, Donahue, what about him? What if Penland's successful in neutralizing him?"

"Have I not told you Donahue's story?"

"No."

"I didn't let Penland in on it, either. Donahue was in the Chaco War, one of the so-called mercenaries we sent down to assist Bolivia."

"I thought we supported Paraguay."

"We did."

"Okay, I'm confused."

"Chaco was an absolute mess," Dillard snorted. "Politicians from all sides, calling in favors, supporting Big Oil, protecting their personal investments. We were hands-off publicly but, in time, learned of our own people heading to militarily support both sides. The Marines and a few civilian ex-military helped the Bolivians…did a damn fine job considering how short-handed they were. That's who Donahue was with. In the end, his unit got double-crossed and he got himself vaporized just as we pulled everyone out."

"If he got himself vaporized, how's he still breathing?"

"I honestly don't know, Buckley. Everyone else died, as best I can tell, at the hands of our own men."

"Our own men?"

"They were under orders to kill anyone aiding the Bolivians."

"Does Donahue know he was fighting Americans?"

"No idea. But, since coming to the D.O.W., he's been nothing but a patriot. I like him, and I believe in him. He rooted Hampton out on his own with minimal resources. And, just like he did with those Chicago mobsters, the man is a frigging survivor. So, let's let Penland and Donahue do their thing down there and we'll just sit back and watch."

"Feeling confident, sir?"

"Yes," Dillard said. "We're going to win this war, Buckley. You know it, and so do I."

"Is your confidence worth losing a conduit mole over?"

Lawrence Dillard dropped back into his seat. "Yeah, Buckley, it is. Penland's played out. Maybe he can clip Donahue. If he can, we'll nab him before he leaves."

"I'll seal Panama."

"But my money's on Donahue."

Lawrence Dillard hung up the phone.

Panama
April 21, 1943

THE TRAIN ride along the canal was far different this time. Everything about it seemed fueled by the promise of a new life. And by adventure. Richard sat in a stifling rail car, the window by his seat down as thick Panamanian air rushed over his newly-bearded face. The skies above were low and gray while jagged shards of lightning crackled in the distance. He could smell the flora of the jungle. Tart smells, given off by plant pollens designed to attract whatever bird or insect the plant needed for its very survival. He could smell the damp, overturned earth of the nearby canal. To his right the superstructure of a gray ship pressed northward, the opposite direction as Richard, moving to the Caribbean side of the isthmus. United States Army Jeeps occasionally passed by his open window, their presence signifying various guard posts and crossings. The train wasn't all that fast, giving Richard time to study the fresh faces of the mostly young soldiers. He absently wondered if any of them had yet seen combat—or if they'd simply lucked out by being assigned here to Panama.

"Sometimes you just have to get lucky," he said to himself, his voice not audible over the rumble of the train. Between his feet, inside his briefcase was the report. "The bomb maker's cookbook," he again said aloud, privately smiling at his cavalier manner. He could yell that he had everything anyone might want to make an atomic bomb and still probably not be heard. The passengers' voices, frenzied with the typical energy of being new arrivals, along with the clacking and banging of the third-world railway created a hundred decibels of brain-jarring dissonance. It also created a layer of privacy.

Feeling a spate of panic over what lay ahead, Richard fought it by surveying the car. Earlier, most of the people he saw boarding the train were from his cruise, although interspersed through the cruise passengers were the mostly Panamanian passengers of a much smaller vessel that had docked at the same time as their ship. He turned all the way around, spotting Frances, staring at him glumly from the back row of the car. She leaned back against the high bench seat, the train's motion making her head rock back and forth as she eyed him steadily. Frances' eyes were sullen and, if Richard wasn't mistaken, he saw a flash of what looked like fury. Her girlfriends surrounded her, laughing and carrying on about something. Feeling a pang of guilt, but not wanting to lead her on, he turned away without expression.

The evening before, after their final roll in the hay, he broke the news to Frances that he needed to be alone once they reached Panama City. He had incredibly important business and, if he finished it in the week she was still there, he would ring for her at her hotel down on the water at Avenida Balboa. But he knew he wouldn't. Once he received his payoff, the only type of woman he would enjoy from then on would be worthy of a modeling gig for *Look* magazine. Tall, high-maintenance women with firm bosoms, trim waists and delicious hips. The type who demand ridiculously refulgent jewelry and expensive dinners. The type who were far more in love with themselves than they ever could be for someone else. He loved that type, because leaving them in a dark hotel room with nothing but a goodbye note didn't bother him a bit.

He shot another glance back at Frances. She'd turned away, thank goodness. Poor girl. She'd certainly served her purpose. The memories of the past days warming him, he closed his eyes, counting the sordid acts he'd talked that gullible Texan lass into doing. She was a number of things, but brainy certainly wasn't one of them. What a trooper, though. Someday she would be a great wife for an average Tex somewhere. And while he'd loved her obedient spirit, he did feel pangs of guilt for occupying her entire cruise in his cabin.

Frances hadn't been a virgin, admitting to him in an alcohol-fueled moment of post-climax transparency that her handsome older cousin had talked her into the sack at a family gathering back in February. Richard had shaken his head but not responded. Damn if she wasn't truthful. Richard's grandmother used to have a saying—*don't tell it all*—mainly for the women of the family. Frances could have benefitted from a relationship with old Maw-Maw.

But giving a girl her first climax was nothing to be ashamed of, Richard countered, trying to give himself some credit as he took positions on both sides of the argument. And boy did she ever yell! Good old Frances bucked and moaned better than a bee-stung calf, her eyes rolling back in her head. The first time he brought her off, her response was so intense he thought she might pass out. And predictably, after that, she couldn't get enough. They'd done it no less than twelve times over the four days, with Frances thirsting for more of the bliss she'd first tasted on the morning of the second day.

Such intense sexual activity, and lack of sleep, had left him spent. He leaned his head back, feeling the wind, enjoying the rumble of the loud car. Sleep washed over him in seconds.

When Richard opened his eyes, he rubbed his face and checked his watch. He'd slept about an hour. He lit a cigarette and leaned back as the breeze pressed on his face. Inside his jacket was the envelope, preaddressed to the post office box. He slid it out, looking at what he'd slowly and neatly penned with his left hand, addressed to Señor Seguro. His thumb moved back and forth over the name and address as a few large drops of rain began to fall. The passengers in the seat behind him began to be pelted by the shower, asking him to please close the window.

As he stood, using his fingers to unlock the clips on both sides of the window, he noticed Frances speaking to the man across from her. He had tan skin and black hair. As the man leaned forward to hear her, his back stretched the cheap fabric of his white dress shirt, displaying his thick muscles in a wide V-shape. Richard finally got the clips undone, shutting the window. He nodded at the thanks from the passengers behind him, dragging on his cigarette as he eyed Frances. Whatever the man was saying was making her laugh. She did not glance at all in Richard's direction.

Fifteen minutes later, after Richard easily leapt from the right side of the slow-moving train, he eyed the platform from his hiding spot across the tracks, trying to spot surveillance. The platform, however, was far too frenzied to pick out anyone who might have been watching for him.

But what Richard did see was Frances, still chatting away with the large, tan-skinned man as they made their way into the station. He was carrying her suitcase. Frances seemed entranced with the big man and, for whatever reason, the sight made Richard's stomach churn.

Setting his feelings aside, Richard waited for the cover of another train before he slid into the teeming urban jungle known as Panama City.

Miami, Florida

THOUGH SHE'D been granted a seat from Chicago to Miami on a Pan American DC-3, the people at the travel agency had made no promises to Vivien about her travel from Miami to Panama. There were several sailings from Texas and Florida, but none for another day. Add to that a three or four day voyage, and Vivien felt she simply didn't have that much time. Now that she'd made the decision to go after Richard, she wished she could wave a magic wand and be there without further delay.

Yesterday evening, after her arrival, the manager at the Pan American desk warned Vivien there were no seats available for tomorrow's lone flight to Panama. He'd given her a glimmer of hope, however, telling her that most of the seats on the DC-3 had been blocked off by the military. "If they don't use them, my dear, I'll make sure you're at the top of the list."

She'd been at the airport, known as Pan American Field, since seven this morning. It was now nearly noon and the flight would be boarding soon. Though she knew the manager was tiring of her asking, Vivien waited her turn and asked him the same question she'd already asked four times today. "Has everyone checked in?"

The manager closed a bound book and nodded. "The gentleman in front of you was the last one. I'm very sorry."

Vivien deflated. "And the next flight is tomorrow?"

"Yes'm, at this same time. As I already told you, it's booked, too."

"There's nothing else?"

"There used to be two flights each day, but now only one." His face showed a trace of optimism. "Have you checked the flying boats at Dinner Key?"

"No."

"One moment," the desk manager said, lifting his telephone. As he talked, he arched his eyebrows and nodded at Vivien.

After a moment he held the phone in his hand and said, "They have a seat. The flight leaves today at four. It has a stop in Havana Bay and is a slower overall flight, but the accommodations are sumptuous."

Vivien clasped her hands together. "Thank you!"

He told the person on the other end of the line to wait while he scribbled figures on a notepad. "I can refund you for this leg of your flight and then you'll have to pay them the full amount at Dinner Key."

Wary, Vivien asked how much it would cost.

"I can refund you sixty-eight dollars. The overnight flying boat will cost you three-hundred seventy dollars."

She stared at the desk manager, unable to speak and trying not to cry. "I can't afford that," she whispered.

"Should I tell them to let someone else have that seat?"

Feeling her lips trembling, Vivien nodded. She searched for a tissue and, not finding one, wiped her eyes with the back of her hand.

"If I were you," the manager said when he hung up the phone, "I'd take the refund from this leg of your flight and get myself booked on a saver fare of one of the cruises. I know that's not as fast as you were hoping for, but at least you'll have some peace of mind and the price should be about the same."

The soldier who had been in front of Vivien had stepped back to the counter, seeming to be waiting to ask the manager a question. He'd watched the exchange and seemed affected by Vivien's tears.

"Excuse me a moment," the desk manager said to Vivien. "Yes, sir?"

"I was going to ask you if all my men are sitting together."

"Yes, sir. You have sixteen seats, all together."

The man wore the khaki dress uniform of the U.S. Army. On his shoulders were shiny silver full-colonel's eagles. He turned to Vivien and, seeing her tears, produced a handkerchief.

"Thank you," Vivien whispered, dabbing her eyes.

"I couldn't help but overhear some of what you said," the colonel said. "You're trying to get to Panama?"

"Yes," Vivien blurted, her response a combination of a laugh and a cry. "And I feel like a fool."

"Why's that?"

Vivien handed the mascara-stained handkerchief back. "Mister, you don't want to know my problems."

The colonel turned to the Pan American manager. "How long do we have before we board?"

"About fifteen minutes."

With a kind smile, the colonel patted Vivien's hand. "I've got time…lay them on me."

Vivien sniffed a few times, finally taking steadying breaths. With a trembling smile she looked at the colonel and said, "I'm trying to get to Panama because I think my husband—my philandering husband—faked his own suicide." She let that sink in for a moment, nearly amused by the colonel's widening eyes. "I think he ran off with every dime we have, leaving me in debt and utterly humiliated. And every time I try to explain, or wonder what I'll do if I do actually find him, I feel like an absolute fool."

The colonel digested this information. "Normally, I wouldn't believe such a tale. But you, young lady, don't strike me as a liar." He turned to the desk manager. "If I were to give up my personal seat, could I be assured of a seat on tomorrow's flight?"

"Might I see your orders, sir?" After he'd glanced at them he nodded. "Yes, sir, you're a four-zero priority."

"Who's on tomorrow's flight?"

After riffling through some papers, the desk manager said, "They're all three-zero priority."

The colonel nodded and turned back to Vivien. "My men and I are catching a ride from Panama to catch a ship and rendezvous with another unit somewhere in the Pacific. But we're not due to leave Panama for a few days." He smiled. "Giving you my seat will allow me to spend one more night with my wife and girls up at Camp Murphy, in Jupiter."

Vivien couldn't believe her luck. Fearful there would be a catch of some sort, she turned to the desk manager. "Am I truly able to have his seat?"

"Absolutely," the desk manager said, jamming a stamp onto a stiff paper ticket and handing it to Vivien.

Vivien opened her arms to the heavens and, for lack of any other way to celebrate, she hugged the colonel, giving him a wet kiss on his cheek. Following their embrace, she asked for the handkerchief again, wiping her lust-red lipstick from his face.

"While I'm thrilled over your kind gesture, the last thing I want to do is send you to the doghouse for your last night home."

After giving the colonel a final hug, and even hugging the desk manager, Vivien gave the porter her suitcase and boarded the DC-3 when called. The flight was to be seven hours long.

Foolish or not, she was headed to Panama.

Chapter Ten

Panama City, Panama

BERND VON DANZIG shed his suit coat. The gunmetal gray clouds did nothing to diffuse the heat, making him consider stripping away his soaked dress shirt, too. He stood in a filthy alleyway behind the police station, told to wait there by the police captain. A white feline stood watch outside of a rubble pile. Behind the cat Bernd could hear the mewling of her kittens. The buildings on both sides of the alleyway were cheaply built and in disrepair. Tainted water, which might have been urine, flowed by his feet on both sides of the alley, trickling slowly to an unseen low point somewhere to the south.

"This is as bad as Mexico City," he mumbled to himself, imagining himself back in Germany, the snow falling on his face while he relaxed in one of Germany's natural spring baths. Then he pictured himself being bathed and pampered in the spring by two nude female attendants. No, make that three...

Bernd felt like pacing but it was too damned hot. Instead, soiling his sweat-drenched shirt, he leaned against the sooty stone of the building, situating himself in the sliver of a shadow at this miserable mid-afternoon hour.

He'd found the correct post office box. Finally! But the damned thing was empty. Now, perhaps the information he needed was on its way, but in the meantime, he planned to do all he could to cover every angle. And that meant starting with the source—finding Richard Hampton.

The rusted door at the rear of the station opened, the hinge grating on the metal of the door. The captain stepped out, donning his peaked cap. He adjusted the brim to a satisfactory angle, wiping his fingers across the shiny brim in a practiced motion. When he stepped down the two steps from the building, Bernd realized how diminutive the man actually was. Earlier, in the Panamanian Police's excuse for a lobby, the captain had spoken to him from behind the desk—it was obviously raised like a pharmacist's platform. But now he was able to get a true view of the high captain without the benefit of the height-altering dais.

Bernd himself was nearly two meters tall, six-feet-two-inches by imperial standards. This man had to be at least a full foot shorter. Wearing a short-sleeve uniform, he had a round belly underneath a broad, laborer's chest. His arms were tan and loaded with old muscle, the forearms showing the striations of strong tendons and overdeveloped brachii. His face was wide and flat, rounded like the moon and covered in pock marks. But it was the eyes that made the captain stand out. Panamanians typically have brown eyes. The captain's, however, were the lightest brown Bernd had ever seen, to the point he would actually describe them as golden. They seemed to be backlit, glowing, like the eyes of a crocodile. The captain wore a polished gun belt with the requisite dual pistols hanging over each hip. Despite his wee size, he carried the air of a man who would be confident in any situation. Stepping closer to Bernd than social graces typically dictate, he tilted his chin up as he spoke.

"I'm here, aren't I? Get on weeth it." His English, while accented, was quite good.

"You speak excellent English," Bernd said, forcing a smile and defying his dominant nature by trying to get off on a good foot with this little man.

"What do you want, gringo?" the captain asked irritably.

"I want you to help me find someone."

"Have they been keednapped?" he asked, frowning as if the problem was as menial as a case of jaywalking. "Eet is standard practice here and in due time you will get a ransom dem—"

Bernd stopped him cold by producing a wad of American five dollar bills, banded straight from the bank. He held the money in front of the small captain's face, literally running it under his nose before sliding the wad into his front pants pocket.

"What I need, Señor Captain, is not exactly police business. It's not a kidnapping, but rather a search…a search of a much more *personal* nature." Bernd smiled adoringly, as if he were talking to a close friend. "And to perform it properly, sir, I need a professional policeman like you." He placed a hand on the man's thick shoulder, giving it a friendly shake. "A professional who has the means and the know-how to assist me, and who will enjoy the significant monetary compensation I'm happy to provide."

The captain glanced down at Bernd's cash-laden pocket before staring upward through his golden eyes. His outlook seemed brighter. "And who might you be looking for, Señor?…"

"Lancaster," Bernd replied in his smooth British accent, smiling with only his mouth. "And I am looking for a man of about my age, maybe a few years older. He may, or may not, be traveling under the name of Samuel Fields, an American." Bernd produced a sheet of folded demitab paper. "His description is here." Then a copy of the photo he'd found in the safety deposit box. "And here is his photo."

The Panamanian policeman took both items, looking first at the photo, uttering a low hum that was more of a grumble. He opened the sheet, quickly scanning what Bernd had written before unbuttoning his breast pocket, sliding both inside. "And, *when* I find him, how much would you be willing to pay?"

"Before we get to that, I'm assuming he will choose to stay at one of the local—"

"I will find him!" the captain growled. "What will you pay?"

Bernd paused at the outburst. "A hundred dollars."

"Two," the captain said after a moment.

"One-twenty."

The captain spit on Bernd's shoes and stalked away.

"Captain," Bernd called out, fighting the urge to yank out his pistol and kill the little prick.

The captain stopped on the steps, his eyes on the door.

"Two hundred," Bernd said, stepping to him. "But I want you to start immediately. If you include other policemen, keep my identity quiet and do not expect further compensation."

Remaining on the steps, the policeman, his eyes alight, turned to Bernd.

"I'm staying at La Cascada," Bernd said. "I want a report tonight, tomorrow morning, and tomorrow evening."

The captain smacked his lips, making small sucking sounds. He didn't blink, didn't flinch. Eventually he hummed again as appeared his habit when thinking. Finally he said, "Theese is no deal, Señor Lancaster. You must double your amount. That was a wad of fives, five-hundred dollars in total."

"You just said two hundred," Bernd objected, taking a step forward.

Stepping down off the step, the captain sneered as he moved before Bernd. Suddenly, in what had to have been a practiced movement, the little man's powerful right arm clamped on Bernd's wet shirt, twisting it and pulling him down toward him as his left hand pressed one of the revolvers to Bernd's neck.

"Five hundred or I will throw you in the bowels of my jail theese very second," the captain snarled through clenched teeth. "I'll do eet, and I will tell *los maricones* down there that you begged to sock my cock…that you want cock…that you need cock." The corner of his mouth turned upward. "You won't live to see the sun go down."

Bernd allowed the little man to shake him as he spoke. He watched as the captain huffed while he waited, not unlike a peacock displaying his plumage. Bernd raised both hands in a show of peace. "Five hundred, Señor Captain. Absolutely."

The captain released Bernd's shirt, holding the gun aimed from his waist.

Bernd backed away.

With a nod, the captain said, "I weel call you tonight, La Cascada, ten o'clock. Be waiting, Señor Lancaster."

Bernd walked away, a private smile on his face as he pondered how exactly he would eventually murder the captain. It would need to be slow and deliberate. Bernd would want to see tears and hear plenty of begging.

And back in the alley, thumbs hitched inside his gun belt, Capitán Ernesto Garza of La Policía Panameña stood watching Bernd go, wearing a guileful smile of his own.

WHILE BERND negotiated with the captain, another gringo, this one a haggard-looking American with a large scar on his neck, was also in the bustling San Felipe neighborhood paying a visit to the very same police headquarters. Upon finding the captain unavailable, he was speaking with one of the station's three lieutenants. Coincidentally, the man with the scar and the other gringo—the one speaking with the captain in the alley—were separated only by nine inches of police station back wall.

The scarred American and the lieutenant, a narrow-faced man with an aquiline nose, sat in a dingy white room used for meetings and interrogations. The room was almost perfectly square and contained no windows and only two dull bulbs for light. It smelled of pungent, concentrated piss, made worse by the fact that the temperature in the room was at least a hundred and ten degrees. The air was heavy and unmoving.

Sitting there, acting purposefully obtuse, the Panamanian lieutenant, Gonzalez, eyed the drained American and his scarred neck—the scar was quite large, plunging down into his neckline. Gonzalez noticed the American's hands; they were trembling. Sweating profusely in a suit meant more for a cold climate, the shaky American had begun in a polite manner but, upon encountering resistance from Lieutenant Gonzalez, like most self-respecting Americans, he had begun to turn forceful as if the world owed him courtesy and respect. He arrogantly requested a list of all American and English speaking travelers from the city's travel prefecture by 3:00 P.M. on the following day, demanding cooperation from the Panamanians.

Gonzalez sucked his teeth. Studied his fingernails.

"Well, can you do it?" the American asked in an exasperated tone, opening his trembling hands.

"Do what, señor?"

"Get me the list from your prefecture."

"This could take several weeks," Gonzalez answered, producing a pocketknife and scraping dirt from under one of his fingernails. "What did you say your name was?"

The American scowled. "Donahue, United States Department of War." He opened his credentials, smacking them on the table.

Gonzalez inventoried his English vocabulary, searching for just the right comeback. "And you realize, Señor Donahue, that your identification says 'United States', while you now sit in the venerated Republic of Panama?" He punctuated this with a thin smile.

"I do realize that, sir, and that's why I've made every effort to be deferential. But it is you who have begun to stonewall me." The American, Donahue, used a handkerchief to mop sweat from his face. "I'm sure you know, if I really want to cause a stink, I can go directly to the governor of the American Zone, a man who certainly holds enough sway to crush you if he so desires. I know him personally. In fact, he owes me a favor." He leaned forward, opening his shaky hands in a sharing gesture. "So, enough threats, okay? Just get me the list."

"What is this in reference to?" Gonzalez asked warily, realizing. If Donahue were telling the truth about being friendly with the American Zone governor, a notoriously ruthless man named Conway, cooperation might not be a bad idea.

"It's a case of Allied security, lieutenant. And it's highly sensitive. I'd tell you more but I can't." He flattened his palms on the table. "Now, I'm sure you realize this, but Panama's a member of the Pan American Union, meaning your republic is my nation's ally...so I know you'll be eager to assist, lieutenant."

Gonzalez rubbed his chin, nodding thoughtfully. He truly hadn't realized that Panama and the U.S. were on the same side. It made sense, given the U.S. warship traffic in the canal. But Gonzalez didn't read the paper too often. In fact, he could have cared less whose side Panama was on. He lit a brown cigarette, eyeing the disfigured American. "Wouldn't it be easier, señor, if you were to simply tell me who you're looking for? This would save you precious time and allow Panama, *your* nation's ally, to participate."

The American had been holding his head to the side much of the time, concealing most of what looked to be skin grafts from a bad burn. After hearing this, he turned straight on to Gonzalez. "Very well, then. Want to write this down?" He paused a moment while Gonzalez removed a nib pen and unscrewed the cap.

"His given name is Richard Hampton, probably here under an alias. About six feet tall, maybe a hundred and ninety pounds, blond hair, blue eyes, and his skin is quite tan for an American. He's in his mid-forties and would probably be considered handsome due to his angular features. And he has a fondness for women, prostitutes especially. I don't know if he speaks Spanish. But what I do know is—" The American stopped speaking.

Despite his trembling, he was very still before he tilted his head upward, his bleary eyes wide as he stared at the cracked plaster of the ceiling.

"Señor?" Gonzalez asked, cocking an eyebrow.

The American made him wait by raising a finger. He went into his breast pocket, retrieving a small booklet. Licking his finger, he went back through the pages, eventually stabbing a page. His face brightened, seemingly illuminated by some inspiration. "The man we're looking for was here once before, last December." He glanced at his notes, scribbling the exact dates. "He's certainly not using that passport, which was the one attached to his given name." He stopped, licking his lips, eyes darting all around. Again he nodded. "But he came back, he had to have come back, just a few weeks ago, when he returned with the deep tan. And that trip wasn't listed on his real passport."

"What does this mean, señor?"

"We take the prefecture's list of travelers who are here now and we cross-reference them with the list from two weeks back. There's a chance of a few duplicates, but probably not too many, given how difficult travel currently is with the war and all."

Gonzalez nodded. "Theoretically, even if your man is traveling under an alias, this would give him away." He wagged his index finger. "That is, unless he is using multiple fake identifications."

The American shook his head. "He doesn't even think he's being followed. I'm willing to bet he'll be under the same identification he was under two weeks ago."

They spent several minutes discussing all points of the procedure. Donahue gave Gonzalez his hotel information, telling him he would leave word with the front desk if he was to be gone for any length of time.

"This sounds like an excellent plan, señor." Gonzalez placed the pen on the paper, crossing his legs tailor style. He interlaced his hands, resting them on his knees, staring at the American, making his expression placid. Silence fell again.

Sweat beads rolled down the American's head and face. After a moment he asked, "So, can you do it?"

"Possibly," Gonzalez replied after a pause.

"Possibly, based on *what?*" The American seemed incredulous that the cooperative air had left the room so quickly.

"I heard your threats, señor. Perhaps they have merit, perhaps not. But what I do know, what I'm quite sure of, is that you don't have *time* to make complaints to governors and such. While you're standing in line, the American you seek will be busy working against you." He smiled warmly, taking a pull on the cigarette, speaking as smoke billowed from his mouth with each syllable. "And that, señor, would be a shame when your requests could be carried out quickly and with great efficiency."

"A bribe," the American said flatly.

"Señor, please," Gonzalez replied, drawing out his words and making a tamping down gesture, as if bribe were far too ugly a term.

The sweaty American spoke flatly, saying, "I don't know what else to call it."

Gonzalez touched his finger to his lips, looking away to draw inspiration. When he found the correct phrasing, he nodded and spoke with a tone of magnificence. "I believe the best English word to describe a gift such as this is *tribute*. Tribute to our assistance. Tribute to our customs. Tribute from your nation to our republic…one ally to another."

"How much?"

"One hundred dollars, American, by tomorrow at three P.M."

The American shook his head, again moving it down and to a position to cover his scar. "Fine," he mumbled, standing and using his sleeve to wipe sweat from his face. He jabbed a finger at Gonzalez's notes. "Call my hotel if you produce the list any earlier."

"That would cost extra, señor," Gonzalez replied.

The American exited the room, slamming the door behind him. Lieutenant Renaldo Gonzalez casually finished his cigarette, using the cigarette to direct an imaginary orchestra as he spent the money in his mind. Three new suits, tailor-made, in peaked lapels like he'd been seeing in the recent mobster moving pictures he so adored. Plus, two new pairs of loafers, *cordobán y negro*, and a dress apiece for his mistress and his wife.

A hundred dollars was nearly what Gonzalez made in a year.

"Gracias a Dios," he murmured to the quiet room. He crushed out the remaining nub of the cigarette and stared at his list. Oh, how he loved those loathsome Americans.

AFTER A satisfying stroll around the block for fresh air, Lieutenant Gonzalez walked to the captain's office, finding him rather distracted as he sat with his boots propped on the window sill, slurping from a sweaty bottle of Balboa beer. Next to the captain, as it was every day at this time, sat a bucket of cold water loaded with more beers.

Gonzalez crossed his hands in front of him, dipping his chin. "Sir, I need to speak with you."

"Can't you see I'm busy thinking?" Captain Garza said irritably, lifting the beer as proof. He didn't turn to look at Gonzalez, but instead took a long sip. Then he belched.

Lieutenant Gonzalez was Garza's closest friend, if Garza had such a thing. The two men took part in a multitude of bribes and shakedowns together, using a system not unlike the structure of a traditional crime syndicate. Lieutenant Gonzalez had risen to his police rank not by being an excellent policeman, but by being a top producer. A producer for Captain Garza, of course. Garza was the don, rarely getting his hands dirty unless the prospects were sizeable. Gonzalez managed their schemes, backed by half of the police force and nearly the entire underworld of the southern side of the city. While they did sometimes find enough time to actually prevent crime, window dressing usually, both men knew where their true pursuits lay. But occasionally a friend of theirs would be murdered, or some deviant might harm a child. These situations had to be dealt with swiftly, and with great prejudice. Even men like Garza and Gonzalez, crooked as they were, had standards.

"Are you still here?" the captain asked, using the quiet voice which typically presaged full eruption.

"Yes, I am, captain," Gonzalez answered firmly. "And don't you think, señor, that by now I know when you don't want to be disturbed? Don't you think, after all these years, I'm not so stupid as to interrupt you when you're *thinking* unless there is something of great importance to speak to you about?"

Garza turned his head, his pock-marked face solemn but unable to hide a flicker of curiosity. "What is it?"

"The Americans sent someone to see me. They're looking for a man."

Garza screwed up his face. "You interrupted me because another of their whore-mongering sailors has gone missing? I'll bet this bucket of beers he's either dead or in the *prostíbulos* with the rest of the gringo miscreants."

Gonzalez straightened. "Respectfully, señor, I feel insulted."

The captain looked him up and down, turning his attention back to the window, staring down the street at the cobalt Pacific. A shapely woman walked by, causing him to lean forward, grunting from the stretch. He leaned out the window, viewing her like a hungry man eyes steaks in a butcher's case, sitting again when she disappeared.

Gonzalez waved his hand. "Do you want to hear this?"

"Just say it, damn it."

"The American who was here isn't some local military officer looking for a sailor from a ship. He was from their War Department…which, by the way, proves why the United States exists to even have such a thing…but he traveled here on some sort of urgent search for a man, and he's willing to pay at least…*at least*, captain…a hundred dollars for a list of all foreign travelers."

Garza lifted the beer and paused, holding the opening in front of his mouth. He turned, saying, "Looking for a man you say?"

"Yes, señor. He wouldn't tell me why, but I get the feeling it has something to do with the war."

The captain's cruddy boots hit the floor with a loud plunk, sending bits of dried mud and horseshit flying. His lips parted as he looked up at his subordinate with great intensity. "Do you have a description of this man he seeks?"

"I've even got a name," Gonzalez answered urgently, sensing his superior's energy.

"Describe the man," Garza commanded.

The lieutenant removed his notepad, reading slowly. "Mid-forties. Fairly tall, blond hair and blue eyes. Tan skin…more so than the pale variety gringo. Handsome and well dressed, with an appetite for hookers."

Captain Garza's breaths were audible. He stared out the window again, finishing his beer and allowing it to drop to the floor with a clunk. After considerable time, he turned back to Gonzalez, his face breaking into a rare smile, his gold incisors matching his eyes in what could only be described as a wicked grin.

"If your American is willing to pay a hundred dollars, and the Englishman who I *just* met with earlier will pay five hundred…imagine what they will actually pay if *we* capture this man and hold him for ransom."

"Sir?" Gonzalez asked, confused. "What Englishman?"

The captain unbuttoned the top pocket of his shirt. From it he removed the folded-over demitab paper, handing it to Gonzalez.

Unfolding the paper, the lieutenant stared at the description of a man, written by a foreign hand. It was almost word for word with the notes he had taken. The captain dug into the pocket again, this time producing a photo. He handed it to Gonzalez, who studied it.

"Wouldn't you say, Renaldo, that both men are seeking the same person?"

"I would, señor," Gonzalez breathed.

"Yours, the American, said the man's name is Richard Hampton. And mine said he is traveling under the name Samuel Fields."

Gonzalez nodded his understanding. "So we know both names he uses."

"Meaning we have the advantage." Then, doing something he'd never before done, Captain Garza reached into his beer bucket, removing a beer and biting the top off. He handed it to his subordinate. "Have a cerveza, and together we will think. We will think about how to find this American man. We will think about where to hide him when we do. And we will think about the unmatched ransom we shall make from him."

Gonzalez accepted the beer, waiting as the captain bit the top off another for himself. The two men clinked the bottles together, sitting that way until the sun disappeared behind the squat buildings to the left, replaced by thick clouds that promised heavy rain and lightning.

As the first large drops began to fall, the two policemen didn't move, just sitting, drinking, thinking.

April 22, 1943

VIVIEN HAMPTON exited the very same train at the very same stop her husband had a day earlier—only, unlike him, she didn't leap from the far side of the train. After all her excitement over getting the colonel's coveted seat on the Pan American DC-3, the pilots were forced to divert their landing to Colon last night due to storms fifty miles to the south over Panama City. They landed at an airstrip near where the cruise ships dock and provided train vouchers to the handful of civilian passengers. After going through the cursory customs station at the busy port, Vivien lugged her bag to the nearby train station. There had been a final evening train leaving, but Vivien, again with no priority and being at the back of the throng, was unable to get a seat. She spent the night on a bench in the train station and took the first train this morning.

While she'd been energized yesterday morning, the challenges of getting here had sapped her enthusiasm. Last night, as she dozed on that slat bench, whatever enthusiasm she had left had devolved into something that resembled dread as she now stood on the train platform, keeping back from the crush as people searched for their large bags. She felt utterly foolish for coming here.

What if Richard's suicide *was* genuine, his body still back in Illinois, hung up in some eddy, trapped under the flotsam and jetsam that lingered on the remote shores of Lake Michigan?

Maybe his body had been found by now.

Maybe the investigators would start to wonder why she'd run away.

Maybe what started as a routine suicide could morph into a homicide investigation—based on the fact that Richard Hampton's wife, attractive and young, hadn't even waited for his body to turn cold before cutting and running.

Closing her eyes, she tilted her head back—she'd always made stupid decisions when she was angry. And even if Richard had faked his death, what the hell was she going to do if she did luck up and find him here in Panama? Who would she tell? Could she even go to the local police, assuming they spoke English, and file a police report? *Yes, officer, I realize you're busy with a million ships going through your canal—not to mention that your little sliver of a country happens to be overrun by drunken sailors and spoiled travelers pissed that Europe's no longer open for business—but could you please stop with all that and go and arrest my husband, then arrange to extradite him back to America? Why? Well, because he faked his death, of course. I saw him, officer, with my own green eyes. He's alive and well and shacked up with three of your bubble-butt whores in his hotel room. Where did the supposed crime take place? Well, there's nothing supposed about it, but since you asked, it happened in Chicago. Chicago? It's in the United States, of course, why does that matter? What do you mean it's out of your jurisdiction? So you're telling me even though he's stolen all of our money, and because he's spending it here on your whores and liquor and cigars, you're not going to do anything about it?*

Vivien wiped perspiration from her brow, pressing her lips together as she halted her pessimistic reflections. "Yeah, that'll go over like a charm," she murmured below the din.

A fight nearly occurred directly in front of her between two locals: a short man in his fifties and a woman twenty years his junior. Had someone been taking bets, Vivien would have wagered her meager net worth on the woman; she outweighed the man by at least two-hundred pounds. They were arguing over a piece of luggage, both gesticulating wildly, inching closer by the second before one of the rail workers appeared with an identical grip. Wide-eyed, the little man realized his error, looking as if he'd just been made to eat a lemon. Without a word he turned and ambled away with his suitcase.

"*Tú pequeño hijo de puta!*" the woman yelled at him as he walked away, making an obscene gesture with both hands. The remaining crowd of locals laughed as they gathered their things.

"Why am I here?" Vivien whispered to herself, feeling somewhat better at the visible reticence of other Americans to enter the frenzied quest for luggage by the native Panamanians.

When the crowd had eventually dissipated, she stepped forward and retrieved her grip, immediately approached by a fawning man of about twenty. She'd noticed him earlier, standing off to the side as if he were waiting on something. He wore a broad smile on his narrow face, bowing over and over, telling her in broken English that he would carry her bag and find her a taxi for only a dime. Her bullshit detector ticked up a hair but she was too tired to object. Vivien placed her bag down on the dusty concrete, returning his smile with a small one of her own, nodding. She followed the thin man as he walked at a diagonal angle offset by the heavy piece of luggage. He wore a tattered black suit and appeared to be a porter. Perhaps he worked on tips alone.

They exited the ramshackle lean-to building that was the train station, turning right onto a wide avenue. Vivien took in the simple architecture of the adjacent buildings, straight lines gabled by sweeping false fronts. The tallest building she saw was only two stories. The sky was already white-hot with late morning heat. People slept in shadows on the far side of the street, lounging in the cool dirt as if they were in their own bedroom. The young man turned right into a narrow alleyway, saying the word taxi over and over as he pointed. She followed along, her mind still occupied by the persons on the street when she realized the alley appeared to lead to a dead end. It was quiet here, and dark. The porter, or whatever he was, had stopped and turned.

His smile was gone.

"Dame el bolso," he said with eerie confidence.

"What?" she asked.

"El bolso!" he screamed,stabbing a pointed finger at her purse.

He wants my money, she realized, feeling a burst of fury hit her bloodstream as if it had been mainlined through a port, her patience all but gone after Richard's alleged stunt and the many hours of grueling travel.

Cat quick, the man dropped her suitcase and lunged at Vivien's purse. It was slung over her shoulder. She gripped it fiercely as he tugged at it, faintly aware of his filthy curses intermingled with her own protestations. Just when it occurred to her that she should scream, the man punched her, catching her in the cheek just below her left eye.

Vivien had always heard that it was the anticipation of a punch that was worse—far worse—than the pain of a punch itself. And as the bastard swung again, this time only glancing her ear since she ducked, it occurred to Vivien—just like her mother had instructed Vivien twenty years before when she'd been picked on—that she should quit crying about it and fight back. She still clung to the leather strap with her left hand and, being right handed, she unleashed a strong right hook, catching the skinny punk flush on his jaw. Though she hadn't been able to set her feet, the punch had been clean, sitting him down as his brain spiked for a moment when his jaw pinched down on his hypoglossal nerve.

"Get away from me!" Vivien screamed at him, leaning forward as his face was struck again, this time by her spittle.

The young man stood, rubbing his jaw. His face was indignant as he shouted Spanish obscenities back at her. Rather than talk, she took a puncher's stance, satisfied when he took two cautious steps backward, in the direction of the street. But before she could react, he grabbed her suitcase, running away and turning up the street, away from the train station. Vivien, in her low heels, gave chase. The alley was made of cobblestones, worn and rutted. This was a problem. Vivien's heels, despite being rather wide at the rear, kept catching.

The thief got away.

After she fell for a third time, scraping both knees, Vivien staggered back to her feet. The palms of her hands were scraped and bloody. Her cream-colored skirt was soiled and torn at the bottom and her stockings were now useless. She gingerly touched the back of her hand to her left cheek, feeling the warmth and puffiness from where the little prick had hit her.

Refusing to cry despite the tears that were welling in her eyes, Vivien walked from the alleyway, turning left and trudging back into the station. After finding a uniformed railway attendant, she tried to explain what had happened. He spoke no English and her Spanish was limited to twenty or so words.

Frustrated and ready to simply move on, she searched until she found the actual taxi stand.

"Dónde?" the driver asked her three times.

Police or hotel? Long reports and painstaking translations—or a soapy bath and a nice meal? Wrestling with what to do, she finally leaned back and gave him the name of her hotel.

Vivien Hampton was many things, but she wasn't stupid. She assumed she wouldn't receive much attention at the police station, and she was right—although, had she gone there and, after complaining of the assault, gotten around to her husband and his description—she might have set off a chain reaction of events. But she didn't go to the police, which turned out to be a critical decision.

So, with her meager amount of remaining money and no possessions, she decided to go to the hotel with the hopes that the manager could help her with the police. The long voyage and the mugging had left her grubby.

As the taxi puttered eastward, Vivien hoped and prayed her room had a nice clean bathtub.

Unfortunately for her, it didn't.

Chapter Eleven

IF THERE was one thing Richard learned in the aviation industry, it was the value of testing. Back at Omicron they tested everything. Alpha tests. Beta tests. Stress tests. Tests under normal conditions. Cold. Heat. Pressure tests. Tests under positive gravitational conditions. Negative, too. There could never be enough testing.

Naturally enough, he'd carefully tested the all-important Panamanian postal service on his most recent trip to the Republic. On three consecutive days he'd mailed three separate letters, all from the same mailbox, all to the same post office box. The contents of the envelopes were clearly marked One, Two, and Three. It had taken three days for each one to reach the post office box—in order, One, Two, Three—and although the final one had actually taken four days, the extra day had been Sunday. The mail didn't run on Sundays. Because of that, Richard had given the postal service the benefit of the doubt. Three business days. Not bad for a crime-ridden third-world country.

With the results of his testing giving him confidence, he'd mailed his letter yesterday shortly after his arrival—*the* letter, the one to the little man pretending to be British who was going to pay him a quarter-million dollars—getting it in the mailbox a half hour before the sleepy-looking mailman pushed his cart by, unlocking the box and adding the small pile of letters to his till. Just to make sure the mailman didn't get robbed, Richard had followed him as he'd finished his route, ambling to three more mailboxes before finally reaching his postal station in Pueblo Nuevo. Now, why it took three damned days for a letter to be sorted and placed in a post office box thirteen blocks away was beyond Richard. But he couldn't change the Panamanian Post, so he decided to be patient. What choice did he have?

Last night, refusing to get a hooker (he was swearing them off…a wealthy man shouldn't have to pay for personal satisfaction) he'd had a surprisingly excellent dinner at La Parilla, a bustling restaurant in Casco Antiguo. Afterward, he'd made a pass at a Panamanian woman in the adjacent bar and struck out miserably. He'd then visited two nearby nightclubs, making what he'd thought were solid runs at three separate women—an American, an Argentinian (the prettiest of the bunch), and a frumpy Panamanian who should have certainly taken him up on his offer. None of them had shown him any interest. In fact, the dowdy Panamanian had blown him off as badly as he'd been rejected in years, making him decide that her reaction was probably a defense mechanism, subconsciously developed due to her lack of beauty.

Though it had been very late when he got back to his Calidonian hotel, he studied himself in the full-length mirror. His body was in fine shape for a man of his age. No paunch to speak of, and his chest and arms were still nicely muscled from an adolescence of athletics. But his chiseled face was heavily lined, more than usual, and there were bags under his eyes. Richard knew he had the ability to look good; the problem had to be a lack of rest. Sufficiently drunk, he'd rummaged around in his bag, finding the powder the doctor had prescribed him a year ago. He ripped one of the dose packets open, depositing the white powder on his tongue, rolling it around in his mouth as it turned to a bitter paste. Following a glass of murky water he was out cold, stark naked. It was rest he wanted and rest he received, not waking today until nearly noon. He guzzled two more glasses of water from the pitcher, happy that there was no hangover, only a vicious cottonmouth. Slipping on the previous night's clothes, Richard made his way downstairs, asking the clerk to have his room cleaned and to please put two more pitchers of boiled water beside his bed. The local water, un-boiled, could kill a man whose insides weren't accustomed to it.

After a light lunch and a gloriously strong cup of locally grown coffee, Richard went back to his room and donned his favorite pair of bathing trunks. Feeling fresh and rested, he took a towel and strolled to the waterside park overlooking the polluted Bahia de Panama, sunning himself as he feasted his eyes on the crowd of young Panamanian women further tanning their already bronze skin. Their striking images created licentious thoughts in his mind, giving him a painful erection. He rolled to his stomach to conceal it, the pain of the hard-on cementing for him the notion that he would soon have to do something about it. Before leaving, of course, he approached the nearest group of sun worshipers, telling them he was new in town and inviting them, one and all, for dinner and drinks—his treat. They looked at one another, giggled, collectively shrugged and murmured the requisite, "No hablamos."

Just a slow start, Richard thought as he made his way back to the hotel. But he could feel the flush in his cheeks, the tightness of his chest. And the pressure in his balls.

This adventure was not beginning the way he'd hoped. Now he wished he wouldn't have set up this blind box stunt; it was costing him three days…three days without the money.

Three days without *his* money.

So it was early in the evening as he lay in his stifling hotel room, the overhead fan impotently stirring the thick air, that Richard talked himself out of self-pleasure and into paying chubby Frances from Waco a visit. Funny how a day can change a person's perspective. Yesterday he'd been spent, having done everything with her that his creative mind could sexually envision. In actuality, he'd been tired of her, not even wanting to think about Frances. Not about her oversized, but admittedly taut, body. Not about the way she moaned low and deep when she climaxed, like a cow stuck in barbed wire. Not about the way she liked to cuddle afterward. Or the way, when she kissed him, she cleaned every square inch of his mouth with her overactive tongue. He hadn't wanted to think about *any* of it.

But that was yesterday.

Now as he lay here, staring down at his naked body, over the muscles of his chest, past his trim and freshly tan abdomen, he thought of Frances' firm skin, responding under his fingers; he remembered her wide hips, the way she would thrust them upward as she was on all fours, craving the pleasures he doled out in heaps—all of these thoughts melded together, washing away whatever contempt he'd had yesterday, evidenced by his hardening manhood, levitating as if operated by invisible wires, the truest signal a male can give.

Frances…

He shut his eyes, picturing the look on her face when she opened her hotel room door. She'd punish him for at least an hour. She *was* a woman after all. But after a genuine apology Frances, good old Frances, would grudgingly forgive him for leaving her alone her first day. In fact, just like he'd envisioned her doing when she someday got married, he was banking on a blowjob at the end of his penitent hour. If he didn't get one she was going to be mighty disappointed at their first copulation of the night. Those girls out by the bay had gotten him so inflamed he didn't think he would last very long with their nubile brown bodies still dancing on the movie screen of his mind.

There could have been a large coiled spring under Richard, given the speed he bolted from the bed. He gathered his toiletries, making sure he put his cologne in the bag. It was almost seven-thirty; mealtime here occurred later than back in the States, starting after eight and going until sometime around midnight, even later on the weekends. He was briefly struck with the fear that she might not be in her room but shoved it aside. She's young; young girls don't go out until late. She'd be there, secretly waiting on him although she probably wouldn't have admitted it to her friends. They could have a nice meal together and then, just to spice things up, Richard could take her back to the seaside park where he'd sunned earlier. They could do it over the sea wall. Frances learned on day two of the cruise that she liked it best from behind. He could walk her around to the outer part of the bay, past the eddies, out to where the water was clean. The waves would crash below them, covering their bodies in delicious saltwater. Maybe some other couple would see them from a distance, so aroused that they'd have to stop and attend to their own pleasures. Hell, maybe they would come over and the four of them could come back to the hotel and have a real good time together. Richard stopped what he was doing, tilting his head back to the ceiling and the slow moving fan. There was a smile on his face; he was warm with anticipation.

It was a grand plan. It would provide him with the release that he so urgently needed.

With a towel wrapped around his waist, Richard whistled his way down the hall. He planned to shave off his beard in the tub, hoping the cool bath water would lock in his fresh tan.

Things were looking up.

Richard had no idea how wrong he was.

WITH SURPRISING speed, another powerful evening storm moved over Panama City, headed northeast, blowing in from the Pacific. On his third day of sobriety, feeling somewhat better, Rollie was pleased with the speed at which he'd been able to cover a slice of the hotels, restaurants, and bars of the large Central American city. The restaurants had begun to fill up shortly before eight. As he'd learned yesterday, all it took was a flash of his credentials to make the deferential employees dip their heads, allowing him unfettered access to their establishment. None of them even questioned him, probably used to imperialistic law enforcement from the American Zone.

He wore his largest fedora, the brim pulled low over his head, his neck concealed by an out-of-fashion silver cravat. He'd shaved his six days of beard, leaving a burgeoning moustache in a wide, outside the mouth style. It wasn't his idea of an excellent disguise, but in case Richard might remember him as a face from Chicago, he didn't want to take any chances.

Rollie ducked under the slanted awning of a restaurant, the water cascading downward as he wiped his wet face with the cravat. The rain was so hard it was creating a flash flood, debris and horse manure floating by, the water awakening smells from the dry streets that would typically only emanate from an outhouse pit. Even with the pounding rain, Rollie was parched. He'd been walking for two hours without a drink of any sort. Hoping the squall would pass, he stepped into the bar of the restaurant, his head low as he surveyed the dim establishment.

The restaurant was deep and narrow, with a traditional bar running half the length on the right. Constructed mostly of blond woods and bamboo, the light wood was offset by the dim light from table candles and hurricane lamps along the left wall.

All of the tables seemed to be occupied, mostly by couples and a few groups of four. There was one long table at the rear with ten graying revelers, celebrating a birthday or an anniversary. With a trained eye, Rollie quickly surveyed each shadowy profile for Richard Hampton, seeing no one who remotely resembled him. Lightning cracked nearby, making many of the patrons jump, the women placing hands over their hearts and the men laughing with one another the way men do when they're scared collectively shitless but hide their fear by ridiculing the women. Glancing outside as the storm raged, Rollie decided to take a break in hopes it would pass within the hour. He bellied up to the bar, ordering a Coca-Cola and studying a matchbook as he awaited the sugary international drink that, for whatever reason, typically seemed to make his condition feel slightly better.

Lit a match. Tossed it in the ashtray. Lit another. Placed the matchbook on the bar; created a coil with his middle finger; flicked it down the bar; watched it slide to a stop a few inches from the end.

"Will you be eating, señor?" the bartender asked, popping the bottle cap and pouring the small drink over ice.

"No, thank you."

Rollie took a long sip of the soda before he pressed on tired eyes with his thumbs, wondering what might await him when he returned to the States. Nicholas Penland didn't like him; that much he was sure of. Rollie didn't really give a damn about his standing in the War Department but did feel a bit foolish for emptying his bank account on the charter flight down here. Funny how something that could seem so grave one day could seem so insignificant just a few days later. He flexed his left hand, feeling the old scars as they fought against his tendons, trying to prevent flexion despite his years of self-rehabilitation. Across the bar and the gap where the bartender worked, behind the cooler and the rows of liquor, was a mirror, etched around the edges in a lacework of a tropical vine. Rollie reached around his neck, untying the cravat and staring at his image.

Haggard. Worried. Drawn. Pale.

Regarding the morphine, he knew he wasn't out of the woods yet. He'd hardly slept since he'd begun this crazy trip. But his waking condition seemed to have improved. It was almost as if his body had finally made peace over the fact that there was no opium on the way. Now, if only he could get through the night…

But there was more than just a morphine sulfate dependence going on here. Narrowing his eyes at his reflection, Rollie attempted to go below the surface. What was going on inside his head? Why such impetuous action? Was there some subconscious anniversary that had passed, escaping his notice? Maybe it was his age? Do men go through the same mid-life change as women, but strictly in a mental passage, and not physiological? And why now? Why did he suddenly decide to challenge his boss in what would almost certainly result in a job-surrendering disciplinary action, or worse?

He shook his head, letting out a long and whistling breath. There were no answers. He was simply tired. Tired of bullshit. Tired of taking orders.

Tired of taking drugs to sleep. Tired of paying for another human's touch. And tired of letting assholes like Richard Hampton go free just because some bureaucrat had sacred cows to attend to.

He eyed the mirror. A lift of his chin showed the grotesque scar.

"Yeah," he said aloud, zoning in on the real problem. He was tired all right…tired of being Rollie Donahue.

Rollie finished the Coke and ordered another. The bartender said something about being named Jose, and just to call out if he wanted to order anything else. Rollie gave him an index finger salute and drank deeply, allowing the carbonation to linger on the back of his tongue as it burned his throat in its quest to descend. He lowered the glass for a moment, repeating the action almost immediately. He already felt better, the sugar hitting his stomach and giving him an immediate shot of energy.

Suddenly, something made Rollie want to look to the left, into the restaurant. The urge was powerful and magnetic, a sensation as ancient as man himself, as curious as the fleeting, yet potent, feeling of déjà vu or a dead-on premonition—it was the distinct feeling of eyes looking at him—boring into the side of his head.

Making himself act with discipline, he retied the cravat, struck with an odd feeling that he knew the sonofabitch who was staring at him, burning him down with his eyes.

Rollie lowered his right hand, under his still-wet suit coat, reaching under his arm and placing his hand on the satisfying grips of his Colt .38 Super. He took a breath, held it, and slowly turned.

His eyes widened.

As it typically was, his intuition had been correct. There *were* eyes on him. He recognized those eyes, all jade green and sparkly. They didn't belong to a sonofabitch after all. They belonged to a lady. A beautiful lady.

Vivien Hampton sat twenty feet away, one hand rigidly clasped over another, her face a mask of indignation despite the blue and pink bruise that puffed the fine cheek under her left eye. A tremor passed through her face. Just then, his timing about as bad as it could be, her waiter breezed in with a plate of something or another, setting it before her with a flourish as he lifted the food's cover. Rollie watched as Vivien pinched her lips together, summoning patience as the waiter appeared to be asking her if she needed anything else. He saw her mouth the universal one-word declination.

And then Rollie watched as she stood, spiking her napkin into her chair as if she was trying to embed it in the wood, before she began stalking in his direction.

EL HOTEL Destino was one of the multi-colored budget jobs down by the water in the Casco Antiguo neighborhood. Casco, as Richard learned on his first trip, was mainly a low-rent tourist neighborhood, a south-jutting promontory loaded with hotels, bars, and rip-off casinos with such bad player odds that they would make an Atlantic City casino boss blush.

The evening storm had just passed; Richard had ridden it out in the lobby of the Encantador Hotel on the Avenida Balboa, making a mental note to stay there at some point after receiving his money. He didn't even realize that such a fine establishment existed in Panama, easily as nice as some of the swankier hotels back in Chicago on North Michigan. The storm had raged for thirty minutes, but now, even as evening set in, the streets were nearly dry as the resident tropical heat evaporated the water away in minutes. And though he'd managed to avoid the storm, his cream-colored linen suit hung from him as if he'd been made to stand under a shower. The humidity of Panama was oppressive. But it was of no matter, thought Richard. Frances didn't care how he looked dressed.

While he was riding out the storm in the Encantador, Richard smoked a rather acrid Panamanian cigar and made note of a fine little seafood restaurant attached to the hotel. He flirted with the aging hostess who had probably been quite comely fifteen years ago, making a reservation for two at nine-thirty. This would give him a full hour to apologize before cajoling Frances into a bout of expedient fellatio. Then they could dine at the lovely establishment before heading to the park and living out his fantasy, bent over the sea wall.

He paused at the walk-up to El Hotel Destino, tossing the remaining cigar into a wet planter of tropical flowers. From inside his coat he produced a packet of mints, pressing one onto his tongue and sucking vigorously. He studied the hotel, squat and wide like the new motor lodges Richard had seen back in the states, designed with its room doors to the outside and the three levels of breezeway balconies all running to a center stairwell. Richard would have to rely on the person at the hotel desk to give him Frances' room number, or to ring her room in the unlikely event they came equipped with telephones. From his wallet he removed a dollar bill, cupping it in his left hand in the event he needed to convince the clerk that he meant the girl no harm, and giving him her number was certainly not an invasion of privacy—especially to an American.

As he began to move inside, he happily realized his preparations were for naught. One of Frances' girlfriends he'd met on the ship—Richard didn't remember her name—flashed by on the third floor, giggling as one of the college boys from the cruise chased her, whipping and popping at her tan legs with a rolled up towel. She paused at the end of the balcony, turning and laughing as college boy lassoed the towel around her before kissing her in a moment of playful passion. When the kiss finally ended, Richard yelled up to the girl.

Her smile faded as she stared down at him. The college boy saw Richard too. He backed up, leaning against the concrete of the hotel, silent the way many well-raised young men are in the presence of an older male.

When it became apparent the girl wasn't going to speak, Richard yelled, "What room is Frances in?"

"She *doesn't* want to see you," her friend replied in almost a normal tone, barely audible.

"I'm here to apologize," he said, making sure his affable smile was broad enough to be seen over the distance. "Just please tell me what room."

The girl made a pointing motion to the very room she stood in front of. It was on the top left of the hotel, the southernmost room with dual water views to the south and to the east.

Richard started moving, waving his thanks. He was halted by the girl's final statement. She and her boyfriend were heading into the room adjacent to Frances' when she stopped and yelled down, "I wouldn't come up here if I were you."

Richard looked up at her. She shook her head at him one time, her action pronounced, moving to her neck's side to side limits.

"Why do you say that?" he asked. No answer. The friend just stood there, staring, her look ominous. Was she playing some sort of college game with him? Richard remembered those days well. Nothing more than beefed-up versions of grade school playground games. And despite having years of education under their belts, college kids were worse about it because they thought they knew everything. Richard rubbed his forehead, remembering when, at twenty-five or twenty-six, the shocking revelation hit him that he actually didn't know shit.

He shrugged, waiting on her answer. She gave him another shake of the head.

Despite the friend's trying to run him off, she was damned cute, though. Standing up there in short, stark white shorts, her legs long and tan and shiny. He almost wished he was heading into *her* room for a roll in the hay, rather than the near-battle he was going to have to endure with Frances. The friend had backed up and was lingering in her doorway. He eventually acknowledged her now silent warning with a tug of the brim of his finest Borsalino Naples hat before pressing forward to the stairwell, taking the stairs by two despite the heat.

A thought struck Richard on the top flight of stairs, making him slow down. There had been a certain tone to the friend's voice. It wasn't the standard warning of a pissed-off woman. Lord knows if anyone knew that tone it was Richard. Rather, it was more of the type of tone someone used when danger was in the air. A warning. Like a lifeguard might use to a swimmer bounding toward the water when the ocean was ripping with a deadly tide. Or when one of the chemists back at Omicron used the same voice, telling Richard he'd better not touch this or that. So what had that leggy girl been trying to tell him? Frances couldn't be pregnant, could she? They'd ceased being careful after the second time, but not even a week had passed since then. There was no way she could know such a thing by now, could she? He was halfway up the final flight when he crunched down on the mint, shaking his head at his ridiculous reticence. There was nothing to fear. Just a quick apology, a nice meal, and then the fun could begin.

Who knew, maybe the leggy gal pal was jealous? She was probably used to getting the man, so it might be bugging her that she was stuck with a pimply-faced, narrow-chested college boy—almost surely a minute-man—while her heavy friend Frances was enjoying all varietals of ecstasy, leaving her with more working bedroom knowledge than a person might get on a bawdy trip through the Orient.

Eyebrows arched, Richard made a mental note to find out about the friend's opinion of him. If she *was* jealous, it certainly could lead to all sorts of interesting possibilities before the Texas gals had to cruise back home.

When he reached Frances' door, he adjusted his hat, cocking it in the Hollywood fashion. Then, to display his confidence, he rapped on her door loudly. Authority means a lot. For a moment he heard nothing, then caught the thump of feet coming off the squeaky bed followed by footsteps. The chain slid off the door. The knob turned. Frances opened the door.

Her eyes went wide upon seeing him. She was covered in a beach towel, her pale skin now bright pink from the sun. The towel was cinched above her chest, making the skin pooch out over the top due to the towel's tight constriction. Frances' hair must have been wet, because it was all done up in a turban. Richard thought he could smell the aroma of soap and lotion. She'd just bathed.

Perfect.

"Hi, Frances," he said, giving her a modest smile. "I just couldn't stay away."

All he received in return were two blinks. She held the door fast, only six inches of space.

"Did you hear me, gorgeous? I said I couldn't stay away from *you*."

"So I see," Frances said flatly, her mouth a dash.

"Let me come in so I can explain."

"No."

"Frances, please…I really did have important work to do. But it's done now and I've got two days to do nothing but—"

"Stop it," Frances said, cutting him off and letting out a long breath. "It's different now. You should just go."

Richard inserted his light brown derby shoe into the door, widening it a bit. With his best naughty smile he pushed into the room, pleased as she backed up with a resigned look on her face. He knew that look. It was definitely resignation, layered with worry. She was resigned because she had no defenses against his charms, and was probably just worried that he would leave her again. He felt his own pang of anxiety, wondering what the hell he was going to do when he was someday too old and too ugly to play this game.

He reached for her. She pulled back.

"You shouldn't be here," she said softly, head still moving side to side, but just barely.

"Oh, come on," he replied, putting a finger under her chin and lifting it. "I didn't mean to hurt you, Frances. My presence here should demonstrate for you how magnetic your allure really is." He took two daring steps, his body inches from hers as he grasped her hand, touching it to the elevated rigidity in his pants.

Frances' mouth opened as she seemed to stifle a small gasp. And, like he had when they first met, that's when he knew he'd struck gold. He pressed his face to hers, kissing her deeply. As he came up for air he moved down her neck with his tongue. "I couldn't stop thinking of you."

"Why did you leave me, damn it, why did you leave?" Frances' voice was a moan, loaded with regret as she placed the back of her hand to her forehead. "You ruined everything."

"No," he said, his head back a fraction, eyeing her. "It's okay, darling. I'm here now."

It appeared she wanted to tell him something but instead closed her eyes, defenselessly accepting his kisses.

The room was a simple square, wallpapered in a tacky, nicotine-tinged tropical print. The bed squeaked as he pushed her backward, both of them falling onto the lumpy mattress. He'd had girls like Frances before, the type that, for whatever reason, were completely vulnerable under his spell. They didn't come along often, and he usually bored of them quickly, but they were still something to marvel over and damned fine to call on in a pinch. There had been one, maybe fifteen years before, Julia Cornwall of Milwaukee. She had the prim and plain face of a young librarian, right down to the horn-rimmed glasses. But underneath her modest clothes had been the lithe body of a cheetah with a spirit to match. They'd carried on for a while when she was in her early twenties, but after that, long after she was married with kids, any time Richard paid her a visit she would acquiesce, powerless to his presence.

As Richard kissed Frances, he recalled one fall day when he was passing through Milwaukee in the early afternoon. Feeling a stirring in his pants, he'd turned off the main road, consulting his address book before getting service-station directions to Julia's home. It was a tidy little house on a quiet street, the leaves around the house all raked up, showing green rye grass that fronted the house like Richard's personal welcome mat. Just like Richard did tonight, he had rapped on Julia's door confidently, satisfied at her stunned reaction upon opening it. Without saying a word, he had stepped inside, listening to her meek protests, babbling that the kids would be up from their naps soon. He had kissed her as she spoke, feeling her stiffen in his arms. They had stood that way for a full minute, her tension melting away as her hands began to roam. When the kiss ended, still without a word, he spun her around, right there in the hallway, lifting her skirt, sliding down her stockings, and going to work as she gasped. They ended up on the floor of an adjacent room, Julia thrashing and moaning the way she always had. The entire sordid deed had taken less than ten minutes. As a child cried in the back of the house, Richard got dressed and gave her a final kiss. His only words to her that day came as she sat there looking bewildered in the afterglow. "Someday, you naughty woman, when you least expect it, I'll be back again," he said, tugging on his hat and leaving.

The memory of that chilly October day warmed Richard, inflaming him as Frances' now eager hands roamed his body. He managed to get the towel off of her, his tongue lolling over her neck and breasts as she tugged him to her. He could tell what she wanted. Ah, to hell with it, he thought, blowing off his desire for only oral pleasure. In a deft motion, Richard undid his trousers and shifted them down his legs. She was whispering "please" over and over. He'd known he could make up with Frances but hadn't anticipated it might be this easy.

"Hurry," she said.

"I don't think it'll take long."

"Just hurry, and then I'll fix everything."

The action had begun—but her words gave him pause. "What do you mean 'fix everything'?" he asked, lifting his head back to see her.

"Never mind. Just hurry, then you have to leave." She pulled her head back, looking him eye-to-eye. "Please finish and leave and then I'll come find you tomorrow. I'll fix everything."

They stayed that way for a moment before he gave a small shake of his head. *Whatever.* He could concern himself with her problems at a later time; for now he was exactly where he needed to be. His first strokes were long and deliberate as he closed his eyes, thinking of baseball statistics and snakes and wrinkly old women. She pulled on his buttocks, trying to speed him up. He had hoped to last longer but could see the beginnings of the flashes of light behind his closed eyes. It amazed Richard that, despite having had thousands of orgasms—hell, tens of thousands—he still sought them with the same lustful greed he had when he was thirteen, either when tossing-off in his tree house with a stack of nudie pictures he'd found behind the gas station, or in the grubby hands of pimply-faced, sixteen year-old Doreen Mills in her momma's tarpaper hovel down the street. He could feel it starting to happen, followed by that incredible sensation as his product left him, swimming into the deep to do their one and only duty.

Frances screamed.

He kept his eyes clenched, but for a fraction of a second wondered why *his* climax was causing such a reaction to Frances. He kept on thrusting, not wanting to interrupt the electric pleasure of what was turning out to be an incredibly intense moment of pleasure.

She screamed again, almost as if her own ecstasy (*or terror?* a small voice inside him interjected) was intended to tell him something.

He finally stopped, the waves of bliss having moved on, taking great breaths and wincing as he disentangled himself from her. In the scant light of the room he could see that she wasn't looking in his eyes like she had done each time they'd made love on the ship. Her right hand was balled into a fist, much of it inside her mouth, as her head trembled. But it was her eyes that sent a new wave through his body—this one a distinct wave of fear rather than orgasmic pleasure. Frances was looking beyond him, over his shoulder, her eyes wide enough to display the whites over and under the irises. Feeling as if his neck was controlled by a rusty gear, Richard turned his head to follow her gaze.

Standing in the open doorway was a massive figure, the sky around him the deepening blue of the Panamanian twilight. His head was covered in short but thick black hair. His skin appeared to be quite dark, especially at this evening hour, but even despite the lack of light, Richard could make enough of the features of his face to determine he was a hard man. Hard and rough. Almost certainly a local, the man's face was a mixture of features he'd come to associate with Hispanics and Indians, especially the sharp nose like so many American Indians possessed. His neck was as wide as his head and his shoulders were dual bowling balls. He stood at least six-feet-three and probably weighed somewhere north of two fifty. The man was well-dressed, looking as if he was here to pick up Frances for a night on the town. A small bouquet of yellow flowers tumbled from the man's massive hand to the floor.

And as the big man ceased watching and started moving, Richard recalled him as the man he'd seen making Frances smile on the train.

Oh shit.

In the two seconds before the first hammer-fist struck his back, it all came clear to Richard. Frances, heartbroken Frances, had been crestfallen when Richard informed her he couldn't be with her in Panama. Sitting there on that train, her friends all coupled up with the college boys, this Panamanian brute had made eyes at her. Perhaps, in her fragile state, she'd smiled in return. And like so many millions before her, on the age-old rebound, Frances had taken him into her bed in an effort to get back at Richard, but mainly as a cure for her own loneliness.

The problem, especially for Richard, was a Panamanian brute such as this one hardly ever had a chance at an American girl. He would likely kill in order to keep her.

All of these thoughts occurred to Richard in a split second, his line of thinking cut off by two of his ribs cracking when the Panamanian hit him in his back with all the power of Thor.

Frances screamed again. Richard did, too.

LIEUTENANT RENALDO Gonzalez was leaving at ten. No matter what.

The clock on the wall had just loudly clicked past nine when he used his secret key to let himself into the captain's office, finding two of the captain's daily Balboa beers floating in the bucket. Unable to bite the caps off due to his already-cracked molars, the lieutenant nearly broke the lock on the captain's window as he eventually jimmied the first cap off.

A young officer appeared in the doorway, breathless. Whatever he was about to say was precluded by his obvious surprise at finding Gonzalez in Garza's office, drinking the captain's beer.

"He knows I come in here," Gonzalez said sharply, reading the younger man's face. "What the hell do you want anyway?"

The junior officer's eyes cut away, as if he'd already forgotten what he came to say.

"What?" Gonzalez said, his voice rising. *"What?"*

"Señor, we got a message from one of the reefer snitches. Your man has been spotted or...at least a man fitting his description."

Gonzalez allowed the open beer to fall back into the bucket, sending warm water and a geyser of foamy beer soaring. "Where?"

"Walking up the stairs at El Hotel Destino...you know it?"

"Yes. Are you sure?"

"Por supuesto, señor!"

Gonzalez knocked him out of the way as he ran by, the soles of his dress shoes betraying him on the tile floor of the lobby, sending him sliding into the wall. Paying his fall no mind, he was back up and out the front door in seconds. His trusty BMW R32 took only two kicks before he twisted the hand throttle to the stop, rooster-tailing road silt onto Avenida Sur, yelling a prayer of thanks to Mother Mary for allowing the hotel to only be a half mile away.

Rather than use the inadequate horn, Gonzalez yelled ahead to keep the evening strollers out of his path.

UPON SEEING Vivien Hampton, and reading her fierce expression as she stalked in his direction, Rollie turned straight ahead, his head down, studying his fidgeting hands.

She moved into his space, shoving the adjacent barstool backward as she spoke through clenched teeth. "Well, well, well...welcome to Panama, Mister Donahue of the Chicago Police Department. Oh wait..." she said, arching her brows as Rollie turned slightly, "...Panama's just a bit out of your jurisdiction, isn't it?"

Rollie was well aware of his carotid artery thumping against the hardened scar of his neck. He managed to swallow, his words a croak when he spoke. "I realize you think I'm duplicitous, but I never lied to you Missus Ham—excuse me," he said, recalling her terse request that she not be called that. He cleared his throat. "I never lied to you, *Vivien*."

She listened to his explanation with a scrunched up face. "That's a *lie*. You came in my house waving a badge telling me you had a few more questions."

His pulse wasn't getting any softer, feeling as if some kid were thumping his neck every half-second with the end of a school pencil. Knowing he couldn't speak any further until his heart settled down, he reached inside his jacket, removing the slim bi-fold credentials and sliding them toward her.

Vivien snatched the credentials from the bar, opening them as she slid back away from his view. Rollie closed his eyes as each of his hands massaged the other. She was behind him for what felt like a minute before he saw the barstool next to him being turned. She eased herself up into the seat and sat sideways, facing him.

"I have an obvious question, Mister…or Agent…or whatever you call yourself, Donahue."

"I thought you might," he managed to say, distracted by the memory of that night when Vivien had paraded around her house in the sheer gown.

"If you really *are* with the Department of War, what in the world would you want with my husband?" She halted any response with a raised finger. "And part two of that question has to do with Richard's death…which you obviously don't believe occurred. Do you?"

Rollie tried several times to clear his throat, eventually taking a sip of his soda. "No ma'am—" He saw her eyebrow cock. "Excuse me. No, *Vivien*, I have a strong suspicion that he's still alive. And I also—"

"Then why didn't you say so when you were in my living room?" she snapped, looking like she might start crying.

Rollie exhaled slowly, making his cheeks expand like a blowfish. He gave a quick shake of his head. "Honest to God, I would have liked to. But the stone-cold truth is that I've been following your husband for some time, and to tell you *that* at that time wouldn't have been a good idea at all. I needed to get confirmation first…at the time I had none."

"And do you have confirmation now?"

He thought about it a moment. "No, I don't."

"But you *think* he's here?"

Rollie looked at her. "Yeah, I do think he's here. But Panama, despite seeming small on a map, is chock full of places to hide. He could be anywhere."

Vivien studied him. There was a period of silence before she finally spoke. "But, if I'd known you were coming here, I never would have made such a foolhardy move as coming here myself."

"I'm sorry."

"What?" she asked, cocking her head. She stared at him as if he were a curious being from some unknown planet. "What did you just say?"

"Just that I'm sorry."

Almost imperceptibly, her chest hitched with a suppressed chuckle. "Novel hearing that from a man," she whispered, not directing it at him.

Rollie didn't respond to that, eventually asking what happened to her face.

"It looks better than it did earlier," she replied, peering in the bar mirror. "Took me hours to find a handful of ice in this overheated city."

"What happened?"

"I fought off a mugger."

Rollie arched his brows when she showed him the fresh scabs on the knuckles of her right hand.

"Also scraped up my palms and my knees," she said. "He took my suitcase and all my things, so tomorrow I have the joy of using what little money I have to buy clothes."

"Where was this?" Rollie asked, glancing outside.

"Easy, tiger," she said, patting his arm. "I'm sure the kid who robbed me has long since moved on to his next victim."

"Well, can I at least help you in some way?"

She shook her head and grew quiet, her gaze distant. Then, after a moment of viewing him in the mirror, she said, "You'll pardon me for being direct, but you look different than you did back in Chicago."

"I haven't slept much."

"I can tell," she said, eyeing him for a moment longer before she looked away.

They sat there, eyes off in different directions, neither saying a word for what would have been an uncomfortable period for most people. Vivien eventually broke the silence when she slid her barstool backward, dropping her feet to the ground. She took two steps back in the direction of her table before she turned and gestured to Rollie, her brows arched. "Well, don't just sit there, Donahue, bring your beer and come sit with me. My food will go bad."

Her tone was the type not to be trifled with. Rollie made a motion to the bartender who glanced at Vivien, winked, and gave him an approving nod.

Half a Coca-Cola in hand, heart still hammering in his chest, Rollie made his way to her table.

ROLLING OFF the bed turned out to be a bad move for Richard Hampton. As Frances slid backward against the headboard, he spun to the floor to avoid another of the bone-crushing hammer fists from the jilted Panamanian. With no breath in his lungs and stabbing pain from his broken ribs, his means of escape were highly limited. Bringing himself to all fours, Richard was able to see the swift kick coming but was powerless to stop it. Added to all that was bad about the situation, as the foot rushed forward, Richard noticed they were cowboy style boots, the toes pointed and curled slightly upward behind polished steel tips.

Had he not pulled his head backward, the kick would have caught him in the throat and probably killed him. But by jerking backward, the arc of the Panamanian's kick continued upward, catching Richard on one side of his chin.

When Richard was a boy, he loved eating the shiny pieces of peanut brittle every September at the state fair. His favorite part were the lumpy peanuts, interspersed through the sugary delicacy, a soft piece of glory mingled randomly in the crunchy treat. He'd always chomped down on the candy, unlike his friends who would break it in their hands, then roll a manageable piece around in their mouth until it softened enough to bite. Not Richard. The crunch from the peanut brittle was unmistakable—brain-jarring—a sound that passed through his skull with the noise of an internal gunshot.

Richard's jaw shattering sounded exactly the same way. Only louder.

The brute stepped to his side, open handing Frances, sending her crashing over the other side of the bed. Empty bottles and an ashtray were collateral damage, one hitting Richard on the head.

Other than the grinding sound coming from his face, Richard was aware of Frances' crying and the Panamanian's brahma bull-like breathing. Trying to prop himself up, Richard's arms failed him as he collapsed onto his face, doing more damage to his now unhinged jaw. The angry local drove the same boot into Richard's side, cracking more ribs and making Richard quickly forget about the pain in his skull.

Probably realizing Richard was no longer a threat, the man turned to Frances and began to berate her in surprisingly good English. If Richard's hearing was accurate, the Panamanian was crying as he spoke all of the typical things one might expect to hear, not from a man who just met Frances, but rather from a long-cuckolded husband: *How the hell could you do this to me?*...and...*What did I do to deserve this?*...and the sappy...*I loved you the moment I met you*...and Richard's favorite...*Does he make love to you better than I do?*

Feeling as if he might vomit (from the kick—not from the Panamanian's surprisingly saccharine pleas) Richard slid backward, hoping his aggressor wasn't paying attention.

He was.

The boot sailed in for a third time, again striking Richard's jaw and this time completely dislocating it. It was so far out of line Richard could actually see it protruding to the right side of his face as the bottom left row of teeth connected with his top right for the first, and hopefully only, time in his life.

He imagined the big Panamanian, speaking his excellent English, wearing a candy striped suit and top hat, barking in front of a small tent back at the Illinois state fair. *"Step right up folks, come one, come all, pay your nickel and make your way into the tent to see the amazing man with the diagonal face!"*

Richard rolled to his side, moaning through his crooked maw, exposing his abdomen to the Panamanian as both hands surveyed the ruins of his face.

Frances was back on her feet, pulling at the Panamanian's meaty arm and pleading for him to allow Richard to leave. She pulled her larger lover in the direction of the bathroom but he didn't budge. Richard's eyes turned up, locking with his aggressor's. The man glowered down at him, his beady brown eyes impossible to read in the scant light.

"Please," Richard whispered, unsteadily raising his hand for mercy.

"Vete a la mierda, gilipollas," the man said in his native tongue, his words sounding far more manly than they had when he pleaded with Frances. Before he allowed himself to be pulled away, he unleashed one final kick to Richard's stomach. It wasn't as hard as the ones before it, but it caught Richard perfectly, several inches below his diaphragm.

Richard coiled on himself, gasping for air as the troubled couple went to the rear of the hotel room, the bathroom door clicking shut as muffled yells could be heard from both of them. Richard gasped for air, finally propping himself on his elbows in an effort to get the hell out of there before the Panamanian came back out.

Using his butt as a slide, he pushed backward, managing three good slides which got him closer to the open hotel room door. And that's when a man appeared in the doorway, breathless, as if he'd been running. Richard's head fell to the floor as he looked up at the man from an upside down perspective, a Panamanian judging by his skin. Quite suddenly, as if he'd been injected with a large quantity of morphine, Richard realized he felt no more pain. Appreciating that his appearance was probably ghastly, Richard lifted his right hand to his jaw and shoved it back—almost back—in its normal position, the bones grinding in the process.

Again, there was no pain.

He took a deep, wet breath and tried to sit up, instead, feeling a welling inside him unlike anything he'd ever felt before. On reflex Richard turned his head and vomited an incomprehensible amount of dark blood onto the carpet, watching the river of the rosewood-colored vomitus with an odd, detached fascination. Smacking his lips (strangely pleased that they were again in alignment) he appraised the remaining salty blood in his mouth, tasting very little stomach acid with it. He knew, at this point, that his insides had ruptured and the remainder of his life was probably down to seconds and not minutes.

The man who'd entered the room was carrying a pistol, a revolver with a long barrel, keeping it aimed at the bathroom as he knelt over Richard. Richard watched as the man's eyes widened at the sight of the coppery-smelling blood. He took several steadying breaths, adjusting the pistol in his fingers as he appeared momentarily unsteady.

"Is the man who did this to you in there?" he rasped.

"Yeah," Richard gasped, resting his head on the floor, able to see the man's handsome, slightly haughty features. Blackness began to rim the corners of his vision. He knew he didn't have much time. He lifted his hand to the man's knee, tapping it to get his complete attention.

"How'd you know I was here?" Richard asked, suddenly aware of his great thirst.

The thin man licked his lips, eyes cutting between the door of the bathroom and Richard. "Listen to me," he said sharply. "Why would two different men come to the policia offering us money to find you?"

The blackness was pressing now over the center of Richard's vision, blurring his sight. He could feel his heart pumping like mad, probably confused that there was hardly any blood to pump. His midsection, with most of the body's organs, was the largest intersection of blood in the entire body. A massive hole there could cause a person to bleed out even faster than a sliced artery in the neck or groin. All these things occurred to Richard, almost clinically, as if he were viewing the scene from a distance. While he thought about this, he could hear the Panamanian again asking about men looking for him. The curiosity of who they might be zipped by like a common crow on the breeze, so unimportant at this, his final moment of life.

"What do they want?" the man yelled, jarring Richard with his hand.

Though his eyes were open, Richard could no longer see. He tried to take a deep breath but was unable, hearing the sucking sound as only a small quantity of air went down his throat. With one final effort, he said two words:

"The notebook."

"The notebook?" the man asked. "The notebook?" He shook Richard several times before pressing his hand to his neck.

Taking off his hat, the man stood, removing his handkerchief and wiping the perspiration from his brow.

Richard Hampton was dead.

Chapter Twelve

AS HE sat with Vivien, Rollie declined any food. He fought with himself internally, a man who thrived on a mission, feeling a complete failure for getting so easily made by Hampton's wife and for stopping his search in order to watch her break bread—he was already behind due to his slow start here in Panama. Averting his gaze, he struggled over the ethics of the situation. So what if he was made? There was nothing he could do to stop it, and now that the curtain was down, why not get her unvarnished perspective about Richard? Heartened by his rationalizations, Rollie realized that Vivien just might hold the key to everything he was trying to learn. Again feeling her potent gaze upon his face, he turned back. She was sipping her water, those green eyes coolly leveled into his soul.

"Why are you so upset?" she asked when she lowered her water.

"Upset?"

"I hope you don't play poker, Mister Donahue," she remarked. "Not with that face. It looked as if you were having your own personal war behind those beautiful eyes of yours."

Words hung up in his throat as if caught on a rusty nail, not because of her seeing his angst, but because of her glorious compliment. He managed a forced laugh and sipped the table water rather than reply.

Vivien's nostrils flared as she pulled in a breath. "I'm going to ask you some questions and I want the truth." She pushed her plate to the side and dutifully placed the silverware at the four o'clock position.

"What sort of questions?"

"Primarily about the reasons you've been following Richard. And then, in return, I'll permit you to ask follow-up questions of your own."

Rollie thought about it for a moment. The agent-side of him screamed *absolutely not! Don't tell her a damned thing. Leave her where she sits, stand up, leave, and forget she ever saw you. The rain has stopped and it's still early enough that you can cover seven or eight more bars before the night is done. Go now, old boy. Get those size elevens in motion and haul ass.*

But, on the other hand, his practical side countered his instinct, informing Rollie that his career was likely over. *Your ass is cooked!* No one defies Nicholas Penland. Rollie knew, as soon as he got back, he would almost certainly face a summary review board. It wasn't like he didn't leave a trail—Penland would have it all right there in front of him, using one of those neat little folders he favored. Rollie could just see him, reading the evidence against Roald Donahue, sheet by sheet, making crisp accusations like "dereliction of duty," "willful and unlawful disobedience," and the one that would be the career-killer, "desertion of duty during a time of war."

Vivien was saying something but Rollie didn't pause his train of thought to try and comprehend it. Although he'd known it all along, it struck him that he might well go to jail over this. Penland could even request a penalty of death, though Rollie didn't think it would go that far. If Rollie spoke in his own defense, he could make a strong enough case to the jury that he viewed Richard Hampton as a threat to national security. They might give him some symbolic jail time, but it wouldn't be much.

Regardless, as his practical side had laughingly yelled at him, his ass was cooked. Indeed.

So why shouldn't he answer her questions?

When he looked back at Vivien, she was holding an unlit cigarette, shaking her head. "Like I said, Rollie, you should never play poker."

Screw it.

"If you've got questions," he said flatly, "then I've got answers. There may be some questions I can't answer. If so, I'll tell you."

"No lies?" she asked.

"No lies."

Rather have their little deposition at the table, Vivien paid her dinner bill and led him back into the bar. They sat in a comfortable sitting area, in adjacent high-back chairs. And Rollie answered everything she asked.

MARIA FUENTES listened to the man, an Argentinian, handsome and probably loaded, drone on and on about himself and his shipping company. He talked about his travels to Europe, to the Orient, to the Middle East. He bragged about how fast his company had grown, despite the imperialistic Brits who'd done everything they could to keep him down. When she'd thrown obvious signals that she was ready to leave and be alone with him, he'd ordered another round and said, "First, let me tell you about my newest facility at the Port of Santos."

While he prattled on, Maria looked out the window of the dimly-lit seafood restaurant. The storm had passed. What had at first seemed like a good idea—inviting herself into this man's bed—now made her stomach turn. He'd probably want to describe his actions in detail prior to doing them. Finished with this meeting, she held up a finger, stopping him.

"If you'll excuse me," she pronounced with a fake smile, "I just remembered someplace I was supposed to be."

The man stood up. "*Mierda!* You're leaving?"

"What's my name?" Maria retorted harshly, watching as the man's eyes searched while his mouth silently moved. "You don't know it, do you? You don't know it because you're too busy talking about yourself."

"But, but I—"

"You missed your chance." Leaving him with the bill and his half-told story about his Brazilian facility, Maria breezed out the front door, deciding to check a few more bars and restaurants on her way back to her hotel.

"Maybe I'll get lucky," she said to the clearing sky, having no idea how prescient her quip actually was.

LIEUTENANT GONZALEZ stared at the lifeless form below him—the gringo's rapidly paling face was starkly framed in the deep carmine spread all around him like a liquid blanket. Gonzalez searched the man's clothing. There was a passport in the jacket on the floor, the sleeve steadily soaking up blood. Samuel Fields, of Illinois…so he *was* traveling under the alias the

Englishman told Garza about. No big surprise. The picture was attached, stamped by the U.S. State Department. Gonzalez tucked the booklet into his jacket and stood.

Taking a steadying breath, he crossed the small room, the barrel of the revolver leading the way. He knocked, announcing his official presence. All arguing that had been coming through the door immediately ceased. There was a moment of silence before the doorknob turned and he was admitted to the bathroom by the wide-eyed giant.

From his belt he produced a pair of shiny handcuffs, rattling them as he told the large, trembling man to turn. After cuffing him, Gonzalez had them both stand against the rear of the small bathroom, in the stained tub. The lieutenant propped himself on the small sink, keeping both people at gunpoint.

Suspecting the large man had problems with rage, Gonzalez could see the adrenaline had all but left him now. His lower lip quivered while his face was saturnine, staring downward into some unknown place. Next to him the girl leaned against the stained tile, a towel wrapped around her broad body. She seemed bewildered, her eyes nervously darting from the gun to Gonzalez and down to the towel that covered her. There was a welt on her cheek; someone had struck her. Despite being heavier than normal, she was quite attractive, with an innocent air about her. What had probably begun as a vacation fling had degraded into this.

Gonzalez had seen it more times than he cared to remember. Tropical air, sunshine, and plenty of alcohol. Combined, they created an effective formula for high drama.

The interrogation took only ten minutes; Lieutenant Gonzalez immediately believed both of them. The man was what Panamanians would call *"agricultor inteligente"*, literally translated as farmer-smart. The country was loaded with them: simple people who made the economy plod along, most of them desiring to trade a hard day's labor for enough pay to feed themselves and their family. Despite his brutish appearance, the giant seemed fairly well-spoken, having probably finished at least seven or eight years of school. Judging by his accent he was from well outside the city, to the west, if Gonzalez was forced to bet on it. When asked, he told Gonzalez his family was in the millstone business—a fitting profession if they were all his size. He had traveled by cargo ship to Caracas, selling a load of Panamanian stone to the Venezuelans. On the way home, on the train from Colon, he met this

American woman, Frances, who found him desirable. With the gun barrel pointed at his head, the big man cried like a five year-old, blubbering about dreams of marrying her, and how it enraged him to come to her hotel to find that vile gringo rutting on top of her. When the large man finished his story, Gonzalez, disgusted at the man's show of womanly tears, threw a wad of toilet tissue at the girl and asked her to wipe his face. When she was finished wiping the tears, Gonzalez turned his attention to her, now speaking English, relaying a brief version of what the big brute had said.

"Is this all true?" he asked.

The girl peeled away a length of toilet tissue, dabbing her own eyes as she nodded. "I don't know anything about Emilio's family business or his trip to Cara...Cara."

"Caracas."

"Yes, Caracas. But all that you said after Emilio and I met on the train...all that is true."

"Did Emilio hit you?"

"Yes."

"Are you okay?"

She bit her lower lip and nodded.

"Who was the man you were in bed with?"

Her eyes widened. "How is he?"

Gonzalez searched around with his eyes as he considered his angle. "He's being attended to but his mouth is heavily damaged so I cannot speak to him. *Who* is he?"

Relief passed over her. "His name is Sam. He's from Chicago." The mention of the man's name brought on more blubbering from the giant, quelled by a flick of Gonzalez's Smith & Wesson.

The lieutenant turned his attention back to the girl. "Sam from Chicago. Very good, my dear. And where did you meet Sam?"

"When we boarded the ship in Texas, the Arosa Star."

"Did he say what kind of work he does?"

She turned her head for a moment. "Yes, he said he had left his job and was moving down here for good. He said he was done working."

"And what kind of job does he have?"

"He never said."

"You're *sure*?"

The young woman nodded, a flash of shame passing over her face. "We didn't do much talking on the ship."

"Did he ever mention a notebook?"

"A notebook?"

"Yes," Gonzalez answered, taking a step closer, the gun still trained on the man. "A notebook. Did he *ever* mention one, or did you *see* one?"

Her eyes darted back and forth as she appeared to be searching her brain. She finally looked up. "No. He never mentioned one, and I never saw one."

"Are you certain? *Think*."

"There was a briefcase."

Gonzalez swallowed thickly. "Describe it."

"It was new, light brown, made of soft leather. He was always fussing over it and carried it whenever he left the room."

Nodding profusely, Lieutenant Gonzalez used his free hand to pat her arm in support. "Very good, my dear. Excellent work. Do you know where he was staying?"

She shook her head emphatically. "No, that was why I was so mad at him. He wouldn't tell me."

"Are you positive?"

"Yes."

His face inches from hers, his teeth grinding, he asked again.

"Yes, I promise!" she cried.

After several more questions, Lieutenant Gonzalez was satisfied he had learned all he was going to learn. She had no reason to lie. He commanded the man to sit, un-cuffing one of his hands and reattaching the cuff to the exposed drain pipe under the sink. Still inside the bathroom, he shed his coat and covered the girl's head. Keeping his coat wrapped tightly around her head, he led her from the room, carefully leading her around the coagulating pool of blood, pulling the hotel door shut as they walked into the breezy Panamanian evening.

"Do you have somewhere else to stay?" Gonzalez asked, lowering the coat and draping it around her.

"Where's Sam? Why were you covering my eyes?"

"When we just walked through the room, he was being attended to by a doctor."

"But why couldn't I see him?"

Gonzalez licked his lips. "Two reasons. Your Panamanian friend broke his jaw very badly. The doctor had given your friend an *anestésico*, so he is unconscious and the position of his jaw would be disturbing to delicate eyes." He ran his tongue over his teeth, lowering his voice an octave. "The second reason is highly sensitive."

The girl cinched the coat over her escaping bosom. "Oh?"

"Your friend is in a great deal of trouble, miss." The lieutenant searched his mind, deciding to modify a case he'd worked early in his career, involving an Irishman. His brown eyes came back to hers. "He was planning to blackmail you."

"Blackmail? How?"

"Samuel Fields makes a habit of seducing women for his, ah, carnal purposes. Young women. Women with parents wealthy enough to send them on trips to Panama." He lowered his voice again, now whispering. "When you were aboard the ship, did you engage in, ah, sexual activity in his room or yours?"

She quickly chewed a fingernail, shame washing over her face. "His. I had a roommate on the ship."

Gonzalez suppressed a smile. This would work. "And are your parents wealthy?"

"No, not wealthy at all. My father is a professor, but I think we're just average."

"My dear, an American professor is extremely wealthy compared to most of the world. Here the man would live like a king."

Troubled, she nodding her understanding.

"Would it be possible for you to get twenty dollars per month?"

"I don't understand where this all—"

"Just answer," he snapped.

"Yes, of course."

"As best I can tell, Samuel Fields has used the same con on at least thirty women, all sailing to Panama. Every two or three weeks he goes back to the United States, boards the ship, and does it again." Realizing he was too intense, Gonzalez softened his eyes. "My dear, he tries to find women with a weakness, then seduces them. He has advanced cameras in his room, photographing with great detail every sordid deed they might allow him to perform."

That did it. Her eyes widened; she put a hand over her mouth, no doubt recalling the disreputable acts she'd performed on the ship. During her period of silence, Gonzalez imagined her greedily taking the American in her mouth, or perhaps curiously (and painfully) allowing the American to wedge himself somewhere morally reprehensible. It was all he could do not to smile. He gathered himself. "And this is why I must find his notebook and that briefcase you mentioned."

Choking back tears, the girl's head began to tremble as she said, "What do I do? I've been…I've been so bad. My parents taught me better." Twin tears trickled down her face as she stared into some unknown place reserved especially for the bitten-in-the-ass. "But I thought he loved me. He was so…so…" Her face twisted into a mask of tortured regret. "Oh, what a fool I've been!"

Using his calming charm, the lieutenant soothed her, telling her he would destroy all the evidence before the pictures were even developed. "Your parents will never see these images, my dear. No one will."

"Thank you," she whispered.

"And you're certain you don't know where he was staying or anything else about him?"

"I swear…I promise I would tell you if I did."

He nodded, satisfied. "Where are your friends, my dear?"

She motioned to the door only a few feet away. Gonzalez banged on it, waiting until an attractive young woman answered, staring wide-eyed at her friend's bizarre appearance in suit coat and bath towel.

"There's been a crime next door," Gonzalez said in a tone that asked for no response. "I'm with the Panamanian police and we have some business to attend to. Take your friend inside. I'm going to hand over her things and then I want you all dressed and out of here in less than five minutes or *all* of you are going to my jail."

"What in the world is going—" the girl started to ask, getting cut off.

"*Less* than five minutes or I will take you all in and," he yelled, then lowered his voice midstream, "I can promise you it will be the worst night of your life." A fake smile. "So please. Throw some clothes on your friend here and just leave. Go eat and drink and be merry as you Americans love to say. You're free to come back, but not until after midnight." He turned to the girl named Frances.

"The hotel will give you another room. Just stop by the desk when you *return*."

She nodded.

"Where is your room key?"

"On the bedside table."

He removed his coat from her shoulders, telling her he would probably come back tomorrow before noon for a few follow-up questions. He sent her inside her friend's room and pulled the door shut, rushing back inside the blood-soaked room next door. After finding Frances's suitcase, he ignored the whimpering giant as he stuffed all her clothes and toiletries inside. Gonzalez again knocked on the adjacent door and handed it over half-closed, garments protruding from three sides.

"You now have three minutes," he said in a stern voice, counting four people in the small room other than his witness, standing there, still trying to cover herself with the inadequate towel. The room was littered with all the things one might expect to see from a crowd of college vacationers. Bottles of liquor. Cigarettes. He would lay decent odds that, if he were to rifle the room, he would find lambskin prophylactics and perhaps even a tin of local reefer. Earlier in his career, when money was tight, Gonzalez would come to a room such as this and walk away with five, ten, sometimes even twenty dollars in bribes from American kids who didn't want to get in trouble. He'd even gotten laid before, courtesy of a red-haired New Yorker desperate to prevent her papa from knowing she'd been down here smoking and drinking.

But tonight there were much bigger fish to fry.

Back in the other room, as he stared down at the dead body of Samuel Fields, Gonzalez listened to the muffled sounds of frantic voices next door as the five students scrambled to leave. He could hear the chubby one, Frances, as she continued to say, "I'll tell you later." He smiled as he pondered the excuse she would likely make up. After only two minutes he heard the door slam, pulling the curtain back to watch as the four well-dressed students and the disheveled girl hurried down the stairs and onto Avenida B. He allowed the filmy curtain to flutter back in place, finding Frances's key and dropping it into his pocket.

Gonzalez poked his head into the bathroom, finding the giant still slumped against the wall, softly blubbering. "I'll be right with you," he said in rapid Spanish.

After lighting a cigarette, he knelt over the body of the American, eyeing the handsome yet pallid face, one side of it soaking in the man's thick blood. His shirt was still on, ripped from the kick, and his pants were around his ankles. Taking his time, the lieutenant removed everything from the corpse's pockets, keeping the money and studying the old-fashioned key attached to a round piece of steel displaying the stamped number 210. A hotel key, most likely. He went through the man's coat, checking for anything else that might be useful. There was nothing.

Cigarette clamped in his mouth, Lieutenant Gonzalez gripped his Smith & Wesson in his right hand, holding a pillow in front of it with his left. The pillow would help, as would the inner walls of the bathroom. The room next door was empty. There were no rooms above him and one below him. But it was dinnertime—certainly no one would be in the downstairs room right now. Even so, he'd have to chance it. The cigarette tumbled to the filthy carpet, purposefully dropped by the policeman. In a swift motion, he entered the bathroom with the pillow leading the way, shoving the door shut with his foot.

The big Panamanian was slow, but he wasn't stupid. Seeing the pillow and surely knowing what was behind it, he scrunched up his face and made a sound like a stuck pig. "Oiiiiiiieeeee!"

Lieutenant Gonzalez shot the big man in his head, afterward opening and closing his mouth in an effort to clear his ears. After holstering his pistol, he slid his index finger into each ear, wiggling them up and down.

Giving the hotel room a final glance, Gonzalez kicked the pillow back out onto the carpet and crushed the smoldering cigarette butt. Completely unconcerned with implicating himself through fingerprints, he locked the door from the inside and pulled it shut. Outside, he put the room key into the lock and broke it off, casually walking from the crime scene as he decided how to proceed.

Downstairs, after the requisite threats to the desk clerk, he confiscated the other key to room 330, telling the clerk the room was now a crime scene and if tampered with he could expect immediate transport to the brutal La Joyita prison for a few loving nights with *los animales* in general population.

Satisfied the situation was under control for now, Gonzalez rode his motorcycle back to headquarters. Before ringing for Captain Garza, he wanted to compare the gringo's key to the collection of hotel and guesthouse keys they had on file.

Perhaps he might learn a little more before letting anyone in on his secret.

THEY'D SPOKEN for the better part of an hour. Not once had Vivien Hampton been shocked at anything Rollie told her. The only portion he left out was the part about illegally entering their house and seeing her from the cupboard—somehow he didn't think she would be too pleased with that. When she asked about the missing Panama book, he shrugged, suggesting perhaps Richard had brought it with him. Oddly enough, when it had come to his turn to question her, Rollie deflated as she spoke. The farther she went into her and Richard's troubled past, the more he began to believe Richard might have actually taken his own life.

But what of the partially-burned travel itinerary?

Richard's strange actions? Looking for a tail.

Disappearing for a week, then returning with a tan.

And what did he leave in that lakeside park just over the Indiana state line?

Instinct, Rollie...what does your instinct say?

Without letting the answer burst to the top, Rollie focused on making his mind a blank slate. He closed his eyes in a prolonged blink, staring at the blackness, waiting for complete clarity. Then he asked the question: *Where is Richard Hampton?*

The answer chimed back immediately: *He's here. He's in Panama.*

Suddenly Rollie became aware of their corporate silence as Vivien seemed to have run out of questions.

"Are you okay?" she asked.

Eyes popped open. "Yes, sorry." He cleared his throat. "Where did Richard tell you he typically traveled to?"

"Usually to New Mexico and Tennessee a few times, and lots of day trips to Champagne."

Rollie shook his head. "He might have been lying to you about that, too. He took a number of trips to Dallas and Atlanta. In fact, I was always able to find him booked on airlines each time. He usually took the same flights to each location."

"I can understand why you would think that," she replied. "But he told me about why it might appear that way. Whatever his company was working on was in remote locations. When he and the others…they flew in groups…would arrive in Atlanta or Dallas, they would get whisked away to another airfield and then flown by the Army to some place in the hills of Tennessee or way down in the desert of New Mexico, near the border."

Alarms began to ring in Rollie's head as he tried to comprehend this. "You said *the Army* would fly them?"

"Yes," she replied. "I could always tell when Richard was lying about something. This wasn't a lie."

"Did he say what he was doing there?"

"No, he didn't ever really talk about that kind of thing, but he and his company had been working on it for a while. Something very secret, from what I could tell. And judging by the men who came to our house, something important."

"What men?"

"Military men. They wore civilian suits but I could tell by their hair and demeanor they were military. Richard even said so afterward."

"When was this?" Rollie asked.

"A year ago, maybe a little longer."

"And you have no idea what was going on?"

She shook her head. "Richard's not a good face-to-face liar, but he *is* good at keeping secrets."

He continued on this line of questioning, nibbling in from all angles, unable to learn anything of value. Tomorrow he would have to find a phone and get connected with an operator who knew how to get a call back to the United States. If he couldn't make the call, he'd have to risk arrest by going to the American Zone. There was no other choice. Whatever it was that Richard Hampton was working on in New Mexico and Tennessee *had* to be related to why he was here—again, assuming he was here.

He's here.

Feeling partially vindicated for having the correct gut feeling, Rollie also felt amateurish that Hampton's deception ploy had worked. But how many times had Rollie asked permission to follow him on one of his trips? And how many times had he gotten Nicholas' standard, monotone rejection? "I appreciate your enthusiasm, Kestrel, but your target is low priority." "As are you," Nicholas never tacked on verbally but implied every chance he got.

Rollie had grown quiet as his mind raced. When he became aware of his surroundings again, just as he had earlier, he could tell Vivien was studying him. Rather than look up, he focused on his empty glass.

"Rollie?"

"Yes?"

"Is that your real name?"

"It's Roald."

"Roald," she said slowly. "Don't hear that much."

"Are you complaining?"

Her laugh started slowly at his little bout of self-deprecation. It became deep and throaty and sensual while she still continued to stare at him. Rollie could barely breathe.

"Thank you."

"For what?" he asked.

"For making me laugh. I've done something very foolish in coming here, and I'm thankful to have bumped into you."

"We may have both done something foolish," Rollie replied, adjusting the cravat up over his scar.

Vivien grew quiet again. From the corner of his eyes he saw her hand move a few times, stopping short each time and moving back to her armrest.

On the third attempt it floated the gap between their two chairs as she leaned forward, her voice lowering to a private tone while her hand gripped his wrist.

"I have a feeling that something happened to you once. I have a feeling it was probably quite tragic and I think it has something to do with that mark on your neck." Her hand gave his arm a small squeeze. "Tell me what happened, Rollie."

Typically when someone asked this question, Rollie's introversion transformed to some degree of anger. Internalization, evasion, and usually evacuation were his standard processes for dealing with it—don't respond, be oblique, leave. Then he would allow the steam to seep out over a period of days before things normalized, when the bubble on the level centered itself, when he finally tucked the pain back into that crammed little strongbox located in the depths of his soul.

Watching the inside of the glass, the melted ice in the bottom following gravity to the lowest area as the smooth glass turned under his hand, he realized Vivien's question was different than any he'd ever before heard. And it wasn't just because she was a pretty woman. No, that wasn't the reason. There was something about the *way* she asked it, an indefinable quality, a level of curiosity that had nothing to do with his grotesque external scar; instead, it felt as if she cared about his *internal* scar, the one he carried on his soul. She asked him and touched him with the same level of compassion that his long-dead mother might have possessed. That safe, late night-comfort of a mother appearing next to a sick child—the welcome maternal presence—when mama brought a cool washcloth and murmurs of security to her suffering offspring the way only a mother could. He tilted the glass up, letting the dribble of cool water drop into his mouth.

Eyes finally joining hers he asked, "Do you really want to know?"

"I do, Rollie. I really do."

He gnawed on his lower lip. "I've never told anyone about it. The Army doctors questioned me about it. Strange men from all branches of the government tried, too. I always gave them the same answer: I don't remember anything. They would ask for snippets or shards of my recollections, and my answer was always the same, wiped away by the blast."

"But you do remember," she whispered.

"Yeah, I do. I'll never, ever forget it."

"Tell me, Rollie. Just let it out."

"Why am I actually considering this?" he asked, voice cracking.

"I can tell you actually care about *me*, and not just about finding my husband. I knew it the second you walked into my home. Maybe it's just a little crush, but there was something there and I picked up on it."

Rollie tried to respond but only managed to nod.

"And when you've been with an unloving person for so long, Rollie, to feel someone actually care…it's medicinal."

"I do care, and I understand everything you just said."

"I care, too," she responded without hesitation. "And holding something like this inside is terribly unhealthy. You need to let it out, and to do so with someone who cares." Again she gripped his hand. "Tell me."

There was a moment, as they joined eyes, unlike Rollie had ever had with a woman—or any human being, for that matter. He'd never be able to describe it, not for the balance of his days, but it had something to do with complete and total trust.

Rollie started slowly from the beginning, talking about his recruitment from the Marines for a very special job. He hurried through the tales of the specialized training he and the others had received, followed by their rail and sea voyage to South America, pausing every now and then for her questions. Like most people, she'd never even heard of the Chaco War, her surprise turning to a sort of cynicism when she learned that Big Oil had been behind the warring armies of peasants. He didn't explain much about the war itself, because there simply wasn't much to tell. Speaking deliberately, he summarized exactly what happened at the end of the war: the valley bombing and his subsequent burns and injuries. He explained that he was the only survivor in his platoon and, not only did he have to live with his physical scars, but he was also forced to shoulder survivor's guilt, constantly harangued by the question of whether or not he could have affected a different outcome. Though he'd thought about it thousands of times, the tale sounded foreign actually coming from his lips. Hands gripping the armrests of his chair, he wrapped up quickly, taking steadying breaths as his own silence washed over him like cool water.

"This may sound cold as my first question," she said.

"Ask it."

"Why, Rollie, have you kept all this quiet?"

"Well, as I'm sure you gleaned, it's not pleasant for me to discuss. But I haven't been walking around holding it in due to my own pride."

Her eyes narrowed. "What's the real reason?"

"I was supposed to die in that valley, Vivien. I don't know the details why, but someone on my side struck a deal with the enemy. And after that, every American mercenary—that's what they considered us—who was there fighting with the Bolivians, died. Every single one but me." After a few tries, Rollie managed to swallow. "I was marked for death. And when I showed up back in the United States, damn near six months later, I could have caused problems."

"But you kept quiet."

"I did. Some of the interrogators worked to convince me—without saying so, in so many words—that there was no vendetta, that everyone who died simply died in the course of war. They gave me this job, even tried to give me a medal."

"And you did as they requested."

"I'm a Marine, Vivien. Someone had a reason to send me there, fighting for Bolivia. But then, for other reasons, they must have changed their minds."

Her brow furrowed as she shook her head. "But Rollie, something about all this doesn't add up. Why would they want you to keep quiet? What was so secret?"

"In the final days of the war, I had suspicions. Our numbers were dwindling…we were on the retreat. But then, at the very end, just before the bombing, I heard them."

Vivien was rapt. "And?"

"The men we were fighting were American. The aircraft that dropped the bombs was brand new, cutting-edge, a Curtiss A-12 Shrike."

"Americans attacked you?"

"We'd been fighting them for weeks, but I had no idea they were American."

She nodded, looking away and whispering, "The country you love tried to kill you."

Rollie rubbed his throat and wagged the empty glass at the bartender. "Forgive me, Vivien, but let's leave that story for now." He took deep breaths. "I really don't want to talk about it anymore."

Vivien's face displayed a bevy of unasked questions but she nodded her understanding. Rollie knew, while she was acting as if she understood all he had detailed, her understanding really had to do with why he couldn't speak further about such epic betrayal. When his third cola arrived, he finished his tale by giving her a brief précis of his career to this point, concluding by again telling her that he'd made a foolhardy move in coming here. And like her, he was now busted. Only, in his case, he was probably headed to jail.

"Do you feel okay?" she asked, squeezing his wrist after he finished.

"Actually, yes," he said, doing his best to make his smile appear confident.

"Then can I ask you one more question?"

He nodded.

"It's a toughie."

"Thanks for the warning."

She said it quickly, unfiltered. "Rollie, are you self-conscious because of your scars?"

"Yes," he replied without hesitation. This was another first.

She nodded knowingly. "As I told you at my home, you *shouldn't* be. They're not bad at all."

As was his habit, he'd had his head down upon hearing that a tough question was coming. He lifted it, looking at her. She was sitting in a comfortable position, one leg tucked up under her skirt. Her mouth built into a lovely smile, a reassuring smile that said, "I'm completely serious, Rollie. Forget those scars, forget what you looked like before, and focus on the man you *are*."

"Thank you," he whispered.

"Those scars give you great character, no matter how far down your body they go. But they cannot hide the fact that you're an ethical man…a principled man. And I'll tell you another thing, Rollie…" She seemed to be waiting on him to ask her to go on.

He managed to swallow, finally saying, "And what's that?"

"Something about that scar makes you *more* of a man." Vivien's smile shone like a bright light into his darkened soul. "You're already damned handsome, and the second you left my house last week, my sister and I both mentioned how charming your reserved ways were."

Rollie couldn't control his deep, ragged breaths, coming through his mouth like a person who might be on the verge of vomiting. Feeling claustrophobic, he stood, about to head to the bathroom to throw cold water on his face when her hand locked on his and she prevented him from leaving.

"You see, Rollie," she said, tugging at him as he stood before her, reduced to the mannerisms of a schoolboy, "you've locked yourself in your own little world so long that a compliment from a woman makes you panic."

Feeling ridiculous, Rollie lifted his head, using the same method he did when shooting to calm himself—deep, slow breaths in through the nose, steady exhalations from the mouth. There, finally, he could feel his pulse coming down. He backed up, dropping into his chair. "Vivien, I—"

"Look at me when you talk," she said sharply, cutting him off.

He did, drawing an approving smile. "Vivien, I...I just don't really know how to react to the things you've said."

"You don't have to react, Rollie. That's just it—I'm not asking for a reaction."

Although the exchange had left him spent, he managed a smile and asked, "Did I miss something somewhere?" He cocked his head. "Are you a psychiatrist or something?"

"No, Rollie, I'm just a lonely woman. My husband deserted me, and my father and I haven't spoken in years. I don't seem to do well with men." A tremor danced through the corners of her mouth, making her cheeks twitch. "And if you study me long enough, you'll find my scars, too."

He wanted to reply to that but had no words, none at all. Feeling about as helpless as he ever had, Rollie managed to mumble the words "I'm sorry" before he went back to what he knew, producing a stack of photographs from the inner pocket of his sport coat.

"Back to business, huh?" she said flatly.

Rollie again chewed on his lip, guilty as charged.

"It's okay," she said, leaning over and taking the photos from him, spreading them on the table. "I apologize for being so pushy. Sometimes my damned mouth just works all on its own."

As they leaned over the table, he put his hand on hers. "Thank you, Vivien. For saying what you did."

"I meant it, Rollie." She focused on the photos. "Okay, I've put you through enough tonight. So tell me about these pictures of the scoundrel that was..." she drew in an audible breath, "...or *is* my husband."

Rollie rearranged the photos in chronological order, the timespan evidenced in many of them by autumn leaves at first, then various amounts of snow and the winter clothing Richard wore. "I took these over various times in the last half year."

She worked left to right, top to bottom, stopping at a picture of Richard exiting the Excelsior Hotel in daylight. He was wearing a topcoat and a hat, a satisfied, smug look on his face.

"When was this?" she asked, shaking the photo.

"March, I think," he answered, taking it and glancing at his marking on the back. "Yeah, March fourteenth."

"That was two days after my birthday. Was this in the morning?"

"Yes. He left the hotel and went straight to work."

She stared off in the distance. "On the day after my birthday, he told me he was buried in work and was going to work all night and catch a few hours of sleep on the sofa in his office."

Rollie felt uncomfortable, giving a slight shake of his head.

"That wasn't the only time he stayed there, was it?"

"I've probably got thirty pictures of him staying there or other nearby hotels at different times."

"Were there other women?" she asked knowingly.

"Yes."

"Call girls?"

"I never checked to be sure, but yeah, I'm almost positive they were all pros."

Vivien took the picture, studying it as her features grew harsh with anger. He thought she might crumple it, but instead threw the picture like a discus, the small rectangle knifing through the air as it whirled, sliding onto the stone floor ten feet away. A young woman, a local as it appeared, who had been sitting in the chairs across from them, talking to an older gentleman, bent to retrieve the photo. She was dressed strikingly, her white outfit contrasting against the shiny tan of her skin. She appraised the photo with arched brows, bringing it back and holding it equidistant between Rollie and Vivien, saying something to both of them in rapid Spanish.

Vivien seemed disinterested, her mind in another place. Rollie, however, even accompanied by a beautiful woman, couldn't help but be momentarily captivated by this Panamanian princess.

"I'm sorry, miss, but *mi Espanol es muy malo*."

The young woman laughed good-naturedly, shaking the photo. "Are you American?" she asked in English.

"Yes," Vivien snapped, loading the single word with an unmistakably dismissive tone.

"I saw you throw this," she said, handing the photo to Vivien.

"Thanks, but I threw it because I didn't really want to hold it any more," Vivien replied, again using her "piss off" voice.

"What a coincidence," the girl replied, her head going back and forth between Rollie and Vivien.

Rollie narrowed his eyes, seeing Vivien doing the same. "What coincidence?" he asked.

The girl tapped the photo. "Samuel Fields, the man in the picture."

Rollie's eyes widened. "Samuel Fields, you say?"

"Sí."

"You know him?" Rollie asked, coming forward until his butt barely touched the chair.

Her laugh was sardonic and biting. "Unfortunately I do, and when I find him, excuse my language, but I'm going to slice off his balls."

As Rollie and Vivien sat dumbfounded, the girl stepped back to her older friend and quickly dismissed him. After the disappointed man had taken his leave, she spoke in singsong Spanish to the bartender, apparently ordering a round of drinks before sliding her chair in front of Rollie and Vivien.

"Before I tell you what happened," she said, thrusting her hand first to Rollie. "Allow me to introduce myself. My name is Maria Fuentes."

Chapter Thirteen

ONE HUNDRED and thirty-three hotel keys hung in the box at the station. The dead American's key was long and made of a silver-colored metal, single-sided with rounded bittings. The large end of the key was unique, shaped in a diamond rather than the traditional bull nose.

Lieutenant Gonzalez ran the American's key in front of each hanging key, finding two possible matches and taking them to the Panamanian Police's pathetic excuse for a forensics room. After waiting for the strong overhead lights to warm, he placed both keys flat on an adjacent work table. Upon closer inspection, the American's key was a shade of gray, burnished from years in guests' pockets. He studied the two possible matches, both of which were probably brand new when they were added to the collection, leaving them both unworn and largely unlike the key he'd brought with him. One key was dull silver, the other more of a gunmetal color. This didn't help the lieutenant much; both colors existed on the worn shades of the American's key.

After rummaging through a stir drawer under the work table he found a jeweler's loupe, bending over the American's key to examine the numbers. It was here the lieutenant found his match.

The American's key was engraved, the numbers clearly reverse-beveled into the steel of the key. But the gunmetal-colored key appeared to have been stamped, evidenced by minute amounts of slag on the outer rim of the numerals.

When viewed through the loupe they appeared jagged and menacing, but to his naked eye were nearly unnoticeable. He slid the stamped key out of view, smiling as he eyed the police version of the dead American's key—the engraved one. Attached to it was a hang-tag, upon which was written...

Hotel Azul, Calidonia

Gonzalez knew the hotel well, pocketing both the keys in his pocket and returning the stamped key to the key box. Before leaving, he sent a lone patrolman back to the Hotel Destino, telling him to stand guard outside of room 330 and to let no one near it. He would be by later.

Since the storms had passed and a cool Pacific breeze ruled the night, Gonzalez chose to walk to the Azul, pondering how he could turn this situation to his own advantage.

THE DRINKS had arrived several minutes earlier; Rollie couldn't help but notice Vivien, as she took several large slugs of her wine, staring with distrusting eyes at the buxom Hispanic beauty who was going on about how she'd had a torrid affair with this Samuel Fields fellow, of Chicago, Illinois.

Cutting her off, Vivien shook the photograph in front of the woman. "Are you sure...absolutely sure this was the man?"

Maria nodded with conviction. "Of course I am sure. That is him. That is Sam." She poked the picture for effect.

"Sam?" Vivien asked, looking at Rollie. "When did Richard start calling himself Sam Fields?"

"Richard?" Maria asked, cocking an eyebrow. "That's his name?"

"Yes," Vivien answered flatly.

"What is his real last name?"

"Unimportant," Rollie answered authoritatively, cutting Vivien off before she could say anything. He was trying to get her attention to give her a warning look but Vivien appeared to be stuck between jealousy and bewilderment, having drinks with a woman who claimed to have had a love affair with her husband.

"Are you his wife?" Maria asked, touching her mouth with her hand, concern coming over her.

This time Vivien noticed Rollie's sharp stare. She tightened her lips over her teeth, shaking her head in the negative. Maria appeared mildly skeptical, then motioned to Vivien's bruise.

"What happened to your face?"

"She bumped it on the train. So tell me something, Miss Fuentes," Rollie said quickly. "Whether or not you knew Sam…why is it so important you see him again?"

Maria listened to the question, seeming thoughtful as she turned away for a few moments. Finally she said, "Because, even though I joked about cutting off his manhood—though I would like to—I actually want to be able to tell the men where he is. If I don't, I'm afraid they will kill me, instead."

"Excuse me?" Rollie asked.

"Sí, the men, they threaten me."

"What men?"

"I don't know who they are," Maria snapped. Her face showed pain and frustration. "Just gringos. Mean men who will stop at nothing to find him."

"Americans?" Rollie asked.

"No. They have an accent like English or Scottish. I can't really tell. But I do know it's not American."

"What do they want?"

"They didn't tell me anything, but I get the feeling he's doing some sort of *business* with them." She twisted the word business to make it sound negative.

"Do you have *any* idea what type of business this is?"

She shook her head emphatically. "I do not. But I gathered it was something dirty. Something with the war."

"What makes you say that?"

"Just a guess. There are men and women all over this country involved in information and secrets. These men just seemed like those kind of people."

"Why didn't they just contact him in the United States?" Rollie asked.

"They didn't know how to reach him. That's why they interrogated me with such ruthlessness."

Something about this beautiful young woman was just a bit off-kilter. Rollie made his tone mildly wary as he said, "You know, you certainly seem to speak good English."

She shrugged. "If one hopes to be successful here, one should speak good English. I grew up selling my family's fruit to the Americans at the canal."

Rollie allowed her explanation to stand, finishing his water as he processed this mighty convenient chain of events. He looked at Vivien who appeared a bit haggard. Maybe these revelations were too much for her. He turned back to Maria. "It's late and we've had a long day. How about we meet again tomorrow? Maybe we can help you locate Sam."

"You said his name is Richard."

"*Whatever* you want to call him."

"Is he here?" she asked with a wisp of a smile.

"Here?"

"In Panama."

"Why do you ask?"

"The pictures…you…her…you seem to be looking for him, too."

"We don't know where he is," Rollie answered honestly.

"Then I want to help you find him."

"We can discuss it further. Tomorrow, here, eight in the evening."

"No," Maria said. "Before then. Meet me in La Boca, by the canal. There's a hill there where you can view the ships. Six in the evening."

"Why there?" Rollie asked.

"It has significance to Sam. And I can show you something very important in the canal from that vantage point."

"Look, I'd rather not meet out—"

"You don't trust me," Maria said, pouting, on the verge of tears. "Do you realize what those men did to me? Do you know all I've been through?"

"It's not that we don't trust you."

"When we meet there, you will see the significance," Maria said.

Rollie shrugged, too tired to argue. "Fine. We'll be there." He threw some money on the bar and led Vivien away, quieting her with a raised hand as she peppered him with questions.

When they were outside he spoke forcefully, his voice razor sharp. "Where's your hotel?"

"Some run-down area called Bella Vista. Do you know it?"

They were on the nearest street corner, Rollie staring back at the restaurant to make sure they weren't being followed. "Yeah, I know it because that's where my hotel is. What's the name of your hotel?"

"Sereno."

"We'll find it." Holding her by her elbow, Rollie led her with authority, getting her off the main street quickly. He cut through an alleyway, following it several blocks until they were on Justo Arosemena, hurrying in the general direction back toward Bella Vista.

MARIA SAT back down, waiting until the Americans left. As they walked out she could see the man with the scar holding his hand up as if to stop any questions. Outside, they turned to the east, him leading her by her arm. Assuming he was an experienced operator, Maria knew he would make evasive maneuvers as he moved away from the restaurant. But the woman with him was clearly inexperienced and, Maria knew with little doubt, was the wife of the gringo she and Philip sought. The American man, with his economical manner of speaking and austere presence, had to be with the government. He was looking for Sam/Richard...just like the Prussian who had employed Philip. But looking for him from the other side.

A race to find Sam/Richard, she thought with a smile. And what does Sam/Richard possess that's so important?

Maria toyed with her string of faux pearls, quickly making the decision to try and follow the two Americans. "They turned east," she whispered, knowing that directly to the restaurant's south was the Bahia de Panama. That meant, unless they were to go into another bar, he would be forced to double back through one of the numerous alleyways laid out in a near-perfect grid. Having walked much of the city, Maria knew the only decent hotels back to the west would be found in Casco Antiguo. But to the east there were numerous hotels and much more ground to cover. If they were heading back to the east, however, he would have made his first move to the west before doubling back.

She closed her eyes, dissecting the situation, thinking back to when she first saw them an hour earlier. She'd only taken cursory note of them, because of their skin color, her efforts focused on finding Samuel "Richard" Fields. But now as she thought about it, when she had been sitting there and ignoring the older restaurant patron she'd used as a prop, she remembered looking over at the American man and the woman, at their initial exchange and the way they'd spoken when they first moved into the sitting area. They looked as if they were surprised to see one another.

A chance encounter. And now he was walking her home.

Maybe, just maybe, the man with the scar didn't know where her hotel was. Not until they got out on the street.

So how could he head east to throw off their tail if he didn't know where he was headed?

It was a longshot but, at the moment, a longshot was better than nothing. Maria stepped smartly to the rear of the restaurant, as if she might be headed to the *baño*. Acting as if she knew what she was doing, she turned into the kitchen, surprising the men gathered at the back door, smoking rolled cigarettes as they probably procrastinated over the night's dishwashing. The door was propped open with a broken cinder block. She hurried outside, sprinting through the first section of alley, sending cats scurrying. After a moment she yanked the ineffective heels from her feet. Wincing at the tepid detritus oozing through her toes, she turned to the right and padded through the eastward backstreet, scanning the crossing alleyways for the American couple.

First alley...nothing.

Another...nada.

Again...vacío.

But, at the fourth alley, while she didn't find them in the alley, she saw a flash of the woman's cream-colored getup several hundred yards to the north, on the main street, headed east. Next to her was the tall man with the scar. Cursing herself for wearing white, Maria sprinted up the northward alleyway, ignoring a lewd suggestion from a man on a back porch. At the head of the alley, she saw a crooked street sign marking the avenue as Justo Arosemena. Poking her head out only far enough to see, Maria marked the couple as they hurried east, two blocks ahead and across the street. She stayed still, noticing as the man halted abruptly, appearing to show his companion something in a diagonal window.

He was checking his tail. Maria was right. He was government… a spook.

"Okay, mister," she whispered. "You know what you're doing…but so do I."

When the man with the scar continued eastward, Maria advanced two blocks, light on her feet and feeling a rush of adrenaline as she now could feel herself getting into the mission. She halted, positioning herself behind a folding storefront sign just before the couple stopped again.

"DO YOU really think she would follow us?" Vivien asked, not without a trace of exasperation.

Rollie studied both sides of the street, his hackles up for some reason. "Do you believe in coincidences, Vivien?"

"What do you mean?"

After one final visual sweep of the damp street, he took her arm and pressed on to the east. "I find it a bit fantastic that, in a city of far more than a half-million people, that the exact woman who had an affair with your husband just happened to be sitting across from us when I pulled my pictures out."

Their footsteps clicked on the wet flagstone sidewalk as Vivien didn't respond for a moment. "It does seem to be quite a coincidence, but maybe the odds are lowered because my shit of a husband slept with half the women in Panama?"

He turned to her, cocking his brow as she managed to laugh at what was probably a painful joke.

"And another thing, Rollie…while I do find it to be convenient that she was sitting there, don't forget what a coincidence it was for me to run into you."

"Touché," he murmured.

She pointed up at the hotel dominating the city block three blocks away. "There's my—"

"Don't point," he hissed. Rather than go directly into the hotel, he turned north at the cross street two blocks prior to the hotel.

MARIA HAD been standing on an elevated stoop. She saw the woman point and witnessed the man push her arm down. When they turned to the north, Maria had to fight the urge to follow them. Instead, she stared farther down the street, seeing the lights of a hotel two blocks past where they had turned.

"She was pointing at the hotel," Maria whispered, proud of her assumptions. "Lo sabía."

Moving eastward, she took up a position in an overgrown vacant lot directly south of the hotel. She waited, catching her breath, nestled behind a stack of tires, a prickly bush rubbing at her bare leg. Counting silently, she only made it to thirty before she saw the man and woman flash around the building, disappearing into the secondary entrance of the hotel on the east side.

She straightened, not needing to hide now, saying, "Te tengo ahora, Señor Cicatriz." *I've got you now, Mr. Scar.*

ROLLIE LINGERED by the rear stairs, his eyes wandering over the interior of the unkempt building. The paint on the walls was peeling, drooping down in spots like the bark of a river birch. And while he could see the faint flashing of light denoting a whirling ceiling fan around the corner, the air in the rear of the hotel was thick and still and musty. He could hear Vivien around the corner asking for her key, just as a mouse appeared on the threadbare carpet of the stairs, peeking up from the basement. Rollie stared at the gray mouse, watching as it looked him up and down, its nose and whiskers twitching. Vivien's footsteps were headed his way so he stomped his own foot, sending the mouse scurrying back downward. When she came around the corner, key in hand, he led her up the first flight of stairs, stopping on the landing at the second floor.

"Listen to me and listen carefully. Go straight to your room and bolt the door. If there's a chair in there, wedge it underneath the knob and, no matter what anyone says, do not answer it tonight." He glanced down the stairs. "I'll be back by for you tomorrow, but it may be noon before I can get here. You'll get hungry, but just stay in your room until then. Better hungry than dead." He leaned out over the gap between the stairs, glancing up and down.

"Hang on a moment, Rollie," she interjected calmly.

"Just do as I say," he said forcefully. "See if there's a fire escape outside your window. There probably isn't, but in the event there is, have a plan in mind to head out that way if things turn ugly." In a deft motion he unsnapped his compact F&W .32 from the uncomfortable ankle holster, pressing it into her hand. "That's loaded and ready to go. Aim, pull, shoot and don't waste time in doing it. And be advised that the range or stopping power on that isn't all that great—"

"Stay with me tonight, Rollie."

Pretending not to hear her, he pressed on. "And when you shoot, you keep shooting. Understand? A thirty-two can kill a man but, if you hit him in the stomach or chest, it's going to take more than one shot."

Her face was serene as her hand touched his upper arm, rubbing up and down. "I want you to stay with me."

Oh, but he'd been in his element.

"I…I…that pistol is…Vivien, it's not very, well…"

The chance encounter in the restaurant, the frenzied evasion through the streets of a strange city, talk of escaping out of windows and the loaning of one of his hobby handguns—all of it nirvana to a career warrior who otherwise lived a life turtled inside his shell. He'd actually felt the evening building to something, but to something he was comfortable with. Maybe he'd find someone waiting on him back at his hotel, or perhaps he would even spot Hampton on the walk back. Or maybe it would have been a couple of locals trying to mug him. But in his most reckless of daydreams he hadn't anticipated this; and all his accumulated machismo shattered like thin glass upon her four-word suggestion, leaving him hitching and stammering like a film reel that had hung up.

She handed the pistol back. He accepted it, still searching for a word. Vivien grasped his free hand and led him up the stairs to the fourth floor. Rollie was dumbstruck. The F&W dangled from his left hand, the trigger guard barely attached to his index finger.

The lights seemed to blur together as she led him down the hallway, glancing back at him a few times with the tranquil, mirthful expression she'd taken on. Vivien walked with a light gait, her scraped legs probably making her stride a tad shorter than it would normally be. The key worked a deadbolt which she managed with ease. Inside, the room was just that, a room. It was deeper than it was wide, with a sprung bed to the right and a single table covered in a few store-bought items. The paint on the walls was something akin to pea green and, as pitifully plain as the room was, even though she'd probably spent less than an hour there, it smelled of her, and that fragrance sent shockwaves throughout Rollie's being.

"I lost all my things when that little...when that *excuse* for a man robbed me earlier." Vivien squeezed his hand before letting it go. "Are you okay?"

His nod was short and shaky.

She turned to the table with the assorted items, lifting a toothbrush and a tube of Ipana toothpaste, proffering both to him. "I've only used it once and, unless you don't want to, I don't mind if you use it."

"Vivien, using your toothbrush isn't the...the...um...it isn't what I'm concerned with."

"Then there should be no objections, Rollie. I can handle a lot of things, but bad breath isn't one of them." She physically turned him by the shoulders. "The bathroom's at the end of the hallway. Earlier they had a pitcher of distilled water in there that you can use." She gave him a friendly shove. "Go on."

From the hallway he looked back at her, realizing his face was slack as he floated through this uncharted water like some inanimate log bouncing amongst the rocks on a raging river. He gave his head a quick shake, clearing away the cobwebs. *What the hell am I thinking?* A small measure of relaxation came over him as he realized she simply wanted him to stand guard and nothing more.

Then why does she want you to have fresh breath?

Good point.

Maybe because the room is so damned small, a person with bad breath would stink it up in minutes.

Weak argument, counselor.

You're getting way ahead of yourself. There's no way she's interested in a scarred-up has-been. Feeling somewhat better after his internal argument, Rollie decided that tomorrow he'd put her on a boat out of here. He'd call Nicholas Penland, come clean, then go and meet that alleged local—*what was her name, Maria?*—and get to the bottom of her story.

Rollie tossed his tie around his neck and brushed his teeth vigorously, unaware that he hadn't even rinsed the toothbrush off before beginning.

Only here to stand guard.

Only here to stand guard.

He brushed and brushed and brushed. Then he gargled with the purified water. The hanging towel was dingy. He flipped it over, dampening it and wiping his face. With his head turned to the left, he studied his profile—the good side—noting the bleary eyes, giving them a few tugs to offset the wrinkles brought on by his sleepless nights.

Before leaving the bathroom, he wet his hand, neatening his hair.

His last move was to take a dab more of the peppermint toothpaste, depositing it on his tongue and coating the roof of his mouth.

But he was only planning to stand guard.

Chapter Fourteen

MINUTES EARLIER, Maria spied from the vacant lot. Through the hotel's open front doors, she was able to catch glimpses of the American woman as she retrieved her key from the hotel desk. The man with the scar was nowhere to be seen. The woman disappeared the way she had come. Maria licked her lips while hatching a plan. As she emerged from the lot, scraping her bare feet on the sidewalk, eventually using the frond of a Pindo palm to wipe them, she nodded to herself when she felt her plan was worthy of a try. And even if it didn't work, she now knew the woman's hotel and could stake it out if need be.

Giving the front entrance a wide berth, Maria counted five floors as she crossed the street. She eased up the steps at the side entrance, gingerly stepping inside in an effort to not be seen. The stairs were there, right by the door, so she climbed to the next level, walking the hall to the far end, finding the bathroom. Maria used water from the sink, purposefully smearing mascara down her cheeks. Taking care not to rip her new dress, she lowered the right side almost underneath her breast so that it pressed outward as if someone had tried to pull it down. She made sure the top of her areola was visible, splashing water on her upper chest before slipping her high heels back on. Feeling curiously stimulated by her little ruse, Maria fought back a smile and made her steps loud as she crashed down the flight of stairs, hurrying into the dingy little lobby, screaming for help.

A stunned clerk emerged from a back room, his beady eyes wide as he listened to her hysterics. Those same beady eyes began flicking up and down, alternating between her face and her nearly-exposed breast.

"Young boys, *criminales*!" she yelled. "They're out of control, ripping the fifth floor apart down near the baño. They tried to pull me in there!"

"Boys?" the diminutive clerk asked, gripping the counter.

"Yes! Three or four of them. They can't be more than fourteen years old but they're acting like wild animals. Please stop them!"

He made an initial move to come around the counter but stopped—Maria watched as his fear warred with his desire to appear manly to this gorgeous creature before him.

She moved the Dutch door, swinging it open as she purposefully allowed her chest to brush against him. "Go and stop them, please!"

The man pressed his lips together, cinching up his pants with both hands. With a final glance at her chest, he pushed through the door and turned. "It will be done, my dear."

"Gracias, señor," she breathed, giving him a dusky look.

She heard him as he ran up the first flight, the knock of his shoes slowing considerably by the time he reached the second floor. Knowing he might turn back at any moment, she whirled behind the desk, flipping open the register, frantically running her finger to the most recent entries.

"Vivien, Vivien, Vivien…" Maria whispered, recalling the sharp look the government man had given her when she introduced herself. He never gave his name.

Her finger ran down the page, her bright nails marking the multitude of Spanish names until…*there!*…Vivien McGraw…checked in at 4:55 p.m. She was in room 405.

After flipping the book shut, Maria put her finger to her mouth, tapping her lips. The woman, Vivien McGraw, was in for the evening. She wouldn't be going back out. Maria would begin by following her on the morrow, meaning there was no point in staying here. Ripping a sheet of paper from an adjacent notepad, she pressed it to her lips, leaving a pink kiss, placing it on the desk for the clerk.

Maria might need him again.

She left by the front door, smiling as she headed to her El Carmen hotel.

It had been a good night.

ROLLIE STOOD in the hallway, waiting on Vivien as she brushed her own teeth. The water ran for what felt like an hour as he waited, staring down the hallway as if marauders might appear at any moment. It occurred to him, as a rare smile crept onto his face, that he *wished* marauders might appear. The door behind him clicked.

No marauders.

Bathroom light lit the dim hallway for a moment before she pulled the string. He turned. She was still wearing the tattered cream skirt and her short sleeve blouse; Rollie noticed the skirt appeared loose. When she passed by him, he saw why. The skirt had been unzipped from the rear and now barely clung to the curve of her hips.

"Wouldn't it be easier for you to sleep if I take the chair out in the hallway?" he asked in an unsteady voice, standing under the threshold to her room.

She ignored him, extinguishing the lone ceiling bulb. Rollie twisted his gaze back to the hallway as she began to unbutton her blouse. He could hear the whisper of fabric sliding off her arms and to the floor.

"Would you mind closing the door?"

Without looking, he pulled the door to, feeling resistance from inside as she grasped the knob, pulling the door open.

"Close the door from the *inside*, Rollie."

He blinked several times, studying the stained carpet of the threshold. With great effort he stepped inside, pushing the door shut, his face inches from it. Although the room was dark, light from outside spilled in, casting everything in the room in shades of blue. The air changed ever so slightly, making him realize she was inches behind him. Her arms went around his body, gently turning him.

"I've had a miserable couple of days, Rollie," Vivien said as she pressed her chest to his midsection, tilting her head back to look up at him. "I've taken several flights, struggling to find seats before we were grounded by a storm. Then I traveled by train, was mugged, punched, fell down, and then found out my husband had an affair with a post-teen Panamanian tart." She shook her head, laughing softly as if verbalizing things made it seem funny somehow. Her face grew serious again as she said, "And, if at all possible, Rollie, despite all that's transpired, I'd really like to end this day on a high note." Reaching upward, she slid the jacket off of his shoulders, pausing at the shoulder harness. Vivien moved around him, unbuckling the harness from under his left arm, sliding it off also.

"We shouldn't do this," Rollie whispered, defying the powerful arousal that had enveloped him, suddenly making his opium sickness disappear.

"I really don't care about what I *should* do," she replied, moving with more speed as she undid the buttons of his damp button-down.

Rollie felt a spike of panic. "Wait," he said, pushing past her and crossing the room to the window, looking up. There were no curtains, no shade. He turned and whipped the tattered blanket from the bed, pulling it wide as he prepared to shroud the window.

She was behind him again, pulling his arms down. "Stop, Rollie," she said in a soft voice. "Stop…I want to see you."

"No," he said, jerking his arm away with more force than he meant to use. He stood still, his breath coming in jagged rasps. "It's bad, Vivien, okay? Is that enough for you? It's bad, like something on a horrid monster from a Saturday matinee."

"I said," Vivien started, using an equally forceful voice, "I want to see you." With surprising speed and strength, she snatched his shirt backward, lowering it to where it hung on his hands. Although he resisted, she ripped his undershirt down his front side, exposing his entire torso.

Had someone told Rollie what was going to happen, he would have feared his own reaction. His first thought was that he would react with great anger, and might even strike a woman for the first time in his life. Or would he simply flee the situation? Would he hurriedly cover himself in the blanket, grab his things and leave in the shame he'd come to know so well? There were other versions inside those two possibilities, but that's the scenario he would have bet on. Rollie, however, wouldn't have *ever* predicted his actual reaction, which was to close his eyes and lower his head, inviting the unaccompanied solitude that such a personal posture provides.

"See," he heard her say in a soothing voice. "You're all worried over nothing." Her hands gently probed his scars, touching them the way a person might run their hand over the texture of an old oil painting, just enough to hit the high spots. She ran her hands up his body, past his abdomen, over his chest, onto his neck; both hands moved around him as she gripped him around his lower back. Then, giving him the biggest surprise of his life, she lowered her head, starting at his belly button, tracing a line up his stomach—

right at the edge of his scar tissue—her glistening tongue reaching his chest as her hands moved behind his head, pulling it down to her as her mouth clamped on his.

The kiss transported Rollie back to 1935, the date of his last kiss, eight long years before. For that brief moment, his scars were gone and the eight years of physical and mental pain were excised, their memory erased as if by a wet sponge on a chalkboard. And while her hands roamed in his hair and on his back, Rollie remembered the way Vivien had looked that cool Chicago night as he hid in her cupboard, realizing that, for the first time in ages, a dream of his had actually come true.

Feeling a long-forgotten shot of libidinous manhood, he grasped her under her arms, lifting her to the bed as he lay on top of her, their impassioned kiss continuing.

Though he was far out of practice in making true love, the movement of her legs and her clawing at his still clothed buttocks signaled to Rollie exactly what Vivien desired on this night.

And what he had yearned for since 1935.

LIEUTENANT RENALDO Gonzalez searched every square inch of Samuel Fields' hotel room. He found nothing. He was now sitting in the room's spindly white wicker chair, his eyes carefully scrutinizing the chamber, viewing every single item, having already sectioned the room in quadrants. Gonzalez paused at the vent in the side wall. While there was no heat in Panama, it wasn't uncommon to find a duct system that blew fresh air into the rooms, able to be converted someday in the event that one of the mythical cold weather machines became affordable. Whipping his knife out, Gonzalez hurried to the vent and turned the painted screws which held it in place. Yanking the flimsy metal away, he slung it across the room and stared inside. There was nothing but dusty ducting leading downward into blackness.

He checked the bed, flipping the mattress over. There was nothing in, under or associated with the bed. After looking underneath the small desk, in the event Fields had somehow tucked the notebook under the cavity, he turned his attention to the bathroom. The most obvious place was the stained commode with its reservoir up near the ceiling. He opened the top, pressing his hand into the water, splashing toilet water on his face as he searched with frenzy. Again, nothing.

On his first search he had checked the cheap plywood cabinet under the sink. Gonzalez ripped the door from its hinges, checking again. Seeing nothing in the dark cavity, he looked up around the bowl, even pressing on the bottom and back of the substandard wood structure for trap doors.

Searching his mind, he could think of nowhere else to look—it was obvious the American had stored the notebook and its briefcase elsewhere. Gonzalez left the room, pulling the door shut and locking it. There was nothing to be found here. He made his way back to the station.

Although he had no desire to do so, the lieutenant sent a junior policeman to Captain Garza's El Carmen home.

"Wake him up, loudly if need be, and tell him we have a problem."

The young officer stammered before he got the question fully out. "W-w-what kind of problem, sir?"

Gonzalez looked up, his eyes bloodshot from a lack of rest. "Tell him the gringo we're looking for is dead."

Looking like he wanted to ask a follow-up question, but thinking better of it, the young policeman sprinted from the hotel. Gonzalez pulled the dingy blinds to the side, watching as the officer sped into the night on a bicycle.

Poor kid, Gonzalez thought. *Garza might shoot him simply for bringing him bad news.*

Knowing he had at least an hour before his superior's arrival, Gonzalez stretched out on the floor of his office and, despite his stress, he slept.

MARIA CONSIDERED her options as she walked back to her hotel. It was late and Samuel/Richard was known to love women. If he was here, there was a good chance he'd be in one of the bars at this hour, trying to sate his urges. But Maria may have already struck gold with the wife and the American man. Deciding to get some rest, she continued on to her hotel, wanting to sleep so she would be fresh tomorrow. It was her intention to be onsite in front of the wife's hotel early in the morning. While Maria would certainly go through with the evening meeting at La Boca, she wanted to see where the woman might lead her beforehand.

Maria's El Carmen hotel was low and wide, two floors, with outward facing rooms on front and back. There were a hundred just like it in Havana, simple buildings that could be thrown together by any group of semi-skilled workers with a stack of cinderblock and cheap mortar. The yard surrounding the hotel consisted of low-cut grass, prompting Maria to remove her heels and walk across the lawn, wiping away the traces of dirt from earlier. The dewy grass felt good under her feet, making her again flirt with the notion of heading back to the bars. Something about the wetness on her bare skin made her feel free, made her feel like removing her clothes, made her feel like walking to the first bar and finding a beautiful man to take home and love her.

She stopped in her tracks. Why couldn't she pick someone up? She could satisfy her cravings in ten minutes with the right man. Just a simple roll in the hay (at his room) followed by her quick exit. A smile on her face, Maria whirled around, ready to walk back to the El Carmen business district.

But interrupting her libidinous thoughts was the image of a man, on the lawn, storming in her direction. He'd obviously been following her and was now mere feet away. With her sudden, unexpected turn, she'd exposed him as a tail.

He was coming straight at her, leaning forward in a fast walk.

His expression was the definition of intensity. And danger.

Maria immediately went for her pistol, tucked down in her clutch. She was too slow.

The man was quite large, his hands a battering ram as he shoved her shoulder and upper arm, sending her skidding onto the wet lawn while the pistol flew in the other direction.

She cried out as she clawed the wet ground for a purchase, needing desperately to get to her pistol.

ROLLIE REALIZED he couldn't stop kissing Vivien. While he certainly enjoyed it, he knew deep down it was simply another ploy to occupy her from ogling the scars he'd gone to such great pains to keep hidden. She must have known it too, pulling her head away from his.

"Turn over," she whispered. He tried to kiss her again. "Turn over, Rollie."

Not without hesitation, he eased himself off of her, the cheap springs of the mattress announcing his descent. When Vivien stood from the bed, the depression in the mattress claimed him. She removed her brassiere, the light from outside highlighting the lovely curves of her body. Rollie stared at her face. While it was too shadowy to see her green eyes, he could tell she was looking at him, and on her face was a smile—a giving smile. This was her present to him. Vivien wiggled her hips as she slid her skirt down, removing her underwear next.

Rollie heart pounded with such speed and force that he nearly passed out. He shut his eyes for a moment, controlling his breathing.

Next came his clothes. Vivien managed his shoes and socks without a problem, needing his help with his pants and boxer shorts. As her hands again moved to his torso, focusing on the scarred tissue, her mouth roamed his body.

Colorful fireworks illuminated the room.

MARIA SCRABBLED on the wet grass, trying to get at her nifty little Beretta 34, given to her by Philip as the perfect pistol to fit inside of a clutch. She could see its bluing glinting in the moonlight as the man moved in front of her, blocking her way. He was saying something but she was in no state to comprehend, rage turning her world red. In a swift motion she grasped his left ankle, biting it from behind with animalistic ferocity, doing her best to sever his Achilles tendon.

The man let loose a yell as he wrenched her hair backward, lifting her to her feet. Maria kicked and flailed, quickly subdued as the man grasped both of her arms and held her tightly to him. And that's when she began to hear his words.

"...the man who hired Philip," he growled in accented Spanish. "And unless you want to die right here on the spot I'd suggest you calm down."

She ceased her movement, her wide eyes rising to his. Bull breaths entered and exited her nose with pneumatic force as her racing mind slowed, considering what he'd said. The red that had colored her world like a lens dissipated, displaying a gorgeous specimen of a man, eyeing her in the exclusive manner of the ultra-confident. Finally she asked, "You hired Philip?"

"Yes," he whispered. "And this little scene isn't exactly good for our mission."

"And what is that mission?" she asked, testing him.

"You know what it is," he said, releasing her, glancing around. "Samuel Fields." The man lifted his pants leg, cursing. "Another bite," he said, gesturing at her with his hand, pointing to a scabbed-over wound.

She rubbed her arm, processing what he'd said before. "If you're my contact, then why the hell did you hit me with the force of a sugarcane truck?"

"Like you, I've been out searching for him all day and decided to go ahead and contact you tonight. I knew you were staying here and was waiting on you from across the street. When I finally saw you, I was following you to time out a meet as you entered your room so we could speak in privacy. I didn't expect you to stop and turn, and I certainly didn't want you shooting me with that..." he glanced over at the pistol, studying it for about a second, "Beretta."

"Well, how was I to know you were going to contact me? I was given a number to call if I found anything. That is all I knew."

"And have you?"

"Have I what?"

His eyes studied her. "Found anything?"

She made certain she didn't hesitate when she shook her head, giving him a decisive "No."

The man was tall and had a muscular neck that indicated an athlete's body below his nicely-tailored linen suit. His face was indeed handsome—damned handsome, like that of an actor. His high cheeks and cleft chin appeared to have been chiseled from stone, and the normally tepid-looking

Caucasian skin on his body browned from years in the sun. He wore an oversized fedora, tilted in a self-confident manner and she could feel the sea change as he undressed her with his eyes. She was already sweating, so his good looks combined with her urge for carnal satisfaction made her suddenly aware of her body's physical response to him. Maria tilted her chin upward, moistening her lips.

His moves as lithe as a cat, he scooped up the clutch and Beretta, displaying trust by handing them back to her.

"Thank you," she whispered.

The man grasped her wrists, pulling them effortlessly down to her side. Then he kissed her, his mouth awash in the taste of fresh peppermint.

When he pulled away, Maria stared up at him, her breaths caught in her throat.

¿Quieres más? he asked. *Want more?*

"Sí, mucho más." *Yes, much more.*

He released her left hand, his right hand assertively slipping under her short skirt, touching her body with stunning accuracy. And, as Maria's breath escaped her, he lowered his mouth, licking her neck before he breathed one question. "Which room?"

THE ROOM was warm, the air thick with body heat. Rollie lay back on the bed, Vivien straddling him, resting both of her hands on his chest. She smiled down at him, never moving her eyes from his. There was obviously pleasure involved, but the smile seemed to originate from something deeper than surface pleasure. It was, perhaps, a smile of contentment. Sharp breaths escaped her mouth with each rhythmic movement. One of her hands moved to his face, lingering on his lips before cupping his cheek. She bent over to kiss him before rolling off.

Sensing her desires, Rollie kissed her again as he took up a position on top of her.

THE LARGE Prussian destroyed Maria's new dress as he ripped it off with primal passion. He lifted her with ease, depositing her crossways on the bed. With his tongue extended, he dove to her body, licking all around her around her most erogenous zone, occasionally wandering to other areas. The Prussian stood abruptly, again pulling Maria by her hair, earning a pained grunt as he moved her head to his midsection.

Maria complied, stimulated by his rough nature as he continued to twist and jerk her hair. She gave him a taste of pain in return, occasionally raking him with her teeth as her hands scratched his body.

THEY MOVED slowly and deliberately, with Vivien making satisfied purrs between her whispered compliments to Rollie. She was beneath him, her hands up, roaming his chest and shoulders and back.

You're so muscular. I'm lucky to have met you. This feels wonderful. Don't stop, Rollie...don't ever stop. You've made me very happy.

Rollie clenched his eyes shut, the long gap in his love life irrelevant as he sought to hold out long enough to provide this beautiful creature pleasure. He could feel her hands as they touched his scars, seemingly unfazed by their mutilated image and feel.

The love they were making was perfect. Though still trying to hold out, he risked opening his eyes to look at her. She was so beautiful, a real woman, here in bed with him. She seemed to truly be enjoying herself and was going out of her way to make him feel good.

And though Rollie's heart soared, something niggled at his mind from the deep. Closing his eyes again, he tried to bring it forward.

MARIA WAS on all fours. The muscular Prussian had switched on the overhead light, sliding the cheap chest of drawers in front of the bed so they could view themselves in the warped mirror. Between his deliberate moves, he would smack her on her rear end, pull her hair or pinch her. While there was definite pain involved, Maria was in her element, feeling her coming pleasure, knowing it would be long and deep—the type that had even been known to make her lose consciousness.

She could tell he, too, was getting close. She slid her hand down her belly to provide herself with enough pleasure to try to time her earthquake with his.

The man slapped her back very hard, making her scream out in genuine pain, but she still continued to thrash, feeling a tidal wave of orgasm coming up through her body.

ROLLIE SQUEEZED his eyes shut. The query that had evaded him pressed forward, bolstered by his years of self-torment, centering around the whys and wherefores of this unusual encounter. *Why was this beautiful woman taking such an interest in him? Why did she ask where the scars came from? And why was she looking into his eyes as she lay below him, her hands gently clutching his back as he moved with her?* Occasionally she would raise her head, joining her lips to his. But now she lay back, as if she were trying to press her head through the mattress. Rollie could see the veins and ligaments of her neck as her lips peeled back, displaying her white teeth clenched together.

Vivien was making more noise but he could tell she was trying to stifle the sounds. Her mouth transformed into a round shape as she sucked and blew, her coming moment making her body begin to shudder. As it went on, she lowered her hands to his buttocks, keeping their bodies together.

Seeing all this, combined with the sensation of her adjusting herself made Rollie's surprising stamina crumble. His vision began to spin and, unlike Vivien, he wasn't able to contain his guttural sounds. But, despite his pleasure, the questions over Vivien's interest in him tolled in his head.

MARIA BUCKED, held fast by the big man's cowboy grip on her hair. She could actually feel his passion as it erupted with the denouement of their careless act. Like it always did when she was with a man, her pleasure went on three times as long as his and, even after he'd collapsed beside her, she continued to shudder and moan as blackness nearly overtook her.

Completely spent, she lay in the fetal position, catching her breath, looking at the man as he lit a cigarette and drew deeply.

He joined eyes with her, unsmiling, licking his lips one time. And while he was indeed a specimen to behold, Maria realized at that moment that behind those eyes there was no joy, no scrap of kindness, and absolutely no capacity for empathy.

Testing him, she said, "That was nice."

He couldn't contain the sneer as he continued to eye her through hollow eyes.

"Did you enjoy it?" she persisted.

"Can you just shut up?" he snapped, turning his eyes back to the ceiling and smoking.

She would wager her life he had no family of his own and had certainly renounced his parents and any brothers and sisters. Who knows? He might have even killed them. This man was more like a machine, running roughshod over everyone in his way.

Though young, Maria Fuentes was an expert judge of character. This was a man who would kill at the drop of a hat. Who would maim without hesitation. Who cared about no one, or no cause, other than himself. What might have taken a team of psychiatrists weeks to diagnose, she gleaned in less than a minute, all from staring into those soulless eyes.

Yes, she decided, *he's extremely dangerous*. She knew, if she didn't watch her step, she would be the one who'd wind up dead.

Maria Fuentes had probably never been more right in her life.

ROLLIE COLLAPSED on top of Vivien, feeling sweat pouring from the right side of his body. She held him there, her hands roaming his back, his hair, lingering on his body. Finally, she slid her hands around to his face, pulling him close as she kissed him again.

As kind as she had been, and as glorious as the love they'd just made was, the question bubbled forth again, but this time he spoke it.

"Why?"

Vivien adjusted her body, shifting slightly to the side to view him. "Why?"

"Yes. Why all this?"

"What do you mean, Rollie?"

"Why would you sleep with me?" he asked flatly, hardly increasing his tone at the end of the sentence to indicate it as a question.

"I...I don't really know how to put it into a sentence, Rollie." She shook her head. "You know, your asking me this...especially at this moment...doesn't exactly make me feel like a good person. I thought what we just did was beautiful."

"But I'm hideous," he seethed. "So did you just endure touching me in an effort to get something out of me or to make me back off?"

She lifted her head, her face contorting. "You don't honestly believe that, do you?"

"Well, what else could it be?"

"Rollie, I *only* wanted to be close to you."

"But why did you have to pry into my past?" He stood, feeling all of the pleasure, all of the warm feelings drain from his body, instantly replaced by the pain and bitterness that he'd grown so used to.

Vivien was quiet as he hurriedly covered himself with his shirt and pants.

"Rollie, please calm down."

"Why should I?" he yelled, surprised at his own ferocity. "Do you want me calm so you can get inside my head for a few more secrets?"

She sat up, turning her legs so they fell off the side of the bed. The quiet grew, lingering as she appeared to search for the right words. Eventually she turned her head up, one side of her mouth twitching as if she might be about to cry. "You're only the second man I've *ever* given myself to."

His first inclination was to scream "bullshit!" but he was used to sniffing out liars. It only took a moment's analysis to determine that she was telling him the absolute truth. Her words had the proper effect on him, extinguishing much of his anger but leaving the question remaining.

"Well, I still don't understand," he managed to say in a more reasonable tone.

"What don't you understand, Rollie?"

"Why a woman like *you* would want a man like *me*."

"Because I like you." She enunciated the words slowly. "It's as simple as that."

"Okay, if that's true, then I find it hard to believe. Added to that, why would you care about all I've been through? About my injuries? About what goes on in my mind?" He chewed on his lower lip for a few seconds. "It just feels too…too perfect. Too much of a happy little coincidence."

"Do you think I'm somehow in on things with Richard?" Vivien, her pain showing, began to cry.

"No. No. No," he answered, making a calming motion with his hands and realizing how foolish his accusations sounded. Rollie covered his eyes as he shook his head. "I didn't mean that. I don't know what I mean any more." He stayed that way, trying to make sense of his feelings.

Vivien found her purse, rummaging in it until she produced a near-crumpled pack of cigarettes. She lit one with a match, inhaling deeply and blowing the smoke up in the air as she sat back on the edge of the bed, pulling the dingy sheet over her lap.

After a few steadying pulls on the cigarette, she lowered her head, resting it in her hand as she spoke to the floor. "Rollie, if I had to make a guess, there have probably been many people who would have genuinely cared to hear what you've been living with. As bad as your torment has been, I think you probably built up a little mental fortress to keep all prying eyes out. And while doing that might have saved you from having to answer some painful questions, you also managed to shut out people who probably cared."

Rollie had no words because she was dead on target. He stood there, his open shirt swaying as his heavy breaths were his only movement. His only action was to take one of her cigarettes, lighting it with hers. He sat next to her on the bed as they smoked in silence. After some time he whispered a brief apology which she seemed to accept.

Again they sat smoking, alone with their own thoughts.

"Look at me," Vivien said, breaking the silence in a quiet voice.

Rollie turned.

Her eyes were intense. "You have *nothing* to be ashamed of, do you understand me?"

He stared.

"Nothing at all, Rollie. Look how you made me feel tonight. You made me feel special, and while I think you're a fine man to look at, I value *all* of you. The way you think, the way you talk, the way you rarely smile. That's what makes you the person you are, Rollie. Those scars are no different than the color of your eyes or the tone of your voice. They're only a small piece of you." She paused. "They *don't* define you."

He held her gaze for a long moment, realizing his eyes were wide, his stare intense as he replayed her words over and over.

Vivien crushed her cigarette out in the bedside ashtray, her hand moving to his leg, giving it a quick squeeze. "To answer your original question, I just knew, Rollie, that you were a good man. I still do. That's the real reason I wanted to know you better, because I knew your intentions were good. And layered underneath all that I could see some sort of agony. Maybe I was vulnerable after all that happened, I don't know. But I know one thing…"

He raised his eyebrows as he waited.

"I don't have a single regret," she said, finishing her sentence with a smile.

Rollie crushed his cigarette out. He eased her back onto the bed. He made love to her again. Slowly.

Before she slept, he spoke only two more words.

"Thank you."

Chapter Fifteen

April 23, 1943

LIEUTENANT GONZALEZ opened his eyes. The blackness of his sleep only brightened a bit in the dark room, most of his vision now showing a deep gray other than the figure standing before him. It was Captain Garza, looming above him, his silhouette, dumpy with a taut gut, unmistakable as trace moonlight bled through the window behind him. Gonzalez sat up, rubbing his eyes with one hand while the other retrieved his cigarettes.

"I'm glad you're here."

"How did he die?" Garza said, low and raspy. He was probably drunk.

A flash of light erupted with the match. Gonzalez drew on the cigarette, exhaling the smoke downward as he rubbed his temples. "I got a reported sighting and by the time I got there he was dead."

"How?"

Gonzalez stood, crossing the room and lighting his dim desk lamp. "Just a local yokel, a *patán*...somehow our man and the yokel were screwing the same woman. The yokel caught him in the act and killed him."

Garza seemed to accept this. "Where's the man who killed him?"

"I already questioned him."

"And?"

"He knew nothing."

"Where is he?"

Gonzalez cleared his throat. "He's no longer with us."

The captain gnawed the tip off of a cigar, chewing on the end contemplatively. He walked to the double windows, pulling them open as he stared out to the barren street. "We are due to update our contacts today, you to your man, me to mine."

"I know."

"What do you propose we tell them?"

"We lie."

Garza turned, his belly hitching once. "I figured that, Renaldo. But what shall our story be?"

Gonzalez sucked on the morning cigarette, thinking. He'd already thought about it and now ran through the plan again. Satisfied it would work, he said, "First, we need to be cautious. While we might hold sway here in Panama, these men might kill us without fear, emboldened by the backing of their imperialist governments."

The captain snorted as if he was the only immortal in the room. "Go on."

"We tell them *both* we've captured the American and are holding him."

"That might get their attention, Renaldo," Garza said in a superior tone, "but they're going to want to see him."

Standing, Gonzalez crossed the room to his suit coat. He produced the American's passport, shaking it before smacking it into the captain's hand. "We show them this. We tell them if you or I are harmed the American will be killed…then we start the bidding."

Garza flipped the green passport open, studying the picture before viewing the words and various stamps and seals. A smile grew on his face. "Who do you think will pay more?"

Gonzalez jerked open the door, his mouth aimed down the hall to the patrolman's dayroom as he screamed, "Coffee!" He pushed the door shut, answering his captain with another question. "Who cares?"

"How much do you think we should demand?"

Gonzalez walked next to his captain, sitting on the ledge of the window, shoulder to shoulder, as he finished his cigarette. "All of our scams, our petty ploys, our scrambling to make money for our families. They've put me near the top of the heap and you at the top. But the heap we're at the top of is the poor…the wretched." He turned, gesturing with the cigarette butt up the hill to the posh Bethania area. "Señor Captain, if we ever hope to break from the upper ranks of the poor, if we ever hope to have a beautiful casa, a *palacio*, in

Bethania, with servants and multiple bedrooms and running water…if we ever hope to have mistresses fighting for our attentions…to have our jealous wives be willing to look the other way rather than risk losing us…if we hope to have all that and more, then we need a true payday, such as this one can be."

"You must think this dead man held a great secret."

"Indeed, I do."

"Again I ask…how much do you think this secret is worth?"

Gonzalez licked his lips. "Ten thousand dollars." *And then I will kill you for your half*, thought Gonzalez, making sure his expression remained stolid.

Garza's pockmarked face twisted into a frown upon hearing such a farfetched amount. But slowly, the face melded into a wicked grin as he digested the huge sum, not unlike a great snake that has to unhinge its jaw to accommodate its prey. "Yes," the captain whispered. "Ten thousand dollars, and…each day it's not paid…an *extra* thousand."

They both laughed at this wonderfully wicked plan.

Garza was due to meet his man first, the tall Englishman, in the center of the bayside Parque Urraca at noon. Gonzalez was due to rendezvous with his American man at seven in the evening. In the meantime, they had a lot to do.

A baby-faced policeman arrived with two steaming mugs of coffee. As they clinked the mugs together, both taking a sip, Gonzalez read the captain's face and wasn't at all surprised that he knew exactly what the man was thinking.

He's thinking about killing me too.

AROUND THE same time, Maria awoke to a sharp pain in her stomach. She had been sleeping on her back, the soldier position, which was normally the way she slept. As she blinked away the blurriness and fog of sleep, she could see the Prussian standing over her, still naked. He was leaning over her body. After blinking a few more times, her eyes cleared enough to see that he was brandishing a long, narrow knife—the type she'd seen attached to the end of rifles. It was not a stubby bayonet, either. This was more of a piercing dagger. It must have been hidden in his clothing somewhere because, when they'd quickly undressed, she'd only seen his handgun. Less important, she noticed that in his left hand was a pillow.

The Prussian had positioned the knife just above her navel, poking downward on her taut skin as his sinewy arm shook with tension.

"Know this," he said in Spanish. "I've been watching you, so consider this a test. Fail it, and this knife will come out your back while I clamp this pillow over your face."

Fighting back hysteria, Maria swallowed forcefully. "What test?"

His words were slow, with pauses between each one. "Did you make contact with Samuel Fields?"

"I told you the truth already," she growled, fully awake now and pleased with her anger rather than the fear that most people would display.

"Did you see him?"

"I did *not*."

"Did you learn anything?" he asked with a cock of his head.

"Just stab me," she said. "Stab me and kill me now, you bastard."

He pressed harder, sending a stinging voltage of pain through her as a tiny dot of blood appeared from her stomach. Maria bit her lower lip as she moved her eyes back to him. "Stab me!" she yelled.

"Did you learn anything tonight?"

"I'm not telling you anything until you pull that knife back."

His arm continued to quiver, like an arrow pulled all the way back on a taut bow. She could see deliberations warring behind his eyes before he snatched the blade away, holding it threateningly as he straightened. "You better talk."

Maria dabbed the wound with her finger. "You're a savage."

"You'll get a lot more than that if you don't start talking."

She glared at him as she propped herself up on her elbows. "I met a couple tonight…I think the man is from the American government, and he had a large scar on his neck. They had pictures of Fields." Maria held the "Richard" revelation back on purpose.

"A couple?"

"The man was with a woman, and I think she may have been Fields' wife."

"How did you manage this?"

"Don't worry about how I managed it. But just know I'm meeting them tomorrow." She glanced out the open window to see a strip of pink on the eastern horizon. "Today, actually."

"And what did you learn?"

"I didn't learn anything but I played it perfectly to get more when I meet them."

"Did they give you anything at all?" he asked. She noticed his deep breathing.

"I *said* he must be from their government. He's smart—he wasn't volunteering anything. But it's obvious he's looking for Fields, too."

The Prussian lowered the knife, tossing it on a stack of clothes. He chewed a fingernail, spitting it on the floor as he stood looking at her through slit eyes. "How did you know who they were?"

"Well…" Maria said, purposefully using a patronizing tone, "…when the man with the scar jammed Samuel Fields' picture in front of every person's face in the bar, asking us in English if we had seen him, that kind of tipped me off."

Alarmingly fast, the Prussian grasped her bare arms and lifted her off the bed, holding her suspended. "Are you certain?" he growled. "There can be no mistakes…absolutely no mistakes!"

She pressed her lips together, accepting the situation as it was, telling herself to stay calm. "The picture was him…Fields. The American man is dragging the woman around, looking for anyone who knows him. They're trying to find him just like we are." Bernd dropped her. Maria caught herself as she tumbled to the floor, falling to one knee before standing again. "I'm guessing it's important we find him before they do?"

He'd walked to the open window, lighting a cigarette as he stared out over the city. A full minute passed before he answered her, his head shaking. "You have no idea how big this is. If they find him…"

"Like I said," Maria replied proudly, "I have a meeting with them today."

"The meeting," he said, turning and tossing the cigarette out the window behind him. "The meeting…when is the meeting?"

"Six in the evening."

"Where?"

"You're going to like it."

"Where?" he asked, taking a threatening step toward her.

"There is a hill near La Boca, near the canal."

"Yes?"

"A hill with nowhere to run…nowhere to hide."

"But isn't the American Zone by the canal?"

She made a dismissive motion with her hand. "I already scouted it. The Americans claim both banks of the entire canal but you won't find a soul patrolling anything but the area around the locks."

"With the war they're stretched too thin," Bernd added.

"Exactly."

"You're certain this meeting site is a good one?"

"I was trained by the finest military tactician in all of Cuba," she snapped, faking her bravado. "I know a bald hill when I see one. They will have *nowhere* to go. You can capture or kill them, the choice is yours."

The Prussian smiled. Squared-off white teeth glinting in the scant light. He was no longer the handsome man with a chiseled body and knowing hands. She saw him at the center of a dark aura—the opposite of a halo. This man was pure evil.

His head turned sideways, so he was viewing her from the corner of his eyes, divining her, looking into her soul. Then she watched as his prick began to harden, levitating skyward, pulsing, threatening.

"You would have killed me tonight," she whispered, defying her fear.

"And I still will," he responded, shoving her back on the bed.

The sex was again rough and powerful. Experienced in unwilling sex, Maria made sure her moves and reactions seemed genuine.

But they weren't.

She was no longer remotely aroused by him. She was afraid. Very afraid.

In a hurry to be done with their copulation, she made her language vulgar, her ribald words having the prescribed effect.

And though his was certainly genuine, on this occasion her climax was faked.

LATER THAT morning, as the Cuban woman slept, Bernd donned the previous night's clothes and, after helping himself to a cup of genuine coffee at the café attached to the hotel (and taking the cup with him,) he walked to the American Express office in the central San Francisco neighborhood. Using a stubby pencil, a cigarette dangling from his mouth, he filled out the brief form to send a telegram, along with an accompanying wiring of money, to a man named Dario Cortez in Havana, Cuba.

Bernd paid the extra dollar fee to have the message personally delivered to Cortez, listing his address at a hotel near the center of Havana. The message was meant to appear innocuous, just a few mundane sentences dealing with instructions about the supposed care of the sender's home while he was abroad. This, of course, was code. The money was to pay for a prearranged contract, and the coded message was the initiation of that contract.

The contract itself had been agreed upon an hour after Bernd had hired the little Cuban whore's boss, a haughty Brit named Philip Carlton, a homosexual. Dario, a vicious little local who came highly recommended, was to make sure Carlton and his older lover were together. Bernd's instructions were explicit: kill them and make it look like a murder/suicide. As soon as the Cuban authorities put two and two together, learning the men were lovers, the case would be open and shut.

Once the fussy American Express clerk made certain everything was in order, Bernd counted out fifty-six American dollars—fifty for the contract, five for the wiring and telegram, and one for the personal delivery—signing his false name afterward.

He was due to meet the Napoleonic police captain in a place called Parque Urraca at high noon. Before then, he needed to get some food and additional ammunition.

Despite his "bed head" and disheveled appearance, there was a kick in Bernd's step as he walked back to his hotel. His preparations appeared to be paying off. With the entire Panama City police force hunting for Fields, and

Bernd's plan to kill his American opposition, Bernd's ascension to a high position in the Nazi Party was all but engraved.

Things were looking up.

IT WAS nearly noon before Maria stood from her bed. As the sun moved higher the room had grown stifling, leaving her body sticky from a night of sweating and raunchy sex. Usually by this hour she was famished, but today she wasn't hungry at all. After drinking most of the pitcher of purified water, she made her way to the bathroom where she thoroughly bathed, also brushing her teeth with vigor. She was sore after the marathon session with the big Prussian, and unlike her normal fleshly liaisons, this one did not serve as a warm memory. It occurred to her she didn't even know his name—not the real one or the pseudonym he was probably traveling under.

Back in the room, Maria braided her hair, putting it up to keep it out of the way. As she dressed in her commoner outfit, she focused on each of the things that had bothered her about the Prussian. Indeed, she still considered him evil: a self-serving organism with no respect for human life. While she regarded herself as a person with scant social morals and a skewed sense of allegiance (especially when money was involved), Maria still valued the human heartbeat more than anything on earth. She could think of a number of things she would threaten a person with before she would even consider harming them. She thought back to the big Prussian menacing her with his bayonet. The damned thing had been quivering from pent-up force, making her wonder if he'd actually been hoping she would deceive him just so he'd have a good excuse to kill her.

She lit a cigarette, shaking out the match as she readied her items to leave. Maria paused at the window, staring eastward, back to Cuba, imagining the money she would be due if she delivered this Samuel/Richard to the Prussian. Philip had promised her half and he would certainly pay; she trusted him as much as any soul on earth.

But do I really want to turn someone over to that Prussian maniac? I need to talk this through.

Philip…

If only she could make contact with him. Never before had Maria genuinely feared for her life. That episode last night shook her to the depths of her soul, and to think he wanted sex afterward. The man was an animal. A beast. Assuming the two of them happened to find the American, what then? Would he simply pay her and walk away? An ominous warning from the depths of her mind made her shake her head as she involuntarily whispered, "No."

He would kill her, and probably Philip too. They were nothing to him. Just disposable tools which would have no use after the job was over.

Maria crushed out the cigarette, feeling slightly better for having thought things through. While she was indeed scared of the Prussian, she wasn't hopeless. Before her father died, before she'd even turned ten years old, he did his best to drill an ideology into her head. Often phrased in different ways, the premise was the same: *No one's going to do it for you.*

The room was paid for another week. She left her things other than what she needed for this evening. Hurrying, Maria departed the hotel, seeing people dozing in the shadows as the sun blazed forth overhead. The sky was gassy white, the temperature probably hovering around a hundred degrees. At the next hotel (in case the Prussian had her hotelier in his back pocket) she rang the bell at the desk. When a sleepy clerk appeared, she asked where she might make an overseas phone call.

"You can go to the American Express and try," he said yawning. "Otherwise, I think you'll have to send a telegram."

"Can I not do it here?" she asked, pouting her lips out, resting her bosom on the counter.

"It's not possible," the man said, seemingly unaffected by her show. "Our line is local. Everyone's is."

Dejected, she asked for directions.

Maria proceeded to the one and only American Express in the city. As she learned upon her arrival, like so many other businesses, they were closed from eleven until two for siesta—it was now eleven-thirty. The clerk, however, was not taking a nap. As she viewed from the corner of the large window, she could see him behind the counter, reading while munching from a plate of food, his feet propped up on the desk. He appeared to be in his mid-twenties and bookish, wearing thick spectacles. Flashing a friendly smile, Maria rapped on the door.

He didn't even look up, yelling, *"Vuelve a las dos!"* in the manner of a person who has said the same phrase a thousand times.

Maria licked her lips, cursing herself for not paying more attention to her looks back at the hotel. Her eyes floated downward as both corners of her mouth turned up. *What would I do without my beautiful girls?* With a practiced hand, she flicked open the top three buttons of her mottled cambric shirt. Reaching inside the shirt, she unclasped the cheap hand-woven bra, leaving it in place but allowing it to spread open. She pulled the shirt wide so that half of her breasts were visible and, making her smile dazzling, she drummed on the glass with her long nails.

The clerk's brows lowered as he jammed a finger into his book, irritated by the interruption. His mouth opened to yell as his eyes came up, but the words never came out. Instead, Maria could see him blink several times as he drank in the glorious décolletage jiggling mere feet away.

She clasped her hands in a prayerful motion, mouthing the help-needed Spanish phrase "Ayúdeme." As her *pièce de résistance*, Maria lowered her hands, jutting her chest forward.

After his book fell to the floor, the clerk ran to the door.

FOR SUCH an urban setting, Parque Urraca was lively with nature's song. It was perhaps the size of two or three city blocks, ringed by a stone wall and two-deep around its edge with palm trees and thick flora. Once inside the vegetation, Bernd could see why the captain chose it for their meeting.

The interior of the park was essentially a grassy glade, protected from the stink and bustle of the city—an enclosed urban oasis. Parts of the field were well-worn, probably where the poor youth of the city played fútbol. But it was the birds in the surrounding trees that made all the noise. Bernd looked around him as he walked, seeing colorful fowl of all varieties cawing to their hearts' content. A skirmish erupted in a tree off to his left, causing a hundred birds to reposition themselves as their cacophony heightened. Bernd pressed forward. The captain had obviously ordered the park cleared for their meeting, as dual officers rested on the stone wall at each entrance to the noisy glade.

Surprised that the two policemen at the west entrance had not searched his bag, Bernd felt his heart thudding as he stepped closer to the waiting captain. The little man was standing in the center of the park, thumbs hooked in his belt mere inches away from his twin revolvers. While Bernd was dripping sweat in the broiling heat, the captain appeared as cool as a man standing on the shore of the North Sea. Bernd trudged forward, gritting his teeth at the arrogant posture of the little infidel.

"Stop right there," the captain yelled in Spanish, raising his hand like a traffic cop.

Bernd complied. They were twenty feet apart.

"Place your things on the ground."

Again, Bernd complied.

"Are you carrying a pistol?"

"Two."

"Put them down."

"Not unless you put yours down first," Bernd replied, also in Spanish, slowly wiping facial sweat with the back of his sleeve, careful not to appear to be drawing on the man. He wouldn't put it past this little savage to have a sniper somewhere, hiding in the thick vegetation, the steel sights of an Argentinian Mauser centered on Bernd's glistening head.

"Then keep your hands in front of you and," Garza grinned a smile that contained no humor whatsoever, "whatever you do, don't appear threatening."

Yep, a sniper.

"Come forward so we can speak at a normal tone."

Bernd stopped a few feet from the captain. "What's with the birds?"

"Poachers, Señor Lancaster, they are everywhere in our forests and jungles and these birds, smart as they are, know it. The poachers kill the adults and rob their nests for the tame babies, and they sell them to cute little families in America, and England, and *Alemania*." In Spanish, Alemania means Germany, and the way the captain spoke it, and the way his yellow crocodile eyes twinkled, indicated to Bernd that he somehow knew he was a Nazi. Score one for Napoleon, although Bernd really didn't give a damn what the captain knew. As soon as he had the goods, he planned on never coming back to this overheated slice of hell on earth.

"So the birds are protected here in the park?"

"*Sí*. As am I, Señor Lancaster."

Bernd fought the urge to wipe away a drop of sweat that had beaded on his nose. He cleared his throat once. "Have you found Samuel Fields?"

The captain tilted his head backward, a smug look on his face as he repositioned his thumbs over the shiny brass of his bullets. It was an unmistakable victory pose. "Before we discuss that, señor, I must inform you that things have changed."

"Oh?"

"Indeed. There is another highly-interested bidder for Señor Fields."

Bernd thought about the couple Maria had met. He remembered what she said about the man having a large scar. He eyed the captain as he pondered a bluff, deciding almost instantly to play it.

With an unconcerned laugh, Bernd looked away as he spoke. "You must mean the American, the one with a great scar on his neck." He turned his eyes back, seeing the jolt pass through the captain's face.

Direct hit, you little bastard.

"The scarred American is of no worry to me."

The captain recovered quickly, but the smug look was gone. "Perhaps you *should* be worried. He has offered much more than you have for Señor Fields."

"I'm really not in the mood to be talking about money when you haven't produced anything as of yet."

The smugness returned as the captain chuckled self-indulgently. "And what if I have?"

"Enough games. If you have something, prove it."

Lifting the dirty button-over flap of his breast pocket, Bernd watched as the diminutive policeman slid out what looked to be a passport. He proffered it, the leafy gold letters facing upward. Unable to breathe, Bernd accepted the booklet, knowing what was inside before he even opened it. When he did, he did so quickly, the picture and name confirming what he already knew.

"Where is he?" Bernd asked.

"Somewhere very, very remote, Señor Lancaster."

"And what do you want for him?"

"Ten thousand American dollars." The captain sucked his teeth, eyeing Bernd through slits.

Bernd took the sum without so much as a blink. The vindictive side of Bernd wanted to inform the captain that his bidding war was severely flawed, especially since the American man with the scar would be dead by sundown. But he couldn't do that. Not yet. Not until they had a deal. To do so beforehand would put the Panamanian at a weaker bargaining position, and might cause him to reach out to the American and warn him in an effort to get more money.

Or—definitely the worse of the two possibilities—he might just have Bernd killed.

Over the years, like so many other agents, Bernd had siphoned much of his so-called "enticement and operational" money off for himself, scrubbing the cash clean and tucking it away in a variety of foreign banks under a multitude of fabricated identities. Though he'd done a fine job in creating his nest egg, spending ten grand here would wipe out a third of his net-worth. But, with an opportunity to eliminate the American and perhaps even take Samuel Fields alive, it would be money well spent. Besides, Bernd wasn't yet convinced that this unsophisticated little Panamanian wouldn't slip up at some point. If he did, Bernd would kill him without hesitation. The ultimate coup would be netting Fields and his precious intelligence without spending an American dime.

"Ten thousand, you say?"

"Sí."

"That's too much. I don't think I can get that for you."

"Then I shall go to the American."

Bernd flared his nostrils, pretending to ponder the situation. The only sound for a full minute was the birds. Finally, he said, "If I *can* get you ten thousand?"

"Then we have a deal."

Bernd raised a solitary finger. "But will I have your word you will not speak to the American?"

"Of course, señor. No communication at all."

"Why did you come to me first?" Bernd asked suspiciously.

"We may be under American influence here...but we hate them." The captain extended his thick hand.

"When can I see Samuel Fields?"

"When can I have my money?" the captain countered.

Bernd knew he would have to wire Mexico for it. There wasn't enough time today to do it. "Probably tomorrow, if all goes well."

"You can have him when you bring me my money."

The captain's hand was still extended. Bernd took it and, as he shook it, he said, "I will pay you under one condition."

"And what is that?"

"I want your personal guarantee of immunity if something were to happen to the American, the one with the scar, and any of his associates."

"Ah," the captain replied, pulling his hand back. "Señor Lancaster, for all I care, once we are in agreement and you get me my money, you can chop him up and feed him to the gulls in our shit-infested bay. Is that satisfactory?"

"It is. But for the ten thousand, I want one more thing."

Garza let out a long breath. "What is it?"

"Ten men, armed with rifles and sufficient ammunition."

"For what?"

"Backup."

"When?"

"Today. Good men, who will take orders from me and shoot to kill if needed."

"As much power as I possess, señor, we cannot have a firefight in the city. The imperialist Americans would lose their minds."

"We won't be in the city," Bernd said.

"And where will you be?"

"To the west, in the jungle."

"Ah...I believe this area has become known by a name given by your imperialist people...the hinterland." Garza pronounced it like, *"heenterlan,"* again tipping Bernd to the fact he knew he was a Nazi.

"Ja, *das Hinterland*," Bernd replied in German. "But I, sir, am Prussian."

"I don't care," Garza said flatly. "And I want an extra thousand for the armed men, and I can only provide six, not ten."

Bernd thought for a moment. "Fine. Add in a truck, but not a dollar more."

"When can you pay?"

"I can produce ten-percent today," Bernd replied. "The full amount, as I said, probably tomorrow."

"There will be no Samuel Fields until you produce the full amount, and no men and no truck until the ten percent."

"Agreed. Shall I bring it by the station?"

"I'm going there now, Señor Lancaster."

"Have your armed men standing at the ready behind the station at five this afternoon."

"Done."

"Your men better be good."

"And you better have my eleven hundred dollars."

Both men dipped their head in agreement. Bernd backed away.

"Señor."

Bernd stopped.

"Señor, if you try to double-cross me, I will instruct the entire citizenry of Panama to tear you limb from limb."

Bernd took the threat without reaction. "As I promised, I will pay you today, and I will pay you tomorrow."

As the captain turned to go, Bernd yelled his name. The captain stopped and turned.

"And, señor capitán, if tomorrow, you do not produce Samuel Fields as advertised, I will call down the entirety of my brethren on your pitiful fleapit of a country."

Threats made, the captain laughed as he sauntered away.

Little prick.

The two men headed off in different directions, both wondering how they could get what they wanted without giving all they'd agreed to. Bernd needed to find his Cuban whore so he could update her on the new plan for tonight. The captain needed to find Gonzalez, to tell him to postpone his meeting with the American with the scar.

It was to be an evening to remember.

Chapter Sixteen

Maria Fuentes chain-smoked as she wandered the streets, trying to make sense of it all. She halted in a shady area of a side street, standing under an overhang as she leaned back against the wall, tilting her head skyward in an effort to stop the tears. It didn't work. She flicked the cigarette into a puddle before burying her face in her hands, shuddering.

She didn't want to believe what she had just learned.

The helpful man at the American Express spent a full hour trying to reach Havana. Being siesta, it was difficult to even find operators willing to make the necessary connections. He eventually got through, immediately telling Maria the connection was very bad. She stood there watching him as he yelled the address into the phone, telling his Cuban counterpart to go and retrieve the silver-haired man for an important call.

"If he's not at home, ask any of the locals about the man called *El León*."

"And hurry," Maria whispered.

"Hurry!" the clerk yelled, smiling at Maria.

She clasped her hands together in thanks, rewarding him as her boobs pressed majestically together.

"It's very important!" the clerk yelled as a follow-up. "Leave the line open so I don't have to connect again." With a satisfied nod, he placed the earpiece down and looked at Maria, his eyes still warring over which of her luscious features to focus on.

"My associate says the address is not far away. It should take ten minutes to get there and back."

"Thank you so much, señor." They made small talk and Maria was more than surprised when he didn't make a pass at her. As the conversation grew more mundane, she inquired about his job.

"It's usually quiet unless the sailors come ashore. Today, however," he said with a frown, "even without sailors, it's been quite busy. A bunch of wires and exchanges. But you've made it quite rewarding."

"Thank you," Maria beamed, checking the time. "So, do you think the man in Cuba will do the job as you instructed?"

"I hope so. In fact, I've worked here a year and never sent a cable to Havana, but you're the second person to communicate with Havana today."

"How interesting," Maria said, hardly paying attention. Had she not spent her night sexing a madman, she might even consider a quick tryst with the bookish clerk. He was sort of cute and, occasionally, she enjoyed giving a man a sexual experience he would carry his entire life, still bragging about it in his old age. But black thoughts dominated her mind as she pondered how to handle this Prussian. She was actually flirting with the notion of killing him.

The clerk held the earpiece to his ear after about five minutes, waiting for his Cuban opposite to return, going on to Maria about how he planned on eventually moving to Canada. "They have everything the United States has and more, except they aren't saddled with such a large economic base to guide their thinking. With their copious natural resources, I truly believe they will be the dominant world power by nineteen-sixty, seventy-five at the very—"

He stopped, his eyes cutting down to the phone.

"Is he back?" Maria asked.

The clerk held up his hand. His face darkened, transforming to a horrified expression. "I can barely hear you over this bad connection. Say that again!"

"What?" Maria asked, reading his face.

"Are you sure?" the clerk yelled. "Did you speak with someone who would know?"

Maria's heart lurched. She stepped forward. "What? What happened?"

The clerk continued to hold up his hand as he concentrated on what was being said. "The woman is standing right here. I don't want to tell her that unless you are absolutely certain!" After a moment the clerk nodded resignedly, placing the earpiece back into the cradle.

"What is it?" Maria asked, heart pounding.

"There were police everywhere around the home when the man from our Havana office arrived. He asked several people what had happened, finally learning from one of them that your friend, and another man, were both found dead. Gunshot wounds. He said it looked as if one killed the other, then took his own life."

Maria's hand had reflexively shot to her open mouth. She backed up, a piercing scream erupting in her brain. The clerk had come around the counter, placing a consoling arm around Maria though she barely felt it. Her mind was in Havana, thinking about Philip, with that bizarre Webley & Scott automatic pistol of his still clenched in his hand, lying on the floor of his grand mansion, dead. Enrique wouldn't be far away, probably dressed in one of his beautiful pastel suits. A quarrel that went too far, she thought.

The clerk didn't charge her anything for the call. She could tell he was compassionate as he continued to ask her if she would be okay. Even through her grief, Maria made a mental note to stop back by after this was all over. Perhaps, with all the resources at his disposal, he could help her depart Panama once she fixed the situation with the Prussian.

Since learning of Philip's death, for the past hour, she'd wandered the barrio in a fog of anguish. What on earth could Enrique have said that would have set Philip off that way? And it would have definitely been Philip who would have done the shooting—there was no doubt in her mind about that. While cultured, he had a dangerous temper lurking below the surface. Especially when he was drinking.

Maria dug into her bag, producing the old pocket watch she carried. She had almost another hour before she was due to meet the Prussian. She lit another cigarette, dreading seeing that vicious beast. What was it Philip had called him? A Burgandian? She nearly chuckled at the warm memory of Philip's expansive vocabulary, sucking on the cigarette as she ambled back into the blazing sun of Avenida Balboa.

She froze.

The clerk at American Express. He said he'd been busy. Wires. Exchanges. And I wasn't even the first person to communicate with Havana that day. I was the second.

Pulse pounding against her temples, Maria tossed her cigarette and sprinted back to the American Express. She had one more question for the clerk, even though she felt she already knew the answer.

EARLIER, FOLLOWING the highs and lows of the sleepless night before, the morning had been as glorious as any Rollie had ever enjoyed. Setting aside the deliberate search for Richard, other than keeping their eyes peeled, Rollie and Vivien walked the city after sunrise and enjoyed a breakfast of fruit and strong local coffee at a downtown café. As the two of them had enjoyed their third cup, Rollie spoke further about his experience in the Chaco War, this time doing so in a lucid manner, with no terror or accusations of her prying. His trust in Vivien grew rapidly, making his heart flutter over the intense way she stared at him while he talked.

When the talk of Chaco wound down, Vivien touched the back of his hand. "You didn't sleep last night."

"We were busy," Rollie remarked.

"Afterward."

"I was just on edge."

"I felt you trembling a few times."

Rollie didn't respond.

"Talk to me, Rollie."

"It's embarrassing."

"I want to know."

Eyeing her, Rollie said, "Since my injuries occurred, I've depended on a narcotic to sleep. I also sometimes took it during the day, when things were bad. It was a type of morphine, made from opium. And I haven't had any in five days."

"Why on earth would you be embarrassed about that?"

"It's weakness."

She shook her head. "Rollie, stopping cold is not how you break a habit like that. That's why you look sick."

"It's better now."

"Have you slept?"

"A few naps, here and there."

"Did you take it all the time?"

He shook his head. "No, I did *not*. Mainly only at night or during times when my scars split open. But my body grew used to it at nighttime."

She rubbed his hand. "You need sleep."

They walked back to her hotel in the late morning and, from her purse, Vivien showed Rollie a small white bottle. "This is laudanum."

"What are you doing with that?"

"I don't use it often, but I always travel with it. Take some." She pushed it into his hand.

Rollie stared at the bottle. "No."

"I want you to take some and go to sleep."

"Vivien…"

"You cannot function without sleep, Rollie. I insist you do this."

Vivien had a type of influence over Rollie unlike anyone else he knew. In fact, the only person he could recall with such sway over him was his long-dead mother. He'd taken laudanum a few times when he'd been without his morphine. Suddenly, Rollie's sweats returned, starting at the palms of his hands and spreading to his face and body. His mouth became dry and he could feel his throat constricting. He handed the bottle back.

"I'm fine, Vivien. Please, trust me on this."

She tucked the laudanum back into her purse.

After a moment of awkward silence, Vivien led Rollie to the bed. "We've lots of time, Rollie."

"Yes, we do."

"Make love to me."

A half-hour later, Rollie fell asleep without the aid of an opium-based narcotic. It was a deep, satisfying sleep. Though it was only four hours, the rest was medicinal.

When he awoke, as Vivien still slept, Rollie hurried to his hotel to retrieve his extra pistol cartridges. He stopped along the way, having another genuine cup of strong coffee, unable to get enough after the shortage back in the states. As the caffeine stimulated his mind, Rollie pondered the afternoon's planned rendezvous at La Boca—there was something bugging him about it that he couldn't quite put his finger on. Usually when his gut told him something was wrong—something was wrong. To combat the uneasy feeling, Rollie had learned to be extra vigilant with all preparations.

When he reached his hotel, meaning to change into more utilitarian clothing, his train of thought was derailed by a small stack of correspondence awaiting him with his key. There were three envelopes, all in the hotel's stationery. He didn't pay much attention to the unmarked envelopes, assuming they were just bills, tucking them into the pocket of the utility pants he planned to wear. Though he was in a hurry, the third envelope grabbed his attention—it was marked in chancery cursive with "de la policía" in the center. Rollie ripped it open.

He sat on the edge of the bed and read the note; it was from Lieutenant Gonzalez. The police lieutenant and his men were busy chasing several leads and he would need to push his meeting with Rollie until noon the following day. Unless he heard otherwise, they could meet in the lobby at Rollie's hotel.

Not knowing how long the meeting with the young woman would take later today, Rollie was fine with the delay, though mildly perturbed at the lack of progress. Deciding not to dwell on it, he quickly changed clothes, donning the utility pants and loading both cargo pockets with all eight of his cartridges, each loaded with high-velocity .38 Super ammunition.

Arriving back at Vivien's hotel with a sack of street food, Rollie knocked and announced his presence. She opened the door, asking how he slept.

"I feel so much better," Rollie answered, giving her a kiss. "I think you wore me out."

Once he was in the room, Vivien commented on his outfit—thick utility dungarees, a black shirt, and tanker boots—immediately mentioning her need for something more practical.

"Brought some food," he said, lifting the bag and ignoring her comment.

She took the food, pausing to read his face. "What's wrong?"

"Nothing."

"Did you hear what I said about my clothes?"

"I'm going alone," he said firmly.

"The hell you are."

He shook his head. "No, Vivien. I don't trust that girl any farther than I could throw her."

"Neither do I," she said with a knowing nod. "She's already sacked my *ex*-husband—you think I'm going to give her a shot at you, too?"

"You *already* don't trust me?"

"Okay, that wasn't fair," she replied. "But as far as me not going, it's not even worth discussing…because I *am*."

"Vivien…"

She stepped to him, cupping his head in both hands. "No argument, Rollie Donahue, okay? I am a grown woman and I take responsibility for my decisions. You didn't take my laudanum, and I didn't argue. But this warrants an argument if you persist."

He was silent as he pondered her demand.

"Rollie…" she said in a warning tone.

Exhaling loudly, he nodded resignedly.

After pecking him on the lips, she slipped on her wedges and buttoned her now-dirty blouse, her mouth twisting as she stared down at her clothes. "I'm sure you're so excited to see this outfit again."

Rollie looked her up and down. "You're beautiful."

"Not in this tattered getup I'm not."

"Believe me, you are." He motioned outside. "Maybe we should go shopping at one of the street bazaars, get you some things that are a bit more practical?"

"That's fine, but do you think I need something more practical?"

"This place we're meeting her is rugged."

"Why did she want us to meet her way out there?"

"Like I said…"

"You don't trust her," she finished for him. "Don't you have to meet the policeman later?"

"Not now I don't. Let's eat this fast and go shopping."

Vivien nodded her approval as she viewed her clothes with obvious disdain. "Going shopping is the *second*-best idea you've had all day."

He kissed her; then they ate from the sack of food. It was a struggle for them both, but after eating they managed to disentangle themselves and depart the stifling room.

Unbeknownst to either of them, they would never come back.

A HALF-HOUR before their big payday, Captain Garza and Lieutenant Gonzalez were rewarded with an unexpected visit. Their visitors didn't stop at the front desk, striding by the desk *sargento* with arrogant authority, a transgression that normally would result in their being shot. But these visitors were better armed than anyone on the local force. The first two carried massive American Colt .45 pistols; the trailing four men, all well-muscled United States Army military policeman, each carried their M-1 carbines at port arms. In all, the six men wore grim faces and appeared ready to shoot the first person who protested their presence.

Gonzalez was marking on the blackboard in the room next to Garza's office. Garza was seated, his legs propped up, arguing each point with his subordinate. They were discussing the $9,900 balance of money that was due to be paid to them tomorrow, and how to lure the Nazi into a seemingly safe area where they could arrest him and take the bribe money, plus whatever else he had on his person. They planned to charge him with a number of crimes, including blackmail and sexual solicitation of a police official. By adding these charges, they would eliminate the German as a future threat, and possibly wipe him from the earth, depending on the mood of the animals inside La Joyita prison.

Both men turned as they heard the sound of heavy boots approaching. A loud voice thundered down the hallway, speaking Spanish, saying, "Where the hell is Captain Garza?"

Before Garza could even stand, two men entered the room, one in a sweat-stained suit and the other in U.S. Army fatigues. Behind them, the beefy military policemen stood at the ready, snorting like bulls in a pen. The uniformed officer, a major Garza had seen before, did the initial talking.

"On your feet, captain," he said in Spanish. "Habla Ingles?"

Garza glanced at Gonzalez, who appeared mystified and crestfallen. Whatever this interruption meant, it couldn't be good.

"Habla Ingles?" the major repeated through clenched teeth.

"Yes, I do," Garza replied sullenly, his golden eyes downcast.

"Major Melton, from the American Zone. Behind me are some of my men, and this is—"

"Nicholas Penland," the man in the suit said crisply, cutting the major off and stepping in front of him. "I'm with the United States government, and as a government employee of Panama, our ally and occupied territory, I expect complete cooperation from you. As you know, we're at war and I'm here because of the war. Anything I sense from you that's deemed uncooperative will be dealt with harshly, possibly by death. Do you understand?"

Garza listened to the preamble and asked, "Of what do you speak?"

Penland motioned Garza and Gonzalez to the table, reaching into his jacket and producing a photograph. The man in the picture was posing, unsmiling. It was the type of photo one might find in a service jacket or on a passport. His head was tilted downward, but the large scar on his neck was unmistakable.

Penland stabbed the picture. "This is Roald 'Rollie' Donahue. He is the primary target of my search."

He produced another photo, taken on a busy street yet quite clear. The man was handsome, his fedora cocked as he strode with a cigarette dangling from his mouth.

"And that's the other object of our search. Secondary, but important nonetheless. His name is Richard Hampton, although he is likely here under an alias."

Garza swallowed thickly, turning to Gonzalez, who nodded almost imperceptibly. Garza had never seen Rollie Donahue but remembered Lieutenant Gonzalez's description of him. He had, however, seen the other man's photograph—the one the Nazi called Samuel Fields. And he knew, according to Lieutenant Gonzalez, that the Hampton/Fields man now lay dead in a Casco Antiguo hotel room, rigid and certainly stinking by this point.

"And why do you seek these men?" Garza asked.

Just as Penland was about to reply, a commotion erupted in the hallway. The M.P.'s were yelling at someone who was yelling back at them in Spanish. They weren't letting the Spanish yeller through. Penland stepped into the hallway and stopped the M.P.'s, telling them to take the man's weapon and let him into the room. A Panamanian policeman wearing Great War-era web gear and an old helmet pushed his way past. Garza, eyes intense, shook his head at the man as if trying to pass a message.

The policeman, a sergeant, glanced back at the M.P.'s who had just roughed him up, seemingly bewildered. He didn't catch the gesture from Captain Garza.

"What do you want?" Major Melton asked in Spanish, his eyebrow cocked.

The sergeant moved in front of Garza, dutifully popping his heels to attention. "Sir, the man are assembled in the truck as ordered."

"What men are assembled?" Melton asked.

The sergeant's mouth parted as he glanced at Garza for direction.

"Talk to *me*," Melton growled, jerking the policeman's combat suspenders.

"Señor, we are only following our captain's orders, something about working with a gringo."

Garza and Gonzalez both closed their eyes, shaking their heads.

The major relayed the man's words, in English, to Penland.

"What orders?" Penland asked the major. "And what gringo?"

It was Gonzalez who spoke up, making Garza shoot a death glare in his direction. "Gentlemen," he said in English, taking a step forward. "We are working with a third man, and it's related to the two men you seek."

"Working with a third man to do what?" Penland yelled.

Gonzalez avoided his captain's eyes. He stepped to the table and poked the picture of the man with the scar. "We are working with the third man to find this scarred man in the picture…to find him and kill him."

Penland's nostrils flared. While Garza, an accomplished poker player, expected an explosion of anger, he was quite surprised to see a flicker of pleasure cross the gaunt American's face.

The American, Penland, tapped the picture of the handsome man on the street. "And this man?"

Gonzalez visibly swallowed. His voice was a croak as he said, "He is dead, señor."

Garza, given his expression, might have seen a troupe of ghosts.

But Penland straightened, asking, "Are you certain?"

Gonzalez's smile was obsequious as he said, "Oh, quite certain."

SITTING AT a table as a fan whirled overhead, an untouched pitcher of fruit tea before them, Bernd von Danzig and Maria Fuentes were going over the plan for the third time. He was due behind the police station in ten minutes. The café was only a minute away, and Bernd had his hand clamped on Maria's wrist as he finished his instructions. Using her sharp fingernails she peeled his fingers away, eyeing him with contempt.

"Do you think I'm stupid?" she asked, feeling her face quivering.

He eyed her curiously. "We're repeatedly going over this because I can't leave anything to chance."

"Your plan is simple, which it would *have* to be, coming from you."

The Prussian snorted, appearing more than a little bit surprised at her sudden edge. "Simple or not, can you handle it?"

"I can handle *anything*."

"Repeat it back to me."

"Again? Well, again I ask, do you take me for a complete fool?" She purposefully used a tone that, to a keen listener, might indicate a double-entendre.

The Prussian narrowed his eyes, looking like a person who felt they weren't quite getting all the story. Finally he said, "Just repeat the plan."

"I leave right now. I walk through El Chorillo and, at exactly five minutes before six, I walk to the top of the hill at La Boca and stand there to draw them out."

"Very good. And?"

"And once they arrive, I jerk my pistol from my bag and, without any hesitation, I shoot the man in the groin or lower stomach."

The German nodded but then lifted his finger. "He's highly trained."

"I can draw very fast," she countered. "I told you this already."

"There are arteries where you're planning to aim, so try not to hit him in his upper leg. Between the belly button and his *pequeño* cock would be best."

"Because you want him alive."

"For a while, yes."

"Then I step backward but keep them both under the aim of my pistol."

"And that's when I, and the Panamanians, will arrive."

She arched her eyebrow. "And that's when *Philip* and I get our money?"

"When the job is *done*. This is only part of it."

She glared at the Prussian, never taking her eyes off of him as she tapped out a cigarette. Clamping it in her mouth, she asked, "Should we call him?"

"Call who?"

Maria lit a match and held it to the cigarette, puffing twice before shaking the match and dropping it into the ashtray. "Philip," she said, exhaling into the fan's vortex. "Should we call to update him?"

Bernd's expression was even and without reaction, the quintessential liar. But his pupils constricted immediately, something not even the most accomplished deceiver could prevent. As casual as if they were on a fifth date, he reached over the table, took the cigarette from her and took a long drag. With a glance at his watch and a shrug he said, "There's simply no time."

Maria flashed a dazzling fake smile and stood. "Then it's time for me to go."

He stood also, his tone serious. "Are you sure you can do this?"

"Oh...I'm quite sure I can do my part." She leaned forward. "As you'll soon find out."

"Are you irritated over something?" he asked.

One corner of her mouth ticked upward and then Maria turned and stalked off to the west, walking to La Boca.

Bernd von Danzig watched her go. He stood still for a long time, his eyes narrowed as his mind raced. What had gotten into her? Eventually he looked at his watch again, turning and heading towards the police station.

VIVIEN AND Rollie walked back through the inland portion of the city, making their way toward the canal and the hill at La Boca while navigating the edge of the Panamanian jungle. To their left was an industrial district and, on their right, at the very edge of the wilds, a garbage wasteland. Massive fences had been erected, tilted toward the garbage, aimed at keeping the refuse of the city contained. While Vivien wanted to move inland several blocks—explicitly to avoid the rancid smell—Rollie insisted they stay at the jungle's edge. They had a half-hour before they were due to meet the young woman at La Boca. Ahead of them, the sun sinking down just above it, Rollie could see the hill, the only topographical relief on this side of the canal. Why there? Why would a girl, a dish like her, choose to meet at the edge of the Panamanian badlands?

Vivien's hand found his. She swung it cheerily, beaming at him. He smiled in return, but his mind was troubled. Rollie's eyes wandered back to the dump. Greenish vapors could be seen rising from the filth as the garbage combined with the resident heat to create a mélange of acrid toxicity. But even the noxious wall of waste couldn't hold back the jungle. Tentacles of vines had pressed their way through several hundred yards of rubbish, emerging through the fence and clawing out into the street. Trees erupted through the filth, growing skyward in a sign that the jungle couldn't ever be stopped. Behind the garbage the jungle was a wall of blackness, the only sign of life the cawing of the resident birds.

He tugged on Vivien's hand, stopping her.

"What is it?" she asked.

Rollie stared at La Boca, shaking his head back and forth. "Something isn't right."

She chewed her lower lip, remaining silent.

His eyes were narrowed. "Why would she suggest *that* hill?"

"If I remember correctly, she said it had some connection to Richard. And she said she could show us something important in the canal from that vantage point."

Rollie turned to Vivien. "You've got a good memory. I must have been distracted by you when she said that."

"Or her," Vivien said knowingly. She eyed the hill. "It is quite stark against the flatlands around it. Do you still want to go?"

Rollie closed his eyes, pushing his thumb and index finger against his eyelids, massaging them. After a moment he nodded. "Yeah, I do. But I want to recon that hill from someplace safe."

"Where would that be?"

"There," he said, stabbing a finger at the jungle. Pulling her along, they turned into an access road that cut right through the filth, probably where the garbage wagons entered. Rats the size of cats occasionally scurried across the road, making Vivien yell out in fear, laughing afterward each time. With Rollie holding her hand, they pressed forward, entering the damp jungle a half mile from the hill at La Boca.

Picking their way along, edging toward the hill, Rollie searched for a suitable vantage point.

Chapter Seventeen

IT WAS the exact same alleyway Bernd had met the captain in two days before. North-south, the alley was protected from the setting sun. And with a southern breeze from the Pacific, the evening was quite tolerable. Bernd entered the alley from the north, seeing the rickety old American Mack AC truck, the type used in the Great War by the tens of thousands. Trained in the silhouettes of hundreds of enemy vehicles, Bernd hoped the Panamanians didn't pay much for that old piece of scrap metal. The Americans probably gave them away just to get rid of them.

The truck was facing him as he approached. He could hear the nervous conversations of the men sitting in the back, no different from soldiers of any nationality, outfitted for a battle but clueless as to what the mission might be. Feeling slightly jumpy himself, he produced his pistol, holding it against his right leg as he poked his head around the canvas of the truck to see mostly middle-aged Panamanian policemen in the back. One curled his lip, aggressively asking Bernd who the hell he was and what the hell did he think he was doing approaching an official vehicle.

Keeping the pistol hidden behind him, Bernd slid it into his waist band, appearing completely unconcerned at the challenge. "Where is Captain Garza?" he asked with a sneer, bettering the policeman's crude Panamanian-Spanish with his own high-Veracruzana accent.

"Our *sargento* went inside to get him. Are you the man who we're to help?"

Another one chimed in, nodding. "Gonzalez said he was a *gringo*." He scowled at Bernd, "So, *gringo*, you wanna tell us what the hell is going on?"

Bernd lit a cigarette, ignoring them as he stepped to the rear door of the station. Just before he reached for it, the door banged open, followed by the sound of numerous heavy footsteps coming from inside.

First through was an older policeman, dressed in the same gear as the men in the truck. He was probably the sergeant they'd mentioned. Following him was a senior policeman who Bernd hadn't yet seen, his rank evident by his polished cross strap and belt. He covered his highly-oiled hair with a service cap upon exiting. Garza should have been next.

He wasn't.

Bernd stiffened upon seeing an American exit, dressed in the familiar khaki summer fatigues Bernd had seen in so many Pacific war newsreels. He held a shiny Colt .45 in his hand and walked with a typical American swagger, leering at Bernd as he bounced down the three stairs. The flat ground of the alley revealed him as quite short.

Doing his best to disguise his shock—his mind was clamoring to know what the hell was happening here—Bernd raised his cigarette to his mouth in order to partially conceal his face. The American was followed by four more Americans, military policemen, all as large as Bernd or larger.

Heilige Sheisse!

Well, this was it. Somehow they had discovered Bernd's true identity and were planning to snatch him right here on the spot. He'd be placed in jail for a week before they would move him to the U.S., probably detaining him at Fort Leavenworth or maybe even that maximum-security hellhole he'd read about, located in San Francisco Bay—Alcatraz. He shuddered to imagine what the inmates would do to a Nazi spy. And the interrogators, they'd whip him with a rubber hose until they drained him of every ounce of information—then they'd allow the prisoners to have their way with him until shock took over and he finally passed on without ceremony. The Americans would send word to the Reich, probably through the Spanish embassy that, while his treatment had been excellent, the detained prisoner, von Danzig, died from an unfortunate heart attack due to a preexisting condition.

Bernd cocked his brow. But if they *were* preparing to arrest him, then why did the American soldiers move to the other side of the stairway and fall into a two-by-two formation? And why was the slick-looking Panamanian policemen giving him an "everything's all right, I hope you will still pay us" look. And why was Garza now exiting the building, nodding confidently at Bernd and wearing the same look as his slick partner.

The last man to exit the building was tall and thin. His head matched his body, high and skeletal with a hawkish nose. He had baby blue eyes and the pale skin of a person who spends too much time indoors. The high-quality suit he wore appeared to be worse for the wear, as if it had been on his body for several days. As soon as the man turned to Bernd, his eyes widened a fraction. Bernd took another drag on the cigarette, lowering his head as he exhaled.

What the hell just happened?

Garza approached him. "These Americans are looking for the same man you are." His voice lowered to a raspy whisper. "Our deal is still in play, yes? My men are here, the truck is here, the deal is still on."

Bernd eyed Garza for a moment before dropping his cigarette, grinding it under his shoe. He cleared his throat, putting on his best perturbed British accent as he gestured to the uniformed Americans. "Who the bloody hell are you pillocks? This was supposed to be a discreet job, not a sorry excuse for an American western."

The American officer, wearing the gold clusters of a major, took a step forward. "I hear you contracted these men."

"Correct."

"Then you mind telling me who the hell you are, and where you get off setting up an op in an occupied American territory?"

"Harold Lancaster, of the United Kingdom. And what I'm doing and why I'm doing it is a few notches above your pay grade, *major*."

"Look here, pal," the major said with a twang, reminding Bernd of that memorable young American actor, John Wayne, in *Stagecoach*. "I gotta canal full of Allied ships two miles away that I gotta try to protect with only a handful of M.P.'s. I got every foreign agent from Japan to Germany to Russia to pis-ant Liechtenstein prowling around the *avenidas* of this here city, and you don't get a free pass just because you can put on some fancy East Anglian accent and recognize my rank." He raised his .45 to waist level, not yet aiming it, but punctuating his bluster. "Now either you produce some orders which, oh by the way, I'm going to verify…or you put your fancy hands up against that wall there and spread 'em."

Bernd's eyes flicked down at the Colt. The little bastard had his finger on the trigger and, given his bravado, Bernd didn't put it past the major to kill him here and now. There was a war on—and killing, to certain types, was like a sport. The military police behind the major were tensed, each of them holding their rifles at a ready state. Garza had stepped to the side, mouth parted in dismay as he was no doubt *only* concerned about his payday, probably already wondering if he could somehow pilfer the money in the event Bernd was shot or arrested.

Bernd breathed in through his nostrils, deciding that a power-play was his only option. He could pretend to retrieve his orders, yanking his own pistol out and shooting this sloppy American who was too stupid not to search him before making a speech. And, even though he put his own chances of escape at less than five percent, he already hated the undersized major and would rather go out by killing him in a blaze of glory than tied to a rack in prison.

But then things changed.

"Ease up, Melton. I know all about this Lancaster fellow."

It was the gaunt American, leaning casually against the stone wall as he lit a cigarette, flicking his silver lighter shut, puffing away. Everyone stopped and looked at him, waiting on him to expound.

He didn't. Instead, seeming unconcerned, he picked a piece of tobacco from his tongue.

"You know him?" Melton finally asked.

"I know *of* him—are you deaf?" the gaunt man snapped.

Major Melton appeared hurt, and the mysterious American's stock immediately soared with Bernd von Danzig.

"Well, sir, I…ah…well, I have to say that here in Panama the military is the authoritative body and, well, if the colonel had been in country today he would have—"

Ignoring Melton, the gaunt American looked at Bernd. "I'm Nicholas Penland. We haven't met but I've been working on this with Reginald Lane from over in MI5. He told me you were down here."

Bernd, for lack of anything else to do, nodded, managing to mutter, "Good."

Nicholas Penland clamped his cigarette between his lips, producing a folded sheet of paper from his pocket. He shook it audibly until Melton took it. After a deep drag on his cigarette he said, "That's an order signed by Henry Stimson, the United States Secretary of War. Below Stimson's autograph is the signature of William Leahy, the Chief of Staff to the president. I would have gotten more signatures, Melton, but simply didn't have the time." He snatched the order away and replaced it in his pocket. "Now, I really hate to be a horse's ass and pull rank, but this is a joint operation that we've been working on for ages. You've been a good Joe so far, and if you keep it up you'll get a nice little commendation that'll go a long way to turning that gold leaf to silver." Penland straightened. "What are your questions?"

Melton swallowed. Twice. "Well...how do we help?"

Removing his sweat-stained coat, Penland gestured Melton and the two Panamanian officers to a spot away from the rest of the soldiers. Bernd stood where he was, unsure of what to do until Penland twisted his head around. "Well don't just stand there, Lancaster. Get over here and let's diagram this thing out."

Bernd exhaled for the first time in a full minute. He moved between the men as Penland used a pocket knife to scratch a rectangle into the alleyway's dirt floor. He lifted the knife to Bernd and said, "Lancaster here is hot on the tail of a rogue American named Rollie Donahue. Rollie, now a traitor, worked for me, so you might say I have a special place in my heart to nab him."

"What did he do?" Melton asked.

"He betrayed our country and her allies," Penland replied without hesitation, staring at Bernd as he spoke. "Right, Lancaster?"

"Right-o," Bernd replied, still wondering who this man was.

After handing the pocket knife over, Penland eyed Bernd. "Show us exactly what you've got laid on for the traitor."

Bernd had no clue—none whatsoever—about what was happening here. But knowing a good deal when he saw one, he leaned over the makeshift sand-table, surrounded by his Reich's bitter enemies, and gave the men a workable plan for how they would kill one of their own.

ONCE NEAR the hill's base, Rollie could see why the girl chose La Boca as a vantage point. Completely out of place in the low flood plain, it rose smoothly from the ground, gently rising to an elevation several hundred feet above the wide waters of the Panama Canal's southern entrance. The bottom of the hill was covered in trees and thick vegetation but, for whatever reason, the top half of the knoll was blanketed only in long grass, waving in the evening breeze, breathing as if the hill were alive.

Rollie situated himself and Vivien so that the hill obstructed their view of the canal, but provided him with a viewpoint of the girl's (or anyone else's) likely avenue of approach. On the hill's south and east sides lay shacks and a stubby, leaning water tower that looked like it might topple at any minute. Rollie and Vivien were tucked back into the front line of thick vegetation, gazing due south. Each time Vivien tried to speak to him, he held up his hand, silencing her.

The sleep he'd had had been heaven sent. And now rested, he was unwilling to allow carelessness or impatience to rule him. Rollie scrutinized every trail, every road, and every house that bordered the backside of the hill. He was searching first for human movement, then for surveillance clues of any type. If the girl was alone, he wanted to be supremely confident there was no one behind her, preparing to rush in for the kill. Because, while he knew coincidences occur, Rollie still found it too fantastic that—on the very night he and Vivien arrived—a girl who knew Richard Hampton made what was supposed to be incidental contact with them. Especially in a city as large as this one.

Something besides the sea of garbage definitely stunk.

Satisfied that there was no one nearby, other than a group of children playing, Rollie had just begun to explain what he was doing when the young woman, Maria, emerged from the middle avenue, striding confidently toward the hill. Unlike the night before, she was now dressed like a local, wearing a common shift and flat sandals. Her hair was pulled into a tight bun and, despite her youth, she wore a grim face.

Vivien searched the area behind Maria. "She appears to be alone."

"Let's watch," Rollie replied, placing his hand on her shoulder to keep her in place.

Maria entered the thick ring of vegetation at the bottom of the hill, disappearing completely. As they waited on her to emerge, a distant gunshot behind them made Vivien jump while Rollie turned and peered through the jungle. Birds could be heard screeching in the distance. There was another gunshot, then silence. The second shot confirmed for him that both came from at least a mile away.

"Poachers," he whispered, having read about them in the State Department's mostly canal-oriented brief on Panama. He turned his eyes back to the hill, seeing the woman emerge from the flora of the lower half and steadily climb the hill. It must have been rocky under the grass because, although she made good time, she occasionally had to pick her way to the top. The wind blew her shift against her well-proportioned body as she stood at the summit, turning slowly, waiting.

"Are you ready?" Vivien asked.

"In a minute," Rollie replied, turning away from Maria and again scanning the adjacent area. The kids still played. The shacks stood quietly, their loose tarpaper intermittently fluttering in the breeze. The leaning water tower stood sentry over the area. There was nothing to give him pause.

Although he'd checked it three times, Rollie removed his Colt .38 Super and checked that a round was seated. He took several deep breaths, keeping the pistol in his right hand as he gave Vivien a reassuring nod.

"Let's go."

MARIA CAUGHT their movement as soon as they emerged from the sea of jungle to the north. The man carried something dark in his right hand, surely a pistol. Given the fact that they were hiding and watching told her they were suspicious—and they should have been. The man led the woman westward, entering the thicket around the base of the hill from the canal side. This would allow them to reconnoiter that side of the slope while shielding them from prying eyes on the developed side. The canal behind them would prevent an ambush from the rear.

She was dealing with a smart operator.

Given what Maria had planned, it gave her a small measure of relief.

THE OLD Mack AC was parked five blocks south of the hill, in a small plaza surrounded by dilapidated businesses. The six armed Panamanian police were in the back. The two senior police officers had ridden motorcycles here and were still sitting on them, talking nervously while parked in front of the truck. The four beefy M.P.'s smoked and chuckled over something, parked on the other side of the plaza, shoehorned into the rear of a Jeep. Major Melton, Nicholas Penland and Bernd, still acting as Harold Lancaster, were standing behind the Mack truck, discussing the basics of the plan.

"No matter what," Nicholas said to Melton in a tone dripping with condescension, "do *not* allow Rollie Donahue a single gap to get off that hill. If I know him, he's hating having to even ascend a hill like that, leaving himself so out in the open." Nicholas jabbed a bony finger at the major. "Donahue was a decorated Marine, with plenty of combat experience. Don't let him get the drop on you."

"I thought you said he was a traitor."

"He is, Melton!" Penland bellowed. "But he was born an American, and served as a Marine. That too hard for you to comprehend?"

Bernd looked at his watch. "They're probably in place by now."

"Don't worry," Nicholas replied, still eyeing Major Melton. "Rollie will be late if he even shows at all. His hackles are on end right now, I can assure you. And if he's stupid enough to go up there, he deserves what he's going to get."

Despite the reassurances, Bernd was still on edge. On edge because it was nearly time, and on edge because he was surrounded by the enemy—with no clue about why this Nicholas Penland had taken his side.

Nicholas pointed to the street beneath him as he spoke to Major Melton. "Stay right here and make sure our makeshift squad is ready to take that hill, and give each person explicit instruction about which part of the hill they're to cover."

"Like the sand-table Lancaster drew back in the alley," Melton said.

"Just like that. And make damned sure your overstuffed M.P.'s and these locals know east from west."

Melton made a big show of cocking his Colt. "I'll take care of it."

Nicholas produced a small pair of binoculars, hitching his head to Bernd. "Let's have a look, Lancaster." He led him to the westernmost building, marked by a hand-painted sign that read *Carnicería*. Holding his compact pistol in front of him, Nicholas walked to the door, checking the knob. It was locked.

"Give it a kick," he said to Bernd.

Splinters flew as Bernd kicked the brittle door inward, his pistol out and ready. Nicholas followed, brushing past Bernd. The rickety stairs were at the rear, a straight shot heading up toward the front of the building. Bernd stayed just behind Nicholas and, when they were halfway up, a stunned man appeared at the top, wearing unbuttoned trousers and an undershirt. In his hand was a dangling newspaper. He began yelling in Spanish, gesturing wildly until Nicholas reached the top of the stairs, pressing the three and a half inch barrel of his Smith & Wesson .35 to the resident's nose. Behind the man, down a short hallway, a woman appeared, screaming in sheer terror. Two children, probably fraternal twins, clung to her leg.

"Tell them to shut up and they won't get hurt," Nicholas said, eyes never straying from the man.

Watching his moves, Bernd could tell he was a good operator. "*Silencio!*" Bernd yelled, motioning downward with his hands.

"Good. Now, tell them to go in that room at the end of the hallway. Tell them to lock the door and be quiet," Nicholas said in a calm voice. "All we want is the use of their back room for just a minute. Tell them we only need to get a good look at something behind their home."

Bernd quieted the woman, speaking rapid-fire Spanish as he approached her with his pistol down by his side. He dug into his pocket and pressed a few crumpled bills in her hand. He then pulled the butcher by his upper arm, translating what Nicholas had said, shoving him into the room at the end of the hallway with his wife and kids.

"No one leaves this room," Bernd said in Spanish. "We'll be gone in a few minutes."

The butcher, obviously scared but trying desperately to be a proud man, didn't respond. Instead, he puffed out his chest, tilting his chin upward. He didn't defy Bernd either. Bernd said the words again, and this time the wife nodded, closing the door and locking it with a click.

Bernd walked back to Nicholas. "Done. They won't come out until we say so."

They moved into the back room where Nicholas pointed to the only window. "Open it." Bernd opened the window and stepped back.

Nicholas held the binoculars to Bernd, gesturing to the west. "Recon the hill."

Bernd eyed him through slit eyes.

"Go on," Nicholas said, pushing the binoculars into Bernd's hand. Nicholas still held the pistol in his right hand.

After a great breath, Bernd dropped to his knees, keeping his own pistol in his right hand. With his left, he held the compact binoculars to his eyes and rested his elbow on the humidity-warped window sill, focusing on the hill at La Boca.

"There's my girl," he said, gesturing with his pistol. "No sign of your boy Donahue or the wife. Not yet anyway."

There was a metallic click just behind Bernd's head—the unmistakable sound of a quality handgun being cocked. It was followed by Nicholas Penland's haughty northeastern accent as he said, "Don't so much as twitch, or our butcher friend here will have a lot more than pig blood to clean up."

MARIA STOOD at the apex of the hill, hands on her hips, watching as the couple picked their way up the remainder of the slope. The man arrived first, careful to stay far enough below her level so his profile wouldn't be visible from the other side. The woman stood to his side. Both were winded from the rugged climb.

"I have to tell you something," Maria said without preamble.

The man appeared to read her eyes, his hand coming up.

"Wait!" she yelled without gesturing. "We're being watched, and what I have planned won't work unless we play it perfectly."

"The hell are you talking about?" the man yelled back, his eyes whipping in all directions.

"I'm not Panamanian; I'm Cuban. And I'm also *not* alone."

Again his hand moved, this time aiming his pistol from his hip.

"Please," Maria pleaded. "Listen to me. I don't think he can see you because he's supposed to be behind me, on the front side of the slope." She swallowed, making a small movement with her hand. "But if he sees you with that pistol, the game is up."

"Listen to her, Rollie," the woman said.

The man held his pistol in place. "Then you better explain real quick."

And Maria did, telling the man called "Rollie" everything in less than a minute. She told them about her professional relationship with Philip. She told them she'd performed various assignments before this one. And she told them her mission here: to find Samuel Fields. And just as the man, Rollie, was about to speak, she cut him off with a halting hand.

"But I now know that the man I'm working for here is a savage. He threatened to kill me, and just hours ago I learned that he sent word back to Cuba…"

"And killed your boss," Rollie answered for her, doing so with a knowing nod.

"Yes." Maria felt her eyes well with tears.

The wind whipped and buffeted the top of the hill, making each person's clothes furl and pop. No one spoke for a full minute. Finally Rollie lowered his pistol, tucking it behind his back.

"I'm confused," the American woman, Vivien, said to Rollie.

Rollie took Vivien's hand, squeezing it before he turned back to Maria. "I'm not saying we'll comply with anything, but what do you propose?"

"My plan *will* work," Maria said. "But it involves a bit of deception."

The two Americans looked at each other. "What's the plan?" he asked.

Maria took a step down the hill. "The first order of business is determining if you're a good shot."

Rollie offered a rare smile.

BERND KNEW this gaunt American behind him would shoot him if he didn't comply. He slowly lowered the binoculars and his pistol, turning his head in a smooth motion. After studying the barrel of the pistol, he looked up at Nicholas.

"Place the lenses and your pistol on the floor." Bernd did. "Good," Nicholas crooned. "Now, raise your hands. Do it slowly." Bernd did, slowly. "On your feet," Nicholas commanded, wagging the gun away from the window. The room they were in was a bedroom, and he instructed Bernd to sit on the narrow bed, causing it to squeak.

"I'm quite afraid I don't know why you're doing this," Bernd said, making sure his British accent contained the ingrained Anglo polite indignation.

"I saved you earlier in that alleyway."

"Because you said you knew about this operation," Bernd said.

Nicholas ran his tongue over his teeth, nodding once. "But why I said that isn't what's pressing. The pressing question is, 'Who?' As in, 'Who the hell are you?' And don't feed me any more bullshit about Harold Lancaster in Her Majesty's service."

Bernd shifted on the bed. "Shall I make up a porky then?"

"What?"

"A porky. An enormous lie."

"So they taught you slang, too, did they?"

"They?"

"You know who taught you." Nicholas Penland's face split into a knowing grin. "A fine job they do over there."

"Over where?"

"C'mon, pal...you know, there in Berlin, the section that's under the command of Oberst Lars Ruff."

It was all Bernd could do not to show reaction.

"You can let down your front," Nicholas said. "Just as they did with your English accent and words, they taught *me* all sorts of American slang, vernacular, colloquialisms...regional stuff mainly...before they slipped me into Vermont to take over a dead man's life. That's been," he searched the ceiling, "my word...ten years ago now."

Bernd's throat was so constricted he could barely breathe.

"C'mon, Lancaster. You know what I'm talking about," Nicholas chided. "I believe language is now taught on Prinz-Albrecht-Strasse, although when I came through we were in a small school on Seegefelder, under the watchful eye of Commandant Ruff...surely you remember him. As far as I know, he's still there."

"Those places and names sound *German*."

"Indeed, they are."

"And you're admitting to me that you're actually German?"

There was a very long pause as the two men shared an electric glare.

"Are you?" Bernd asked.

"Indeed, I am German, *Herr Lancaster*. And I have a strong *Vorahnung* that you are, too."

Bernd von Danzig, light-headed, allowed himself several great breaths.

Nicholas raised the revolver, aiming it at Bernd's face, his long finger visibly tightening on the trigger. Bernd had always bragged that he wasn't afraid to die, but while he'd flirted with death on a number of occasions, he'd never been presented with a choice. And as scrawny as this slightly hunched, cadaverous man first appeared, Bernd now had zero doubts that he would blow him away right here and now.

"Drei...Zwei...Eins...*Nul*."

"Ja, Ja," Bernd implored, eyes clenched shut. "I'm Prussian, actually."

There was a period of silence.

After what felt a full minute Bernd opened his eyes, wondering if this was a technique the Americans were using to root out Nazi agents. Perhaps the revolver was loaded with inert rounds and the pressure the man put on the trigger was all for show?

"Prove it!" Nicholas growled, twisting the pistol.

Bernd spit out the first verifying fact that came to him. "Heike von Braunfels...she was the deputy chief of the language school when I went through and, you're correct, officially it was located on Prinz-Albrecht-Strasse but..."

The so-called American, Nicholas, appeared triumphant. "But what?" he asked with a smirk.

"But most of my true learning occurred in Frau von Braunfels's large iron bed."

Nicholas eyed him for a moment, his thumb magically rising to the hammer as he applied even more pressure, uncocking the pistol and allowing the hammer to gently kiss the strike-plate. "Ah, old Heike…how I remember her. She is still insatiable, ja?"

Bernd closed his eyes again, this time in relief, as he exhaled a long breath. "She *was*, but that was seven years ago."

"She's probably fifty by now," Nicholas said distantly, sliding the pistol into his shoulder holster. "Probably gray now and showing some wrinkles. Does she still take the girls too?"

Bernd mopped sweat from his forehead. "There was a saying at the school: unless you're a eunuch, your biggest test will occur with your clothes off."

Nicholas eyed Bernd. "You're *Der Geist?*"

"A ridiculous sobriquet."

"I've read about you in a those coded briefs they send out. Didn't they send you to Mexico?"

"Unfortunately, yes."

Nicholas chuckled as he lifted Bernd's arm. "Come on, stand up," he said, giving him a quick hug and clapping him on the back.

"Were you really going to shoot me?"

"Without question."

"How did you know? What tipped you off?"

"I get fragments of things, bits and pieces. I've known for years that we, meaning 'the Americans,' were working on the atom bomb. But unless one is specifically placed on a team that's working on it, it's impossible to get a whiff of what's happening."

"But how did you know I was getting the designs from the man known as Samuel Fields?"

"Richard Hampton."

"Whatever."

"Rollie Donahue, who works for me, has been following Hampton. He's the one who put it together that Hampton was selling something."

Nicholas pushed a cigarette into the corner of his mouth. "It wasn't until after Hampton was gone that I learned he was involved in the atom bomb project. And I assumed, correctly I now see, that he'd made a deal with our Nazi brethren."

Bernd was troubled. "But if Hampton is dead, who has his data?"

"I'm hoping we'll learn more from the two Americans meeting on that hill," Nicholas said.

"The Americans don't have anything," Bernd protested. "Because why would they even be meeting Maria if they did?"

"How were you to get the data from Hampton?"

"He was to contact me by mail, setting the meet."

"Do you *know* he's dead, or are we just going off of what those Panamanians said?"

Bernd shook his head. "Not for certain, no. I know what you know."

"So he could be alive?"

"Maybe," Bernd allowed. "And if he is dead, I'm guessing he stashed the data somewhere nearby."

"And the Panamanian officers had his passport," Nicholas said. "They are likely the key to finding the data."

Nicholas lifted the binoculars and eyed the hill. "They're all up there now. Rollie Donahue," he murmured, more to himself than to Bernd. "I can see that hideous scar from here. And look at Hampton's wife. No wonder you were so eager to come here, Rollie. Can't find a woman to touch you so you try to be a hero in the hopes one might pay you a nickel's worth of attention." Clucked his tongue. "Not today, Rollie old boy, not today. *Heute ist für deinen Tod.*" Translated, his prophetic declamation meant, "Today is for your death."

Nicholas lowered the binoculars and turned to Bernd. "His scar is his calling card, per se. It's massive, down his neck and body, dating back to a sealed incident when he survived an attack of some sort that killed everyone else." Nicholas snorted. "Someone in our unit felt he was owed a living because of it, so I inherited him. As much as I dislike him, I have to give him credit. He began to piece things together about Richard Hampton that were compartmentalized, things I didn't even know."

Bernd was trying to be patient but gestured to the hill. "It's past time. We can discuss everything later." Snatching the binoculars from Nicholas, he focused on La Boca. Maria was at the very top, the breeze making her pauper's shift whip in the strong breeze. She was now aiming her pistol with both hands, looking back over both shoulders as if she was wondering where Bernd was. Standing on the other side of her, partly obscured by the hill, Rollie and Maria had their hands up.

"Sheisse! She's already gotten the jump on them," Bernd yelled, grabbing his Browning Hi-Power from the floor. "Hurry! I'll explain everything in the truck."

With a claw grip on his shoulder, Nicholas halted Bernd at the top of the stairs. "We will use these Americans and Panamanians to kill Rollie Donahue. He *must* be killed."

Bernd nodded his understanding. "Then we will deal with everyone else?"

"Except the Panamanian officers. They will need to be questioned. After that we can take our time ripping this city apart."

With a mutual grin, the two undercover Nazis thundered down the remaining stairs.

The butcher and his family didn't open the door until the following morning.

"WHAT THE hell are you waiting for?" Rollie yelled, having been standing with his hands up for nearly five minutes.

"He was supposed to step forward soon after I pulled my gun," Maria replied, continually looking back at the alleyway that fed into the base of the hill.

"Was he with you?"

"No, we came independently here in case you followed me." She turned to Rollie. "I only agreed to all this in the hope that you would help me kill him. We *must* kill that bastard."

"If he shows," Rollie remarked.

Maria turned back, stiffening immediately. "There he is." Her Beretta was trained at blue sky, although Bernd shouldn't have been able to tell from his angle. Making her movement pronounced, she nodded once.

The big Prussian stood stone still. Staring up at her.

"*Avanza!*" Maria yelled, frantically waving her free arm.

He just stood there, a shadow, unmoving. She realized what he was waiting for.

Turning, she gripped the pistol with both hands, taking up a shooter's pose. Without moving her mouth she whispered, "Get ready."

Maria pulled the trigger.

Chapter Eighteen

JUST A moment before, Bernd stared up the La Boca hillside, estimating it would take him two or three minutes to summit. The girl was now waving her hand, motioning frantically for him to come. But, because of the angle, he could no longer see Donahue or Hampton's wife. Regardless, and even from such a distance, he was getting a read on the situation—and something about it was wrong.

All wrong.

Scrutinizing Maria, with her wild gesticulations, her actions seemed bogus. Seemed forced.

And the setup wasn't right. She should know to bring the two Americans around so he could see them. She was many things, but stupid wasn't one of them.

Kleine Schlampe...

Something was definitely amiss.

He hadn't trusted her since watching her on the ship, watching the way she'd effortlessly neutered the old codger. And this Rollie Donahue, a trained field agent of the United States, was no doubt armed, probably to the teeth.

Of course he's armed! Bernd's mind yelled. That being the case, why then would this highly-trained American allow himself to be held by a buxom little Cuban with only a pistol? And the fact that she was turning her head for long periods made her even more susceptible to his rushing her.

Maybe Bernd wasn't giving the little tramp enough credit; perhaps she had disarmed him. But even still—Bernd counted...*eins, zwei, drei, vier, fünf, sechs, sieben*—there! She turned for seven damned seconds to stare down at him, *away* from the American. Even if he was twenty feet down the slope he could have easily rushed her in that amount of time.

Now she was nodding, smart enough to make her movements big enough to be visible over the distance.

"*Avanza!*" came her scream, shrill and distant.

Bernd didn't move. She wasn't even sticking to the script.

Finally, as if she remembered her duties, he watched as she turned, took a shooter's position with her seven-shot Beretta and fired, the dart of flame and smoke visible long before the report of the .380 ACP caliber round reached him.

Bernd donned his hat, stepping forward to a concealed spot under the trees at the base of the hill. Using his hands, he signaled the men. They were at least a hundred meters back, standing in the shadows of a hovel, watching. Bernd made a number of hand motions, simply confirming the plan they'd already created. The first was a wiping across his lip, symbolizing a moustache. This represented the Panamanians, all eight of them. He balled his fists, placing them thumb to thumb, then opened his arms. He finished the motion by turning and arching both hands up then down. *You Panamanians, split and go to the far side of the hill.*

His second hand motions displayed twin revolvers which he mimed drawing from hip holsters. *Stupid, oblivious Americans*, he thought. When he'd made these signals up minutes earlier, they were too stupid to realize he was insulting them with a cowboy gesture. He duplicated the splitting motion he'd given to the Panamanians, but finished by gesturing to this side of the hill. *You American cowboys, if you have enough brains to do it, split up and ascend this side of the hill.*

The third hand motion was quite simple. He pointed to Nicholas, then made a V with his fingers and gestured to his own eyes, then touched his own chest. *Nicholas, my fellow Nazi, you back me up.*

His next gesture involved timing and an overarching command. He touched his left wrist, signifying a wristwatch. Then he pointed to himself and made a shooting motion. *Rush them on my gunshot.*

His final gesture involved his thumb, slashing it across his own throat. He did it twice for good measure. After making the motion, he turned, distinctly stabbing his finger three times to the top of the hill, displaying three fingers afterward.

The final gesture was simple and easily understood: *kill them…kill them all.*

ROLLIE WAS down on his stomach, the pistol trained up at the top of the slope. Per his instruction, Vivien was behind him, slithering backward on the rocky promontory.

"Where is he?" Rollie hissed to Maria. "You should see him by now."

Maria searched, her head moving in several directions. "It's getting dark, especially down in the trees."

Rollie looked to his left, trying to gauge his vision against the shadowy backdrop of vegetation below him. He twisted around to see Vivien, now fifty feet below him. While they were indeed in a twilight situation, he could clearly make her out.

"Something's wrong!" Rollie yelled, now unworried about being heard. He kept looking back at Vivien and that's when he caught sight of movement. Emerging from the thick undergrowth at the bottom of the hillside, spaced about two hundred yards apart, were three men. They were just inside the ring of trees, each picking their way up the hillside, carrying what looked like carbine rifles. They were coming up the *backside* of the hill.

Damn!

"Vivien, get up next to me and do it on your belly! Crawl fast and don't rise up over the grass."

Then, as quickly as he dared risk, Rollie rotated himself on the rocky earth, thankful the grass was higher than the profile of his own prone body. *What is happening? Who are those men?* With a distinct feeling Maria had been double-crossed, Rollie looked to his left and saw something that chilled him to the bone.

There were three more men, advancing in the same manner. Due to the scant remaining light, Rollie was able to better make them out.

Panamanian police.

"Mierda!" Maria cursed, her tone more angry than scared.

"Get down here!" Rollie commanded.

Just as she dove in his direction, the first shot rang out.

UNLESS HE'D just made the luckiest shot since the hapless assassins from the Black Hand happened upon Archduke Franz Ferdinand's wayward motorcade, Bernd assumed the little Cuban whore had seen the soldiers or police and tried to dive to safety.

If she hadn't known the jig was up, she certainly did now. Bernd would have given good odds her gunplay was a ruse—it didn't matter—they'd all know momentarily. Her double crossing him was of no surprise, although a part of him was mildly curious to know what made her flip. Perhaps it was the bayonet to her belly in the middle of the night? Regardless, the situation was under control—but he still cursed himself for not bringing a proper rifle. Bernd would have liked to have been the one to squeeze off the fatal shots. Assuming the Panamanians did their job on the back of the hillside, this should amount to nothing more than a Hessian lord's St. Stephen's day boar-shoot. Bernd looked left and right, seeing the Americans, Melton being the closest, crouched down with a bewildered look on his face.

"Did you not hear me shoot? Rush them!" Bernd yelled with fury, gesturing with his pistol.

Melton nodded and shouted a few commands, followed immediately by his over-muscled soldiers charging the bald hill from the eastern slope.

Bernd would also move, but in good time. While he had no respect for the Cuban or her American friends, he also didn't expect any of them to go down without a fight.

And it certainly wasn't going to be *him* taking their bullets.

ROLLIE SURVEYED the hillside, twisting himself to view all angles of the western slope. He gnawed on his lip for a moment, putting his arm around Maria first, then Vivien, cinching them close on each side of his body.

"What's happening?" Vivien asked, her face a mask of fear.

"That bastard double-crossed me!" Maria seethed.

"No time for that now," Rollie answered in a whisper. The closest Panamanian was now a hundred and fifty yards away. "Assume the other side of the hill looks like this side, or worse. In three minutes we'll be surrounded, and I don't think they're climbing all the way up here just to pass around cigars and ask questions."

"They're going to kill us?" Vivien asked, voice rising.

"They already fired on us," Maria snapped.

Rollie turned to Vivien, gripping her chin with his thumb and index finger. "Listen to me. Our chances of survival, if we panic, are zero. We *will* die." He softened his voice. "But if we keep our heads, we may just have a chance. Do you understand me?" Her eyes were wide, her breaths audible, but his words seemed to have effect as she nodded her understanding.

"Okay," Rollie said, looking at both women. "We have a few advantages…shooting down is slightly easier than shooting up, especially with our short-range weapons. And if we stay low, they can't see us until they're right up on us. But they're moving, making them visible. Our only hope is to take down at least two of these men and streak through the hole in their constricting perimeter."

"But what if there are men behind them, in the trees?" Maria asked.

"Don't think that way," he retorted. "What if there aren't?"

"Are you expecting me to shoot this?" Vivien whispered. She raised the F&W he'd given her from his ankle holster, gripping it with only her fingertips, staring at it as if it were a venomous snake.

"Just relax," Rollie said, touching her hand. "I pulled you both close so we can all fire. We'll create a wall of lead." He pointed at the climbing soldier directly below them. "That's our first target. He *will* kill us if we don't do this." Rollie allowed that to sink in for Vivien's benefit. "When I tell you to, I want you to expend every round you've got. Aim straight in his direction but aim high, maybe as if he's twice as tall as he really is. As you shoot, lower the barrel a tad each time until you're aiming head-high on your last shot. And hold your pistol below the grass when you're firing. Just shoot through it. Understand?"

"He's getting close, Rollie," Vivien warned.

Rollie made his voice soothing. "And he needs to be close. As soon as we run out of ammo, I'll help you reload and we'll shoot that man," he said, pointing to a fat one struggling to come up to the left of their initial target.

"I won't have any more bullets," Vivien said.

"I've got some," Rollie answered, angry at himself for not bringing more than he did. "But don't worry about it. If this first volley works, we can do the second one without you."

GUSTAVO JALISCO had no clue where the three people were. Earlier, he'd seen the woman dive down but, especially with the growing dusk, his vision was not what it used to be. Unable to afford eyeglasses, Gustavo knew he was a liability unless he was to get to close range. Putting on a final burst of speed, he lifted his old Colt Lighting Carbine to have it ready to shoot, leaping up and over a rocky outcrop.

He didn't even see the three muzzle flashes until he was falling backward, his neck and shoulder feeling bee-stung as his body hurtled ten feet down the hill. Small rocks tumbled onto Gustavo's body as he took his last breath, pleased that he could now rejoin his beloved wife whom he'd murdered three years ago in a fit of drunken rage.

"FOLLOW ME," Rollie whispered with urgency, hoping his movements weren't disturbing the grass enough to make them visible. Using a textbook low crawl, he skittered forward and to his left, moving twenty feet as the girls followed. It was imperative they get away from their former location and, sure enough, shots rang out from their left and right, the rounds ripping through the high grass behind them like angered hornets. Had they stayed in place, one of those rounds would have certainly found a home.

Rollie chanced a look to his right, seeing the three Panamanians and a man in dress clothes yelling and moving on the hillside laterally. They were shooting as they ran, suppressing fire, their aim scattered and unfocused.

"Reload," he whispered, happy to see the Cuban woman was adept with her piece.

Again he gripped both women, aligning them next to him on both sides. After wiping sweat from his face, Rollie turned to Maria. "Same procedure, okay?" She nodded.

"What about me?" Vivien asked. "I think I used all my bullets."

"I've only got a few more rounds for your pistol. Just sit this one out."

"He's in range," Maria whispered, gesturing to the heavy policeman below them.

Rollie turned his head back and forth, making sure to make eye contact with both women. "As soon as this next one goes down, stay low, zig-zag, and follow me the hell off of this hill. If you fall, if you break your arm, if you split your head wide open, *get up*, keep moving, and worry about it later." He turned his hand so that it was up and down like a blade, gesturing to a single point of the broad waters of the Panama Canal, right at a bend. "We're already facing the canal, so just keep going 'til you get there."

"Why the canal?" Vivien asked.

"Because if we try to double back, we're going to run into these men. And the canal is surrounded by the American Zone and, in the American Zone I'm hoping we'll find safety."

The rushing Panamanian was seventy-five feet away, his grunts audible as he struggled to climb, firing every few steps. Rollie held his hand on Maria's arm as the man knelt to load the long tube magazine.

"Ready?" he whispered. Maria confirmed with a nod. "Wait 'til he comes up." There was silence as they waited. Rollie looked all around them. They would be overrun in no more than a minute. This *had* to work.

"Rollie," Maria whispered, squeezing his arm. The policeman was up and moving.

"Here we go. Three, two, one, *fire*."

The two of them followed the same procedure, with Rollie realizing he should have reminded her not to shoot too high this time since the man was much closer. Fortunately, near the end of his own clip he saw the man spin to his left and disappear into the high grass as a bullet put him down.

He ejected the cartridge on his heated Colt .38 Super, ramming a third one home and raking the slide. Rollie yelled for the women to go. As they all stood to run, the heavy Panamanian who had just been felled clambered to his knees with a primal yell, lifting his Colt Carbine directly at the onrushing Rollie. Rollie had been covering their backside with his head and pistol aimed up the hill. He turned just in time to see the policeman's bad intentions. Before he could even get his own Colt around and aimed, the man's neck erupted in a shroud of foamy pinkness, sending him tumbling onto his back for eternity.

Still running, Rollie looked over at Maria, running to his left. "It wasn't me," she yelled. He turned back to Vivien, wagging her pistol as she leapt down over a cluster of rocks.

"I had one left!" she yelled with a triumphant smile, sprinting ahead of him.

As the last of the daylight departed, they bisected the remaining men, descending the hill in thirty seconds, ignoring the lead flying in their direction.

"Go, go, go!" Rollie yelled as he reached the tree line. He stood just inside its black shadow, surveying his pursuers' silhouettes as his chest heaved. And for that split second, despite the imminent danger and all that came with it, Rollie felt magnificent. The sky beyond the hill was that glorious shade of deep purple just before the blackness of night takes its full hold. When shadows seem darker than normal and people are nothing more than obscure cut-outs awash in a deep sea of twilight. It reminded him of Chaco, forced into that final valley, before the double-cross, before the burns that charred his body, when he and a small team of capable men held off hundreds with only a few rifles and an unequalled will to live.

But there was something else about this time of day, perhaps embedded in the human psyche. As far back as he could remember, whenever he was in a natural environment, the coming night always made his skin tingle. It took him back to the final moments of long summer days, when Rollie and his childhood friends would convert their daylong game of war into a final match of hide and seek after the sun made its departure, the boys hurrying to get as many rounds in before parents started yelling their names. He remembered, just before joining the Marines, the summer nights in Pasadena, when he'd been lucky enough to accompany a girl on a long evening walk up to Eaton Canyon—his skin tingling due to the anticipation of what the night might hold. Long ago, maybe young males associated the electricity of twilight with a coming hunt, or perhaps illicit sexual liaisons they would do their best to initiate under the cloak of darkness.

Either way, Rollie felt wonderful and relished the adrenaline as it mixed with his blissful feeling for his new lady friend. No matter what happened, even if it killed him, he vowed to himself to deliver her to safety.

The Panamanians were several hundred yards behind him, not even pursuing. He could see them huddled up, well out of range of his Colt, all of them gesturing wildly to one another as their shouts filled the night. They certainly didn't look the part of a motivated enemy.

Nearly ready to run, he peered around the left side of the tree, straining his eyes to see if anyone was pursuing from the far side of the hill. He was just turning when a new threat froze him in his tracks. Clattering around the hillside, rushing like mad bulls, were a number of large figures set off by two distinct accoutrements, both glowing like torches in the night. Like any former soldier Rollie would have recognized the initials, centered on both items, anywhere, at any time of day. The large soldiers' dark helmets were ringed in bright white. Gripping each man's left arm was a black patch. And on both items were the emblazoned letters *M.P.*, standing for, of course, military police.

The United States Army Military Police.

Oh no...

His pursuers weren't just Panamanians, there were Americans, too. And they were shooting at Rollie, yelling at one another, coordinating their movements. When one would stop to shoot, the others could clearly be heard yelling deadly phrases known to soldiers of every sort:

"Kill him!"

"He went in between the two large trees! Kill his ass!"

"Drop that bastard. Put more lead in there!"

For the second time in a decade, American soldiers were trying to kill Rollie Donahue.

Just as he regained enough sense to haul ass, he felt something like a hot poker jammed to his neck. His next sensation was the ground striking his back, and then thick warm fluid soaking his neck and face.

Behind him, waiting on him in a clearing, the two women screamed.

"I GOT HIM!" yelled one of the M.P.'s, his voice heavy with what sounded like an Arkansan twang. "Laid that som'bitch out!" The other running M.P.'s congregated around him as several of them stuffed chaw into their mouths from the same pouch, laughing and congratulating the one who had dropped the running man as if they were on a drunken autumn raccoon shoot.

Bernd arrived at their gathering first, with Nicholas coming around from the other side. The M.P.'s' characteristic American imprudence was shocking to Bernd, even though he was looked upon as cavalier by his rigid German counterparts. He ripped off his fedora, throwing it at them, standing taller than all but one—probably one of few men on the Isthmus of Darien who could actually physically intimidate the assembled group of titans.

"You shot one, but did you get all three?" Bernd yelled, jerking the shooter's cross strap and flinging him aside. "And where's your damned commander?"

Major Melton arrived from the side Nicholas did, after him, both men winded from running around the entire hill. Melton bent double for a moment before straightening.

"I'm right here, and if you touch one of my men again, you and I are going to have a serious problem." He was pointing, his voice tense and shaking with anger.

Bernd listened to the insult before turning to Nicholas who gave him a slight nod. Bernd eyeballed the American major, saying, "Real lead out there tonight, Melton. I understand this is a tad dodgy for you, but my word is final out here, and if you need verification of that, ask Mr. Penland."

The major's eyes moved around the motley crew. His soldiers, typical of lower enlisted, stood quietly while watching the terse exchange between the men of authority. Melton drank them in before turning his head to the Panamanians, just shadows now, standing in a cluster well back of the soldiers. He shot a glance at Nicholas before turning to Bernd, putting his hands on his hips in a defiant pose.

"Let me tell you something, pal, there's two dead Panamanian policemen up on that hill and the rest of them are now scared stiff. These Panamanians don't understand our war and the two who died up there probably did so unnecessarily. To boot, in case you didn't see their backsides when the shooting began, the two local police commanders, Garza and Gonzalez, have taken a French leave, meaning they're probably smarter than the rest of us." Melton wiped sweat from his eyes, lowering his voice and saying, "And like those two cops who just lammed it, I'm not so damned sure I want to risk my career by shooting at people I don't even know."

The major turned to his men.

"That said, who *were* the three people up there? Anyone get a good look?"

The M.P.'s glanced around at one another before one stepped forward from the rear. Bernd couldn't see any features of his dark face other than the fact it was shaped like a frying pan.

"I was closest to 'em, sir. To me theys looked like a man and two women. I didn't see 'em shoot the Panamanians neither. All I seen was 'em runnin' like spring deer down this here hill. Bein' honest, I couldn't bring myself to shoot at the women. The man stopped in thems trees and that's when Fender here dropped him with a clean shot."

"And while we're all here jacking each other off, he's probably up and gone with his two women!" Bernd screamed, interjecting himself.

"No way, sir," the M.P. continued. "He's dead for sure. Neck shot. Even in the dark I seen his red blood go a'flyin'."

Major Melton moved deliberately. He clicked the safety of his Colt and holstered it, pressing the leather flap over the brass stud of the holster's base. "My men and I are off this operation until I get proper orders from a *military* commander."

"Major," Nicholas said softly, "I'm here under the authority of the Office of Strategic Services and the Department of War. Right now, I'm more authority than exists on this entire peasant finger of land and, unless you want to live on the inside of a cell until 1973, I'd suggest you—"

"Saddle up, men!" Melton yelled, turning to his M.P.'s. "We're headed back to the Zone to sort all this out."

Nicholas raised his .45, aiming it at Melton's back. "Major Melton, I can shoot you for willfully disobeying a lawful order by a proper authority."

Melton turned as slowly as a minute-hand, a sideways smile appearing as he stared without fear at Nicholas. He spat at his feet and said, "Something stinks here, sir…stinks like hell. And that's why you're in such a panic to kill those three, isn't it now? I'm fluent in Spanish and heard bits of the whispers of those two Panamanian officers. They had already *talked* to this man we're after tonight. Said something about the *highest* bidder."

"Enough with your blabbering," Nicholas said, still aiming the pistol. "Get on your knees and interlace your hands on your helmet."

"Negative. I'm not buying this bullshit bluff from you and your spook buddy, here." He began to back away. "You can go ahead and try to court martial me if you like…can't wait to see what the brass has to say about it. But for now, we're headed back to the Zone. Let's go, men—we'll check on the ones who were shot before—"

Nicholas Penland shot the Army officer, the .45 sounding like a wheeled Parrot Rifle at close range with the rocky hillside as an acoustic backdrop. Nicholas didn't aim to kill him, but instead lowered the Colt and blew the major's knee nearly in two, dropping the smaller man in a screaming heap. He turned his pistol to the assembled M.P.'s, all of them taking a few steps backward with looks of disbelief at such extreme action.

"Anyone want to question me now?" They were silent. "Someone tourniquet his knee and cuff him. I'll send the medics for him later."

"You bastard!" Melton growled at Nicholas while the M.P.'s jumped into action. "Sonofawhore suit-wearing bastard!" His curses continued, modulated by deep guttural snarls as he tried to deal with the furious onslaught of pain.

After half a minute of urgent whispers among the scrambling M.P.'s, the talker of the modified squad raised his head, his hands holding the tourniquet on Melton's leg. "Sir, we can call back to the Zone on that there radio. And maybe we should anyway, jus' to *verificate* all you done said."

Nicholas, expecting this, turned to the large radio, about the size of a loaf of bread, lying in the grass. There were two more shots from his Colt, blowing the handheld SCR-536 radio to bits without even a spark from the battery.

"We do this alone, men. Finish that tourniquet and get assembled." Nicholas turned to Bernd. "Lancaster, go police up those constabularies and get them over here."

Crickets and cicadas ruled the night as two of the men tied off the lever of the tourniquet to Major Melton's upper leg. Melton had finally fallen silent, his only sound the wet rasping of his breath.

"Can I give him a few sticks of morphine, sir?" one of the M.P.'s asked.

"Leave him all the dope you want. Maybe he'll overdose." Nicholas illuminated his narrow face with his lighter, firing up a cigarette. With smoke escaping his mouth he said, "It'll save him a court martial."

MINUTES BEFORE, just after Rollie was shot, Vivien told Maria to move to the other side of the trees and wait. Then Vivien padded back through the damp forest, thankful for the resident humidity as it silenced her footfalls over the ground vegetation. She found Rollie where he had fallen, his face and neck slick with black blood. He was stone still. Choking back a sob, she chanced a quick look outside of the tree line, seeing a group of what looked like soldiers congregating a few hundred feet away, their black shadows showing them to be much larger than the men who had been on her side of the hill. While she couldn't hear what they were saying, nor did she try, their yelling and frustration was evident. And they were speaking English.

"Rollie," she whispered, dropping to her knees beside him. "Oh, my God, Rollie." The blood covered one side of his face, visible only by its shine. Vivien couldn't tell if he was breathing, touching her hand to his chest.

She nearly screamed as his eyes sprung open, his sclera so white they seemed to glow.

"What in the hell are you doing back here?" he hissed.

Vivien lurched backward, covering her heart with both hands.

"My God," she hissed through clenched teeth, "I thought you were dead."

"Hardly," he replied, propping himself up on his elbows. "Once I realized I'd been shot, I laid here, pistol down to my side. With ten shots, I gave myself half-decent odds of taking at least half of them…whenever they finally stop bickering long enough to come over here to see if they actually killed me."

She lowered her head to his chest and sobbed quietly.

"C'mon, get up," he said, running his hand through her hair. "Cry later, okay? That'll get you killed out here."

Vivien lingered for a moment, lifting herself and taking deep breaths. "How can you sound so chipper after being shot?"

"Bah, passed right through me," he answered, his hand going to his neck. "That's the benefit of having a half-inch hide of scar-tissue." He dug his hand into the damp of the earth, producing a handful of mud and organic humus, smearing it on his neck, working it in. "There, that ought to stem it for a bit."

Rollie came up to a crouch, his pistol extended at the group of men standing on the hillside. Right then a flash erupted, followed by the thundering report. A man fell to the ground screaming a torrent of curses. The flash illuminated the group, confirming for Rollie that they were military police, along with two men in street clothes.

"They're shooting each other," he whispered, as fascinated as if he were watching a good movie.

"Rollie, come on," Vivien whispered, tugging at his arm.

"Wait," he said, his eyes squinting at the scene as if it might help him see better.

After a moment, more pained screams, and a few muffled voices, two more shots rang out. The flashes created by the pistol, aimed at the ground, lit the group of men bright as day a second at a time.

The gunshots had been fired at an object and not a person—but far more pressing to Rollie was the unmistakable profile of the man shooting the gun, illuminated by the flashes. Tall. Hunched. Roman nose on a gaunt face.

"Holy hell," Rollie breathed. He would recognize Nicholas Penland anywhere…his superior…his boss…

His pursuer.

Chewing on his bottom lip, ridiculous, nonsensical thoughts raced through Rollie's mind. The man on the ground, shot by Nicholas, had been an American. Rollie could recall the quick views of his uniform from the three flashes of gunfire, the images burned into his mind as if by light-sensitive emulsion. Why was Nicholas here? And, more importantly, why in the hell was he shooting Americans? Those two colossal questions were only overshadowed by a need to get Vivien to a safer area. He turned to her, dread rising inside him as he gestured her to get going.

Rollie took a final look back, still unsure of what was going on before he followed her.

Nicholas Penland, here in Panama…

…coming after me.

Rollie took off after Vivien, darting through the trees and tropical thickets, to the west, to the canal.

Chapter Nineteen

Once Bernd summoned the four remaining Panamanian policemen, Nicholas led the men forward to where Rollie had fallen. Each person trained his weapon on different fields of fire—the area where the body was presumed to be the most dangerous part, requiring the working end of one rifle and two pistols. After a few moments of searching, Nicholas instructed everyone but two of the M.P.'s to be ready to shoot into the woods. He had the two M.P.'s light their hand-torches, telling them to sweep the area for the body. As they did, Nicholas closed his eyes for a moment, murmuring a German prayer that Rollie would be found dead so he could focus on the two women that had run off. Catching them (with only Bernd's assistance) would be a cinch.

"Blood right here," one of the M.P.'s yelled. He hadn't spoken before, his distinctive voice deep and gravelly. He crouched to inspect the bodily fluid. "Not too much, either."

"Look," the other one said. "Footsteps all around here."

Nicholas and Bernd peered into the undergrowth, seeing two different sets of prints, one of them probably a woman's. The impressions were scattered in the area of blood with two distinct trails leading to the west.

"The man isn't dead and now they're running," Bernd said. He glared at Nicholas. "The quicker we do this, the better."

Nicholas nodded his understanding, bringing the group of men in, adding gravity to his voice.

"Men, I didn't want to do what I did to the major back there, but I cannot overemphasize the importance of this mission." He made eye contact with each of the Americans as Bernd translated to the Panamanians. "The man we're after is trying to get ultra-sensitive information to the Germans. We tracked him here and had tried to take him alive in the city over the past few days. When that didn't occur, we brought you in." More translation. "If he escapes, and I *cannot* overemphasize this, it will cause the Allies to lose the war." He swept his eyes over the lower rim of La Boca as Bernd continued to translate for the Panamanians. "Do you understand the gravity of the situation?"

"Who is he?" the drawling M.P. asked.

"He *was* my employee," Nicholas said, adding an ashamed tone. "Greed got to him. And by being here, doing what he's doing, he has proven that he is willing to kill all of you, and your families back home."

While Bernd again translated, another M.P. asked, "What do you mean by families? How would he do that?"

Nicholas and Bernd shared a quick look. *Why not?* Bernd's look said. *We're going to have to kill them anyway.*

"We've been working on a super-weapon for years," Nicholas said, flicking his cigarette into the wet brush. "We're essentially there and, in the meantime, the Nazis have been trying to build one, too, but they're a few years behind. If they learn what we know they'll jump ahead of us and they'll use this super-weapon, maybe against London, maybe against New York, maybe against your hometown." He paused for effect. "And I can promise you, when detonated, it will flatten an entire city and melt the skin from every person within many miles."

Nicholas allowed Bernd to explain this to the Panamanians as he studied the faces. Most were sufficiently grim. It was time to move to the next phase.

"Now, believe it or not, men, despite this tattered suit, I'm a fully-trained infantry officer. We're going to move to the canal in split squads, one north and one south…" he lowered himself to the muddy floor of the thick copse, smoothing the footprints and blood with his hand, creating another makeshift sand-table under the lemon light of the hand torch. "We'll use the canal as the backstop, creating a pincer attack from north and south." Using a stick he gouged two lines for the canal, then made two rectangles with an X inside, and a dot over each rectangle, to indicate each of the two squads. "We'll open up outside these woods and move in diagonally so they can't get back into the woods here, and once they're rounded up against the water, you M.P.'s use those rifles and kill them."

"What if they surrender?" an M.P. asked.

"Kill them anyway, no questions."

"The women, too?"

"Those two women would slice off your family jewels and feed them to the fish in that canal," Nicholas replied crisply. "Trust me. They're as bad, if not worse, than the man we're after. This is wartime and there's no time for clemency."

There was silence among the M.P.'s as Bernd translated. Finished, Bernd looked at Nicholas and rubbed his fingers together. Nicholas nodded. From his pants, Bernd produced a wad of American bills, counting out fifteen hundreds, making three neat stacks beside his sand-table.

"Five hundred per head, that's the reward," he said in his best British accent.

"What about those two cops that ran off?" one of the M.P.'s asked.

"He's right," Nicholas said to Bernd. "They betrayed us and, based on the whispers Melton heard, they're obviously in cahoots with Donahue."

Bernd added two more $500 stacks, telling the Panamanians, using excellent slang, that their bosses dicked them over good. He then asked them if they would have a problem icing either man.

The Panamanians were all wide-eyed, staring at the enormous sums of money. Though none of them appeared comfortable, none of them objected, either.

Split into two squads, one led by Bernd, the other by Nicholas, a ragtag group of loose allies set off toward the Panama Canal. The men of each squad had no idea they were being led by two Nazi spies, headed to kill two patriotic Americans and a Cuban sympathizer.

Behind them, already forgotten, Major Melton, semi-conscious from shock, rolled to his side in agony. His battered leg scraped a Cecropia root, the motion dislodging his tourniquet.

He died two minutes later.

LIEUTENANT GONZALEZ rushed back through the thickets, finding Captain Garza frantically peering through a clump of elephant ear. Garza whirled, aiming his handgun, his wide crocodile eyes returning to slits.

"Good way to die," the captain hissed. "I heard numerous shots. What the hell's going on?"

"The lanky American shot the American Army officer, Melton…shot him in the leg. I watched and heard everything." Gonzalez leaned forward, hands on his knees as he took several large breaths. "They have our men, *capitán*. They laid *our* money on the ground as a bounty on the three from the hilltop…and as a bounty on *us*."

"*Qué putas pasa?*"

"My sentiments exactly."

"Where are they now?"

"They split into two squads."

"*Hijos de puta.*"

Gonzalez mopped his forehead with a handkerchief and said, "I think we need to find the large American, the one I spoke with, and we offer to tell him everything."

"In exchange for what?"

"Money, of course."

"And our men, with these double-crossing gringos?"

"We communicate with them somehow, let them know the men they're with aren't to be trusted."

Garza again peered through the plants. "I can see the canal from here, I can see La Boca. But what I cannot see is the two squads you mentioned. If we're going to get out in front of them, we must go now."

"Come on," Gonzalez said, rushing off to the southwest. He led his captain on a diagonal path through a field of cane, getting ahead of Nicholas Penland's M.P. squad in a race to the southern mouth of the canal.

THE WATER near the southern entrance to the canal was wide like a lake and serene on this night. A half-moon rode low on the western horizon, sending wavy white streaks of light across the water, reaching over the slow-flowing surface as if finger-painted by a child. The insects were unbearable, however, swarming the group of three to the point that Vivien seemed on the verge of losing control. Their conversation consisted of urgent whispers, the reality of what was happening affecting each of them in different ways.

"Stop waving your arms," Rollie whispered patiently. "I know the mosquitos are stinging you but you're making too much motion. With this moon coming up those assholes back there can see you."

Maria, her pistol extended, was turned opposite Rollie and Vivien, focused on the path. "Come on…come to mama," she whispered.

Rollie searched the area with his eyes, shaking his head. "We're now in the American Zone and the canal should be under high security."

"How did you get here?" Vivien asked.

"I told you," Rollie said, "by airplane."

"Well I took a train in from the other end of the canal and the only time I saw soldiers was around the locks."

"She's right," Maria said. "I saw the same."

"Shit," Rollie breathed. "The locks are miles up the canal. We've got to get there but, if we stay on this side, we'll get intercepted."

Maria turned stared across the broad expanse, shaking her head. "I can't make it," she said.

"Yes, you can," Rollie replied in a calming voice.

"I'm not a good swimmer," she whispered. "You two go. I'll stay back here and kill that murdering Prussian sonofabitch and anyone else I can get a bead on."

"No," Rollie said. "Now, we cannot go south so Nicholas will certainly anticipate us heading north. Even though that's what we must do, we've got to cross the canal first."

Vivien raised her hand to swat a fresh swarm away before biting her lip and abstaining. "He's the one you were surprised to see back there?"

"Yes."

"What surprised you?"

"Nicholas is my boss. While I can honestly tell you I never trusted him, I can also say I'm bewildered as to what's going on." He turned his eyes skyward, the verbalizing of the situation making him think more clearly. "And the large men with him…those were American Zone military policemen, and he *shot* one of them. That tells me he started at the American Zone and told them who-knows-what about us."

"Why would Nicholas, an American, shoot one of them?" Vivien asked. "It's crazy."

"He shot him in the leg…a message," Rollie said, rubbing his stubble. "If he's using wartime authority, creating a panic…I could see Nicholas, devious type he is, using such an incident as a tool."

"A tool of what?"

"Fear," Rollie said flatly. "It's his specialty."

Maria was scurrying in the underbrush at the water's edge. She came back with a torso-sized piece of driftwood, dragging it in the water, smiling when it floated. "Can I use this?"

As Rollie told Maria yes, Vivien grabbed his arm. "But what could Nicholas have told them to make them come after us?"

"Let's assume he already found Richard, but Richard had already made his exchange. Who, other than you, me, Maria and Richard knows about his transgressions?"

She was silent a moment. "No one…that I know of."

Rollie nodded. "Nicholas, my boss, didn't want me coming here. In fact, he threatened me if I did. So that tells me one of two things. Either he's trying to cover up his screw-up, or…" he pulled in a sharp breath as it hit him, "…or he's working for someone else."

"Then how could he get the backing of the American Zone, if he was working with someone else?"

"He's got high credentials from the O.S.S. and the Department of War. Guy like him walks into the Zone commander's office and they'd all fawn over him." Rollie bit off a curse as it all became clear to him. He nudged Vivien to the water. "They're probably getting close. Go. Start swimming."

"What about the current?" Vivien asked.

"It's calm." He positioned Vivien next to Maria. "Don't splash when you kick. Move slowly and patiently toward the moon until your feet touch ground on the far side." Rollie watched as Vivien offered Maria a few words of encouragement before the two women set out, both of them holding the driftwood. Vivien's kicks were more efficient, making them turn sharply before they got in sync. He could see the young woman, Maria, eventually seem to relax as the pair settled into a nice stroke.

Rollie crawled back to the watchman's trail, peering in both directions and then through the high grass. At first he saw no one, puzzled why Nicholas and his assemblage of men hadn't yet given chase.

He looked out over the water. The women were already a quarter of the way across.

When he turned back to the trail, he heard a rustling, and what sounded like whispers. The sounds were coming from the north. He adjusted the Colt Super in his hand, crouching low, waiting.

GARZA WHISPERED torrents of curses, creating combinations of lurid phrases unlike anything Gonzalez had ever heard. They were on their knees, moving forward as quickly as they could. Every few minutes, in a loud whisper, Gonzalez would say, "Señor Donahue!" It carried almost as far as a normal voice.

"We're going to get shot," Garza seethed.

"Halt," came a firm, yet unseen, voice. Both men complied. There was a gentle rustling of grass before the voice said, "You're both about two seconds from meeting San Pedro."

Gonzalez glanced back, seeing Garza's yellow eyes wider than he'd ever seen them. *"Díselo!"* Garza hissed.

"Señor Donahue, it is Lieutenant Gonzalez and Captain Garza."

There was no response.

"Señor, we left the American and the...the *other* man to come to you."

"You double-crossed me," the voice from the grass said. "You told me you were working leads and I would see you tomorrow. And the next thing I know I see you down below La Boca, sending a squad of your *own* armed police up after me and my companions."

Gonzalez wilted, dropping to his belly as his mind raced for an explanation. He spoke into his folded arms. "When I left you the note,

Señor Donahue, I believed everything to be true. The other man was joined by a second man…from your government. They forced us."

There was a long moment of silence.

"Señor?" Gonzalez implored.

ROLLIE HAD a good bead on the talker, Gonzalez, and could hear enough fidgeting and rustling to know that the other one, the captain, was just behind him. He guessed them to be fifteen feet away, on the trail, separated from him only by the high grass. Gonzalez was going on about some man from the States who used his authority to…

Rollie's head snapped skyward as a thunderbolt struck him.

The fleeting thought that had been evading Rollie for the past several hours finally, thankfully, leapt forth in his mind.

The envelopes of hotel stationery—he'd been so interested to see the one marked *de la policia* that he'd never taken time to look at the other two, which he'd initially written off as hotel bills or messages from the concierge. He pulled the crumpled wad of damp envelopes from his cargo pocket, holding them in his left hand so he could maintain the grip on his Colt, alternating his vision between the papers and the high grass swaying in the moonlight.

"Señor?" Gonzalez pleaded. "Señor, please…we can still help you."

"There's a gun with extremely high-powered bullets trained on both of you, Gonzalez. The gun is held by a man who's unafraid to die and is thoroughly pissed off. That said, advance to be recognized. And do it carefully."

The two policemen, their faces and clothing so covered in dirt and mud and dead grass that both men looked identical, slithered around the edge of the thick grass, both of them wearing sycophantic smiles that seemed incredibly out of place. There were no guns in sight, so Rollie chanced a quick look in the other direction, seeing a slow wake being generated by the two women, now halfway across the canal.

Rollie turned back to the two policemen, keeping the .38 Super steadily aimed at Gonzalez's nose. "Tell me about the two men who *forced you* to join them?"

"The first one calls himself Lancaster, señor. He came to see the captain at the same time you spoke to me. He portrays himself as English."

"Is he English?"

"The captain has his doubts, señor."

"And the other?"

"Nicholas Pen...Pen..."

"Penland," Rollie said flatly. He'd hoped his eyes were playing tricks on him earlier, but he knew better. And this confirmed it.

"You know him, señor?"

"Yeah, I know him."

"Señor, he went to the American Zone, commandeering soldiers and telling your own American people that you are a spy. But, after all the shooting, when Captain Garza and I finally talked," the sycophantic smile returned as he smoothed mud through his hair, "we questioned which of these men who'd come to us seemed more trustworthy? The answer was, of course, you, señor."

Gunshots cracked through the stillness of the night, making all three men flatten themselves on the ground. It registered to Rollie that these shots originated across the canal. Again, like earlier, distant birds shrieked in protest.

"Cazador furtivo," Garza said, rising to his knees and shaking his meaty fist at the sound.

"Poachers?" Rollie asked. Gonzalez nodded.

"Señor," Garza asked, his respect obviously feigned. "May I remove my pistol to guard our rear?"

"No," Rollie answered firmly. "Tell me about Samuel Fields, also known as Richard Hampton."

The two men looked at one another. Gonzalez swallowed. Garza pursed his thin lips and gave an infinitesimal shake of his head.

"What?" Rollie snapped, twisting the Colt at Garza.

Fear registered on Garza's mud-covered face as he answered without hesitation, saying, "He is dead, señor."

Rollie blinked several times, adjusting his sweaty index finger on the trigger.

"Señor, you must understand we did not do it," Gonzalez appealed.

"Who did?"

"The man you sought was involved, amorously, with a young American woman. From what I can gather she also had a Panamanian lover, a giant simpleton who would know no better." He sucked air into his thin nose before saying it. "When I reached Richard Hampton he was in the process of dying of his injuries, given to him by the giant simpleton."

Rollie believed him, word for word. He'd had enough practice to spot a liar and could definitely envision Hampton getting himself into a deadly love triangle. Added to that, and working in the interest of transparency, the working end of a pistol has a remarkable effect on people.

"You said he was in the process of dying."

"Sí, señor."

"Did you learn anything during this process?" Rollie asked.

Gonzalez flashed the apple-polishing smile again. "Only one thing, and then he died."

"What was it?"

The two Panamanians looked at one another. "Before I answer, may we reconcile our earlier deal?"

Rollie lurched forward, grabbing a shock of Gonzalez's muddy hair and pressing the Colt to his ear. "I'd suggest you just tell me."

"H-h-he said the word 'n-n-notebook' before he expired."

There was a period of quiet before Rollie said, "Notebook."

"Sí, señor."

Rollie gnawed on his lip. "And did you find this notebook?"

"I searched the room where I found him as well as his room. I didn't find it."

Again Rollie burrowed the Colt against Gonzalez's ear.

"Ayeee," Gonzalez winced. "I didn't find any notebook and that is all I know, I swear to *Cristo*."

"You mentioned two rooms. What room did you find him in?"

"He had been with the young American lady at her hotel, and that was where the Panamanian assaulted him."

Rollie remained silent, deciding to set these revelations aside for a moment as his mind came back to the envelopes. They were beneath him on the muddy trail. He motioned to Gonzalez. "Light that hand torch and keep it low, between your body and the trail." As Gonzalez did as he was told, Rollie twisted the Colt at both men. "One funny move…" He tossed the envelopes at Gonzalez. "Read."

Gonzalez seemed momentarily flustered, but at his superior's vulgar urging, gathered himself and first held up his own envelope questioningly.

"The other two," Rollie said.

His thumb under the flap, Gonzalez opened the first one, his head shaking back and forth. "It is just a hotel bill, señor."

"The other one."

Again he followed the same pattern, thumb under the flap, ripping the paper that had been softened by the resident humidity. The buff paper was thick and damp, the typed letters creating a braille-like effect along the back. The hand torch was wedged under the lieutenant, creating a scant sliver of light between his legs. Rollie could see his eyes moving back and forth as he read; he lifted the pistol, applying an extra pound of pressure to the trigger as he aimed it at Gonzalez's nose. "Read it *aloud*."

Gonzalez nodded, reading slowly, his English quite good. "Roald Donahue…to authenticate who I am without revealing my identity, know this…I work in military intelligence in Washington and I'm well-placed. To provide legitimacy to myself, I've found information about your service, your ordeal, in Gran Chaco. After the war had begun to swing in Bolivia's favor, the oil companies backing Paraguay intervened and there were payoffs among the leadership, eventually sealing Bolivia's fate. That's when most of the Americans were pulled out and they left Gran Chaco for good. Your unit was given up deliberately. I'm certain no one expected you to survive, so I tip my cap to you."

The .38 Super trembled in his hand. Rollie blinked rapidly as he heard this crushing information for the first time. For nearly a decade he'd pondered every angle of what had happened, eventually coming to the same conclusion on his own. But now, to hear it spoken aloud by anyone other than his mind's voice…

"Señor?" Garza asked, yellow eyes narrowed.

"Yeah," Rollie said, his voice cracking. "Go on."

Gonzalez gripped the paper at both edges. "Your superior, Nicholas Penland, is German by birth, Nazi by choice, having begun his secretive mission when he was approximately twenty years old. His family name I don't know, but his Christian name was Günter. Eleven years ago, about the time the war in Gran Chaco was just beginning, and when Nicholas was attending university in Heidelberg, he was recruited by the Ausland-SD and his identity was switched to that of a young American man orphaned in his teens, Nicholas Penland of Vermont. The real Nicholas Penland was murdered in cold blood for this very purpose. The SD would often search for months to find someone who could pass for their spy, and once they did, if everything else matched up, such as the real Penland's orphan status and age, they would kill him or her without delay, usually during a transitory period in the victim's life. Once the body was disposed of, Günter became Nicholas. With no immediate family, and with his just beginning four years away at an American university, no one was ever the wiser to his transformation. In fact, I would wager 'Nicholas' has never been back to Vermont because of this. Like most spies who assume an identity, they typically profess hate for their background as the reason for their unwillingness to embrace past and family."

Gonzalez looked up. "Shall I go on, señor? This is a very long letter…are the words important to you?"

Rollie lifted the pistol, aiming it between Gonzalez's eyes.

Gonzalez nodded, turned the paper over and continued reading. "A little about me: I'm also an agent of the Thousand Year Reich who began my service to the U.S. government many, many years ago—long before Penland. While I might have once worked for the SD, my allegiance to them has become tainted. The United States is my new home, not only because I enjoy it, but also because I know beyond a shadow of a doubt that the Reich will lose this war. Had Hitler not been so greedy, had he only gone east, I believe the world might have made room for him. But the man is a blithering fool and will now be made to pay, along with his drone-like followers.

"It is because of this that I have severed all ties and, upon dispatch of this letter by military courier, I will disappear into the folds of the land of the free where I will create a new life for myself. But, before I do, I wanted to make sure I exposed Nicholas Penland, the lowest form of scum I've ever come across. He has traveled to Panama solely to kill you. What troubles me most is something I've learned. Your director, Lawrence Dillard—"

There was a slight metallic sound, nothing more than a tinkle, at Rollie's ten o'clock. All three men turned their head, only to see a darting tongue of bright orange from the same area. Before the report from the rifle even reached them, the .30 caliber bullet that impacted Garza's skull sounded like a ball peen hammer splitting open a watermelon. With the jacketed bullet's entry and exit, Garza simply twitched once before life left him, dropping him on his back as his knees buckled underneath him unnaturally.

Rollie jerked the letter from Gonzalez's hands, stuffing it into his shirt and jumping into the water. He moved laterally, covered by the thick reeds and grasses at the edge of the canal's mouth. Gonzalez followed him in, turning the other direction as Rollie silently directed him. More shots rang out, their termination marked by vertical plumes in the water, all of them hitting in the area where both men had entered the water.

Twenty feet north of where he'd jumped in, north of where the bullets had struck the water, Rollie felt like a crocodile, the cool safety of the water giving him the advantage as he lurked there, the Colt extended before him, trained knowingly through the high grass at the rustling sounds from the watchman's path.

Sure enough, one of the Americans appeared, stupidly moving into the breach as he held his M1 Carbine aimed out at the water, searching for Rollie. After a few moments, his helmet shook back and forth. "Nobody's here," he said far too loudly. "Nobody but that fat little spic cop, and he's deader'n a doornail."

On later reflection, it might have been a better plan for Rollie to have remained silent. But had he done so, his pursuers could have scoured the canal's edge, rooting both him and Gonzalez out into the open. And while he had no appetite to shoot an American soldier, he could feel the mud poultice on his neck oozing away as the water worked on it. Rollie knew his precious blood would follow and, because of that, he needed to escape sooner rather than later.

The M.P.'s tone, as he continued to speak to unseen individuals about his unrivaled marksmanship, annoyed Rollie. Made him despise the big lug. He made the young military policeman to be a braggart and a bully—a combination seen too often in that particular military occupation. This helped Rollie in his decision to pull the trigger, holding the .38 Super very low in order to conceal any muzzle flash from the remaining soldiers. The powerful pistol thundered in the night, striking just behind the soldier's left hand, held properly in a right handed shooter's position on the forward edge of the M1's one-piece walnut stock. Rollie had no idea whether or not the flattening of the ACP slug had severed the M.P.'s wrist on contact, or if it would need to be removed by a doctor at a later time. The result was better than killing the man, who screamed in a pitch far higher than Rollie would have thought possible.

The M1 tumbled into the water as panic fire erupted from Rollie's left. He crouched low, protected by the height of the muddy bank, seeing Gonzalez doing the same on the far side of the area where the M.P. had just stood. Rollie remained still, holding the Colt at the ready, listening first to the M.P.'s cries and then to the frenzied shouts of the soldiers to his left. From a distant point well up the path, making him realize the attack force had split up, Rollie could hear Nicholas Penland's unmistakable voice as it yelled curse-laden queries about what had happened.

"Sneaky bastards are hiding in the water!" came the nearby reply.

There was more inconsequential shouting and arguing from Rollie's left as he lowered himself under the water, feeling his way back to the south on the muddy bottom until his hands found the hardness of the M.P.'s carbine. Rollie stayed below the water's surface, lungs burning, taking care to continue to move slowly. When he could go no further, he emerged, finding Gonzalez aiming a shiny wet pistol at his head.

"You shoot me and they'll kill you anyway," Rollie whispered, watching as the Panamanian lowered his gun. "I got the rifle right here below the water. Those bastards are scared to step forward to the water's edge now, so if we use the bank as our cover we can swim south—"

Just behind Gonzales there was a splash of water, as if someone had thrown a rock. As both men turned, a cannon-like explosion was followed by a geyser of foamy water, lifting Gonzalez from the canal, cart-wheeling him through the moonlit sky above Rollie's head.

Gonzalez's mouth was wide open as he flew but Rollie couldn't hear him over the detonation. In the moonlight he could see Gonzalez had no legs below the knee.

Shit!

It had to have been a grenade. And if they had one grenade, that meant they had more. It was time to move. Despite his fear, his tinge of shock, and his open neck wound, Rollie took three massive breaths and a bead on the far side of the canal. He jammed his Colt in his pants, slung the rifle over his chest and, staying on the muddy bottom, began to swim.

While he swam, he pictured Vivien.

Reach down, buddy, to the depths of your soul. She's over there, waiting on you. Her for you, and you for her. When you need air, you just remember that, and give yourself five more strokes.

He did.

Guessing his depth was at least ten feet, Rollie took long, smooth strokes, challenging himself—despite the conditions—to see how far he might go without coming up for air, Vivien's face staring at him from behind his eyelids.

Five more strokes.

Five more strokes.

BERND HAD been crouched low, fearful of taking a bullet from one of the two water-borne men. The American just beyond him had tossed the grenade without permission. As it arced through the night sky, as pretty as anything Bernd had seen since the little Cuban whore's pair of nubile tits, he dropped lower in the grass, awaiting the coming detonation.

When explosions occur under water—and this one actually happened at a depth of four feet: three-and-a-half-feet of water and six inches of silt—there is typically a shock wave that is felt a fraction before the water erupts upward. Bernd felt the shock wave go through him, lifting his head to see a man flying through the air, his stump legs trailing tendons and sheared off fibulas and tibias. Emboldened, Bernd rose to his feet as the legless man floated face down.

There was no sign of the American named Rollie.

"The other one's out there," Bernd whispered, his Browning outstretched and ready to shoot.

After a minute of searching, gunfire from the far shore made the members of his squad drop to their stomachs.

A MOMENT earlier, both of them occasionally retching brackish canal water on the tussocks of the western bank of the canal, Vivien and Maria had watched in puzzlement as flashes of gunfire erupted across the canal. They were too far to see Gonzalez's body catapulting through the air, but they saw the plume of water and a second later were treated to the explosion from the grenade.

"Do you have bullets?" Vivien asked, coming to her knees.

"Why?" Maria asked, still coughing.

"Do you?"

"Yes, but we're too far."

"Give me your gun and get down," Vivien said. She took the wet Beretta from Maria, aiming it at the center of the hail of gunfire as she began firing at half-second intervals, unloading five rounds. Upon her shooting, all gunfire behind where the explosion had taken place ceased. Silence ruled the night as Vivien ducked down, having provided cover fire without even knowing it.

Maria suggested they move farther north up the trail.

Chapter Twenty

NICHOLAS PENLAND and his squad appeared on the watchman's trail above Bernd's still prone squad. "Get the hell up!" Penland yelled, eyeing Bernd and the others harshly. "You got put down by a pistol being fired from a half a kilometer away."

"Where's your American traitor?" Bernd asked, accusation dripping from his tone.

"Swimming, I would imagine," Nicholas answered, "since you let him get away." He moved to the bank and motioned everyone to do the same.

One of the M.P.'s knelt above their fallen comrade that they'd pulled from the water's edge. His only sounds were loud, ragged breaths. He'd gone catatonic from shock, his wrist hanging on by a section of skin and a few noodle-like tendons.

"Get up!" Nicholas barked.

"But he needs a tourniquet," the kneeling M.P. objected.

Nicholas knelt to examine the man's wrist, running his own hand back through his hair. "Fine then, he can stay here." He pointed out over the water. "Donahue is out there somewhere. And we either kill him now or we cross this canal and kill him over there. Because killing that sonofabitch is the difference between winning and losing this war." He never stopped to explain to the M.P.'s that he was speaking from a Nazi perspective. "And if we don't kill him, put simply, we're all dead." Nicholas made an elevating motion. "Everyone train your weapon straight out over the water. He has to surface sometime and I'll add an extra thousand bucks for any man who can get the head-shot."

One of the M.P.'s cinched a belt around the man's nearly severed arm, dragging him to the other side of the watchman's path. Leather slings could be heard tensing as carbines came up. The remaining Panamanians, despite their lack of English, must have understood the money part as they, too, took aim, each man steadying himself in a firing position, aiming at moonstruck water in his own personal gamble on where Rollie Donahue might emerge for breath.

SWIMMING BLIND, Rollie could feel the trace of current pushing him slightly north, remembering from school that the Pacific was higher than the Atlantic and, despite the locks of the canal, a small current existed. He allowed it to turn him as he swam with deep strokes, his progress impeded by his boots, his clothing and the carbine hanging from his body.

Lungs on fire, he couldn't hold out any longer. And he knew his aggressors knew he had to breathe at some point, and he knew he might die because of it. Despite such motivation to keep going, an inner mechanism overrode him, defeating his will, making him surface as he sucked great quantities of air in two wet breaths.

The gunfire happened almost immediately. Rollie saw the impact of one bullet just to his right. The bullet smacked the water, sounding like a sharp clap of the hands. That was the one—the kill shot. Six inches to the left and it would have hit him in the back of the head and this would all be over. But it didn't. It missed and now Rollie had new life.

Back underwater, he knew the men now had a bead on his course and were training their weapons on his next likely breath point.

Instead of continuing forward, Rollie turned sharply to the north.

"HOW MANY more bullets do you have?" Vivien asked.

"None."

"What?"

"You just used the rest."

Across the canal, more gunshots rang out. The two women peered through the high grass, seeing a head emerge from the water before it dove back under.

"Rollie," Vivien breathed, both hands going over her mouth.

"HE'S GOING to make it," Nicholas growled.

"We need to hit him with another volley when he comes back up," Bernd replied, turning to the shooters. "Swimming is exhausting work, and don't forget he's already been hit. He won't go far on this breath. You men keep those rifles trained out there and pop his ass when he comes up."

The M.P.'s and the Panamanians stood at the ready, tensed, waiting to shoot. Then, quickly, the moonlit water broke and a head emerged.

All at once they twitched to the ripples in the water, quickly adjusting their aim when a singular dart of orange light erupted from the water. Every man began to fire at the figure that had taken a quick shot and already submerged again. The noise of their volley had blocked out the clipped shout of one of their own as one the Panamanian policemen tumbled forward into the water, hand clutching his chest. The M.P.'s and Panamanians lurched backward, dropping to their stomachs in the high grass.

Bernd and Nicholas, however, stood there, disgusted, not even bothering to find cover. Nicholas stared sullenly at his countryman, who brazenly lit a cigarette, clicking his lighter shut.

"A squad of men aiming at him and he pops up and kills one in a quarter of a second," Nicholas said, his voice dripping contempt.

"He has the advantage," Bernd said, exhaling his smoke into the moonlit night. "We don't know where he is, but he knows exactly where we are."

Nicholas turned back to the glittery water, seeing round ripples where his underling had submerged, probably nearly ready to pop up again and take out another one. He squatted down, motioning Bernd to do the same.

"If we stay here, he'll continue to whittle down our numbers."

"How observant," Bernd remarked.

Nicholas gripped Bernd's wrist, constricting on it, his voice a whisper. "Look, I don't care if he kills every one of these assholes, as long as *we* get him. And as long as he stays on that side of the canal, he's not escaping."

Bernd jerked his arm away. "You say that, but you don't know it. What if he heads north, to the American Zone?"

"We're in the American Zone."

"But there are guards, hundreds of them, north of here, by the locks."

Nicholas turned his head to the north. "Then we've got to head that way, quickly. We can cross and cut them off."

"They *cannot* escape," Bernd whispered, pointing a rigid finger at Nicholas' face. "This will be the most substantial intelligence coup the world has ever seen—and I will not allow it to slip through my hands."

"I—realize—that," Nicholas replied, moving Bernd's hand away from his face. "Perhaps we should quit talking about it and start doing something instead."

"Then lead on."

"Time to move," Nicholas turned and said to the group. "Stay low on the path and move north as rapidly as you can."

"Where are we going?" one M.P. asked, handing a bundle of morphine sticks to their fallen comrade.

"We're going to find a boat, and then we're going to cross, and then we're going to kill that murdering traitor who's damn near across the canal."

They watched as the fallen M.P. jabbed his own thigh with two morphine sticks. To his credit, he'd been lying quietly in the tussocks, his eyes wide and unblinking. He was probably in shock. Once he had the opiate in his system, his eyes relaxed and his good hand unclenched. Bernd began collecting a few of the man's things: his combat knife, extra rifle rounds, Mk 2 grenades. He motioned for the rest of the men to go, staying in his crouch and watching them go.

Once they rounded the bend, Bernd uncapped four more vials of the morphine. Without a word to the M.P., Bernd poked each morphine stick into the M.P.'s neck, watching as the wounded man slipped from consciousness. Bernd then grasped the belt tourniquet and pulled it loose. The M.P. didn't budge. Judging by the rate of blood that pumped from his arm, Bernd gave the man less than five minutes to live. He grasped the M.P., dragging him twenty feet off the watchman's path.

"He ought to be a nice meal for the resident crocodiles and caymans," Bernd said to himself in his Prussian-accented German. Then he ran forward, eventually reaching Nicholas. He stopped him and pointed at a glittering dot nearly across the canal.

"There he is," Bernd whispered.

"Tempting as another volley is, let's keep moving. He's too far gone now."

"If we prevent their northward passage, what's to the west?" Bernd asked.

"Rainforest," Nicholas answered. "Thick, deep, and deadly—the perfect place for us to hunt Rollie Donahue, and kill him."

"I've heard a number of men say that type of thing before…right before they died."

Nicholas turned, arching an eyebrow at Bernd. "Those three are as good as dead. Trust me."

The unlikely platoon of men pressed on to the north at a jog. A half a mile later, they discovered a fisherman's motorboat and made their crossing in less than two minutes.

The hunt was on.

THE FINAL third of the swim took quite a while. Rollie had stayed underwater for so long that he'd exhausted himself. Added to his neck wound, he was quite weak. He slithered onto the western shore of the canal with hardly a sound. Digging his fingers into the mud of the bank, he gouged out another lump of clay and grime, pressing the wad into the bullet wound. Collapsing on his back, taking enormous breaths, he heard the rushing of the girls' feet. Vivien's first words were accusatory but strangely comforting…

"Are you crazy?" she hissed.

Rollie was holding the mud poultice in place as he managed to nod, speaking through his gasps. "I've been asked that a number of times in my life. And I've finally decided that, yes…yes, I am."

When he'd begun to finally catch his breath, the trio crossed the watchman's path, crouching in the high grass while Rollie assessed their ammunition situation. He informed the women that they needed to move north as fast as possible. As soon as the words were out of his mouth, the sound of a small motor filled the night.

"What is that?" Maria asked.

Vivien stood and searched the water. The sound was coming from the north.

"It's them," Rollie said in a tired voice, closing his eyes, his other hand going to his forehead. "They've found a boat, and now they're crossing."

"How do you know that without even looking?" Maria demanded.

"I just know."

"What do we do?" Vivien asked.

"They're going to cut off our northward passage because they know we'll go for the American Zone. Shit!" He fell back on his rear end, suddenly dizzy. "Say, could one of you rip a strip of your clothing so I can wrap my neck?"

Maria stood, pulling the pauper's shift over her head without hesitation. In all the danger, with a group of men after them and with a potentially mortal wound on Rollie's neck, Rollie's eyes struggled for want to turn and view the body that lurked underneath that shift, but stronger than his impulse was the powerful feeling of eyes *on* him—Vivien's eyes—so he did what any smart man would do and closed his own eyes again, taking calming breaths through his nose. He could hear wet fabric ripping and then a rustling of the now smaller shift being slipped on again.

"That should do it."

Vivien lifted his head as Maria worked the long strip around his neck. "How tight?" she asked.

"Until I start choking, then back it off a hair."

"Qué?" Maria asked, not following the idiom.

"Make it very tight," Vivien said. "Okay, Rollie," she said shaking him, "now what do we do?"

"As soon as she ties off this bandage, we've got to head west, into this jungle."

"And do what?"

"Hide."

The sound of the motor stopped. There was a distant splash followed by only the occasional sounds of the night jungle.

"They're coming," Rollie whispered, standing. He held the carbine at port arms, gesturing due west. "You two head into the woods, there. I'll be right behind you."

They did as they were told as he dropped to all fours, using both palms like a bricklayer's trowel, flattening out their footsteps in the wet mud of the watchman's path. Finished, Rollie peered to the north, seeing no one.

But he knew they were there, just beyond the bend, too many for him to have a prayer of killing alone. And he shuddered to think of what they might do to the women if he were dead.

Following the women, he entered the woods, thick and wet and full of heavy fragrances—a rainforest—catching up to the women and telling them to set a steady pace in the direction of the moon, when it was visible. Rollie trailed behind, moving in spurts, facing backward much of the time, his hand on the carbine's trigger, knowing he would need more than luck to singlehandedly eliminate what amounted to an infantry squad.

But that wasn't his preferred plan.

Unfortunately, Rollie didn't have another plan.

Yet.

NICHOLAS AND Bernd moved their makeshift squad into the high grass less than a quarter of a mile north of where Rollie and the two women had come ashore. Their first order of business was an equipment and ammunition check. Earlier, Bernd had taken grenades off of the M.P. and now furtively handed one to Nicholas. The three remaining M.P.'s each had several clips of ammo remaining. The Panamanians weren't outfitted as well, with only a few rounds each. Added to that, Bernd felt they were acting skittish after losing Gonzalez and Garza and their fellow policemen.

"You Panamanians, do you understand what's going on here?" Bernd asked, speaking Spanish. The nods he received were less than confident. He pointed to the south. "Those three people we're chasing are enemies, backed by the Nazis." He patted his breast pocket. "And my offer still stands to pay you for their heads."

The mention of money seemed to quell any anxiety that had crept back in.

"I don't know what the world would do without poor people," Bernd whispered to Nicholas after motioning everyone to the south.

They moved, staggering tactically, watchful for an ambush, as unlikely as it was. The moon was high and bright to the west, illuminating top surfaces in shades of purple. After a distance, the moon also revealed a dark area on the surface of the watchman's trail. While the squad fanned out to provide cover, Bernd and Nicholas swept the hand torch over the area. There was driftwood floating nearby and swirl marks on the path where someone had tried to cover their tracks. Just to the west of the path was a distinct bending of the high grass where someone had gone in—into the bush—into the jungle.

"I can't imagine those women moving very fast through that razor grass," Nicholas said.

"And I wouldn't have been able to imagine that we'd already be down five men...seven if you count the two Panamanian officers who fled," Bernd retorted in a whisper. "So maybe we'd do better to stop underestimating this man and his partners."

"Point taken."

"Let's move out again in two squads," Bernd suggested. "Put one of the better shooters out front and head due west, and stay within sight of one another. They've got to be getting low on ammo so there's no way they can ambush two squads."

Bernd relayed the instructions in English then Spanish. He finished by saying, "If you see anyone, or even hear anyone, shoot first. Do not delay."

As the two groups moved into the jungle, one Panamanian, one American, Nicholas and Bernd stayed back on the path for a moment, urgently whispering.

WHAT HAD been relatively quick progress was halted by a stone barrier soaring from the jungle floor like a concrete wall. Sheltered in vines and thick moss, Rollie tore into its covering, tugging and pulling in an effort to see if it could be scaled. He quickly determined it could not. A person might be able to ascend the vines, but only if he had a death wish. They seemed loose and, with the moss and high humidity, were as slick as ice.

"This way," was all he said, pressing southward around the towering bluff, falling several times as his feet became tangled in the resident vines. Five minutes around the southern edge he located a rocky cut, set at a steep angle, but appearing to provide a slippery access up the face of the wall. He called for quiet, listening carefully. There were no sounds behind them.

"We're not going up there," Vivien said, head back as she stared into the blackness of the steep ravine.

Rollie ignored her. "Maria, you climb first."

"But I can't see anything," she protested.

"Do it anyway."

A gunshot rang out nearby, then another.

The sounds came from the west.

In the scant, deep purple light, Rollie held his fingers to his lips. Just like earlier, birds could be heard screeching, though this time their wings could be heard beating against the high leaves of the jungle. Rollie handed the carbine to Maria.

"Stay right here. Anyone approaches without identifying themselves, kill them."

"Wait," Vivien whispered, but Rollie was gone.

THE BIRDS' cacophony of protest angered Rollie. He had read about the poachers in Central and South America, shooting the adult birds, then robbing the nest of the resident babies. Often, the birds were taken too early and died in transit. But these unlawful bastards worked in volume, and if only half of the babies made it back, they considered it a successful day at the office.

Rollie edged around an impervious thicket and, right in front of him, a sharp beam of light cut the night. It was produced by one of those large handheld lights operated by a battery that could probably start a car. The poacher had set it on the ground and was trying to climb the trunk of a massive tree, using the vines and a special pair of spiked boots to do so.

Rollie moved forward, sidestepping the light. The poacher, fifteen feet above, was cursing the birds. After another minute of his struggling, he moved back down the tree and dropped the last six feet to the jungle floor. Rollie was ten feet away and spoke to him, watching as the man whirled while instinctively raising his small-gauge lever-action shotgun to Rollie's midsection.

The man was short and wiry and wearing a large hat. The vertical light was behind the poacher, throwing a black shadow over his front side, making it impossible for Rollie to see his face.

Although the poacher had turned with his shotgun—probably loaded with light birdshot—at the ready, Rollie was also prepared for action. Because extended from his right hand, his left gripping his right in a proper shooter's grip, was his Colt .38 Super. It was aimed at the poacher's upper chest. Theoretically, if they both fired at the same time (unless Rollie was wrong about the birdshot in the small-gauge shotgun), Rollie would be injured. The poacher, however, after flying backward as if he were jerked by a locomotive, would die quickly from the trauma induced by the powerful ACP "super" round.

It was a classic face-off. Neither man moving. Both standing there, aiming their tool of death, alone in their own little world of how to play out such a scenario. Rollie knew there wasn't much time left before Nicholas and the rest of their pursuers found the girls. He had to do something. His mind searched his two years of university Spanish and the rough form of "Portu-Span" he retained from Gran Chaco.

Your gun is small, Rollie thought. "Tu escopeta es pequeno," he spouted, knowing the vocabulary and structure of his translation was incorrect, but also knowing the man would know what he meant. *And mine is large and deadly.* "Y mi pistola es grande y mortalmente."

The man didn't budge, but he did blink.

I want your light, your gun, and your ammunition. "Yo quiero tu fuego y tu escopeta y tu ammunicion." *I have a great deal of money.* "Yo tengo mucho dinero."

The poacher had been stone still for a full minute, but the second after "muy dinero" left Rollie's lips, a tremor passed through the man. He nearly lowered the shotgun but brought it back up, tensing visibly.

"Cuánto?" the poacher asked in a gravelly voice.

Guns down. "Las armas abajo."

Rollie eased his own pistol down, watching as the man did the same with his shotgun. Displaying the first measure of full trust, more so in the interest of time, Rollie placed his pistol on the jungle floor and straightened. The man did the same.

"Rapidamente, sí?" Rollie asked. He lifted his breast pocket and produced a small wad of bills amounting to around forty dollars, fanning the money in the harsh light of the hand lamp.

"Santa Maria," the man whispered, reaching for the money. As soon as he had it in hand, counting it with his tongue extended like an overheated dog, Rollie reared back and drilled him with a looping right carrying the force of a wrecking ball. The punch had its prescribed effect as the smaller man tumbled to the ground, eyes and mouth open, probably disabled for several seconds as his brain spiked from the instant concussion of a full-on right hook.

Up in the trees, the birds continued to flutter around. Hopefully their mother was still alive to raise them.

"I'll be in these woods every night," Rollie said in his broken Spanish while leaning over the downed poacher. "If I catch you poaching again, they'll find you feeding the fish in the canal."

Rollie tossed the money on the poacher, fighting the urge to inflict more punishment. Knowing time was precious, he grabbed the poacher's shotgun, ripped away his ammo belt and, after switching it off, took the powerful hand lamp.

He hurried back through the woods to the cut in the rock face.

VIVIEN SAT on one of the massive mossy boulders thirty feet up the cut. Maria stood on a broad ledge in front of her, holding the rifle in the crook of her right arm, aiming it downward, her finger on the trigger.

"Do you know how to shoot that?" Vivien asked in a quiet voice.

The young woman's white teeth gleamed as she smiled. "Oh sí, this is a thirty caliber carbine rifle, very common in Cuba. I have trained with it many times."

Vivien closed her eyes for a moment. What she wouldn't give for a cigarette. "Did you really sleep with my husband?"

Maria turned. "No."

"Why did you say you did?"

"We were looking for him."

"Who?"

"The man I work…*worked* for, we were hired by one of the men who is now after us."

Vivien stood. "Where was this?"

"Havana. My home."

"And what did he hire you to do?"

Maria's eyes drifted downward. "To find your husband, here in Panama. To lure him in so that the man who hired us could take whatever it was your husband had."

"Do you know what that was?"

"No," she said, shaking her head. "But it must have been very important."

"But now you don't want to help the man who hired you?"

Maria's tone was emphatic. "No."

"Why did you turn on him?"

Having now been in the blackness of the cut for several minutes, Vivien's eyes had adjusted. And having seen herself do it often enough in the mirror, she could tell when a person was on the verge of tears. The stony face. The slight movement of the lips. The rapid blinks.

"It's okay," she whispered, touching Maria's arm.

"He murdered Philip, my superior from Havana. Philip was the only man who has ever been good to me. He took me in. Fed me. Raised me. He loved me." The end of her statement was barely audible due to her shudders. Vivien put her hand on Maria's back. Maria lowered the rifle and sobbed into Vivien's wet shirt: deep, anguished cries.

"When did you learn that Philip had been murdered?" Vivien asked, surprised by Maria's level of intense sorrow.

"Just today."

Now Vivien understood…Maria hadn't yet had a chance to grieve. There were no sounds from the east, so Vivien continued to hold the young woman, rocking her gently, giving her a small measure of comfort.

Moments later, Rollie came crashing back through the jungle from the west. He ascended the lower portion of the cut in seconds, his arm pointing up the remainder of the cleft. "Let's go," he said, obviously not noticing the moment the two women were having.

"Where?" Vivien asked, still holding Maria in the embrace.

"Up this rift."

"But we can't see to climb. Why don't we just keep going that way?" she protested, pointing to the west.

"Because all that exists that way is jungle, and I think that's what these assholes will think we did. When they keep going, we'll come back down and escape to the north, to the American Zone."

"But Rollie—"

A bright beam of light punctured the night, aiming up the ravine from Rollie's hand. He flicked it once. "Here's your light. They're going to be here *any* second…so, please go."

Maria handed Rollie the carbine and, after wiping her tears, she set off, boulder to boulder, scaling the rock crevice with adequate speed. Vivien followed her and finally Rollie, the carbine and shotgun strapped on his back as he tried to keep the cut lit while he picked his way upward.

Judging by what he could see from the light, the bluff was several hundred feet tall.

And, as he climbed for the summit, Rollie prayed for a miracle; he prayed for safety; and prayed for their pursuers to head further into the jungle. Because, with precious few rounds at their disposal, he had no idea how he could hold them off if they followed.

BERND WAS behind the Panamanians when they reached the rock face. He told them to shut up as they began animatedly discussing where they were—a place known *El Barranca del Demonio*—The Demon's Bluff.

"But, señor," the old one said, wide eyed as he backed away from the vine-laden cliff, his hands waving in front of him. "This man must be truly evil to come straight to the bluff. No one comes here unless they wish to die."

"Ignorant, peasant superstitions," Bernd replied with a dismissive wave of his hand. He craned his neck upward at the blackness of the wall that reached beyond the canopy of trees.

All of the Panamanians were visibly tense, each man having moved away from the bluff. They whispered urgently among themselves.

"Well, they couldn't have climbed it," Bernd finally said in an exasperated voice. "Follow it around to the south so we can confer with the other squad."

Rifles at the ready, and staying well away from Demon's Bluff, the Panamanians picked their way to the south.

WITH THE light as their guide, the climb up the cut wasn't as difficult as Rollie had envisioned, especially after they passed through the canopy of the rainforest. Above the canopy, he was able to switch off the hand lamp. He paused, checking his neck wound. It was bleeding but not heavily, stemmed by Maria's bandage. Around him, at his feet, the canopy of the rainforest swayed and undulated in the blueness of the moonlit night. It seemed to breathe, a living organism, and looked solid enough to invite a person to walk on its surface. Above him the stars punctured the night sky in a million random places, mere pinpricks compared to the glow of the moon. It was still to the west but rising, hard and bright and throwing black shadows in contrast to its empty light.

The women had already reached the summit, about a hundred feet above, and disappeared from his sight. Rollie could hear nothing from below, hoping they'd lost their pursuers. After hooking the hand lamp on his belt, he resumed his climb. The rocks above the tree line were free of the damp moss that covered everything down below. It allowed him to move with much more speed, freeing his mind to work on the problems at hand.

Two more minutes of climbing, he estimated.

NICHOLAS AND the M.P.'s were crouching around the wall when Bernd saw them, making a whistling sound to signal them. An M.P. whirled his carbine around, immediately shouted down by Nicholas.

"Find anything?" Bernd asked, pushing his way to the front of his squad.

"Their trail was obvious, so they came this far," Nicholas said with a note of exasperation. "Now we're trying to determine which way they went from here." He turned his head. "Keep searching," he commanded.

Two of the M.P.'s dutifully hit their knees, the third sweeping a hand torch below the base of the wall, the group working together as they tried to find footsteps leading in either direction.

Nicholas stepped to Bernd. "I don't like this," he whispered.

"But where could they have gone?"

He stepped even closer, speaking only in a tone Bernd could hear. "I've half a mind to *rid* ourselves of everyone here—right now. To go back into the city, speak to the remaining local police, and implicate Rollie and the two women for these murders, and then to focus on finding Richard Hampton." Nicholas gripped Bernd's forearm, moving his mouth inches from his countryman's ear. "With my influence, it would work."

"But if he gets to the American Zone..." Bernd said, not finishing the sentence. "Even with your influence, he could make problems."

"Shit," Nicholas whispered, head tilting back. "This damned third-world country...I'm not even thinking straight."

"Look, there are only three of them and I'm not sure they even have any ammo left." Bernd glanced around, the M.P.'s were still on their knees and the Panamanians were still standing back, now silent, obviously scared. "A man and two women—even with these prehistoric locals, we have *no* excuse for not prevailing."

"The blonde is Vivien Hampton. Who did you say the other girl is?" Nicholas asked.

"Maria Fuentes. As I said, she *was* working for me."

Nicholas was silent for a moment. "Why did she turn?"

Bernd shrugged. "This fellow of yours, I guess he somehow convinced her."

"He's a snake."

"Sir," one of the M.P.'s said. "Footsteps over here, heading south."

Nicholas moved in that direction, wiping his high forehead with a handkerchief. He stared at the footprints in a depression. Multiple sets, leading away, boots and smallish bare feet.

"Everyone on your feet! Haul ass!" Nicholas turned to Bernd, lifting his pistol for emphasis. "They're not getting away."

The group hurried off to the south, led by the M.P.'s, followed by the hesitant Panamanians who were constantly "encouraged" by the armed gringos behind them. It wasn't a minute before they were at the cut, the mossy rocks easily displaying the fresh shoe marks in the vivid light of the M.P.'s hand torch.

"Is there any other way off this rock?" Bernd, speaking Spanish, demanded of the Panamanians.

Staring at the shoe marks on the cut, the oldest Panamanian shook his head. "No, señor. But—"

Ignoring him, Bernd turned. "This is the only way on and off."

"Climb!" Nicholas growled through clenched teeth at the nearest M.P..

Rifle slung on his back, the M.P. hurried upward, followed by the two others.

Nicholas and Bernd shook hands, their eyes communicating the same message: "Now we've got them."

Inching backward, the oldest of the Panamanian policemen shook his head, whispering to his countrymen. "To climb that rock is to die."

He repeated this three times.

Chapter Twenty-One

ROLLIE WAS now only twenty-five feet from the summit, taking care not to misstep. The final portion of the climb was much steeper. He was impressed that the women had done so well. In fact, they'd probably negotiated the cut faster than he had. This last portion, with the rifle, the shotgun and his neck wound, was taking its toll on Rollie.

"Are you okay?" Vivien asked, leaning out over the top.

"Just enjoying the view," he muttered, finding a purchase on a small outcropping and pulling himself up.

"There's good news and bad news," Vivien said. Maria appeared beside her, pointing at something and saying something Rollie couldn't quite hear. Vivien nodded and told her to wait a moment.

"What's the bad news?" Rollie asked, ascending to the next stepping stone.

"There's no other way down. Sheer cliff on all sides."

He stopped, wiping his forehead with his sleeve. "And the good news?"

"There's no other way up, either. And it's beautiful up here."

Rollie hitched with a breath of sardonic laughter. "That's just great. Next time you decide to lay out good news and bad for me, make sure—"

"Rollie!"

The rock next to Rollie's right hand popped, throwing bits of chipped stone and spark, cutting the outer edge of his hand. He heard the crack of the rifle immediately after. Flattening himself against the rock, he peered down, seeing one of the large military policemen just above the jungle canopy, leaning against a boulder and taking aim.

Rollie adjusted his position, not giving the soldier a clean shot. "Get back!" he shouted to the women. "Get back and stay back!"

There was another gunshot, and another. Sure enough, now that he'd moved himself flush with the cut, the M.P. could no longer get a bead on him. Rollie looked up and was temporarily mollified that Vivien and Maria had backed away.

But what was he to do? He was frozen here, and as soon as he started to move his pursuers would open fire. Licking his lips, Rollie reached to his right, grabbing a cantaloupe-sized rock. It must have weighed fifteen pounds. He couldn't chance leaning out, and instead had to make a guess on trajectory based on what he had seen. The ravine was steep, its angle at least seventy-five degrees. If he were to throw the rock out fifteen feet, it would plummet well down the crevice and, even if it didn't strike the M.P., it would create a great deal of noise and perhaps cause other rocks to fall. Most important, it would give them something perilous to worry about. A rock of that size and weight, falling a hundred feet or more, would kill a man instantly.

He adjusted his position slightly, setting his feet. Throwing overhand, Rollie tossed the stone outward, watching as gravity took over, pulling it quickly out of sight.

And that's when his left foot exploded.

Just as he was registering that he'd been shot again, he heard the stone hit, followed by loud shouts from below. But taking precedent over his Cro-Magnon-chucks-igneous-rock defense was the bloody hole in the forward half of his left boot. When his foot had been sticking out from the ledge he was on the M.P. had—probably luckily—put a .30 caliber round right through it.

Thanks to the nerveless skin of his scarred neck, the injury from the bullet that winged him earlier didn't really hurt. This wound, however, started the pain-train off with an initial burst of agony. Basically a signal sent through the various organisms of the body which said, "Something is amiss so here's a spurt of sharp pain to get everyone's attention." It worked. But, now, twenty seconds later, as Rollie put his weight on his right foot and made sure nothing else was exposed beyond the ledge, deep, bowel-watering pain resonated through him, emanating from the hole in his foot.

Clenching his teeth so hard he expected them to shatter, he put weight on his foot, testing it. The initial shot of pain was almost enough to make him let up, but he pressed through it, realizing he could add weight even though the throbbing was intense. He twisted the foot in the moonlight, estimating the bullet had passed through the ball of his foot, dead center, probably breaking at least two of the metatarsal bones.

His anger coming forward, he grasped another rock, throwing it. And another. And another. After the third one he heard a clipped shriek of agony followed by a clattering of equipment and steel. There was another shout from what sounded like a different voice followed by more distant rustling. Then silence. Rollie chanced a look, barely able to see one of the M.P.'s hurriedly descending, disappearing below the canopy. There was another M.P. visible, above the tree line, sprawled on a rock, his rifle dangling next to him. The man's leg was bent unnaturally, like he had a new, forward-bending knee in the middle of his shin. He wasn't moving.

Rollie turned his eyes back to the summit. He'd bought some time. It was now or never. Fighting through the pain, he climbed.

"GET YOUR ass back up there!" Nicholas yelled as one of the M.P.'s scurried off the lower boulders of the cut.

The M.P. supported himself against the largest of the bottom boulders, resting his face against the damp moss as he sucked air. "Sir, he started throwing rocks, big ones."

Nicholas turned to Bernd, his mouth open, stupefied by what he had just heard. "Rocks?" he shouted, turning back. "Did you say 'rocks'?"

The M.P. straightened, gesturing with his hand. "That cliff is damn near straight up. You go up there and try dodging rocks as big as a football. It's like standing next to an exploding bomb when one hits. Hell, I think your buddy up there killed Jenkins."

"Where is Jenkins?" Nicholas asked, hands on his hips.

"He got hit when the rock bounced. I was down below him and saw him fall twenty, maybe thirty feet. He didn't move after that."

Nicholas closed his eyes, rubbing the back of his gun-toting hand on his face and forehead.

"Thoughts?" Bernd asked.

Just as Nicholas was about to reply, the yelling started.

It came from above.

A MOMENT before, Rollie threw his hands up over the summit, grunting as he pulled himself over the top ledge, lying there on his back as he caught his breath and attempted to order his thoughts.

"You're bleeding from your foot!" Vivien cried.

He forced a smile, raising his palm to keep her at bay. "Just let me rest here for a second, okay? That was slightly intense. Just need to remind myself that I'm still alive."

Maria and Vivien conferred, and began to remove his left boot.

"Don't," he said sharply, softening the remainder of his words, "...do that...please. That'll just encourage it to bleed more. If anything, just wrap the laces as tight as you can get them around the top of the boot. That will constrict the blood without being so tight as to kill tissue."

"And your neck," Maria said, touching her makeshift bandage.

"Yeah, I'm leaking all over."

The two women worked separately on his gunshot wounds. His mind attempting to race, Rollie forced himself to think back to summer afternoons, during his childhood, when he'd go fishing. He and his friends, and sometimes his father, would sit on the banks of the slow-moving Miami River, killing hours at a time with a cane pole in their hands. But it wasn't the fishing that was peaceful, it was the time spent together. And tonight, on this bluff, he tried to recall those glorious afternoons of his youth. It was a technique he'd learned years ago—slowing his mind, letting it wander.

After the women were finished working on him, he raised up on his elbows, amazed at what he saw. A heavy chill passed through his ravaged body as he surveyed the surface in the moonlight. About the size of two football fields, the top was similar to the buttes of the American southwest. The area at the top was almost perfectly flat. It appeared to have been carefully sheared from the rock, as if created by a woodworker's plane followed by several rounds of fine sandpaper. Smooth as a ballroom floor, with no vegetation, the plateau was nearly circular in shape. It looked as if, anticipating their visit, a crew of janitors had swept and mopped the entire surface, which was even devoid of sand.

The women were saying something but Rollie wasn't listening. His meditation had worked, and he'd come out of it with one single inclination. Following it, Rollie reached inside his shirt and produced the letter, now soaked from his swim through the canal. Carefully unfolding it, he asked Vivien to hold it flat while he lit the hand lamp.

Whoever had written it had, thankfully, used indelible ink. Mildly smudged, it was still quite legible.

There were only two paragraphs left.

The girls read over both of his shoulders, each asking questions he politely ignored.

After finishing, Rollie refolded the letter and tucked it back into his pocket. He rose to his feet, testing his battered foot. After walking in a large circle, working out the kinks, Rollie turned to Maria.

"I need you to translate something."

She nodded.

"I need you to be able to yell loud and clear, okay?"

Again she nodded.

"Very loud, Maria."

"I will pretend I am angry," she said with a smile.

He led her to the top of the cut, standing behind the lip so they wouldn't get shot, and began shouting to those down below.

THE SHOUTS from above were distant but clear.

"Listen up down there! This is for the American military policemen and the Panamanian nationals."

The woman yelled an immediate translation in Spanish. Bernd growled the word "bitch" through clenched teeth.

"You've been taken for fools! According to the Cuban woman who is with me, the man purporting himself as a Brit named Lancaster is actually a German spy. A Nazi!"

Maria's translation followed. Bernd took a step back as the two remaining M.P.'s, staring upward, cocked their heads in disbelief. One of them turned to Bernd who rolled his eyes as if this were a silly, sophomoric ploy.

"*And the other man, Nicholas Penland, he's been my boss for a number of years at the United States Department of War. I can only imagine what he's told you about me, but I am a patriot and, for you M.P.'s down there, I'm a former Marine. I'll admit I never liked Nicholas, and today I realized why…because I just learned that he, too, is a Nazi spy! And I can prove it with a letter I have up here, in my hands.*" There was a brief pause. "*You men think you're following orders, but you're actually working for a spy.*"

Nicholas shook his head with a wry grin on his face, gesturing upward as the woman yelled the translation. "This is a pathetic parlor trick," he said to the M.P.'s. "Don't be taken in by that traitor."

"*And if you don't believe me,*" thundered the voice from above, "*then start asking both of them questions about their backgrounds. They're trained spies so they have wonderfully thought-out backstories, but you can trip them up on things like World Series baseball scores, and old motion pictures, and which radio shows used to come on Tuesday night.*"

"Bloody nonsense," Bernd said to the group.

Cutting off the woman as she translated, the voice cut through the night with a suggestion that made everyone momentarily freeze. "*Or better yet!*" he yelled. "*Disarm the two of them. Or, try to do it and see what happens.*"

The Spanish translation followed with alacrity.

The Panamanians and the M.P.'s stared at Nicholas and Bernd.

"Give it up, Rollie!" Nicholas yelled, craning his long neck upward with his hands cupped beside his mouth. "How many more people need to die so you can sell your secrets?"

"*Who was that man you shot tonight, Nicholas, you bastard? He was wearing an Army uniform! What…did he figure you out? Was he trying to leave? You men down there need to use your brains! Do you honestly believe he was justified in shooting one of your own? Don't be scared of his fancy title and big words!*"

Bernd and Nicholas were standing shoulder to shoulder. Nicholas wagged his .45 at the M.P.'s. "Tell me you fellas don't believe this line of bullshit. That man is a *traitor* to the United States of America and he just murdered one of your fellow men!"

There was a telling bout of quiet.

Finally, the oldest M.P. took a step forward, raising his rifle at waist level. "I don't quite believe him, sir, but all the same, let's have those pistols just so we can be sure. A measure of trust goes a long way and those people up there aren't going anywhere."

"Yeah," chimed the other M.P..

Nicholas lowered his pistol. He barely nudged Bernd with his elbow. The Panamanians were coming toward him, one of them holding his hand out for his pistol while the other two covered him.

When the M.P. took Nicholas's Colt—handed over properly—Bernd glanced to his left and then followed suit, handing his Browning to the Panamanians. Nicholas spread his hands in a gesture of peace. "Satisfied?" he asked without spite. He then pointed upward. "May I?"

Without waiting, he yelled to the sky, "Forget about it, Roald Donahue, you traitorous bastard! We've let them disarm us because we, unlike you, are these brave men's allies! Now you've nowhere to run and, unless I miscounted, you're damn near out of ammo! So do us all a favor and stop with the games! Give up now and you might avoid the gallows."

"Question them!" Rollie yelled in immediate response. *"They're lying to you and you'll trip them up quickly. If we can't go anywhere, like he said, then what have you got to lose?"*

Nicholas rolled his eyes as he put his hands on his hips in exasperation.

The voice from above continued, saying, *"And search them! Don't be careless. They're each carrying more than one weapon."*

A moment before, when Nicholas and Bernd had been stripped of their pistols, the entire group of men had visibly relaxed, each craning their neck up at the shouts from the man known as Rollie. As soon as he uttered the words about other weapons, the remaining M.P.'s started as if jolted by a small current of electricity. They turned back to Bernd and Nicholas…

But it was too late.

Nicholas had snatched the pin from the M.P.'s Mk 2 grenade before Rollie had suggested they be searched. Following the suggestion he quietly released the spoon, starting the four-to-five-second fuse time, of which two seconds had already passed.

Given his position in the Department of War, even though it was compromised, Nicholas Penland had been privy to many items of weaponry in the U.S. Forces' standard T, O, and E. It hadn't been three months since he'd driven out to Aberdeen, spending a frigid Thursday and Friday with a grizzled old master sergeant, shooting weapons and blowing things up. He'd taken a keen interest in the tried and true Mk 2 hand grenade, discernible due to its pineapple shape and the ring of yellow paint around its neck. It was alleged to have a kill radius of thirty-five feet and a reliable fuse of four to five seconds.

Taking these facts into consideration, and given that the M.P.'s and Panamanians were standing ten feet away, he tossed the grenade between them and slightly over their heads, assuming it would detonate twenty-five feet from where he currently stood. Nicholas knew his fellow Nazi had better be on his toes, lest he wind up in the kill-zone.

After he tossed the grenade, when his murderous intentions were common knowledge, gunfire erupted from one of the M.P.'s, but it arced upward in a spray of panic. Nicholas had already hurled himself backward, and earthward, seeing a blur of motion in the corner of his right eye that told him Bernd had done the same.

The resulting blast (unlike at Aberdeen, when he'd been in the bosom of a concrete-walled pillbox) was cataclysmic. Nicholas felt stabs of pain shoot through his legs as the blast sent him cartwheeling a few more feet in the direction he'd already leaped.

Despite the cobwebs from the explosion, and the shrapnel in his feet and legs, he yanked the .357 snub-nose from his ankle holster, rising unsteadily to his feet to survey the damage and kill any survivors.

ROLLIE HAD been peering over the ledge, about to yell another barb when he saw the flash followed a half-second later by the detonation. The canopy of trees swayed between him and the explosion, and every bird inside of a mile screeched and set to flying. Maria gripped Rollie's arm as the two of them listened to more gunshots followed by a long period of eerie silence.

After a full minute, a voice called out from the jungle. *"Roald Donahue…Rollie…it's all over, old friend. Mister Lancaster and I are alive and well! Go ahead and pat yourself on the back for killing off a partial squad of United States military policemen and a host of Panamanian nationals."*

"You're the one that killed them, you bastard!" Rollie yelled, the words out before he had a chance to consider them.

Laughter, deep and cackling, was followed by indistinct talking Rollie couldn't make out.

"What are we going to do now?"

Rollie turned, surprised to see that Vivien had been just behind him all this time. He led the girls away from the ledge, kneeling to take pressure away from his foot. Placing the shotgun on the ground, he asked Maria to lay the carbine next to it.

"Your pistols," he said. Vivien placed the F&W on the stone floor of the butte and Maria followed suit with her Beretta. Rollie popped the clip on his .38 Super, counting one round in the chamber and two in the clip. He had no other clips remaining. He checked the F&W—empty. He checked Maria's Beretta.

Also empty.

Rollie found two rounds in the Army carbine and only one round in the shotgun. He then checked his pockets, finding no additional ammunition. It must have fallen out during his swim.

After grinding his teeth in frustration, he spoke matter-of-factly. "Well, the simple truth is we have six bullets remaining." A period of silence ensued, the only sound being Rollie's Brahma-bull-breaths as he snorted in and out of his nose, trying to channel his rage. It was Vivien who asked the question.

"Is that enough bullets?"

Rollie didn't respond. Maria mouthed the word "no".

Leaving the two smaller, impotent pistols where they were, Rollie took the shotgun, the carbine and his pistol to the ledge, searching the area around the top of the cut for the best vantage point. He chose a spot to the right, only because it had a small indentation which would give him a better view as he peered down the steep bluff. Despite the light of the moon, he couldn't get a good view of the choke that existed on the single-barrel 4-10 shotgun.

It probably wouldn't provide much in the way of range and certainly wouldn't have much stopping power. He placed it behind the other two.

Prioritizing the other weapons was straight-forward. He would use the carbine first, because of its range, followed by his pistol. The shotgun would remain at the ready only in the event someone reached the summit and, even then, he could only hope to possibly disable the person with a face full of birdshot.

He gripped the carbine, peering out over the edge.

A large, muscular figure could be seen emerging from the tree line.

He was climbing rapidly, staring upward.

A MOMENT before, after conferring, Bernd suggested an aggressive plan of action. With one of the American carbines on his back, fully loaded, he would climb the lower portion of the cut, emerging from the tree line and finding a ledge that would give him room to move around. Having arrived without incident, he unslung his .30 caliber rifle, taking a comfortable shooter's position against a smooth boulder, peering over the hard sights for a head or appendage he might put a bullet through.

ROLLIE WATCHED as the muscular man halted and disappeared. He eased his own carbine out, aiming downward at the spot when he saw the muzzle flash below him. There was a whizzing, angry hornet sound that went right by his ear followed by the sound of the gunshot. He pulled back, realizing he'd just come inches from death.

"Get me some rocks," he said to Maria and Vivien, both crouched just behind him. As the women searched, Rollie moved to the left of the cut, finding the big man looking up to where he'd just been peering over. Just as Rollie was taking aim, the girls came back, their voices dripping with angst.

"There are no rocks up here," Vivien cried.

"There's nothing at all," Maria said in accompaniment, sweeping her hand back over the butte. "Not even a pebble."

Taking another peek, Rollie saw plenty of loose scree thirty feet down the cut, at the first ledge. If there had ever been rocks here at the top, he assumed they'd been thrown off in the millenniums since the bluff was first climbed. And, unless he wanted to try to descend while injured to the ledge below, he was left with six rounds for defense, and nothing more.

But he needed to give the two climbers something to think about.

He leaned out again, taking quick aim in case the man saw him, and squeezed off one of his two rifle rounds.

The bullet ricocheted with a spark, missing the man by a foot.

"Damn it!" Rollie growled, rolling back and staring skyward. He pressed his fingers onto his eyelids, taking slow breaths.

Gather yourself. Cool heads prevail.

Rollie switched positions, easing himself to a cleft at the center of the cut. This time he waited for movement, able to see a portion of the man's head. He squeezed off his final carbine bullet and watched the rock just next to the man's head spark before he heard the zing of the ricochet.

"You're not a very good shot!" taunted the voice from below, right after putting three rounds into the cleft where Rollie's head had just been.

Rollie slid the carbine away, knowing he would have to let the man climb quite a bit before having a prayer with his Colt Super. Infuriated at the situation, he placed both hands on his forehead, pressing against his head with such force that his arms shook.

When he finally sat up, he looked at Vivien and Maria. The harsh moonlight cast strange, gothic shadows on their pretty faces, making their expressions difficult to read. But even with the odd light, he could see an expression in both of them that made his heart beat faster.

It was hope.

"Look, Rollie," Vivien whispered, her hand gesturing beyond him.

He turned, staring in the direction she was pointing—southeast—to see a sizeable, gray shadow slowly entering the southern mouth of the canal.

It was a warship.

Chapter Twenty-Two

BERND WAITED. And waited. He repositioned his own carbine, listening as the leather sling protested the amount of tension he was applying. After seeing the previous shots from above, he decided to focus on the center of the cut and wait for the man called Rollie to stick his big head back out. Several minutes had since passed.

And still, nothing.

Was there some other way off?

Was Rollie Donahue dead?

He looked downward, seeing Nicholas, the man who insisted on killing the three Americans, leaning against the bottom of the cut, using what looked like a pocket knife to dig shrapnel from his leg. Bernd, angered over the delay, found a pea-sized pebble and tossed it. When Nicholas looked up, Bernd pointed at him and touched his own watch. Nicholas lit the still-functioning hand lamp two times.

Two minutes.

Bernd, quite visible in the moonlight above the tree line, gestured to himself, then motioned upward

I'm going up.

Nicholas again flashed the light two quick times.

No.

Bernd watched as Nicholas wrapped something around his leg before cinching his shoe back on. He glanced upward, the top of the cut still free of Donahue. When he looked back down, thankfully, Nicholas was climbing.

ROLLIE HAD removed his shirt, not without noticing Maria's wide eyes at the sight of his scarring. He held the powerful hand lamp in one hand, and covered its bulb and reflector with his bundled shirt. Then, using one second intervals between letters and five seconds between the repeating of distress signal, he sent a lighted message to the ship, hoping her crew wasn't resting (or on shore leave) while some sleepy pilot guided her through.

Dot—dot—dot. *S*

Dash—dash—dash. *O*

Dot—dot—dot. *S*

Pause. Do again.

SOS. SOS. SOS. SOS.

"C'mon…wake up, you squids!"

CAPTAIN LUCAS Villiers knew he should be getting some rest but just couldn't manage it. He'd been through the canal several times, the last when he was XO of the USS Idaho, but never as a captain. And here, standing aboard his shiny new toy, a gleaming Gleaves-class destroyer, the USS Satterlee, Villiers was chewing the fat with the old pilot who'd been ferried out to him. The canal pilot, a man who'd probably navigated this manmade shortcut a thousand times, was still passionate enough about his job to indulge Lucas in all the small details only a true mariner could appreciate.

While enjoying a local cigar, courtesy of the pilot, Captain Villiers listened to him relaying a colorful tale about a British frigate that had grounded near this very spot thanks to a strong gale and too much gin on the bridge. Just as the pilot was assigning blame for the mildly humorous misadventure, the officer of the deck (O.O.D.) rapped on the thick window and gestured to the west.

"Cap'n, signal on the port side."

"Where?"

"Ten o'clock."

Demon's Bluff

Counting the pilot, there were six sailors on the bridge. They all turned their gaze to the Satterlee's ten o'clock, realizing in seconds that an SOS was being broadcast—from land.

"I'll be damned," Villiers said, coming to his feet.

The O.O.D. entered the bridge. "Want us to return signal?"

Villiers stared at the flashing light. Whoever was broadcasting it was dutifully repeating the SOS over and over. The distress call was coming quickly, but with enough spacing to show the operator knew what he was doing.

"Cap'n?"

"Not yet," Villiers said, shaken from his brief reverie. He turned to the pilot. "Is that hill in the American Zone?"

"Technically we control the entire canal and the easement around it, extending a mile each way. Technically. But the true zone begins a few miles up. This area down here, with no locks, is too big to foot patrol other than the mouth. There is a boat, PT-104, on patrol out here somewhere tonight."

Captain Villiers turned, whipping charts to the floor until he found the one he was looking for.

"Don't need that," the pilot said. "I can look at the SOS and tell you where it's comin' from."

"And where's that?" Villiers asked, handing the correct chart to the chief.

"That's Demon's Bluff, a rock that spurts straight up outta the jungle. No other place that high on the west side of the canal, lest you go fifteen miles through the bush."

Villiers lifted his cigar, clamping it in his mouth. Rather than have a signalman reply on the main lamp, he instructed his chief on what to do. The chief hefted the powerful bridge lamp from a storage bin next to the compass platform, plugging the 24 volt device into a receptacle and carrying the electrified device outside to the weather deck.

In a quick reply, the chief signaled a short phrase: *SOS acknowledged. ID yourself to the U.S Navy.*

ROLLIE WATCHED the reply as it flashed in quick order. "Hallelujah," he breathed. His head whipped to the cut.

"Maria, get over there and use my pistol to keep that man at bay, but *only* if he's close. There's only three shots, so use them slowly…very slowly. Just one from that hand-cannon should back him down if he's close. Got it?"

She nodded, running to the cut and peering over.

Rollie was flashing his reply when she fired off a round and screamed what must have been a vicious Spanish insult. He ignored the exchange, focusing on his message.

THE CAPTAIN and the chief worked in unison, writing the message on the next blank page of the logbook. Before Captain Villiers pondered what he'd just copied down, he turned to the pilot and his O.O.D.

"Keep us right here in this general area and use the grease pencil to mark our position on the chart."

"Anchor?" the O.O.D. asked with raised brows.

"Not yet, just linger here."

"Aye, aye."

Villiers turned back to the logbook. The chief had already read it over and was staring at the captain grim faced. Villiers read it aloud.

"I am Roald Donahue from US D.O.W. with two civs. Pursued by two Nazi agents. Time critical. Shoot at bluff."

Villiers read it three times, finally whispering, "Are you kidding me?" Badly needing a shave, his thick Gallic beard made a scratching sound as he rubbed it with his hand. He first looked to his chief. "Sam?"

"Unprecedented, cap'n. Part of me thinks it's a joke and another part of me grows cold thinking about the consequences if true."

Captain Villiers looked back to his ten o'clock, narrowing his eyes as the person on the hill steadily flashed another message.

Hurry

While there was no official Morse representation for an exclamation point, the one informally used by the military was a continuous sound or light, and the operator on the other end did so here, leaving the light on a full five seconds each time he flashed the word.

Hurry!

Captain Villiers snatched the fleet radio from the radio bank, calling ears-only to Admiral Halpert who was aboard the USS Taylor. He was probably through the canal by now, and Villiers hoped he wasn't asleep.

Villiers had a terse exchange with a youthful officer, probably a peach fuzz ensign on radio watch. The little prick wouldn't say whether or not Halpert was nearby, which was probably a good sign. While he awaited a response, Villiers instructed his chief to signal back and ask what action was desired.

The chief began to signal.

Several minutes later an exasperated Admiral Halpert came over the radio. "What in God's name could be ears-only when you're passing through the secure canal?"

Captain Villiers relayed the initial exchange, having to explain it two times. As his chief was writing down the supposed Department of War man's response out on the rail, Villiers dipped his head as he listened to Halpert's judgment.

"There's not enough in what you're telling me for *you* to do anything. Hell, what could any of us do? I'll notify the American Zone and let them respond accordingly."

The admiral's voice could be heard talking on another radio, relaying the information, before he came back to Villiers.

"Message sent."

"Aye, sir. Will you stay on the radio for a short while? At least until this plays out a bit?"

The radio squelched as the admiral exhaled. "I was in the rack, cap'n. I'll agree to sit here long enough to have a cigarette and a glass of water. That's how much time you've got."

"Aye, aye, sir."

Villiers cut his eyes to the pilot. "Ever seen something like this in all your journeys through the canal?"

"Never," the man answered immediately, with a humorless laugh.

"Think it's genuine?"

"Have you been in the city before?" the pilot asked.

"Nope."

"It's spy central out there," the pilot said, scratching a match on the steel handgrip by the depth gauge. He gestured to the east as he touched the match to his cigarette. "Hell, there's a Philip Dorn and a Joan Crawford passing messages on every street corner in that city. The Zone tells us that no less than ten undercovers are watching what passes through the canal at any given moment." He took a quick pull on his cigarette and nodded once. "So, yeah, I do think it's genuine."

Villiers didn't respond. He turned and walked out to the rail, grasping the chief's shoulder. "No go on any action. Admiral called the Zone and told them to send a patrol of ground-pounders over."

"Shit," the chief answered, drawing the word out so it sounded like *sheee-attttt*. His shoulders sagged as he lowered the lamp to let it hang from its cord.

"You believe this guy, too?" Villiers asked, gesturing to the hillside.

"Aye, sir," the chief breathed. "I do, and I believe he and his two civilians are in a deadly situation up there."

There was a much smaller flash from the butte. Then, seconds later, a distant report.

"Gunshot," the chief said. Villiers could see the veins in the chief's big hands bulging as he gripped the rail.

Then a message flashed from the hill.

Nazis advancing. One bullet left here. Shoot at bluff

Again the message was followed by a long, continuous beam of light to signify an exclamation.

Villiers tossed his cigar overboard in disgust. "That damned admiral. Signal back and tell them they'll just have to wait for the grunts from the American Zone." Villiers dipped his head and walked back into the bridge, punching the steel throttle housing as he did.

JUST ABOUT the time Captain Villiers had begun to speak with the admiral, Maria had squeezed off one of the remaining pistol rounds. Vivien low-crawled beside her, taking a quick peek over the edge. She looked at Maria who was covered in sweat, breathing as if she'd just sprinted a mile.

"Where is he?"

Maria touched her free hand to her lips, speaking in a low whisper. "They've both climbed almost all the way up, down on the next ledge. They're tucked back where I can't see them."

"How many bullets are left?"

Maria's face was grim. "One here, one in the shotgun."

"Come on, dammit!" Rollie shouted behind them, his frustration aimed at the ship as he continued to signal.

"Stay focused," Vivien breathed, patting Maria on her shoulder and sliding the shotgun next to her bare feet. She spun backward and hurried to Rollie.

"What are they saying?"

"Some bullshit about the fleet commander not being able to authenticate if we're for real or not."

"That's the Navy for you," Vivien said, throwing up her hands. "Always by the book." Behind her, Maria slid to a new position as she angled for her final shot from the pistol. "They're right below her, Rollie," Vivien said, touching his shoulder. "And there are only two rounds left."

"Once the rounds are gone, our only hope is—"

As he was talking, Vivien's mouth opened wide, her hand instinctively rising to cover it. Eyes wide, her face was as taut as if she'd just seen a ghost. On such a beautiful face, her expression of sheer alarm would have halted a battalion of men. It froze Rollie midsentence.

"What is it?"

Her eyes turned to the ship. "My father…"

"Your father?"

"My father, yes."

"What about him?"

"He's an admiral…remember? We're estranged because of Richard."

"You didn't tell me he was an admiral."

"I don't talk about him much. We haven't spoken in years."

Rollie turned away as he considered this. His free hand pulled downward on his mouth as his mind raced. "Okay," he said, nodding. "Okay…tell me something that *only* you and your dad could possibly know. Make damn well sure no one else on this earth could know this. And give me his full name."

She told him the name and, after a brief pause, the story. He made her condense it. They did this twice, whittling it down to an essential amount of words. Just as they almost had it ready to transmit, Maria squeezed off the last round from Rollie's pistol, screaming the insult *coño* as she did.

"They're coming," Maria yelled. "Thirty feet down!"

"Get the shotgun ready," Rollie said.

"If you had more bullets, Rollie," came Nicholas Penland's cocksure, laughing yell from over the ledge, "you'd be raining them down on us!"

"Let him think that, then shoot his ass when he's a few feet from the top," Rollie said in a voice just loud enough for Maria to hear. And, as fast as he dared transmit, he sent Vivien's father's name and her condensed story to the ship in the canal.

When he had only a few words left to send, he heard a plunking sound near the cut.

It was followed by an explosion.

"HOLY SHIT!" the chief yelled, having just copied the long message. He was at the rail when the long transmission was halted by the orange blast from the hilltop. Villiers ran back out from the bridge just as the thunder hit them shortly thereafter.

"Grenade," Villiers whispered.

"Cap'n, you need to read this," the chief said, handing over the message.

Captain Villier's head moved like the carriage on a typewriter as the O.O.D. and pilot read over his shoulder. "My God!" the captain yelled, sprinting back inside and jerking the fleet radio from its holder, simultaneously telling the chief to ring battle-stations.

"Pan! Pan! Pan!" he yelled, cutting into the command net. "Flash traffic for Zulu-Six-Alpha."

When the admiral came back on the line, Villiers said, "Sir, have the radio in your hand to relay fleet HQ as soon as I give you this. We're down to seconds here."

After he read the authentication from the person on Demon's Bluff, twice, he lowered the radio and turned to the chief.

"Chief, I want you to call down to the mount-five-one," he said in reference to the Mark 12 deck gun. "Load AAC and have them dial that hill's coordinates and height in just as the man on the hill asked for. Listen to me for corrections. Go!"

The chief ran to the bridge ladder and slid down on his arms.

Captain Villiers instructed the chief to signal another message.

Should our guns start at bottom of hill and work up?

There was a brief pause before the flashed reply.

Injuries here. Ignore prev target. Now shoot top of hill southmost location.

Where is your pos?

Top of hill southmost corner. Shoot now

The final phrase transmitted from the hill was followed by one continuous light.

"He wants us to shoot on his own position," Villiers breathed incredulously. He snatched the handset from its peg and shouted, "What's the damned status from fleet?"

IN ANNAPOLIS, Maryland, Rear Admiral Shelby "Shep" McGraw shuffled through his quarters, switching off lamps. Leaving only one on in the entrance hall, he walked into the kitchen, filling a glass of water to place beside his bed. He was due a wakeup call at five A.M. and knew his car would be there a half hour after. While he should have gone to bed earlier, Shep didn't sleep well these days. He hoped he could get at least four hours.

Though his current posting wasn't as lively as being at sea, the Severn River Naval Complex was incredibly important to the Navy's mission. And tomorrow was to be a long day.

While communications had made leaps through the 1930's and early 1940's, getting a message from a ship in the Panama Canal to Maryland, even for the United States Navy, was no small task. It required a series of relays back to the American Zone who, in turn used a landline to patch back through Washington, connecting with Severn River and, finally, the admiral's telephone.

In the bedroom, under the covers, Shep closed his eyes, trying to set aside the worries of his job and his failed personal life. As sleep nibbled at the edges of his wakefulness, his bedside phone rang, sending rusty nails gouging down his spine.

"Sonofabitch!" he yelled, starting at basso profundo and ending with spinto tenor. He threw the covers back, slung his feet over and growled a less than warm greeting into the phone.

As he listened for half a minute, Shep McGraw's face went through four distinct permutations.

Anger.

Surprise.

Fear.

Determination.

"It's her!" he yelled, standing so quickly he almost yanked the phone from its cord. "Tell that destroyer to fire right damned now!"

"Aye, aye, sir, hold the line," came the fast reply from the commander on the other end of the line.

Having no earthly idea how his oldest girl might have found herself in a deadly situation in Panama, and doing his best not to try to make sense of it, Shep McGraw did something he hadn't done since he was twelve, more than forty years ago, in one of the pews at St. Agnes Church in Chicago. Cradling the phone at his shoulder, he dropped from the bed to his knees, leaning on the mattress.

Shep McGraw, hands tightly clasped, prayed aloud.

THE NAZIS had thrown a grenade to the top of the cut. Maria, upon seeing it hit and roll, shoved it back over the side like a hot potato. But the grenade hadn't fallen far before it exploded, raining rock and shrapnel down upon everyone on Demon's Bluff. Because she had been so close, Maria got the worst of the blast and the resulting collateral damage. Her lower leg and knee were injured, bleeding from numerous wounds. She'd seemed most concerned with her ears, touching them as she worked her jaw.

Rollie had abandoned the signal lamp, moving to her and taking the shotgun with its one final shell. He peered over the ledge to see that, despite having surely been showered with loose rock, Nicholas and his partner were again on the move.

The top of the cut was the steepest portion, but Rollie remembered it having numerous footholds. The two Nazis were at the highest portion, tucked underneath the outcropping just below the last ledge of rock. Sweat dripped from Rollie's face, mingling with the blood on his neck as he alternated his vision between the cut and the warship in the distance. It was still lingering there, blacked out and silent. He readjusted his sweaty hands on the shotgun, wondering if the authentication they had transmitted was sent in vain.

Vivien was huddled with Maria, several feet back. Maria's Spanish curses were the only words being spoken, alternating between cries of pain to great distaste for the Prussian down on the cut. Rollie took another look over the ledge, damning the poacher for not leaving him more rounds. Nicholas and the other man must have known he was there because they weren't moving, their bodies far enough back so he couldn't see them. Rollie stayed alert for another grenade...

Wait...the grenade!

He turned his head, eyeing the nearby surface. What had been so pristine earlier was now littered with geologic debris from the grenade's explosion moments before. The blast had dislodged hundreds of rocks of all sizes, the pattern of the detonation easy to see in the indigo light, littering the top of the bluff near the cut. Rollie waved his hand to the women, putting his finger over his lips and motioning for them to gather all the rocks they could. He took one in each hand, good throwing rocks about the size of a biscuit. Perhaps he could save that shotgun round just a little longer.

There was a stirring below him. After adjusting his position ten feet eastward, he saw the muscular man fifteen feet down, scampering up the last section. Rollie hauled back and slung the jagged rock, nailing the big man in the back between his shoulder blades with a meaty clunk. The man howled in pain, slumping forward as he slid back down to the ledge while gunshots flamed up from Nicholas who was just beneath him. Rollie dropped to his stomach, grinning, using the edge as cover.

There was a brief period of mostly quiet, the only sound being the growling of the struck Prussian. Then Rollie could hear a bit of muffled whispering, in German.

He thought about the letter, about Nicholas being a Nazi spy, "outed" by one of his own brethren. Rollie had never liked him and could see why his fellow Nazi didn't either.

"I knew you were out of ammo!" Nicholas finally yelled, followed by the clicking of a fresh clip sliding into his pistol. The slide raked, ramming a round home as he said, "You can pelt us with rocks all night, but sooner or later we're going to get up there and kill you and those two little—"

Rollie bolted upright again, sending the other rock hurling downward. He couldn't see either of them so his rock missed—but it shut Nicholas up. As he was accepting more rocks from Vivien, Rollie noticed a flashing in the distance. It was the warship, sending a message. Rollie watched the light, signifying letters of Morse Code. He picked up the tail end of the message.

...oming

The message was followed by a long flash from the lamp. An exclamation.

When he saw the huge orange flash and resulting smoke from the deck gun, he realized what the message had been:

Incoming!

Rollie chanced a glance downward. The two Germans had their backs to the ship. They didn't even know it was there!

Time to move.

At one second post-firing, Rollie jerked the shotgun from the ground, pointing to the north and yelling for the girls to run. Immediately after, the sound of the gun firing reached them. Rollie wondered how long the Nazis would take to realize what was happening.

At two seconds post-firing, Vivien motioned for him to come but Rollie shoved her and yelled for them to go.

At four seconds, with Maria draping her arm over Vivien for support, the women began moving as quickly as they could to the north. Almost simultaneously, Rollie hurled two more rocks before limping to the hand lamp, knowing the incoming round was almost certainly on its downward arc.

At six seconds post-firing, as he limped in a modified run, he began to hear one of the most frightening (or joyful) sounds in the manmade world: the otherworldly ripping of air signifying incoming artillery destruction. Movies used a whistle, and the round did indeed whistle, but not at all like the typical Hollywood portrayal. The actual sound was far more menacing, filling the area with clamorous noise that promised impending destruction on a Biblical level. It was why artillerymen nicknamed their battalions with monikers such as "Steel Rain" or "Death From Above". Sure, the fighter squadrons and Airborne units received much of the glory, but until a man stood downrange and experienced the fear of an incoming round, it was impossible to imagine the destruction and psychological impact artillery—especially massive naval guns—could achieve.

At eight seconds post-firing Rollie was exactly sixteen feet past where the hand lamp had been, and that's when the round struck. He was precisely thirty-seven feet from the ledge, and the resulting blast sent him airborne, heels-over-head, not unlike a circus daredevil fired from a cannon.

Fortunately, the firing officer on the ship had obviously used a good terrain map and known the elevation of the bluff. Due to the close range, he'd lobbed the projectile (which had thankfully provided Rollie and the girls enough time to clear the area) but it struck the cliff too far to the northeast, at least by fifty feet. The high-explosive round detonated below the ledge, sparing Rollie any injury other than the jarring from his half-flip and extreme pain in his ears. He rolled over, flicking the switch of the hand lamp and laughing in relief when it switched back on. Using the switch (as his shirt was probably shredded back near the ledge) Rollie sent a quick message to the ship, hoping they could see the light through the lingering cloud of smoke and dust.

Same range adjust 5-0 yards your left multi rounds hurry

Rollie left the lamp on and placed it on the ground. He rose to his feet, shotgun at the ready as he limped back toward the cut. When Rollie was twenty feet from the ledge, he was halted by a tugging at his arm. The girls had come up behind him. Rollie's ears were ringing so loudly he hadn't heard them until Vivien grabbed his arm. Rollie shouted at them to go to the far side. He saw both women's eyes widen, their gaze looking past him.

It could mean only one thing.

Whipping around, silhouetted by another glorious orange flash of the deck gun behind him, Rollie saw Nicholas Penland summit the bluff. A rifle was slung over his back, his pistol coming up in his right hand. Despite being gangly and hunched and known for his pristine suits and corpse-like complexion, with half his face bloody from either one of Rollie's rocks or the explosion of the naval round, he now looked every bit the part of a deadly Nazi commando. There was a snarl on his face as he took quick aim, abruptly cut off by the blast from the shotgun held at Rollie's hip.

The dastardly poacher, probably because he typically shot high up into the jungle trees, had thankfully placed a full choke in the shotgun, extending the effective range. Just as Nicholas' round fired, the shotgun blast struck him in the face, catapulting him backward and over the edge.

After Rollie himself was flung backward, struck by a freight train courtesy of Nicholas' pistol, he saw the deck gun flash a third time, and another emerging silhouette, this one the muscular Nazi. The big man stopped halfway over the ledge and took a wild shot at the group. The round missed, but it dropped the women to the ground in fear as the Prussian pulled himself to the summit.

Despite the intense pain, which seemed to be coming from his shoulder, Rollie's mind was turning and he knew the ship's projectile was due any second.

As he yelled for the women to run, there was a darting flash of light fabric from the corner of his eyes. He instinctively reached to stop her, but Maria timed her rush perfectly and, despite her leg wounds, she covered the remaining distance in a few seconds. Vivien screamed a protest, held back by Rollie's good arm. The Prussian had his carbine up and probably did strike her when he shot, but a jacketed rifle round isn't a stopping projectile and Maria's momentum was too great.

Even with the ringing in Rollie's ears, and the warning of the incoming round, he could hear Maria's shriek, not unlike the death yells he had heard from his own men determined to hold their ground in Gran Chaco. It was a shriek that said, "Principle over life." It was a shriek that said, "I'm not afraid to die." It was a shriek that said, "I refuse to let you beat me, you evil sonofabitch." And despite the anguish of seeing Maria go flying over the ledge, with the big Nazi in her grasp as she executed a textbook tackle, Rollie would have given anything to have had a picture of that man's horrified face, screaming in fear as he tumbled backward to his death.

One second later the cliff exploded, the Naval projectile striking exactly where he had requested. It was followed by another, then another, then another.

Rollie—his body battered by bullets to the neck, shoulder, and foot—pulled Vivien to him, situating himself on top of her. The rounds were striking well below the ledge, sparing them from direct shrapnel, but the resulting debris from the hillside was cataclysmic, leaving him further pummeled as each round showered his backside with rock.

When the thunder stopped, Rollie was vaguely aware of Vivien's sobs before he lost consciousness.

Chapter Twenty-Three

April 25, 1943

TWO DAYS later, on Easter Sunday, Rollie awoke.

The first thing he noticed was the starchy, clean white sheets, abrasive against his skin. His foot was elevated and bandaged, crimson at the heel of the bandaging where gravity encouraged the blood to weep out. White tile all around him. Too much. Like an asylum. Indescribable thirst. Pain from every joint and fiber.

Rollie heard a sound escape his throat as he adjusted himself, blinking his eyes into better focus. Ten feet away was a man he instantly didn't like, staring back at him through beady eyes. The man sat erect in a steel chair a few feet from the bed, dressed in his buttoned-up gray suit. His skin had the pallor of a person who sat in a windowless office all day, arriving before sunup and leaving after dark. Rollie would give great odds the man had hands softer than a baby's butt. Even with the tidal wave of explosive memory attempting to flood Rollie's brain, it bothered him that a persnickety, judgmental little man like this would be assigned to watch him.

Thoughts of Vivien took priority over his distaste. "Is she okay?" Rollie whispered, surprised at how dry and feeble his voice was.

"Who?" the man replied.

"Vivien," Rollie replied, setting off a painful coughing fit. He could hear a commotion in the hallway, with the expected "he's awake" coming from numerous voices.

"She is in satisfactory condition," the man replied perfunctorily, his face turning to irritation as the door burst open.

Rollie saw an admiral, a two-star general, and more suits and uniforms than he dared count, all pressing in from the hall.

"General, we've been over this," the beady-eyed man said as he stood. Rollie watched as his diminutive guard unbuttoned his coat, placing his hands on his hips with the jacket winging backward. It was a defiant pose. Rollie knew the man was subconsciously trying to make himself appear larger, not unlike a blowfish or a puff adder, doing his best to make up for his bodily shortcomings.

"Been over it hell," the general replied gruffly. "My damned hospital you're standing in. It's Easter Sunday and I've got dead men littered all over that jungle out there." He whipped his head to Rollie. "I wanna talk with you, mister."

Rollie had raised his head slightly, but allowed it to fall back into the pillow. He winced at the throbbing from various zones of his body, sorrow reaching him as he recalled the dream-like vision of the young Cuban woman flying over the cliff. He smacked his dry tongue against the roof of his mouth.

A doctor pushed his way to the front. After asking Rollie a number of questions about how he felt, he asked Rollie if he wanted any sort of painkillers.

"Have I had any?" Rollie asked.

"None. We gave you anesthesia when we did surgery, but no pain medicine. Your lady friend was quite adamant about it."

Rollie smiled and declined all pain medication.

When the doctor took his leave, the suits and uniforms crowded around Rollie.

"You boys get me some water and flip my pillow, and we can talk as long as you want."

They did, for four days, off and on. Rollie spoke with all of them, always under the watchful eye of the initial beady-eyed man, or one of his cronies. The interviewers hung on his every word, seemingly relieved by the same story Rollie repeated again and again.

On the second day of his wakefulness they allowed Rollie to see Vivien, albeit briefly. Thankfully, she was in good condition, suffering only from cuts and bruises and, of course, the anguish over what they'd endured. They were given an hour to visit. After they'd talked a few minutes, she leaned close and whispered to him she had the letter that had been in his pocket.

"When did you get it?"

"Up on that bluff, before we were taken off in something called a heli…heli…"

"Helicopter."

"Right."

Rollie gripped her arm. "Don't let *anyone* know you have the letter."

"Don't worry, it's well-hidden," she said with a wink.

At the end of the hour, Rollie instructed her about a risky "shopping trip" he wanted her to take on the local streets. He didn't see her for two more days but, when he finally did, she winked at him and gave him a thumbs-up. *Success.*

The investigators—Army, Navy, Department of War, and a group of men who wouldn't identify themselves (but were watched closely by the D.O.W. men)—did their best to piece everything together based on his testimony. Of the most interest to the D.O.W. investigators was why Rollie believed Penland was a mole. Rollie never told them about the letter, only telling them that he'd simply, "figured it out."

They never readily admitted it.

On the fourth day, after allowing Rollie to enjoy a warm visit with the captain and the master chief from the USS Satterlee, men he credited with saving his and Vivien's lives, the D.O.W. men were back, appearing even grimmer than they yet had.

"We cannot find the information Hampton was allegedly here to sell to the Germans."

"Oh?" Rollie asked, now sitting up. He had bullet wounds in his neck, shoulder, and foot. The neck was sewn up and deemed "deeply superficial", whatever that meant. The bullet that had struck his shoulder luckily had passed cleanly through the narrow gap between his clavicle and shoulder blade. Both injuries, so he was told, would heal quickly. The foot, however, had two broken bones, each splintered from the bullet's passage. Since the injury was so far from his heart, the doctors were quite concerned about infection, but Rollie could see the Army doctors' concern wane with each passing day. All in all, he felt much better and was already toying with the idea of taking a walk down the hall as soon as he could bribe someone into slipping him a set of crutches.

"Without this evidence against Hampton, your entire story is in jeopardy, mister," said the other D.O.W. man, crooking his finger at Rollie. Throughout the questioning, he had been the asshole of the two. Rollie rolled his eyes at their theatrics. He flung his legs over the side of the bed, wincing as blood rushed to his wounded foot.

"You've obviously scrutinized Nicholas Penland," Rollie said knowingly. "You know he was a German mole." He lowered his right foot to the floor, taking his weight as he held his hands remain on the mattress to steady himself. "You've certainly scoured Richard Hampton's office and home and car, and you retraced his fake suicide, no doubt proven by his body here in Panama." Giving himself a small push with his hands, Rollie pirouetted and allowed himself to fall (a bit roughly) into the bedside chair, stifling a grunt from the brief shock to his battered body. He let out a long breath, looking up at the wide-eyed men. "You've taken testimony from those in the American Zone that Nicholas Penland commandeered a group of M.P.'s, and later killed them. You've also probably identified the muscular Nazi who good old Saint Nick was working with, probably through another mole *you* have planted in Berlin that you'll certainly never admit, to me anyway, that exists."

Rollie reached up to the adjacent table and retrieved his water. He leaned back, slurping it as he adjusted his bad foot over his good one. He sighed loudly, purposefully, annoyingly after the long slug of water. Placid expression evaporating, brows lowering, Rollie raised his gaze to the one who always acted like a putz. "In jeopardy, my ass. Maybe I'll just sit down and write a letter to the Washington Post and tell them that you two dumbasses allowed a German spy to infiltrate our government at the highest level."

The putz stepped forward, his voice rising as his normal tone grew to a yell, "Why, you arrogant, washed-up nobody!"

"Question," Rollie asked, raising a finger. "What have you done to provide for the *families* of those killed in this incident? Killed because *you* permitted a spy to be admitted as one of our own."

The question halted them. The nicer of the two smirked as if this might have been the stupidest question since someone allegedly asked, "Other than that, Mrs. Lincoln, how did you enjoy the play?"

Rollie made a dismissive motion. "I'm done talking. If you can't see that those people were unjustly killed, I want nothing more to do with either of you."

"There's a war going on," the putz growled. "Your threats amount to intimidations of treason."

"There's *no* war in Panama," Rollie answered. He joined eyes with the man. "And I'm also beginning to wonder, based on the innocuous nature of everything placed under Nicholas Penland's authority, if the D.O.W. knew he was a mole all along, and used him as a conduit." Rollie's hands, gripping the arms of the chair, trembled under great strain. "And therefore, the D.O.W. used me and Vivien, and got a number of M.P.'s, Panamanians, and a Cuban killed because of it."

While the D.O.W. men were trained to show no reaction, Rollie caught enough tells to believe his assumption was correct.

He leveled a finger to the door. "Now get the hell out of my room."

The men looked at one another for a moment. "This isn't over," the nicer one said. They left with their heads down.

"And send Vivien in here!" he yelled after them.

April 30, 1943

DURING THE late morning of the seventh day, the doctors pronounced Rollie well enough to leave the hospital. By the time he'd finished packing his small bag, an entourage of suits awaited him outside his hospital door. They were all due at the American Zone's Albrook Airfield at 4 P.M. for a long, multi-stop flight back to the United States. Rollie summoned the D.O.W. men to his room. When asked how long they would detain him and Vivien back in the U.S., the D.O.W. men wouldn't give him a firm answer, saying only, "We'll let you know when we know."

"Am I under arrest?" Rollie asked.

"This is a situation of great national security," the nicer one replied, "and we have authority to detain you both for as long as is deemed necessary."

"Then, if you want my full cooperation, I've a request," Rollie said.

"What is it?"

Rollie's request was quite simple: allow him and Vivien to dine at a restaurant of their choosing before departing.

"Why?" the putz asked.

"Because I'm in love with her, pal. And I'm tired of talking to her when rubes like you are hanging around. It's not as if we'll get any free time when we get back."

"Out of the question," the nicer one said.

"Fine. Then get out until we leave because I need to write those letters to the editors I told you about."

The D.O.W. men grudgingly relented, but only if Rollie and Vivien traveled with an entourage. A compromise was eventually reached and, rather than the large entourage, Rollie and Vivien were allowed to dine with a single escort: a lanky D.O.W. agent with a crew-cut and an ill-fitting, cheap suit. Rollie correctly made him as a fellow field agent though he didn't know the man personally. The three of them took a taxi to the restaurant where Rollie and Vivien had first run into one another, the same one where they met Maria. The restaurant was empty at this time of day, the staff visibly annoyed at having to work during siesta.

After leading them in, the maître d' irritably directed them to a linen-covered table in the center of the establishment.

"You're going to sit with us?" Rollie asked the D.O.W. man.

He shrugged. "Sorry pal, strict orders."

Nodding resignedly, Rollie sat, leaning his crutches over a chair from another table. He allowed his right hand to join Vivien's left, under the table, as the two shared a private look. She barely shook her head, her expression worried. He eyed her for a moment, allowed his mouth to tick upward, and nodded once. As the escort was ordering his food, Rollie mouthed the word "relax" to Vivien. He never engaged the escort, who kept to himself while Rollie and Vivien chatted about what had been going on with the war. There had been a key Allied victory in Tunisia and the Allies were finally making headway against the U-boats in the Atlantic.

When they'd eventually finished the excellent lunch of seafood and local vegetables, Rollie lifted his crutches and climbed to his feet.

The escort made a halting motion. "Wait a minute, Donahue. Where do you think you're going?"

"To take a leak. You wanna come hold it for me?" This drew a giggle from Vivien.

The escort stood. "I've got to go with you."

"Suit yourself," Rollie said with a shrug, thumping off in the direction of the baño. The man turned to Vivien, pointing to the floor. "Stay here."

She didn't respond, only flashing a smile that women give to men when whatever they just said was utterly ridiculous.

The bathroom was modern for Panama, with two private stalls and a sink. Rollie went into the far stall and relieved himself, making sure to let his stream hit the water so his escort knew he was genuinely performing the act.

"Where you from?" Rollie asked.

"Minnesota."

"Cold up there," Rollie replied, smiling at his fake banter. When he bent to flush, he dropped his crutches loudly, falling to the toilet as he spun into a sitting position. He howled in pain, overdoing it like a person would if they had re-broken a bone.

"What happened?" his escort asked, moving outside the stall.

Rollie only grunted, muffling a curse and panting loudly.

"Stay back," the escort said, kicking in the wooden door only to find Rollie aiming a street-purchased Savage pistol at his head. Rollie had never handled a Savage before and enjoyed its compact feel, not too unlike its near-twin, the Luger. While he had zero intention of shooting, he couldn't let his escort know that.

"I *will* shoot you," Rollie said. "You're dealing with a wounded man, betrayed by his country and confused from a fog of pain. They might give you a harsh reprimand for losing me, but if I can pull off what I hope to pull off today, no harm will come to you, friend. That much I promise. Hell, to save yourself you can even tell them I had an accomplice in here waiting on you. I won't refute it."

The escort's right hand was frozen halfway up his torso. Rollie knew what he was thinking—he could see the bulge of the man's Colt under his left arm. Rollie slid his index finger over the trigger. "You pull that pistol, pal, and I'm going to shoot you. I've broken lots of things but my right hand works just fine."

The escort's hand edged back down.

"Good. Put your hands behind your head." The D.O.W. man did. "Now, turn and kneel."

The escort stood perfectly still.

"I've no desire to hurt you. But what's happening here is bigger than me or you. I'll admit, I probably won't kill you unless you try to draw that Colt. But I will lower the barrel of this nifty little Savage and put a thirty-two slug in your knee. So you can comply, and get out of this mess…and believe me, you will…because the government wants to keep this story quiet." Rollie arched his brows. "Or you can stand there and be Billy Badass and get your leg halfway cut in two and then own a game leg the rest of your life. You might be lucky, up in Minnesota, to find a job sitting beside some frozen lake charging two bits for people to go ice fishing." Rollie smiled a humorless smile. "So do me and you a favor and just put your hands on your head and kneel."

The escort blinked several times as he pondered Rollie's monologue. Visibly displeased, he turned and knelt. Rollie yanked the cuffs from under the man's coat, securing one of the man's hands behind his back, pulling the other down so the cuffs were latched around the lower post of the stall. Using white surgical tape, Rollie bound the man's mouth three layers thick. He retrieved his written explanation from his own pocket, holding it up for his escort.

"This is for the D.O.W. men. Once they read this, you won't be in trouble." He leaned down and tucked it between the man's shirt and jacket. Outside the bathroom, Rollie reached in his other pocket, retrieving the single sheet of paper on which, in bold grease pencil, he'd written *Fuera de Servicio*, and below that its English equivalent, *Out of Order*. Using two small pieces of surgical tape, Rollie affixed it to the door and moved as quickly as he could back to the table.

Vivien was standing there, purse in hand, anxiously waiting.

"Did you have enough to pay?" Rollie asked as they left.

"Barely."

As they left through the back, Rollie was thankful to see the maître d' was nowhere to be found. Two servers were folding silverware into linen napkins, neither of them bothering to look up.

It took the two Americans five minutes to get a taxi. When they did, in the backseat, Rollie situated his crutches before telling the driver to go directly to the Hotel Azul. Hand on his throbbing head, he leaned back, closing his eyes for a moment.

"You okay?" Vivien asked.

"I will be when this is all over." He lowered his hand. "Are you certain the matches you found were from this hotel?"

"Positive," she replied, her voice a bit distant.

"Yeah, they questioned me about the Azul, too."

"I remember how betrayed I felt," Vivien whispered. "Richard going off to some exotic location without even bothering to tell me."

Rollie hadn't taken the time to ponder all Vivien had been through. Setting aside the violence they'd both endured, he hadn't even stopped to consider the grief she might be experiencing after—two different times—learning her husband had died, whether or not she loved him. He held her hand, rubbing it with his thumb.

"Are *you* okay?"

She leaned her head against his shoulder. "I am now."

A silence fell over them as the cab puttered to the west, the water off to their left as the hill at La Boca loomed nearby. Beyond that, its flat summit towering over the carpet of rainforest, Demon's Bluff stood sentry over the south opening to the canal. Rollie lifted her hand, gesturing to the two elevated terrestrial features.

"From there to here," he whispered.

She viewed both of the formations, her eyes cutting back and forth. After a moment, she closed her eyes, again leaning against him, taking steadying breaths.

Rollie watched as she fought to stifle her tears.

GIVING THEM no more than an hour before they would get tracked down by the D.O.W., Rollie planned to pull no punches at the Hotel Azul. He and Vivien blew through the front door of the Calidonia hotel, with Rollie demanding to see the hotel register of the last three months.

"Señor," the clerk replied, a hand-rolled cigarette bouncing between his lips, "I am afraid that is not—"

The Savage .32 aimed at his nose immediately silenced the clerk. His brown eyes watered as laces of cigarette smoke enveloped his head. Rollie jerked his head at Vivien, who stepped through the door beside the desk.

"Where?" she asked.

Without moving his crossed eyes from the pistol, the man visibly swallowed before tapping the yellowed book under his hands. "Th-th-this book has all g-g-guests from this year."

Rollie lowered the pistol. "See, that wasn't hard, was it?"

After a relieved smile, the man's eyes rolled back in his head. Then he fainted, hitting the wooden floor with a thud. Vivien leaned down, flicking his cigarette off his black vest.

"Find the dates," Rollie said, glancing back at the door.

She thumbed through the register, going back to March, running her hand up and down the pages, stabbing her finger. "Here it is! Samuel Fields, room 210."

"Now, check the last two weeks."

Her eyes went back down as she thumbed forward. After a minute of searching, Rollie watched as her finger again poked the paper. "Here it is. He rented the *exact* same room again."

Rollie whistled lowly. "This has gotta be it. Get the key."

"Wouldn't they have been smart enough to check back to see if he'd been here before?"

"Sure they would have, but they never found the notebook." Rollie paused. "To me it always felt like they thought the Nazis had already taken delivery of the intel. Regardless, let's get that key and find out."

Vivien turned and retrieved the key from the square shelf of cubby slots.

"Stay here with the clerk," Rollie said, handing her the Savage and taking the key. "When he wakes up, explain that nobody is here to hurt him."

"What if one of the guests comes?"

"Help them," Rollie replied with a smile, moving out the door as quick as he could manage.

THE HOTEL wasn't much different from the others in Calidonia. Some of the hotels blunted their harsh angles with rounded corners or archways, but not the Hotel Azul. Painted (of course) powder blue, this one was three levels high, with all of the rooms opening to the outside. Rollie could imagine the brochure, offered through travel agencies back in the States, depicting the Azul as some regal tropical hotel with beautiful guests and sumptuous views.

As he negotiated the upper level of the stairs, he looked across the hotel lawn at the actual view. In a shallow tidal pool between the hotel and the bay was a herd of malnourished goats, eating the nubby stalks of picked-over pampas grass and crapping everywhere; beyond the herd, the winds had pushed the floating sewage westward, so that it collected in the turbid swirls created by the jetties off of the isthmus.

Just gorgeous.

Rollie used the key to rap on the door of room 210. He should have checked the register to see if it was empty. A squeaky bed spring provided him his answer.

"No service!" came a yell from inside. Sounded American.

"Open up," Rollie said, rapping on the door again.

Muffled curses could be heard before the chain slid from the lock. The door jerked open to reveal an olive-skinned young man with short dark hair and an inhospitable look on his face. He was about five-eight and maybe a hundred seventy-five pounds. Both arms were adorned with bold tattoos and his face, littered with fighting scars and a crooked nose, marked him as one tough hombre. The young man wore khaki boxers, of military issue, and a pair of dog tags. Rollie immediately pegged him as a military boxer, either a Marine from a ported ship or perhaps Army on furlough from the American Zone.

With no weapon and no Department of War identification (it had been seized), Rollie tried a new tack. He played the young man straight. As Rollie explained the non-sensitive points of what was happening, telling him he needed to search the room, he watched as a dark-skinned woman stood from the bed, concealing herself with the sheet.

"Happened to you?" the young man asked, looking Rollie up and down.

Rollie glanced down at his leg dangling between his crutches. "I had a bit of an accident."

"I'll say," the soldier said, eyeing the bandage on Rollie's neck.

"May I come in?"

"So all you need to do is search the room?" the soldier asked in what sounded like a Brooklyn accent.

"Yes."

"What for?"

"I don't exactly know. Could be a book, a film canister, any number of things."

The young man ran his tongue across his teeth, making a sucking sound. "How long?"

"Fifteen minutes should do it."

"This guy you told me about, you think he hid it good?"

"He worked for an aircraft company and had an engineering background, so yeah."

The soldier pulled the door open all the way, making an inward motion with his head. "Yeah, I ain't got nowheres to be 'til port call tomorrow. Kinda tapped out…for at least the next few hours anyway." He winked at Rollie.

Rollie crossed the threshold. "Hopefully this won't take long."

The young man eyed Rollie's foot. "You're in bad shape…how 'bout I help you search?"

Rollie's lips parted to decline the offer before he stopped. "Why not?"

He glanced around the room, smelling cigarettes, sulfur from matches, and the unmistakable aroma of fresh sex. The woman emerged from the bathroom, now only covering her lower body with the sheet. She was pretty, with a rounded face and the smallish, deflated breasts of a woman who had once nursed a child. Rollie looked away.

"Say hello to Rosa."

"Hi Rosa," Rollie said, eyes down, studying the carpet.

"Hola," Rosa replied cheerily. It seemed this interruption was a welcome diversion from what was probably a routine day for her.

"Just stay on the bed and relax, doll," the young man said to Rosa. "We gotta find something." She flopped down, opening the drawer next to the bed and removing a tattered tourist magazine, thumbing through the pages with the thin pillows stacked behind her.

"What's your name?" Rollie asked.

"Torciano."

"Boxer?"

He struck a classic boxer's pose. "Former Camp Lejune middleweight champ."

"Former?"

"Twenty-four now...boxing's a young man's game. Chin got shook. Lost three of my last four fights."

"Getting old's rough, isn't it?" Rollie asked, dropping his crutches and kneeling in the front corner of the room. He began tugging on baseboards, vowing not to leave a square foot of the floor, walls, and ceiling untouched.

Seeing what Rollie was doing, Torciano started at the opposite end of the outer wall, doing the same. Behind them, half-naked Rosa hummed a pleasant tune as she flipped through the magazine.

"You mind if I ask you a question?" Torciano asked, working his way around the door.

"Go ahead."

"Th'hell kinda accident happened to you?"

"Had a little problem about a week back. Took a few bullets."

"That's the fresh shit, ain't it? I really meant that old scar above your neck bandage."

Rollie felt the stabbing pain associated with the age-old question, but strangely, this time it flitted through him and was gone like a vapor. He came up to his knees, pausing as he made himself ponder the Marine's question again.

His ego didn't feel bruised.

There was no tightening of his chest.

No churning in his stomach.

No murderous thoughts or feelings of self-pity.

It was just a question. It stung for just a moment, but nothing more.

Smiling to himself, he leaned forward again, clawing at the wall and baseboard, tugging at the filthy carpet as he spoke. "The scars on my neck run under my collar and down half of my body. They're nearly a decade old. Got blown all to hell in a war no one knows about."

The soldier had pulled the lone chair over, standing on it, working his way around the top of the door molding. "What war?"

"In South America, place called Gran Chaco."

"You're right…ain't never heard of that."

"I used to wish I hadn't heard of it either…but now it's a part of me. Just like your boxing career, wins and losses, is a part of you."

Torciano continued searching as he said, "Other than that scar, did it leave you with any…you know…permanent damages or any crap like that?"

Rollie paused and looked up at him. "Nah. Other than these fresh gunshots, I'm fine now."

They shared a laugh only two veterans could understand and continued to banter as they worked their way around the room. Rollie, due to his infirmity, kept to the low side of the room. Torciano, with his chair, worked the high side including the ceiling. With Rosa standing, they checked the bed, the mattress, and the box springs. Finding nothing in the bed, they scrutinized every piece of furniture, every inch of floor, wall, ceiling, the entire base board, the two electric sockets (which Torciano removed after unscrewing them with his knife), and the sill and molding around the window and front door.

The impossibly tiny bathroom was next. Rollie went over every single tile and checked every crevice, despite the accumulated grit and clinging pubic hairs. Torciano worked on the old-fashioned toilet, scouring each component, examining his hands afterward with a curled lip. Rollie went under the cheap sink, running his fingers around the crevices under the bowl.

Nothing.

Back in the main room as Rosa, still topless, leaned back on the bed, hands laced behind her head, placidly studying the two men, Rollie scratched his head while Torciano shook his.

"I don't think it's here."

Rollie gnawed on his lower lip. "Give me just a little longer." Determined not to leave any stone unturned, he eyed every wall of the small room starting at the top, scanning left and right, working his way down each wall in the same pattern a person might mow a lawn. After doing the inner walls, as he scanned the outer wall, Rollie stopped on the door.

His reasoning for searching here in the first place was the privacy a hotel room provided. If a man wanted to hide something, to really hide it, he needed the privacy only four walls and a roof could give. Then he could drill, hammer, and chisel to his heart's desire. Eyes narrowed, Rollie thought things through. The front door—as a hiding place—wouldn't afford any sort of privacy because it would have to be open.

But the bathroom door would.

Dropping his crutches, he hopped to the door, making a fist and rapping on it. Like most cheap inner doors, it was hollow.

Rollie searched around the perimeter of the door, feeling with his fingers. He dropped to the floor again, peering into the crevices around the jamb, seeing a few tiny pieces of wood shavings that a maid's broom couldn't get to. He pulled himself back up, steadying himself with the knob.

"Could you grab that chair for me?" he asked, trying to remain calm. The door opened outward. Rollie pulled it open, then used the top to hold on as he hopped on top of the chair with his good foot. There along the top of the cheap door, very faintly, was a rectangle within the rectangle. He tried to pry it open with his fingernails. It was too tight. But with Torciano's pocketknife, Rollie was able to pop the top, realizing it had been lightly sealed with wood glue.

He handed the piece of wood to the wide-eyed Torciano before staring down into the cavity of the hollow door. A tiny nail had been tacked into the top of the door, just under the lip of the false top. Around the nail was a piece of string. Rollie lifted the string, which was slack until it took the weight of something white. As the object ascended to the top of the cavity, he realized it was wrapped in a towel—probably to keep it from bumping when the door was opened and shut.

Grasping it with his hands, he pulled it out, yanking the towel off to reveal a black notebook. Still standing on the chair, he opened the notebook, reading the foreword as his heart thudded in his chest.

The foreword was typed in plain, uncomplicated English with a very clear message: *The Americans are very close to finalizing an atom bomb and, with the contents of this notebook, Nazi Germany can catch up and, combining it with their own knowledge, surpass the America and her Allies.*

After getting Torciano's full name and thanking him and half-naked Rosa for their help and hospitality, Rollie stuffed the notebook into his waistband and limped off back to the front desk.

There was one final thing to do.

IT MUST not have been the first time the desk clerk at the Hotel Azul had been held at gunpoint. After going back downstairs and finding the clerk and Vivien having a pleasant conversation, Rollie made a deal with the man. He would give him his remaining money, $62.11 (a figure that made Vivien's new friend cover his heart with both hands) in return for his providing them a room while agreeing not to reveal their presence to the police or the Americans, who would be frantically searching the city at any moment, if they weren't already. The clerk even agreed to bring them some food, homemade from his family table, provided they could wait until sundown.

As the clerk busied himself with their bogus paperwork and a key, Vivien said, "You mean those men scoured that room and found nothing? But you, even in your condition, found what Richard hid?"

"I got lucky, for sure. But I also know, especially since Penland and that big Nazi died, that their motivation wasn't as high as it might have been."

"Or, maybe you're just better than them?" she asked.

He squeezed her hand.

Rollie's final request of the clerk was the use of the hotel telephone. Checking the notes he'd taken during his meeting with the partial crew of the USS Satterlee, he asked the clerk to phone the number written at the bottom of the page.

"Most calls back to the U.S. don't get through," the clerk warned.

"Just try, please."

It took several minutes of negotiating the various operators before the clerk nodded victoriously, telling the operator to wait a moment. He covered the hand piece. "I've reached an American operator but this is a military number we're calling. The person at the number is asking who is calling?"

"Vivien McGraw," Rollie said clearly.

The clerk mentioned her name, waited a moment before nodding again, and handed Rollie the phone. Rollie passed the phone to Vivien and listened to her stilted exchange. Vivien's expression was wooden as she spoke about what had occurred today, unapologetically asking her father to arrange for furtive transport back to the states, to Washington D.C.

"I don't want to listen to any of that right now," she said sharply. She looked at Rollie and rolled her eyes. "No, I won't. Right now I just need you to do this. Believe you me, what we're bringing is incredibly important." She listened a bit more before her eyes filled with tears.

Rollie watched her for the better part of ten minutes, Vivien not speaking the entire time. It was as if the icy, protective wall she'd created melted before his very eyes. At the end of their conversation, Vivien politely told her father she looked forward to discussing things with him. She thanked her father, twice, and gently placed the phone back in its cradle. Vivien dabbed her eyes with a tissue.

Rollie then paid the clerk as promised, hoping the man didn't plan to double-cross them—but having no choice but to trust him. They made their way to the room, eating the food he brought them, staying there until four in the morning.

At that time they were awakened by a polite naval commander in civilian clothes. He led them to a black Chevrolet and drove them all the way to the port at Colon.

Chapter Twenty-Four

Annapolis, Maryland
May 14, 1943

ROLLIE SAT on the green sofa by himself. Vivien sat opposite him, on the other sofa. Seated next to her was her father, Rear Admiral Shelby "Shep" McGraw. While Rollie could see a slight resemblance, especially around the eyes, the admiral was certainly his own man. With a tightly woven mat of gray hair, his most distinct features were the heavy bags under his eyes. They portrayed a man who knew sadness, who didn't sleep well, and who probably worked too many long hours. With his old sailor's tan and a face that was once angular, the admiral had a gloomy dignity about him. But since their arrival, Rollie had seen the admiral's decidedly lugubrious air brighten with each passing day.

They'd been in his home now for three days. It was just past seven in the evening, the long spring day lingering as the lowering sun threw splashes of tangerine across the coffee table and pecan hardwoods. Rollie glanced out the window, seeing two sailors, officers, smoking and lingering by the white fence surrounding the tidy yard. There had been a steady string of them ever since he and Vivien had arrived. Rollie felt very safe. Just as he was about to continue a conversation with the admiral about Chicago, the phone rang.

"Yes?" Shep McGraw said. He nodded once. "He's definitely alone?" Another nod. "Good. Keep everyone in place and keep this line clear." He replaced the phone and looked at Rollie and Vivien.

"Are you two ready?"

They both nodded.

A moment later a burgundy Cadillac stopped in front of the house. A man in a suit stepped from the passenger seat. There were words exchanged with the two officers before the man in the suit passed through the fence gate and walked to the front door. The admiral let him in. Rollie stood with the help of his cane, listening as Lawrence Dillard, Uncle Spook, rumored to be the brightest man in all of government service, harangued the admiral over his harboring two fugitives, even if one did happen to be his oldest daughter. Dillard then said McGraw had a helluva nerve using a traitor's document as leverage, making a number of hollow threats about all sorts of unpleasantness that could occur as a result. He finished his diatribe by insulting the Navy, complaining about being summoned all the way out here to Annapolis to play grab-ass with commissioned sailors in their nancy whites.

The front door led to its own hallway. Rollie and Vivien couldn't see the exchange, they could only hear it. While Dillard continued to badger the admiral, Rollie eyed Vivien and said, "He's blustering."

"He sounds very angry."

"Because he knows he was wrong."

Admiral McGraw's deep voice reverberated as he said, "Instead of standing out there on the porch whining like some spoiled kid, why don't you come inside and talk like a grown man?"

Dillard grumped audibly, walking in and turning the corner to the living room. He halted, frowning when he saw Rollie.

Rollie said nothing.

"You've got *some* balls," Dillard whispered, a purple vein visibly pulsing in his neck.

Rollie gestured to Vivien and her father. "Let's be proper here, sir. The man you just insulted is Rear Admiral Shelby McGraw, and his daughter Vivien Ham—"

"McGraw," Vivien said, cutting Rollie off and crossing her arms. The look she was giving Dillard reminded Rollie of the look she gave him when she first saw him in Panama. Despite the gravity of the situation, Rollie couldn't help but smirk.

Dillard was obviously on edge, his baby blue eyes continually cutting back to Rollie as he perfunctorily greeted Vivien only.

"Sit there," the admiral commanded, gesturing to a chair between the two couches.

Dillard obeyed, nervously fingering his charcoal homburg as he alternated his gaze between the two men. "You'll excuse me if I'm a bit uncomfortable, but this man is a fugitive," he said, gesturing with his hat to Rollie.

While Rollie wanted to reply with something clever, he remained silent.

"Beyond that, we've got major action in the Pacific, the Aleutians, North Africa, and a major security operation here in the U.S."

"Trident," Shep McGraw said.

Dillard's eyes went wide. "How do you know about that?"

"The Trident Conference," Shep said, glancing at Rollie and Vivien. "Churchill and his delegation are in D.C. as we speak." He turned to Dillard. "While you and your O.S.S. boys might think you have a monopoly on the world's intelligence, some of us actually have to put that intel to use on the surface."

"But the Navy is not in the chain of concern."

"Well, obviously we are," Shep said triumphantly.

Dismissing the notion, Dillard turned to Rollie. "Might as well speak up, Donahue. Because if you do have Hampton's documents...that, coupled with your willing cooperation, is the only thing that *might* save you."

Rollie eyed Dillard for several moments before he spoke. Finally, evenly, he said, "You knew Penland was a Nazi mole."

"My men already told me you believe that, Donahue. It's such a preposterous notion that it doesn't deserve my response."

"You knew," Rollie said with force, his tone inviting no response.

"What happened down in Panama was regrettable. And, even though I didn't know about Penland, we did foil a colossal plot. We also think, in the process, we blew out the Nazis' entire Central and South American network."

Rollie glanced at Admiral McGraw. He looked extremely capable, like a grizzled poker player holding what could have been a full-house or just pocket swans. Then Rollie turned to Vivien. She nodded, brows lowered, her eyes telling him to go for the kill.

"Mister Dillard, I never burned anyone over what happened at Gran Chaco."

"Interesting choice of words," Dillard remarked.

"You know what happened," Rollie retorted.

This time, Dillard had no response.

"And instead of shutting Penland down when you could, you wanted to flush everyone out and you used me, and Vivien, as bait."

Dillard's lips whitened as he pressed them together.

"And I have proof."

"Yep," the admiral jibed, sneering at Dillard.

"What proof?" Dillard asked.

"A letter…a letter from another mole very high up in our intelligence network. A mole, Mister Dillard, that you obviously don't know about," Rollie said in a patronizing tone. "Despite being on the same side, this mole hated Penland…probably rivals."

"This is horseshit," Dillard blurted.

"It seems this gentleman—this other mole—has grown to like our ways, and would like to stay here."

"Show me the letter."

"I'm keeping it," Rollie said. "The admiral will help me keep it safe and you can be assured that we'll do all sorts of things to make sure, if something untoward were to happen to us, that it would find its way to the public eye."

For the first time since he'd arrived, Dillard's façade showed palpable weakness. "We'll come back to that. But I came here because I was told you have Hampton's notebook."

Rollie nodded at Vivien. She stood, walking to the tall secretary and opening its top drawer. From the drawer she produced the notebook, carrying it back and handing to Lawrence Dillard. He eyed it for a moment, opening it, carefully studying the first page.

Rollie watched as Dillard stopped breathing for long periods of time. He licked his thumb and turned to the second page. Then, the third. Rollie looked to Vivien and then to the admiral, who gave him a small nod.

"It's far more comprehensive than you thought," Rollie said.

Dillard looked up but gave no indication.

"Keep it. I'm quite certain you won't show it to a soul because, if you did, they'd realize how close you came to giving away a secret that could have turned the war." Rollie reached into his jacket, removing a white envelope and shaking it. "With the letter from the other Nazi mole is a high-quality copy of that notebook. If you would like to ensure that they remain hidden forever, you'll agree to the terms in this envelope."

"You're going to try to bribe me?" Dillard asked.

"Not at all," Rollie replied calmly. "We're giving you a chance to try to make a few things right."

Dillard closed the notebook, crossing his arms.

Rollie again wagged the envelope. "I want the government to pay the families of each of the victims that died in this foul-up thirty years' salary in one lump sum. That includes the Panamanian national police, the American M.P.'s and their commanding officer, Major Archibald Melton."

Dillard's mouth opened to object before Rollie cut him off. "You run a shadow agency in our government. I'm quite sure you can think of some secretive way to scrub the money through a law firm or two and call it some sort of life insurance policy each man had purchased, without his family's knowledge. And the amount of money is an absolute pittance when viewed against what was at stake. There can be no objections over this demand."

Dillard cleared his throat. "I'm not yet agreeing, but go on."

"The men who reacted to us from the USS Satterlee, they get promoted, immediately."

Dillard arched his brows. "If I were to agree, then that request is easy." His open expression turned to a grimace as he steepled his fingers, pressing them to his lips. "I'm waiting on the finale…whatever it is *you* want."

"The Cuban woman who died, Maria…"

"Yes?"

"We want to know all there is to know about her. And if she does have family, they will be compensated, too."

"And what of your personal demands?"

Rollie placed the envelope on top of the notebook, tapping it once and leaning back on the sofa. "I just want my job back."

Dillard slowly lowered his steepled fingers. "And?"

Rollie shrugged once. "That's all."

"Just your job?" Dillard asked, clearly surprised.

"Yes," Vivien answered for Rollie. "But I have a few demands of my own."

Dillard turned to her.

Vivien was sitting demurely, legs crossed, her right hand gripping her father's. "I can't control what my former husband did, Mister Dillard. He was an unscrupulous man who fooled me for many years. For the moment I am a widow, but I've met someone very special." She looked briefly to Rollie, smiling at him. "And while my beau might be too humble to ask for anything, I am going to ask for two additional things."

Dillard leaned forward, sliding the notebook and the envelope in his own direction. "And what might they be?"

"That my future husband's record not be stained at all. He had a hunch. He followed it, emptying his bank account to do so. And he *saved* our country the horror of that notebook falling into enemy hands."

"It appears he may have contributed," Dillard said, admitting this with briefly closed eyes.

"Not just appears," she corrected. "He initiated the operation, saw it through, and finished it."

Vivien held Dillard's gaze until he nodded.

"Therefore," Vivien continued, "I feel Rollie deserves to be repaid his money, deserves a promotion…and deserves a raise."

"Is *everything* you told my men true?" Dillard asked Rollie.

"I gave them the unvarnished truth, only I didn't tell them about the letter from the second Nazi mole."

Dillard turned back to Vivien and said, "I can't promise anything until—"

"Bullshit," the admiral interjected, drawing the objection out in true Navy fashion.

Dillard lowered his head, closing his eyes in an almost prayerful pose. "Have *any* of you breathed a word of this to a living soul?"

The admiral spoke first. "The men outside and the ones who were following you today are all Navy from Severn River. They have no clue what this is all about, other than a request for security."

Rollie was next. "And the only person who knows about the notebook is a Marine boxer named Anthony Torciano. He's a buck sergeant, based on the USS Shaw. His name is in that envelope, too."

"Who the hell is he?" Dillard asked with a wrinkled nose.

"Doesn't matter. He has no idea of the notebook's contents, but he's a good kid and an asset to our military. My final request is that he be promoted and given a chance to attend officer candidate school."

Lawrence Dillard stood, perching the Homburg on his bald head. He pressed fingers onto his eyes, rubbing vigorously. "I'd better get the hell out of here before you people ask me to wave my magic wand and make all the moving pictures start appearing in Technicolor."

"I just want your word," Rollie said, extending his hand.

"There's no fine print in here?" Dillard asked, lifting the notebook and letter.

"No fine print. Of course, the future salaries of those who died will adjust for promotions and inflation. Everything is exactly as we just said, and I want proof of all items once they're executed in *timely* fashion."

Dillard nodded, accepting Rollie's hand. "Timely meaning?"

"Weeks."

Dillard nodded again. He pumped Rollie's hand several times. "You have my word."

"My requests aren't on the sheet," Vivien said. "Please make sure—"

"Trust me, my dear," Dillard said, cutting her off and displaying his first genuine smile. "I doubt I'd ever forget *anything* you might say."

"Thank you," Rollie said, echoed immediately by Vivien.

Dillard jabbed a finger at Rollie. "Take another week off. And then, a week after this coming Monday, I want to see you bright and early in my office. We'll send to Chicago for your things."

Eyes narrowed, Rollie cocked his head.

"Well, didn't you hear your future wife, Donahue? She just got you a damned promotion. I don't have anything for you in Chicago, so you're moving to D.C."

Rollie looked at Vivien. She smiled and gripped his hand. He turned to the admiral, who was beaming, almost surely at the prospect of having his once-estranged daughter close by.

"I'll be there, sir," Rollie said.

"And although you think you've already been through the meat-grinder, plan on a very, very long debrief. In the meantime, keep your collective mouths shut." As Dillard opened the door to leave, Vivien called out to him. She sauntered over, gripping the lapels of his lightly pinstriped charcoal suit, straightening them.

"Yes m'dear?" he asked, lifting the Homburg from his head.

"I have a sister. She lives in Detroit."

"Yes?" he asked, looking wary.

"If she moved here, to be close to her father and me, do you think you could help her find a job?"

Dillard's cheeks expanded as he blew out a loud breath. "Have your fiancé send her résumé to my office and make sure she references your name *only*." He turned to Rollie. "Your first order of business is keeping your persuasive wife away from my office. Understand?"

"Yes, sir."

"Let me get out of here while I still have my pants."

After Dillard had gone, the three of them sat on the back porch, having a celebratory pitcher of lemonade in the dusky Friday evening.

Rollie remained quiet, listening as Vivien and her father continued to work through their troubled past. It went past her father's objecting over Richard. Apparently, things between Vivien's parents had never been very good. In some ways Rollie felt for the admiral. But, just like he'd told the boxer at the Hotel Azul in Calidonia, the past is a part of a person.

While father and daughter continued to speak, Rollie thought about his own family, and how their existence now seemed distant, like a fading dream.

He dangled his hand off of his chair and, although she wasn't even looking in his direction, Vivien's hand lowered, instinctively finding his.

"Vivien Donahue," Rollie whispered, so low no one else could hear it.

As she and her father discussed something about a Thanksgiving many years ago, Rollie smiled in the growing darkness.

Family.

                                THE END

Acknowledgments

Before I thank the many people who helped me with this book, let me start by saying that I'm fully aware there are no towering buttes at the mouth of the Panama Canal. While this book may be loaded with mistakes and errors, the Panamanian butte was deliberate, a figment of my imagination. I appreciate accuracy in fiction. But…it is fiction, after all. And given the harsh world we live in, I think, every now and then, we all need to allow our imaginations to run off and have a little fun.

I can usually recall where the idea for a story came from but, with Demon's Bluff, I honestly don't remember. I started writing it when I was on a business trip to Philadelphia. The first scene I wrote was Richard Hampton's introduction, when he was planning his escape. The second scene I wrote was Hampton's death, due to his weakness for women. After that, Rollie was born, and the story came alive and filled in naturally.

But it was in the middle of my first draft when I discovered the Chaco War. If you have a moment, look it up and read about it. And if you have any interest in a Rollie Donahue prequel, please let me know. I've got some ideas about a story set during the Chaco War. It involves Rollie, Big Oil, and the corruption that found its way into that war that cost so many lives. To this day, it's a war that few, outside of Bolivia or Paraguay, know about.

On to my helpers:

John Humphries was the first person to read this story. He gave me three suggestions, all of which I added to the tale. His insight, as usual, was spot-on.

Scott Hortis also gave me some good advice and even took it so far to cast the movie. If only Scott knew Steven Spielberg.

Phillip Day, one of the finest story editors I know, read it next. He helped me flesh Rollie out in a way that I hope helped you connect better as a reader.

I'd like to thank my military advisors, Colonel Robert Browning, USMC (ret.) and Rear Admiral Ronald Wilgenbush, USN (ret.). Their advice was critical to my manuscript and any military errors that still exist are of my own doing. Specifically, some of the naval scenes from the canal involved a little artistic license from yours truly.

Elizabeth Brazeal is my editor and had to use several red pens on Demon's Bluff. Again, any mistakes in this book are mine, not hers. She's the best.

My beta readers, Laura Hortis, Jan Hillhouse, Karen Vaughan, and Ann Brown helped me find the straggling mistakes. And Sarah Humphries, Spanish speaker extraordinaire, corrected my numerous Spanish errors. *Mi español es muy malo.* Thanks to each of you.

A huge thanks to Sean Madden for creating the unique and über-cool cover art. The red and blue overlay is a representation of the Panamanian flag.

Finally, I'd like to offer an enormous thanks to my readers. It's a humbling, wonderful experience to connect with people who have enjoyed my books. A year ago, when my first book, The Diaries, came out, the initial response was very good. Readers emailed me. They connected with me via the web. Great reviews trickled in. Then, after a while, a few bad reviews began to surface. Not too many, but just the occasional reader that didn't connect with me for whatever reason. After some time it occurred to me that such a thing is to be expected. If I connected with every single reader, my writing would probably be vanilla. Perhaps even boring.

While what I write may indeed bore some people, I write these stories my way. My mind may be twisted, my plots may be laden with holes, but the stories themselves are unique. The way you read them, other than minor tweaks or improvements, are how they come to me. They're not written according to a formula. They're not written to appease anyone. They're strictly written for entertainment—and I hope you've been entertained.

Sharing these stories with you means more to me than I can ever describe.

Feel free to connect with me on Facebook. You can find me on Twitter, too, but I rarely tweet. You can also email me at chuck@chuckdriskell.com. I hope to hear from you.

Thank you.

About the Author

Chuck Driskell is a United States Army veteran who now makes his living as an advertising executive. He lives in South Carolina with his wife and two children. *Demon's Bluff* is Chuck's fourth novel.

Made in the USA
Monee, IL
09 June 2021